China
Gold

To Ruth

Enjoy

Don Stratton

Don Stratton

To Pauline
My muse and the love of my life

An orchid in a deep forest sends out its fragrance even if no one is around to appreciate it

Confucius

China
Gold

1

HUNTER MCCOY STARED AT THE EMPTY SHELF ON THE WALL trying to grasp the unthinkable. His dad, Ed McCoy, murdering a man—and then beheading him.

No way.

Yet the samurai sword the Japanese colonel had surrendered to Hunter's grandfather so many years before was obviously missing. Was it possible someone had used it that morning in a grotesque murder fifteen hundred miles away?

No, he thought, answering his own question again. *Not possible.*

For the past four years, from the time Hunter had purchased the cabin in Michigan for his dad, the sword had been on that shelf. He'd never kept it anywhere else. Now it was missing, and his dad had been arrested for beheading a man with it, in Florida.

Ed McCoy had used the one phone call they'd given him to reach Hunter. Unable to hide the anxiety in his voice, he'd told him that two Sarasota County Sheriff's detectives had come to their house on Casey Key that morning and arrested him for the murder of a man called Scott Harrison.

During the brief call, he'd explained that he and Henry and two neighbors had recently formed a local men's book club, and they'd been reading the new book by a famous World War Two historian and author, Scott Harrison, entitled *Surrenders In The Pacific.* One of the scenes Harrison described was the Japanese colonel surrendering his airbase and presenting his sword to Hunter's grandfather at the end of the war in China.

His dad told him that Harrison had been found murdered at his home on the key the night before just a few miles away from their rental house. He'd been beheaded, and a bloody samurai sword was left at the scene. They told him that Harrison's calendar showed an appointment with Ed McCoy along with his Casey Key address and phone number for about the time of the murder. Even worse, the police told him his fingerprints were on the sword.

Hunter experienced an uneasy sense of impending doom. This was no coincidence. The man beheaded by a sword with his dad's prints on it was not just *any* man. The guy had written a book describing, in detail, the surrender involving his own grandfather.

Hunter promised his dad he'd get a flight to Florida as fast as he could. He called Sawyer International Airport, just south of Marquette, but the best he could do was schedule a two-stop flight the next morning at 11:45, arriving in Sarasota at 8:23 p.m.

Next he called his friend detective Wally Osborn of the Sarasota Police Department. He explained what had happened and told him he'd be arriving there tomorrow and asked if he could recommend a good lawyer for his dad. Wally said to check with him when he arrived, and he'd give him a name.

Finally he called Henry and told him he'd be there tomorrow night.

With his dad's prints on it, the sword probably was his. Still, Hunter couldn't leave until the next day anyway, so to make sure it really was missing and hadn't just been misplaced somewhere, he decided to do a thorough search.

If Hunter had one skill, beyond all others, it was finding things that were lost. If the missing sword was here and not in Florida at a murder scene—he'd find it.

He planned to do a complete check of the entire property. He'd also look for any signs there might have been a break-in. If the sword wasn't here, someone obviously had gotten in and taken it.

Is anything else missing?

He started outside and walked the perimeter of the two-acre property. The cabin was on the shore of Lake Superior between Marquette and Big Bay, between County Road 550 and the lake. A single gravel driveway led from the county road to the cabin which was on a cliff overlooking the big lake below. There were three outbuildings: a two-car detached garage, a small shed, and the new free-standing sauna that Hunter had just finished building as a surprise for his dad.

Most of the property was covered with tall pines, and the ground was reddish-brown with fallen needles and cones. He circled the property, slowly working his way inward. The first building he encountered was the new sauna. Nothing unusual there. Next was the tool shed. Nothing missing or out of the ordinary. Similarly, he found nothing exceptional when he examined the garage and his dad's car.

At the house he walked the perimeter, examining doors and windows for signs of tampering or a break-in, again finding nothing. He checked the alarm system. It was working perfectly. He knew his dad had successfully activated it before leaving for Florida six weeks earlier, because it had been armed when he'd arrived three weeks ago. Thinking of one more check he had to make, he called the monitoring company they'd been using for the security system.

"Peninsula Monitoring, how can I help you?" the serious male voice answered.

"This is Hunter McCoy at Rural Route 42, off County Road 550. I need you to give me a continuity report."

"Of course. What period of time are you talking about?"

Hunter gave him the dates for the three weeks when no one was supposed to be at the cabin—from the day his dad had left for Florida with his best friend, Henry Lahti and set the alarm to the day Hunter arrived three weeks later and found it still armed.

"Our records show only one interruption during that period, on September twenty-first, from 1:05 p.m. until 3:16 p.m."

"Did the alarm go off?"

"No, sir, it was a coded entry."

There it is. Someone disarmed the system, got in, and took the sword.

"No other interruptions?"

"No, sir. That's it. Is something wrong?"

"I don't know, but I'm going to find out."

Hunter hung up and had to conclude that someone, somehow, got the security code, shut down the system on September twenty-first, spent two hours at the cabin, took the sword, then rearmed the alarm and left.

But he figured two things were seriously wrong with that scenario. One was the two-hour time frame. The cabin was small. The sword was highly visible. It would have taken an intruder unfamiliar with the cabin no more than a few minutes to find it. What was he doing the rest of the time? The second and possibly more serious problem was how had the intruder gotten the code in the first place?

Putting that disturbing thought aside for the moment, he walked to his dad's room and looked around again. Had the intruder taken anything else? He searched the cabin again. Of course, he wasn't familiar with all of his dad's personal stuff, but he tried anyway. Though even if he did manage to identify something, it was always possible his dad had taken it with him to Florida. After all, he, and Henry were going to be down there for several months. Hunter finished his search, unable to identify anything else missing.

Before going to bed that night, he recoded the alarm but didn't sleep well. He knew his dad wasn't a murderer. Someone was clearly trying to set him up. But who would do that, and even more confusing—why?

When he finally drifted off to sleep in the early hours, his dreams shifted to an old nightmare he'd hoped was long behind him, the devastating episode of the clandestine raid he'd led as a Marine captain to a cave in the mountains of Pakistan to abduct the terrorist leader Mahmud e Raq. The raid had been successful, but his younger brother, Sergeant Gary McCoy, one of the team members, had been killed, and to Hunter's everlasting shame, he'd been unable to find and return his body.

In the morning he awoke in a sweat, shaken by the nightmare. For years after the event at the cave, he'd been haunted by the image of Gary being lost in the mountains and his failure to bring him out. He'd vowed that never again would he let anyone in his care be harmed in any way.

Over time, he'd come to realize that his need for putting himself in harm's way—the frequent "Find-and-Correct" work he did when his duties at the medical school allowed it—was somehow an inner search to atone for his failure to save his brother.

Now it was his dad in desperate need of his help. He silently vowed that he wouldn't fail again.

2

AFTER DRAINING A MUG OF STRONG BLACK COFFEE, Hunter packed a small bag, locked the cabin, armed the alarm, and headed out to the garage. He intended to drive to the airport, leave the car there, fly to Florida, and stay until this mess with his dad was cleared up.

As he looked at his dad's vintage Camaro he noticed something was wrong—the car was sitting too low. He looked down; the tires were flat. He walked around the car. All four were flat. The night before when he'd moved the car from the driveway into the garage, the tires were fine. A careful examination revealed that each one had been pierced by a sharp object near the top.

Immediately on alert, Hunter scanned the garage. No one there. He raced back into the cabin and retrieved his Beretta from its storage place. He searched every room of the cabin again—nothing. Whoever it was, if they were still around, had to be outside somewhere. Just as he opened the cabin door to begin searching the property, an enormous explosion blew him back into the house.

Recovering, he looked out and saw the garage—what was left of it—engulfed in flames.

What the hell?

He raced out with his gun ready, executing all the combat maneuvers he'd been taught over a lifetime. If that was a bomb, and it was set off remotely, someone had a visual on the garage. He scanned the woods in all directions. Nothing. He looked over the cliff onto Lake Superior below. He saw no small craft offshore.

If the blast had been intended for him, they might have seen him go into the garage but didn't see him race back to the cabin for his gun. They could have detonated it, thinking he was still in there.

He checked the woods, the sauna, the shed. Empty. Frustrated, he returned to the cabin and called 911. The Fire Department arrived ten minutes later, followed by a Marquette County Sheriff's car. Hunter was glad to see it was being driven by Sheriff John Destramp himself.

While the firemen got after the garage, Destramp walked up to Hunter, and the two men shook hands. Hunter had known him for years.

"What happened here, Hunter?" the sheriff asked, waving his arm at the inferno.

Hunter was barely able to make out Destramp's words. His hearing was off from the blast. He wiggled his fingers in both ears trying to get it back.

"I don't know, John, but I'm sure it was deliberate. My dad's car was in there with all four tires punctured. They were fine when I parked it in the garage last night about ten. I checked the surroundings thoroughly after the blast and found no one."

"Any idea who'd do this to you?"

"No. But, I'm wondering if it's related to some serious trouble my dad's having now in Florida."

"Ed's having trouble? What kind of trouble?"

"Let's go in the cabin while they work on the fire. We can talk in there."

On the way, Hunter continued to wiggle his fingers in his ears, trying to regain normal hearing. John Destramp had known his dad for many years, from the time they'd both been with the Michigan Department of Natural Resources. While Ed McCoy and Henry Lahti had gone on to become game wardens, Destramp went into law enforcement with the Sheriff's Department, eventually becoming sheriff himself. Over the years they'd all stayed in touch with each other.

Hunter told Destramp about his dad's arrest and the missing sword.

"What? You're kidding."

"I wish I were. And there's more. Someone got in here using the security code while Dad and Henry were in Florida, and I was at the med school in Virginia."

"Did Ed know the victim?"

"No, but the guy apparently wrote a history of Japanese surrenders at the end of the war. One of them involved my grandfather in Wuchang, China. You know that story."

"Yeah, I've heard your dad talk about it. So you think this fire out there in your garage is related to Ed's troubles?"

"I don't know, but if we assume that someone broke in here, stole his sword, and then used it to murder the author of a book that mentions my grandfather and the same sword, it looks like a frame to me. Maybe," Hunter continued, "whoever is doing this figured that blowing up his garage and car would add a little icing on the cake."

Just then one of the firemen came in. He nodded to the sheriff, then addressed Hunter. "Are you Mr. McCoy?"

"Yeah. This is my dad's cabin."

"What have you got, Charlie?" The sheriff asked.

"We've got the fire out and under control, but I think you need to get a forensics team out here, Sheriff. I'm no expert, but that fire was definitely caused by an explosion, and I believe it came from under the car. It *wasn't* the fuel tank."

Destramp nodded. "Thanks, Charlie. I'll call them."

Charlie nodded and left, returning to his men.

"All right, Hunter, I'll get my people on this right away. What are you going to do about Ed?"

Hunter checked his watch. It was now a little after ten thirty. "I've got an eleven forty-five flight out of Sawyer to Sarasota. I'm going to see how I can help him, including getting a lawyer." Then, he added, somewhat wistfully, "Of course, I was going to drive Dad's car out to the airport and leave it."

"Tell you what, I'll drive you and call my forensics people on the way. From here that's an hour drive at highway speeds. Grab your stuff. We'd better get going if you're going to catch that flight."

With lights flashing and Destramp at the wheel, highway speeds were seriously exceeded.

3

HUNTER RENTED A JEEP AT THE SARASOTA/BRADENTON INTERNATIONAL AIRPORT after the flight from Marquette. It was 9 p.m. and the fall sun had already set before he'd begun driving on US Highway 41 in the dark, looking for Blackburn Point Road, one of two routes over the intracoastal waterway to Casey Key.

Six weeks earlier he'd rented the house for his dad and Henry. Located near the south end of the Key, it was known locally as the Kingston house after the couple who built it in the 1930s. The two friends had quickly moved in for the winter. Hunter had flown them to Florida for their first visit to the state a few weeks earlier after he and Genevieve Swift had completed the case they referred to as Wicar's Legacy, at the Ringling Museum of Art in Sarasota.

This was the first time the two old buddies were going to escape the cold and snow of another Upper Peninsula winter by spending the entire season in Florida. Hunter had easily been able to afford it, and it made him feel good.

A few weeks after his dad and Henry had moved into the Kingston house, Hunter had flown to the UP from his own place in Charlottesville, Virginia, to build the surprise sauna for his dad. While Hunter had actually paid for the cabin, all public paperwork showed that his dad owned it and occupied it year-round. Hunter's link to it was a closely guarded secret held by his former employer, the Defense Intelligence Agency. This was to protect Hunter when he needed a safe house. But he'd also try to make it up there to visit and do repairs whenever he was able to get away from his duties as professor of physiology at the University of Virginia School of Medicine.

FORTY-FIVE MINUTES AFTER LEAVING THE AIRPORT, Hunter arrived at the Kingston house. The two-story wood-frame structure had a plastered exterior painted white, and the yard full of huge live oaks offered plenty of shade from the Florida sun for a table and several lawn chairs. A carport covered in vines nestled between the gravel driveway and the house. The barrel-tiled roof was green, flecked with black mold. The house was illuminated by a bright full moon as Hunter stepped out and knocked on the door under the small arched portico.

Henry answered quickly and greeted him with a big smile and a hug. "Hey, Hunter," he said, "you found us."

"Hi, Henry. Don't look so surprised. I picked this place out for you, remember?"

"Yeah, I know, and it's been great too, least up until now," he said somberly, the smile disappearing as fast as it had appeared at the welcome sight of his best friend's son.

Hunter was glad Henry was here with his dad for many reasons, not the least of which being that the two men had been the best of friends as long as Hunter could remember. Both were native "Yoopers" born and raised in the Upper Peninsula of Michigan. They'd gone to school together, were Marines in Viet Nam together, and returned to the UP to marry local girls and start their careers together with Michigan's Department of Natural Resources.

After Hunter unpacked his stuff from the rental Jeep and brought it into the house, the two men sat at the kitchen table.

"Did you find out anything about Ed?" Henry asked. "The sheriff wouldn't tell me anything. If you hadn't called last night, I'd still be in the dark."

"I know, Henry. I'll see him in the morning and tell you all about it after that."

"Thanks, man. Since the cops showed up yesterday and arrested him, I've been sick with worry. I couldn't even give him an alibi for the time they say that writer fella was murdered. I was out fishing with our neighbors, Jim Furlow and Joe Palma, and your dad stayed home."

"None of this is your fault, Henry," Hunter said. "I *did* learn something, though, someone broke into the cabin and stole Dad's sword. They might have taken some other things too. I don't know. I couldn't tell."

"But the alarm should have gone off."

Hunter nodded. "Yeah. But it didn't."

He told Henry about the two-hour service interruption in the early afternoon on September twenty-first.

Henry shook his head in confusion. "But the alarm should have been on all that time."

"That's right," said Hunter, "and it was. But someone used the code and disable it for two hours. They apparently got in and stole the sword at that time."

"Jeez, why would they do that?" Henry said. "You say nothing else was missing?"

"Not that I could tell."

"How about your stuff? Anything gone there?"

"Again, not that I could see. But there's something else, Henry. Just as I was leaving the cabin this morning to head for the airport, someone blew up the garage and Dad's Camaro. The blast knocked me over at the cabin door, and the garage and car were completely destroyed. One of the firemen who came was sure it was a bomb under the car. John Destramp's investigating."

"Jesus," Henry said, "Are you all right?"

"Yeah. Hearing's still a little wonky, but I'm okay."

"Ed loved that car."

"Yeah, I know."

"Do you think they're related—the break-in and the bombing?" Henry asked.

"At this point I'm assuming they are."

The two men were silent each thinking about what that might mean.

"So," Hunter said, as much to himself as Henry, "if it does turn out to be Gramp's sword they found at Scott Harrison's crime scene, how did it get there, who did it, and just as important, why?"

Henry threw up his hands. "Can't imagine anyone who'd do this. It makes no sense at all. I don't like this, Hunter."

"I don't like it either, Henry. Seems someone's going to a lot of trouble to set Dad up for murder."

Henry frowned and shook his head. "Again, I can't think of anyone who'd have any reason to do that. I mean, anyone associated with the war from that time has gotta be either dead by now or some old guy in his nineties. It makes no sense."

Hunter nodded in agreement.

No sense at all.

IN THE MORNING, HUNTER WAS HAVING COFFEE with Henry when his phone rang. The screen showed it was Jason Turtle, the postdoc he'd left to run his research lab at the medical school in his absence.

"Hey, Jason, what's up?"

"Hi, Hunter," his associate said in a strangely somber tone.

Uh oh, Hunter thought. Now what? "What's going on?" he asked.

"I don't know. Something's fishy with our funding."

"Our National Institute of Health grant on vascular disease?"

"Yeah. We just got a letter from our grant administrator in Washington saying our funds are frozen until further notice."

"What? I don't understand."

"I don't either. It just says—wait, hold on, let me read it to you."

Hunter waited as paper rattled.

"Okay. Here it is.

"This is to inform you that due to irregularities in the withdrawal of salary funds, your grant is immediately frozen until our investigators have completed their inquiry into the possibility of fraud.

Jack Busbee, Research Fund Administrator National Institute of Health, Washington, DC."

"Possibility of fraud? What's he talking about? What fraud?" Hunter demanded.

"I don't know, Hunter. That's all I have. The letter came this morning."

"Does this guy have a phone number?"

"Yeah." Jason gave it to him.

"Okay. Listen, Jason, I'll start with him. I'll call you back when I know what's going on."

"Okay."

Hunter hung up and called the number. After three transfers, he finally reached Jack Busbee.

"Mr. Busbee, this is Hunter McCoy. My lab just got a letter from you this morning, freezing our funds. Would you tell me what this is all about?"

"Let's see. Give me a minute. What's your name again?"

"Hunter McCoy, Department of Physiology, University of Virginia, School of Medicine, Charlottesville, Virginia. Your letter mentions the possibility of fraud. I don't understand."

"Yes, here it is. Your grant application stipulates salaries for three people—yourself, Hunter McCoy, Ph.D., and two assistants, Jason Turtle, M.D, And Cal Wright, Ph.D."

"That's correct," Hunter said, confused. "So what's the problem?"

"The problem, McCoy, is that another individual, named Gilbert Aker, has also been drawing a salary, a rather large salary, compared to the three of you."

"That can't be right. No one named Gilbert Aker works for us. I don't know anyone with that name. Your records have to be wrong."

"Really? Have you checked your personal bank account lately?"

"What, my bank account? Why?"

"Because for the past month, this 'Aker' has been drawing a salary of five thousand dollars *a week* and depositing it in one of your savings accounts, the one you call the 'Find-and-Correct Fund.'"

Hunter was stunned. "What? None of the three of us gets a weekly salary from the grant at all, much less five thousand dollars."

"Exactly. And until we get to the bottom of this, your funds are frozen. When our investigation is complete, you'll be hearing from us."

When the man hung up, Hunter sat holding his phone, completely confused.

What the hell is going on here?

4

THEY WERE HOLDING ED MCCOY AT THE SHERIFF'S South Office in Venice. Hunter got there at eleven, still puzzling over the crazy allegation of fraud involving his research grant.

How could someone be drawing funds and depositing them in my account?

And who the hell is Gilbert Aker?

On arrival, he was ushered into a prisoner waiting room. Within minutes, a guard brought his dad in and then stepped back to the door to afford them some privacy. Ed McCoy was dressed in a jail jumpsuit that somehow made him look smaller and more fragile then he really was. Father and son sat across from each other at a plain table.

"Well, this hasn't been a lot of fun, son," Ed said trying to be nonchalant but unable to cover the underlying anxiety he obviously felt.

"We'll get you out of here, Dad. This is completely bogus." Glancing at the guard, Hunter lowered his voice and said, "Gramp's sword is definitely missing from the cabin."

Ed frowned. "That's not good."

"No, it's not, but if the one left at the murder scene turns out to be yours, of course it would have your fingerprints on it. It's your sword."

"I'm afraid that's not all, Hunter. They say they've got copies of emails between Scott Harrison and me, in which I threatened him. They've traced the emails to my laptop."

"Where's your laptop?"

"It's up in the cabin in my top dresser drawer, under the socks and underwear. I didn't bring it down here. I wanted to sort of 'be off-the-grid,' so to speak. You know, just relax."

If I'd known that yesterday I could have checked to see if it was still there.

"Tell you what, I'll call John Destramp in Marquette and ask him to send a deputy out to check."

"Good idea."

Hunter told his dad about the two-hour interruption in the security system when he believed the sword was stolen. Then he told him about the pierced tires, the bombing of the garage and the loss of his beloved Camaro.

"Oh my God, Hunter, who'd do that?" His father's voice shook with desperation.

"I don't know, Dad, but I'll find out. Wally Osborn called me this morning and gave me the name of good local attorney. I've got an appointment with him for later today. I told you about Wally before. He's a homicide detective with the Sarasota Police Department. I worked with him on the Ringling Museum case last summer. He's a good man and like me, a former DIA operative. He recommended J. Michael Lannigan. Says he's a top criminal lawyer."

TWO HOURS LATER, SHORTLY AFTER LUNCH, Hunter entered the law offices of J.M. Lannigan. Wally Osborn told him he'd learned the hard way what a good criminal defense attorney Lannigan was. On no fewer than three occasions, Osborn and the Sarasota DA had been convinced they'd had enough evidence to convict an arrested suspect, only to find that Lannigan was better at getting him off then they were at getting him convicted.

Over the years the homicide detective and Lannigan had developed a strange relationship based on mutual respect. Osborn was impressed with the attorney because he didn't rely on cheap tricks. Instead, he was just damned good at what he did. He and his PI, Stretch Jones, would dig deep and somehow find convincing evidence that his client was innocent. Evidence that held up and couldn't be ignored.

Lannigan's law office was in a little house—at least seventy-five years old—in downtown Sarasota, surrounded by newly constructed town homes whose front doors were no more than ten feet from Fruitville Road, one of the city's busiest arterials.

Surprisingly, when Hunter arrived at the office and stepped inside, the road noise completely disappeared. The house was a one-story, wood-framed craftsman, painted robin's-egg blue. When he introduced himself, Lannigan stood up behind his desk and reached across to shake hands. He was as tall as Hunter's six-foot-two. He appeared to be in his late fifties. The man had a wide smile, a full head of thick black hair going seriously gray, and a strong grip.

"Have a seat, McCoy."

Hunter looked around and found what must have been the "client's" seat—a chrome kitchen chair with a torn padded plastic seat and back. He sat, and Lannigan did the same behind his desk. The office was lined with metal file cabinets and bookshelves that held a small TV set so old it actually had a tube in it. Then Hunter saw a flat screen TV on the other wall and realized the old set was there as an antique.

"So, what can I do for you, Professor? May I call you Hunter?"

"Hunter's fine," he said, wondering how Lannigan knew about the title. "I'm here about my dad, who was arrested for the murder of Scott Harrison two nights ago."

"Yeah, I read about that, chopped with a sword in his own house."

"Right."

"So," Lannigan said, clasping his hands behind his head, sitting back in his chair, and gazing at the ceiling, "tell me the story."

Hunter told him everything ending with the phony email exchanges.

Lannigan held up his hands, still staring at the ceiling with his eyes closed. "Not phony. The emails actually exist, but your dad didn't write them."

"Exactly," Hunter said. "So what's going to happen to him now?"

"Since they've already arrested him for murder, a judge will determine if he's eligible for release under bond. But the chances are slim, since it's a first-degree murder charge. If you want me to represent him, I'll get on that right away."

"Okay, let's do it. There's something else, Mr. Lannigan."

"Just Lannigan, please."

"Lannigan it is."

"Well?"

"Just so you know, I'm going to be looking for evidence that my dad is innocent."

"And just so you know, I have an investigator, Stretch Jones, who works with me, and I intend to use him on this case."

"I understand," Hunter said, "but—"

"Hold on now, Hunter. Just relax," Lannigan said with a smile. "I'll be more than happy to have your help. As you've probably figured out, Wally Osborn called earlier and told me all about you *and* your background. He explained that you were employed as an agent with the Defense Intelligence Agency of the Department of Defense, tracking down international criminals with intent to harm the United States. He told me you also have official detective status with the Virginia State Police for the purpose of giving you access to Interpol and its vast resources. Further, each agency retains you on an ad-hoc basis in order to be able to activate you when they need your special skills. I also know about your personal "Find-and-Correct" work. On top of all that, you're a medical school professor."

Hunter nodded, silently thinking, *This guy is definitely the right man for the job.* Lannigan went on to explain about his fee, and Hunter agreed.

"All right, here's what we do next," the lawyer said. "I'll find out when the bail hearing is and be there to do my thing. I'll also see what additional evidence the sheriff has linking the crime to your dad. Then I'll meet with him at the jail, tell him I'm representing him, and what I plan to do. Meanwhile, you go do your thing and report back when you learn something."

Hunter got up to leave, and Lannigan came around his desk, limping and walking with the aid of a cane.

Seeing Hunter's surprised expression, he simply stated, "Polio when I was a kid."

Hunter drove toward Casey Key, contemplating his next move. It was beginning to look like he'd be here for a while, so he stopped off at a Bealls department store and bought several pairs of slacks, shorts, shirts, underwear, and lightweight Florida shoes. Then he headed back to the house to tell Henry what he'd learned.

The Kingston house, on the intracoastal waterway, had a third bedroom that Henry and his dad were currently using for storage. It had a single bed, and, with a little rearranging, Hunter turned it into a room for himself. After filling Henry in, Hunter called John Destramp.

"Hi, Hunter. I have a little info, but not much. My people tell me the explosion was a bomb, placed directly under the driver's seat. They can't be sure, but they believe it was remotely detonated rather than through a timer. So if he or they had you in sight and were trying to kill you, they missed."

"Or," Hunter said, "if they were watching, maybe the intent wasn't to kill me but to send some kind of message instead."

"What kind of message?" Destramp asked

"I don't know. I don't understand any of it. But can I ask a favor? Dad tells me they have a series of emails between him and the author in which he threatened the man. The authorities claim the emails came from Dad's laptop, which he says is in his top dresser drawer. Could you could send someone out to the cabin to see if it's there?"

"Give me the security code. I'll do it myself."

TWO HOURS LATER DESTRAMP CALLED BACK.

"His computer's not in the top dresser drawer, or any other drawer for that matter, or anywhere else in the cabin."

5

"HUNTER MCCOY?" THE GRUFF VOICE ON THE PHONE ASKED.

"Yes. Who's this?"

"This is Detective John Bolt with the Charlottesville, Virginia Police Department."

Hunter groaned. *Now what?*

"What can I do for you, Detective?"

"We've had a series of complaints about some possible criminal activity at your apartment. I need to go over this with you, but you haven't answered your door."

Complaints? Possible criminal activity?

"That's because I'm currently in Florida. I don't understand. What kind of complaints?"

"They're actually quite serious, and I'd prefer to talk with you in person. When will you be back in Charlottesville?"

"I don't know. I expect I'll be here for some time; I have some business to deal with. I don't know how long it's going to take, and I don't know when I'll be back. Come on, Detective, please explain. What's this all about?"

"Look, Doc, I know you're a professor at the medical school, and I want to give you the benefit of the doubt. All I can tell you is the allegations are serious, and it's in your best interest to get back here and see me as soon as possible to address them. Where are you staying in Florida?"

Hunter ignored the question. "That's it? You're not going to give me any more than that?"

"I can tell you this," Detective Bolt said, "if the allegations are true, you could lose your job, your career, and spend some major time in prison. I'd get up here as soon as possible if I were you."

"I'll be there when I can," Hunter said and ended the call.

What the hell is going on here? First, Dad gets arrested for murder. Then the NIH shuts down my research grant because of supposed fraud. Now this?

It was beginning to dawn on Hunter that the principal target of recent events might not really be his father after all. Maybe it was someone trying to destroy *his* life and everything he held dear.

IN SPITE OF HIS OWN CONFUSING and—mounting—personal problems, Hunter knew that right now he had to focus on his dad. It was time to meet the detective working the Harrison murder case. He found him back at the Sheriff's South Office.

Detective Otto Skaggs was a fit-looking, tough cop, about five eight, with a crew cut, a stone face, and a look that said, "I don't believe a word you're saying." He didn't appear happy to see Hunter when he introduced himself as Ed McCoy's son.

"What do you want, McCoy?"

"I'd like to review the evidence you have that warrants my father's arrest."

"Oh, you would, would you? I'm afraid that information is strictly police business. Take it up with your attorney." He broke eye contact with Hunter and returned to the work on his desk.

At six-foot-two, Hunter towered over the relatively short detective sitting at his desk. He just stood there, staring down at him. Finally Skaggs looked up and said, "Is there something else I can do for you?"

Hunter ignored the man's belligerent tone.

"Just for the record, Detective, you haven't done *anything* for me yet."

"Look, McCoy, I told you, talk to your attorney."

"I have, Detective, and I'm working the case with him."

"You're working the case? What does that mean?"

"Lannigan is defending my dad, and I'm one of his investigators."

"Really. Are you a licensed PI in the state of Florida?"

"No, but I *am* a detective with the Virginia State Police, and while I don't have authority in Florida, I do have knowledge of investigations and he's asked for my help. I don't plan to violate any Florida laws."

Hunter showed Skaggs his credentials.

Skaggs checked them over slowly and carefully, handed them back, and said, "See that you don't."

After a thoughtful pause, he begrudgingly continued. "Look, McCoy, we've got your father's sword at the murder scene and his prints are all over it. We have emails from his computer threatening Harrison if he doesn't pay him for the rights to using his grandfather's story. He's got means, motive, and opportunity. End of story."

"End of story? Really? Well how about this. That sword was in my dad's cabin in Michigan when he came down here for the winter six weeks ago. It was gone when I got up there three weeks ago. During the three weeks between his leaving and my arriving, the alarm system was fully activated, except for one interruption on September twenty-first, from 1:05 p.m. until 3:16 p.m. I believe that someone got in and stole the sword at that time."

"And you know this how?"

"You can contact my security monitoring company up there and they'll give you that information."

"So you say. But even with that so-called interruption in service, there's no proof the sword was even there during that three-week time. Your father undoubtedly brought it down here with him when he arrived *six* weeks ago."

"He certainly didn't. The friend he travelled with can attest to that. Then there's the situation with the emails. If those emails were dated during that same three-week period, my dad didn't write them. He left his laptop computer in Michigan. I had the Marquette County Sheriff go out to his cabin to see if it was still there. He just reported that it's gone. I believe it was stolen along with the sword."

Skaggs pulled a file out of his desk and leafed through it.

"We have copies of several emails between your dad and Mr. Harrison in which he specifically demanded money in return for Harrison's use of his father's story in the book—he looked at his notes—'*Surrenders In The Pacific.*'

"Our tech people say they came from a laptop computer registered to Edward McCoy. We also have several emails from Harrison to your father in which he specifically says he'll pay him nothing and to stop bothering him. Then, your dad sent him an email threatening him if he didn't pay up. And Harrison's digital calendar shows he had an appointment with your father at the time he was killed."

"Anyone could have put that on his calendar. When was it added?"

Skaggs paused. "We'll check on that."

"What are the dates on the emails?"

"Now *that* we have. September twenty-fourth—first email from Ed McCoy to Harrison asking for money. September twenty-fifth—Harrison responds that your grandfather's story is public information. September twenty-sixth—Ed McCoy threatens Harrison's life if he doesn't pay. In the reply on the same day, Harrison says, 'Get lost.'"

"There you have it." Hunter said. "They were written while my dad was here, and his computer was up north."

Skaggs shrugged. "So you say, but your sheriff friend just said it's not there, didn't he?"

Damn.

"Again, like the sword," Hunter countered, "it must have been stolen during that two-hour interval on September twenty-first."

"Or—he took the laptop and the sword with him when he came down here," Skaggs countered. "You'll have to do better than that, McCoy. My case holds. Your father stays in jail for murder."

Skaggs paused. "Since you're here, McCoy, how did Scott Harrison get the information about your grandfather for his book? Did he interview you or your dad?"

"I don't know, Detective. He didn't talk to me. He may have met with my dad, but Dad never mentioned it if he did. More likely Harrison got it from an article about my grandfather's experience in China at the end of the war that appeared in the *Upper Peninsula Post.*"

Skaggs thought about this then said, "So your contention is that your dad left his computer in Michigan when he came here six weeks ago."

"Yes. He said he left it in his top dresser drawer, under his socks and underwear."

"And you say it was stolen during that security interruption you referred to."

"Yes."

"And you also believe that someone other than your father had the email exchange with Harrison using this stolen computer."

"Again, yes."

"Well then 'Detective' McCoy, how do you explain the fact that after we got a warrant to search the house your dad's renting here in Florida—the so-called Kingston house on Casey Key—we found this very same laptop computer, the one you say he left in Michigan. And guess where we found it? In the top drawer of his dresser under his socks and underwear."

Hunter had no comment.

"Any ideas, McCoy?" Skaggs said with a barely disguised smirk.

STILL IN A SOUR MOOD AFTER LEAVING Skaggs's office, Hunter returned to the Jeep and punched in a number on his cell that he knew by heart and didn't keep in the contact list on the phone. A woman's voice answered, "McMurtle Manufacturing. How may I help you?"

"I need seventeen front-end loaders by noon tomorrow. Can you help?"

"Just a moment, sir."

After a wait of several minutes, a strong male voice said, "Hunter, what's up?"

"The cabin's been breached."

"When?"

"September twenty-first. Someone got the security code, got in and took my grandfather's samurai sword and my father's laptop computer. The sword was used in a killing in Florida, and my father's being held on first degree murder charges in the case."

"September twenty-first?"

"Yes."

"Wait for a call."

"Thanks."

Hunter had just called Deacon Wogen, the Secretary General of the Defense Intelligence Agency of the United States Department of Defense. Several years earlier, before he'd become Secretary General, Wogen had recruited Hunter from the Marine Corps to become an intelligence agent with the department. Hunter had served in that capacity for seven years before leaving to go back to graduate school for a Ph.D. in physiology. Later, when he took the position as assistant professor at the University of Virginia School of Medicine, Wogen approached him again and asked if he'd be willing to return to the department on an ad hoc basis, in the event they needed somebody with his unique combination of skills in cases that might involve higher education. He'd agreed, and they'd activated him twice since then. Each time he'd dealt directly with the Secretary General.

Wogen had always known about the cabin safe house registered in Ed McCoy's name. Hunter had given the Secretary General the security code in the event they needed to reach him and were unable to do so otherwise. The house and all its paperwork and the security code were locked in the DIA's secure computer system. But now it appeared that someone had gotten into that system and found the location and the code.

Hunter wondered what Deacon would find. He'd always had a special relationship with the man and trusted him completely. As he drove into the driveway of the Kingston house, the return call from the Secretary General came in.

"Your digital file was accessed September nineteenth by William Packard, one of our computer people with the highest security clearance. He'd have had no reason to do that as he had no authorized connection to you. On top of that, the man has disappeared without a trace. We're still looking.

We examined his computer use during that time, and yours was the only personnel file he looked at. Now that we know what he did, we'll do a thorough investigation on our end to learn all we can. I'll have Karen call you when we learn something."

"Thank you, sir."

"What are you involved in, Hunter? One of your "Find-and-Correct" things?"

"Not yet. But, there are other strange things going on and I'm not sure if my father is the target or if I am."

He told the Secretary General about his troubles with the NIH grant and the Charlottesville Police.

6

IT HAD BEEN A WEEK SINCE THE FUNERAL of Laura McCasey. Her daughter, Emma Johannson, was going through her mother's things trying to make the inevitably difficult decisions about what to do with all her "stuff." Emma's daughter, twenty-five-year-old Carrie Johannson, was helping her.

"This is going to take a while, Mom," Carrie said as the two women were working their way through the old house that Emma had grown up in and Carrie had loved to visit as a child.

"It sure is. Your grandma lived in this house most of her life after leaving the convent. Every corner has something in it. I'm not even sure where to begin."

The house had two stories with a full basement, a main floor for living, and a large attic, built about 1910. As a child, Carrie had loved exploring that basement. It was a vast and wonderful place. The walls were large stones, cemented together, rather than the cinder blocks or poured concrete common today. Those stones gave the place a cave-like feel that Carrie'd found irresistible as a child. Whenever her mother or her grandma couldn't find her they'd eventually head down to the basement, and there she'd be.

"Maybe we should split up and take different parts," Carrie said. "Each of us could separate stuff into piles. If it looks like junk, put it in one pile. If it looks like something we might want to keep, it goes in another. If it's something to give away to Goodwill or the Salvation Army, it goes in a third. What do you think?"

"That sounds good. Then we can look at each other's piles before we make final decisions."

Carrie nodded in agreement. "I'd like to start in—"

Her mom laughed, finishing the sentence, "The basement."

"You remembered?"

"Of course. We couldn't keep you out of there as a kid. Go ahead. Knock yourself out. I'll start upstairs in the attic, and we can meet later on the main floor."

Carrie bounded downstairs and was immediately flooded with memories of days gone by. Years ago, her grandparents had converted to oil heat but the basement still contained an old coal furnace that squatted in the center of the room, its large twisted octopus-like ducts reaching up to disappear into the floors above. Her grandfather's workshop was in a separate long room in one corner. She knew there'd be no need to deal with his shop tools, as those had all been given away many years before following his death.

Two hours later she'd been through everything and had her two piles. There'd been no need for a third, as she hadn't identified anything that the family might want to keep.

About to go upstairs to find her mom, Carrie took a final look at her "give-away" pile and her gaze fell on what appeared to be an old travel cooler, the kind you'd take on a picnic. She hadn't bothered to look inside. What the heck, she thought, let's see.

To her surprise, inside she found an old leather sack with a drawstring, and under it, a single envelope. Curious, she picked up the sack and opened it. Inside were seedpods, fifteen or twenty of them. To Carrie's trained eye— she'd recently received her Ph.D. in botany from Ohio State University—they looked like orchid pods. They also looked old as did the sack holding them. Intrigued, she examined the envelope, which also appeared to have been lying undisturbed in the cooler for years.

On the cover, in her grandmother's easily identifiable handwriting, she read, *"The Story of Dr. Li Qiang Chen."*

Carrie sat in one of the old chairs she'd put in the give-away pile, carefully opened the envelope and extracted a long letter in her grandmother's handwriting. She began to read.

I'm recording here the events that led up to my being given the sack of seedpods by my dear friend, Dr. Li Qiang Chen. I'm doing this while the events are still fresh in my memory. Dr. Chen and I met while I was still Sister Mary Margaret of the Sisters of Notre Dame de Namur, during my years at the convent in Wuchang, China. Dr. Chen, an elderly Chinese physician, treated patients during the Japanese occupation in WWII.

In 1940 his clinic had been destroyed by the Japanese, but he continued to treat his patients as best he could. Because of my background in nursing, the mother superior asked me to invite him to use the basement of our convent as a makeshift clinic from which he could treat his patients, many of whom were parents of the children in our school. In return, he was asked to provide medical help to the nuns, when needed.

Dr. Chen agreed. The dear man never took payment for his services, only asking for enough food to sustain himself in return. During the time he worked out of the convent, I'd heard some amazing reports from the parents of his young patients of a treatment he'd developed for childhood diabetes. Not just successful treatment and management of the disease, but a prevention of its development to full juvenile diabetes. This was so incredible, I was naturally skeptical.

Dr. Chen raised orchids, found new species, and was constantly testing them for medicinal use. I learned that orchids had been used in Chinese medicine for centuries. With Western medicines scarce or unavailable during the war, he often had to rely on these old Chinese herbal treatments but was always searching for new medicines and experimenting as well. It was just his nature.

When the war drew dangerously close to Wuchang, we were told by the Catholic Bishop in Ohio, where the motherhouse was located, to evacuate to Burma until the war was over. We did, but Dr. Chen stayed on, and continued his good work for the poor people in the city. I remember saying goodbye to him thinking we'd probably never meet again.

In September 1945, after the Japanese surrendered, our superiors felt it was once again safe to return. When we arrived we were shocked to find that the convent and school had suffered extensive damage and neglect. Nevertheless, with the help of local Chinese citizens—many who were in Dr. Chen's debt for care he'd provided their families—we were soon able to get up and running again.

Miraculously, Dr. Chen was still there, and it was wonderful to see him again, although we were saddened to realize that the war, and age, had taken their toll on him. The kindly old man was rapidly deteriorating.

Another surprise was the presence in the convent of an American soldier, United States Army Technical Sergeant Karl McCoy. He was about my age, and he'd been abandoned by his commanding officer after the surrender. The Japanese told him he could stay at the convent, which except for Dr. Chen, was empty at the time. He and the doctor became friends, with the sergeant helping the old man whenever he could.

One day, about three weeks after we returned from Burma, Dr. Chen asked to see me. He was lying on his bed—a miserable cot, really—in terrible shape. I'd had enough experience as a nurse to know he was dying and had only a few days to live. Sergeant McCoy was with him, comforting him, when I arrived. Shortly he took me outside, away from the old man's hearing.

"Sister," the sergeant began, "Dr. Chen just asked me to find some things he's hidden in the basement and to give them to you. One is a small sack of seedpods from a new species of orchid he discovered in the mountains, and the other is his research notebook. He told me they represent his life's work and contain a successful treatment to prevent the development of juvenile diabetes, and he wants you to take responsibility for them."

As the sergeant went to find them, I returned to the bedchamber, such as it was, and the old man took my hand. He told me the sergeant would soon give me the seedpods and the notebook. He also said that it was critical to keep the sack, which contained the very valuable orchid seedpods, cool and dry. If I did, they would last for years. He pleaded with me that when I returned to the United States, I was to wait for a visit from his younger brother, Huan Chen. I was to give Huan the sack of seedpods and the research notebook. It would then be Huan's responsibility to see that they were made available to medical researchers.

When Sergeant McCoy returned, he gave me the sack of seedpods but said the notebook was missing. It wasn't where the doctor told him it would be.

A few hours later Dr. Chen died, and two days after that, his older brother, Bao Chen, came to claim his body and belongings. Sergeant McCoy and I rounded up Dr. Chen's few personal possessions, along with the old man's diary, and gave them to his brother.

In accordance with Dr. Chen's wishes, I kept the sack of seedpods in order to take it back to the States and wait for Huan Chen to come and collect it.

Once Bao Chen left, Sergeant McCoy and I again conducted a thorough search of the convent basement but were still unable to find the missing notebook.

Sergeant McCoy told me about his experience at the airbase. He said that he'd been abandoned in Wuchang shortly after the surrender, by his captain, who had flown them in to take over the Japanese airfield for Allied use. But the captain decided it wasn't yet safe to do so and flew off, leaving the sergeant on his own. Then he told me that he had gone onto the base, and the Japanese colonel had formally surrendered the airfield and his squadron by presenting him with his samurai sword. He'd even shown me the sword.

Shortly after the death of Dr. Chen, Sergeant McCoy, who'd not had any contact with American units during all this time, returned to the base, where the Japanese officers still had some pretty sophisticated radio equipment in working order. He told the radioman that he needed to contact the Americans.

He was amazed when the man was actually able to contact an American ship in the South China Sea. The radioman told them about the American soldier in their midst who needed to return to his unit. Authorities on the ship determined that Sergeant McCoy's unit was currently in Singapore, and they arranged for an American TBM to fly in and pick him up.

When the plane arrived, and Karl met and talked with the pilot for a few moments, he started laughing and told me it would probably be a quick trip back to his unit. I asked him why, and he said, because the pilot had just introduced himself as Captain "Fast Eddie" Falcetti.

We said goodbye to each other at the airport, and I never saw him again.

*It was only after Sergeant McCoy had gone that I
finally came to understand what I think happened to Dr.
Chen's missing research notebook. Shortly after I'd
returned from Burma, an American officer, a Captain
Malport, showed up at the convent asking about Sergeant
Karl McCoy. I told the man that he was in town shopping
at the market and would be gone for several hours. Dr.
Chen was already ill and indisposed at that time.*

*While we waited for him to return, we talked about Dr.
Chen and his work with the sick and injured during the
war. I spoke of the amazing successes that his patients
reported after being treated by the doctor. I'm sure I
mentioned the success with juvenile diabetes. Shortly
afterward, I was summoned back to the school and left
Captain Malport in the basement clinic to await the return
of Sergeant McCoy.*

*I'm thinking now that the man found the notebook and
believing that if the stories about a successful treatment
and prevention of juvenile diabetes were true, it could
contain valuable information and might be worth a lot. I
now believe that he was also the same man who'd
abandoned Sergeant McCoy earlier.*

*In any case, I intend to follow as much of the old
man's dying wish as I can, I'll keep the seedpods cool and
dry and wait for his brother, Huan Chen, to collect them.*

July 15, 1948
Laura McCasey
(Formerly Sister Mary Margaret, SNDdeN)

7

Casey Key, Florida
Present Day

THE MORNING AFTER HIS DISCOURAGING MEETING with
Detective Skaggs and reluctantly acknowledging that
Lannigan was in the best position to learn about any
additional evidence the sheriff might have implicating his
dad, Hunter decided on a different approach. He'd go see
Jenny Lahti, whose mega-mansion was right next to Scott
Harrison's place on Casey Key. Maybe he could learn
something there.

During the drive Hunter recalled how two years
earlier, Jenny Lahti had hired him to find the missing body
of her recently deceased husband, Charlie Lahti. Charlie
had been Henry's brother. Charlie had died while he and
Jenny were on vacation in Italy, and the international
funeral company, *Final Care*, had arranged to process the
body and ship it back to Venice, Florida for the funeral.
Only the wrong body had been delivered.

In the course of tracking down Charlie's body, Hunter
uncovered an international scheme involving a nefarious
neurological institute in Italy. The case had also turned out
to involve deceit, murder, theft, and international crime.

Jenny had been more than generous in rewarding
Hunter for his help in the case. Over the years, Hunter had
done very well financially investigating situations like hers.
It was one of the reasons he was currently considering

retiring from the academic world and devoting himself full time to this "Find-and-Correct" work. The only thing holding him back was that he loved doing research and he loved teaching.

Jenny answered the door herself. "Hunter," she cried, wrapping him in a huge hug, surprised but delighted to see him. "Is it really you? Come in. Come on in. I was thrilled when you called and said you'd like to come over."

"It's great to see you too, Jenny. How are you?"

"Good, good. Gosh, this is my day for unexpected visitors, it seems. And what an amazing coincidence. You're not going to believe this. Come on in. The last time I saw you, you and your lovely lady, Genevieve, were on your way out here, to this very house, to spend a few days together after your great adventure involving *Final Care*. How is she, anyway?"

As they walked through the palatial entryway to the inner part of the house, Hunter wondered what she meant by the coincidence of "unexpected visitors."

"Genevieve's fine. After she completed her one-year exchange program as a curator at the Ringling Museum of Art in Sarasota three months ago, she went back to her job as a curator at the Louvre in Paris."

When they entered the lavish living room of the house, Hunter saw that Jenny already had company, an attractive young Asian woman seated demurely on a sofa.

"Hunter, let me introduce you to Billie Chen." Then addressing the young woman, she said, "Ms. Chen, this is Hunter McCoy, the grandson—if I'm not mistaken—of Karl McCoy."

At this, Ms. Chen gasped a sharp inhale, and put her hands to her face, and began crying. "Oh my God, Mr. McCoy, are you really Karl McCoy's grandson?" she gaped at him with the most anguished, imploring face Hunter could ever remember seeing. "Maybe *you* can help me."

Eyebrows raised, Hunter looked to Jenny for an explanation of the young woman's odd behavior.

"You'd better sit down, Hunter, and let Billie explain for herself. Go ahead, dear."

Hunter sat and stared at Billie Chen, waiting for an explanation. It took her a few minutes to compose herself. Then, between sobs, she began to tell her story.

"A little over a month ago, a man broke into my apartment in Chicago and demanded to know the location of my great-grandfather's research notebook from the war."

Hunter interrupted. "Who was your great-grandfather, and what war?"

"Please, Hunter," Jenny interrupted, "it might be better if you let her explain at her own pace."

"Of course, go ahead," he agreed, wondering what this was all about.

"My great-grandfather was Li Qiang Chen, a Chinese medical doctor and scientist during World War Two in China. I have his diary. In it, he explains that he successfully treated his young patients who presented with early childhood diabetes without insulin and in most cases their disease arrested after several months."

Hunter was astonished. As a medical scientist, he knew this was highly unlikely, but if true, it would represent a monumental medical advance.

The young woman went on. "I had no idea what the intruder was talking about. I'd read my great-grandfather's diary, and while it makes a few references to his research notebook, I've never seen it. The man said he'd read Scott Harrison's book and tracked me down as Dr. Chen's great-granddaughter.

"Scott Harrison?" Hunter turned to Jenny. "Your neighbor, the man who was murdered a few days ago?"

"You know about that? Oh, right, the papers, I suppose."

Hunter thought for a moment before answering. He'd known about Dr. Chen from stories his grandfather had told him about his time in China at the convent. Was this woman really his great-granddaughter?

"It looks like both of us have a story to tell, Ms. Chen." Deciding to keep his dad's arrest to himself for the moment, he said, "Go on."

"I told the horrible man I didn't know anything about any notebook. Then he threatened to kill my brother and his family if I don't get it for him."

"He threatened to kill them?" Hunter said, astonished.

"Yes. I told him I didn't have it. I'd never even seen it. He told me I'd better find it, or he'd kill them all. Said he'd contact me later. Then he left."

The young woman shook her head. "Mr. McCoy, Mrs. Lahti, I'd never even heard of Scott Harrison or his book, so after that, I thought I'd better read it. He mentions my great-grandfather's notebook in the part where he describes the story of *your* grandfather, Karl McCoy.

I decided to come here and ask Scott Harrison himself if he knew anything more about it. But when I got here today, I found his place surrounded by crime scene tape and policemen everywhere. They told me he'd been murdered. I just broke down on the spot. Mrs. Lahti saw me and took me in about an hour ago."

Jenny nodded. "I asked her what was wrong, Hunter, and she told me the story she's telling you now. Go on, dear."

Billie Chen dabbed her eyes with a tissue and went on. "My great-grandfather's diary mentions an American sergeant, your grandfather, who stayed in the convent during the time he was there. They'd become friends."

She stopped and stared at Hunter.

"I can't believe you're his grandson, and you're actually here. Do you know anything about this notebook?"

Hunter ignored that. "This man, the one who threatened you, when did this happen exactly."

"Like I said, a little over a month ago."

"Can you be more exact? Give me the actual date?"

She took out her cellphone, and Hunter could see she was looking at the calendar and doing some processing in her head. Finally she said, "I believe it was September fifteenth, why?"

He ignored this too. "Can you describe him?"

"Yes." Then she described him for Hunter and Jenny.

"That's good." Hunter stood up and said, "Excuse me for a moment, I need to make a call."

He stepped out into the great hall as the two confused women looked on. Once out of hearing range he called Lannigan.

"I may have come across something useful." He went on to explain about Billie Chen and the man who threatened her, a man who'd presumably have a powerful motive to confront Scott Harrison and maybe kill him.

"If he beat up the author and demanded the notebook, he'd clearly want to shut him up after that. If we can show the cops that someone else had a motive to kill Harrison, their case against my dad would weaken considerably."

"Yes, it would. Where are you now?" Lannigan asked.

"I'm at Jenny Lahti's, Scott Harrison's neighbor. I did some work for her a few years ago, and I wanted to see if she had any info on Harrison that might be useful."

"Tell you what. I was on my way over to the DA's, but I'll need to interview Ms. Chen first. Can you bring her here, right now?"

"Let me check. I'll call you right back."

Hunter returned to the living room.

"Jenny? Miss Chen? I have something to tell you both. My dad, Ed McCoy, the son of Karl McCoy, has been arrested for the murder of Scott Harrison. They're holding him in jail right now. He didn't do it."

"That's terrible, Hunter," Jenny exclaimed. "Why would they think he did it?"

"As you know, Jenny, from the story in the newspaper, Mr. Harrison was beheaded by a samurai sword."

"I know, how horrible. He was such a nice man. How could anyone do such a thing. The story said they'd arrested a suspect, even printed his name, but I didn't make the connection to you?"

"The sword was apparently my dad's too. We think it was stolen from his cabin in Michigan on September twenty-first."

Turning to Billie Chen, he said, "You told us the man who threatened you was looking for your great-grandfather's notebook."

"Yes."

"So after confronting you and not getting it, he must have figured his next best hope would be Scott Harrison himself. You did say Harrison mentioned the notebook in his book. And with all the research writing such a work would require, the man might have figured, like you did, that Harrison may have come across it. So he confronted the author, and either got it, or didn't but couldn't risk leaving the man alive to tell anyone."

"But why try to frame your dad?" Jenny said.

"That, Jenny, is the big question."

8

LANNIGAN WAS WAITING IN HIS OFFICE when Hunter and Billie Chen arrived just before noon.

"Thank you for coming, Miss Chen," the lawyer said, offering the young lady the only chair he had for clients. Hunter stood. Billie repeated her story. Lannigan sat back and thought for a moment before asking questions.

"You believe you can give the police an accurate description of this man who threatened you?"

"Yes."

"And you say he broke into your apartment demanding a notebook that belonged to your great-grandfather—Lannigan looked at his notes—Li Qiang Chen?"

"Yes, that's correct. Then he threatened to kill my brother and his family if I didn't give it to him. I couldn't. I'd never seen this notebook."

"You'd never seen it, or you didn't know about it?"

"I've never seen it. I only knew about it because of the reference to it in my grandfather's diary."

"How did you come by this diary?"

"It was passed down in the family and it finally came to me."

"I see," Lannigan nodded. "You said your great-grandfather's diary mentioned the notebook. What did it say exactly?"

The young woman reached into her large purse and brought out a leatherbound book about four by six inches, obviously old, and quickly found the reference. It was, of course, in Chinese, so she translated for them.

"The process for refining the medicine that I've used to treat juvenile diabetes is detailed in my research notebook. It's linked to the Glorious Store in a most ironic way."

"Does that make any sense to you, Miss Chen?" Lannigan asked.

"Only that the notebook has the formula for making a medicine."

"What does he mean by 'Glorious Store'?"

"I have no idea."

The lawyer got up from his chair. "All right, here's what we'll do. I've already called the DA and rescheduled my appointment for this afternoon at one. I've just got time to make it if I leave now. I'm going to find out how strong their case against your dad is, Hunter, before I bring up Miss Chen's threatening man. They may have additional evidence that they didn't share with you when they arrested him, maybe something beyond the incriminating laptop.

"When I'm ready, I'll call and meet you both at the jail, where you, Miss Chen, can give your description to the police artist. I'm sure Detective Skaggs will want to question you and take your statement. Go have lunch somewhere and wait for my call."

Hunter took Billie Chen to the open-air restaurant at Marina Jack on the waterfront in downtown Sarasota, overlooking the yacht harbor and Sarasota Bay. No sooner had they sat down at a table when the young woman began to cry. Hunter waited her out and was about to speak when a waitress showed up to take their order.

"An unsweetened iced tea and the crab quesadilla for me," Hunter told her.

Billie looked up at him, questioningly, so he said. "Try it, it's very good."

She nodded to the waitress, who wrote their order down and left. Hunter turned back to Billie.

"What's wrong?"

Drying her tears with a napkin, she said, "If the man who threatened me is the one who did this horrible thing to Mr. Harrison, he could do the same to my family. How am I going to be able to stop him?"

Hunter thought about that for a moment. "Well, if Harrison did have the notebook, and whoever killed him got it, or at least knows where it is now, he'd have no further reason to harm them, or you, for that matter."

Then, as if it had just occurred to her for the first time, she asked Hunter, "Is it just a coincidence that you, Karl McCoy's grandson, and me, Dr. Chen's great granddaughter, just happen to meet at the same time that Scott Harrison is murdered?"

"What's your point?"

"I don't know, really. It just seems like an odd coincidence," she mused out loud. "Maybe it's not. I mean, you're here because your grandfather's sword was stolen and used in a murder for which your dad's been arrested. That's perfectly logical."

Hunter nodded and picked up from there. "And you're here because a man demanding your great-grandfather's notebook threatened your brother and his family if you didn't get it for him. So you came here to see if Harrison could help you, maybe show it to you or tell you where it is."

"Yes. That's it exactly."

They sat quietly for a moment considering it all.

"And our grandfathers knew each other," Hunter said.

"Yes, they did." She smiled. "Great-grandfather wrote in his diary that he'd become friends with an American soldier who was staying in the convent. The nuns, who'd been sent to Burma to escape the conflict, allowed him space to run his medical practice during the war. He wrote that the man's name was Sergeant Karl McCoy."

"That jibes with what my grandfather told my dad and me," Hunter added.

Billie eyed Hunter tentatively

"What is it?" he asked, sensing she wanted to ask him something but was holding back.

"Do you have your grandfather's things? You know, anything he may have brought back from the war?"

"Oh, I see where you're going with this. No, he never brought back a notebook. The only things we have from that time is the sword, or, I guess more accurately, we did have it, and several personal items that he passed on to my dad."

"Personal items?" she asked, perking up. "What do you mean?"

"One was an interesting old bone pipe that he'd carved some names on. In those days, if you were in the military, you were forbidden to tell your family or anyone else where you were, or where you were going. They kept a strict code of secrecy, just as they do today.

"There was an old slogan, 'Loose lips sink ships.' We now know that my grandfather left Norfolk, Virginia on a troop ship in 1944 for the Far East theater. The names he carved into the pipe bowl and stem reflect the places his ship passed through on the journey to China. Places like Gibraltar, Giza, Aden, and Bombay, but no notebook I'm afraid."

The waitress brought their iced teas and said the quesadillas were on the way.

Changing the subject, Hunter asked, "So what do you do in Chicago?"

"I own a travel agency. It actually was my husband's. He died two years ago—pancreatic cancer—and I run it now. He really grew the business on his own before he married me seven years ago. He was fifteen years older. I have good people running it for me while I'm here. What about you?" she asked. "What do you do? Do you live in Florida?"

Hunter had been waiting for this. Oddly, he wasn't sure how to answer. He was still a medical school professor, even though he was on leave with the possibility it might become permanent. He did technically live in a loft apartment in Charlottesville, Virginia, where the university was, although that would change if he decided to quit permanently. Thinking of his apartment he was temporarily jolted back to the reality of Detective Bolt's call about serious complaints.

"I live in Charlottesville, Virginia, and I'm on leave from my job at the medical school at the University."

"Are you a doctor?" she asked, surprised.

"A Ph.D. I teach and do medical research."

"Why are you on leave?"

"It's complicated."

"Oh," she said, eyeing him curiously, but leaving it alone. "Okay."

Hunter's phone rang. It was Lannigan.

"Meet me at the jail pronto. Bring Miss Chen and do not—I repeat—do not let her out of your sight for a moment."

"What's going on?"

"I'll tell you when you get here."

9

HUNTER KNEW THE DRIVE DOWN US HIGHWAY 41 to the sheriff's office, just south of the city of Venice, would take about forty-five minutes from the restaurant on the bayfront in Sarasota. Lannigan's admonition to not let Billie out of his sight amped up his surveillance. He was checking the rearview mirror when Billie's cellphone rang.

She took it out of her purse, checked the screen, and answered. "Charles, hi. Are you okay? I've been so worried. I know, I know. I did. I didn't call the police, but I have someone—"she glanced up at Hunter—"I have someone helping me now. I'll tell you about it later." She listened and then said, "Yes, for sure, and you do the same. I'll talk to you later."

"Your brother?" Hunter guessed.

"Yes. He's worried. After the break-in and the threat, I called him and told him to be careful. He wanted me to go to the police right away, but I thought it would be better to try to find the missing notebook first."

"So, what about your brother? Does he know anything about the notebook?"

"No. He's never even read the diary. He's never shown any interest—until now, of course. He doesn't read Chinese either. Says we're Americans and we speak English."

"What about your parents? Did they speak Chinese at home?"

She laughed. It was the first time Hunter had heard her laugh, and he liked it. "Only when they wanted to keep something from us kids. My dad was Chinese, and my mother was mostly Japanese. Unlike Charles, I wanted to know what they were saying so I paid attention, and even took Chinese in high school. Believe it or not, the Chicago school system actually offered a course."

She regaled him with stories about growing up Chinese-American in Chicago until they pulled into the parking lot at the Sheriff's station at two-thirty. By then they were both laughing continually.

Once inside, the seriousness of the place immediately darkened their mood. By the time they were ushered into an interview room, all previous lightheartedness had evaporated completely. Soon Detective Skaggs and Lannigan entered, and everyone sat down, Hunter and Billie on one side of the table, Skaggs across from them, and the lawyer pulled up a chair on the end.

Skaggs began. "It's 2:38 p.m., October twelfth. Present are Billie Chen, Hunter McCoy, J. Michael Lannigan, and me, Detective Otto Skaggs. Miss Chen, tell me about this break-in at your apartment in Chicago."

In considerable detail, she described the events of September fifteenth. reporting as much of the exact words the man had used as she could, right through to the threat to her brother's family if she didn't give him the notebook. Skaggs interrupted only twice during her recitation. Once he asked why she thought the man didn't threaten her directly, but only her brother and his family.

"I don't know. I guess he thought that would be more leverage. My husband is dead, and I don't have any children. The only family I have left is my brother, his wife, and their three kids. I suppose that's why."

The other interruption occurred when he asked why she hadn't gone to the police.

"He told me not to. He said find the notebook, or your brother's family is dead. I couldn't take a chance."

At this point, Lannigan asked a question. "Miss Chen suppose you actually somehow managed to find this missing notebook. What then? How were you supposed to contact this man? Did he give you instructions?"

She paused here, as if this was the first time the thought had occurred to her. "I don't. . . know. I guess. . . I don't know. He said he'd contact me. I don't really know."

"It's been a little over a month. Has he contacted you at all during this time?" Skaggs asked.

"No."

"Seems pretty casual for a guy threatening murder of an entire family if you don't come through," he added.

Lannigan interrupted, "Detective, I think it's time you tell Miss Chen what you found at the crime scene."

Skaggs continued to stare at her for a moment. Then, with a sigh of resignation, he opened a folder he'd placed on the table, held up a clear plastic bag containing a bloodstained note written in block letters, and laid it before her. "This was found lying under the sword used to behead Harrison."

He said he didn't have the notebook either.

"My God," Billie cried. "The monster."

"That looks like a direct threat to you and your family, Billie," Hunter said. "My guess is, he'll be contacting you soon, since the note obviously suggests Harrison was a dead-end."

Hunter looked at Skaggs. "Detective, was Harrison tortured? Did it look like the killer was trying to extract information?"

Skaggs straightened up and looked defiant. "That information is not for release to the general public."

"Come on, Detective," Lannigan interrupted, "we have every right to know this."

Defeated again, Skaggs said, "Yes, Harrison had clearly been extensively tortured before his death."

Then, in a complete change in attitude from his earlier defensive posture, Skaggs addressed Billie in a softer tone. "Miss Chen, I strongly suggest that you inform the Chicago police about your break-in and the threat to your brother's family. They can put them on a watch list. But that won't be enough by itself. If your brother can afford it, he should also hire someone to do twenty-four-seven surveillance of his house. If you'd like, I can have my people recommend someone for you. Also, if you and he have alarm systems, make sure they're activated at all times."

"Thanks, Detective," she said. "I will."

"Now, I think it's time to tell Miss Chen and Hunter what else you've uncovered," the attorney added.

Skaggs nodded. "This morning my men were working the crime scene at Harrison's house when the phone on the desk in his study rang. My sergeant picked it up, and a disguised voice on the line said, *'Tell the bitch she'd better find the notebook. There are other swords.'"*

Billie's face went pale and she began to topple back off her chair just as Hunter grabbed her and prevented the fall.

Skaggs hit his recorder and said, "This interview is terminated at 3:15 p.m."

Hunter took Billie outside and walked her around for a while until she regained her composure. "You going to be all right?"

"What am I going to do? I don't know where it is. I don't even know where to begin. I mean, Mr. Harrison was my only hope."

"Well, apparently Harrison didn't know either, or he would have told the murderer."

Her eyes welled. "What am I going to do?"

"Let's start with giving your description of the man to the sketch artist. Skaggs said to go in and do that when you're ready. Do you feel up to it now?"

"I guess so. I don't know what else to do." she answered.

Back in the building, the detective and Lannigan were standing and talking by the front desk. It looked to Hunter as if they were arguing. When Hunter and Billie approached, Skaggs took Billie's arm. "I'll bring you back to the artist. It should take about forty-five minutes."

When they left, Lannigan and Hunter sat on a bench on the far side of the room, where they could talk out of earshot of others.

"Hunter, you told me that your sheriff friend in the UP couldn't find your dad's computer where he said he'd left it, in that top drawer of his dresser."

Hunter nodded. "Right. So whoever put it under his clothes here was likely the same person who broke into the cabin and took it, along with the sword."

Lannigan sighed, looked down, and then looked directly at Hunter. "Unfortunately, they found more than just the computer when they searched the Kingston house on Casey Key."

Hunter waited, anxiously.

"They found a man's blood-soaked shirt and pants in a plastic bag in the back of your dad's closet, behind a footlocker. The DA told me the blood is a match to Scott Harrison's."

10

CARRIE JOHANNSON PARKED IN THE EMPLOYEES' LOT at the Selby Gardens Botanical Center on the bay in downtown Sarasota. Her blond ponytail bobbed back and forth in synch with her light step as she approached the entrance. The guard on duty recognized her instantly and flashed her a big smile. "Top of the morning to you, Dr. Johannson."

In response, Carrie amped up her own smile. "Thanks, Earl, top of the morning to you as well."

"Gonna work hard today?" he asked jokingly.

"Always do," she answered, setting her course for the lab. Today, for the first time since she'd started her position as a botanist at the Selby four months before, she finally had time for an important project of her own.

She and her mother had both agreed that even though she wasn't a medical botanist and didn't have Dr. Chen's research notebook, she'd have to be the one to deal with the sack of seedpods she'd found in the cooler at her grandmother's house. She'd have to be the one to carry on with his work, since his brother obviously never showed up to collect them. If they really contained the secret for a miracle treatment for diabetes, they had to be handled with extreme care.

Carrie had no way of knowing whether the seedpods had actually been kept cool and dry for all those years since the war, but if they had, there was an outside chance they might still be viable.

She was pretty sure they actually were orchid seedpods but would check with Bruce Fembro, one of the other botanists on staff—and an orchid specialist—to see what he thought. If they were, she knew she had her work cut out for her.

Most amateurs don't raise orchids from seeds for a good reason. It's a time-consuming, delicate process, fraught with the possibility of seed contamination and failure. Plus, she would need some pretty sophisticated and expensive equipment to do it properly.

Still, Grandma's letter said these seedpods were important, and she *had* promised the old Chinese doctor on his deathbed, so Carrie was going to give it her best shot.

She found Bruce at his bench, looking over jars of orchid seedlings he'd been preparing for an upcoming show. He looked up and smiled when he saw his visitor.

"Hi, Carrie."

"Hey, Bruce, how are your babies coming along?" Bruce was the best orchid flasker in the house, but he'd been having trouble getting this new hybrid variety going.

"I think the little darlins are actually going to make it. I'll know in a few months. What have you got there?" he asked spotting the bag Carrie was holding.

"I don't know. A mystery, I guess."

"Yeah? What's the mystery?"

"Well, they're seedpods, probably orchids, but I'd like you to take a look and tell me what you think?"

"Sure, but let's step out of the sterile room first."

They went to a bench, where Carrie took out a pod and placed it on a clean paper. Bruce examined it and asked, "Where did you get these?"

"Well, sort of from my grandmother. She died a few months ago, and I found them in a cooler in her basement while going through her things."

"Hmmm. It looks like an orchid pod. Where did she get it?"

Carrie told him the story.

"You mean these are that old? Really? From World War Two?"

"Apparently so. There was supposed to have been a research notebook with them that explained all about them, but she never got it. Here, let me show you my grandmother's letter that came with the pods." She unfolded the letter from 1948 and waited as Bruce read it.

"That's heavy," he said when he'd finished reading. "If he actually found something to prevent the development of juvenile diabetes—and it's actually in these seedpods—that'd be huge."

"Exactly," Carrie said, "and I've been doing some homework. There's no cure for juvenile diabetes. Insulin is the only treatment, but it's not a cure. There is also nothing that can prevent the development of childhood diabetes once it's diagnosed. And insulin was probably not available to a poor doctor in Japanese-occupied China during the war in the nineteen forties. Without insulin or a viable alternative, his young patients with the disease would all have died."

"So why did the doctor's brother never show up?"

"I don't know. But now that I have the seedpods, I feel obligated to try to carry on with them." She looked hopefully at Bruce. "Do you think it's possible they're viable and I could grow them?"

"I don't know. I guess we could give it a try and see."

Carrie grinned. That was exactly what she'd wanted to hear. Bruce had said "we" could try. That meant she'd benefit from the considerable expertise of her friend and co-worker.

"Let's put them in the cooler," Bruce said, "and tonight, after work, we'll get started."

Like Carrie, Bruce was single and had no one to get home to, so staying late for a little freelancing wouldn't inconvenience anyone. So later, after five o'clock, they met in the sterile room of Bruce's lab.

Carrie watched as Bruce first carefully sterilized the seedpods with a bleach solution.

"This is necessary," he explained, "because a single bacterium or fungal spore can contaminate and overgrow the slower-growing orchid seeds. Now, when I open these pods, I'll do it in the laminar flow hood over there." He pointed to a large boxlike structure with glass doors.

"So the seeds don't run into any more contamination?" Carrie asked, even though she knew the answer.

"Right. From this point on sterility is our friend. The laminar flow hood will reduce the chances of contamination to almost zero."

"Then you grow them on agar, right?" Carrie asked.

"Yes. Remember that orchid seeds contain an embryo and virtually no endosperm—the plant equivalent of a yolk. So virtually all nutrients must come from the media, in this case the agar on the bottom of these sterile jars."

Carrie nodded. "But how do they do it in nature? I mean, when the seed pods open and release seeds, where do they naturally get their nutrition to germinate and grow?"

"In nature, orchids must immediately establish a symbiotic relationship with a special type of fungus if it is to grow and survive. The fungus supplies the nutrients."

"Bruce, do you think there's a chance these guys might actually make it? I mean, if they're that old?"

"I don't know. They should be able to last years and even decades if stored under the proper conditions. I guess it depends on how well your grandmother followed the doc's instructions and stored them. In any case, it might be worth a research paper just to see if we can do it."

"How long do we have to wait in order to know?"

"If they're viable, it could take two to twelve months, with alternate cooling and heating to get germination. Then three months after germination, the protocorms in the seed plate will have grown in size and number and start to get leaves and roots. That's when we transfer them to spread flasks, four plants per flask, prepared with fresh media so they can start to really develop. Typically they'll spend three months in the spread flasks, and then we transfer them into final 'replace' flasks, where they should complete their seedling growth in six months."

Carrie shook her head and said with mock surprise, "So you're telling me we won't have our answer by tomorrow?"

Bruce chuckled. "Listen, hotshot, knock it off. I know you know all this stuff; it's just fun to repeat it."

"Yeah," Carrie admitted, "I know, and even then, we won't know for another year or two after deflasking the seedlings and sending them to the greenhouse, what the flowers—if any—will look like."

"Too bad you don't have his research notebook."

"Yeah, too bad."

11

THE DARK GRAY WALLS OF THE SHERIFF'S STATION, mirrored Hunter's growing sense of alarm as the evidence against his dad continued to pile up. While Billie worked with the police sketch artist, Hunter and the lawyer continued their discussion. Lannigan tapped Hunter on the knee. "Someone's going to a lot of trouble to frame your dad for murder."

"Yeah."

"Still no ideas who or why?" the attorney asked.

"None. I can't imagine my grandfather had any enemies, much less any who'd want to hurt my dad. After he got back from the war, Gramps married my grandmother and went to work as an electrician. They lived in Calumet, in Michigan's Upper Peninsula. Later they moved to Marquette, where my dad was born. When my grandmother died, Gramps lived alone in their house until his death last year. He never mentioned any enemies."

Lannigan ran his fingers though his thick black hair and sighed. "Well, I'll put the same question to your dad. Your grandfather might have told him things he never told you."

"Possibly," Hunter said, "but there's something else I can't figure out." He walked to the window that looked out onto the police parking lot. "Are we looking for someone who, for some unknown reason, is primarily focused on framing my dad for murder, or is something else going on?

"That blood-stained note left with the sword suggests the threat was directed at Billie to find the notebook. That strongly suggests that the guy who beheaded Harrison is the same man who accosted her in Chicago. So if we start from that assumption, then the *real* motive of the killer is to find this notebook for some reason and framing my dad for the murder is simply a way to take the focus off himself."

Lannigan nodded. "But why your dad *specifically*? I mean, that took a lot of planning and work to somehow get into the cabin in Michigan, take the sword and the computer, then leave them at the murder scene in Florida."

"Exactly," Hunter agreed. "That's the flaw in the argument. He could have just killed Harrison and left, trying to leave no clues. This elaborate scheme to frame my dad must have a purpose of its own. It's way too personal to *not* to be personal, if you see what I mean."

"I agree. Which, I'm afraid, brings us right back to where we started."

"There's something else," Hunter said. "I don't know if there's a link or not, but it's beginning to look suspicious. Someone may be going after me too."

"What do you mean?"

"My lab at the medical school has a grant from the National Institute of Health that's funding part of my vascular smooth muscle research. Our funds have just been frozen because someone has been regularly drawing a salary illegally and depositing it in my bank account.

"Also, the police in Charlottesville, where I live, have been receiving complaints about my loft apartment. They won't tell me what the complaints are over the phone. They want to see me in person. The police claim that the charges are serious enough that, if true, I could be facing serious prison time."

Lannigan leaned back and let this new development sink in. "So somebody's setting you both up?"

"It looks that way."

"And you have no idea who or why."

"None."

They heard a female voice coming up behind them.

"Hunter, I did it."

Startled, they both looked up as Billie Chen approached. Apparently finished with the sketch artist, she sat down and joined them.

"I was surprised how much I remembered," she said. "The police artist was very good at helping me recall details. When we were finished, her sketch was so good I was actually frightened again at the image of the man she'd drawn. It's definitely him. Here look."

Hunter and Lannigan examined the copy of the artist's sketch.

Hunter tried to reconcile this sketch to the description Billie had given to him and Jenny at her house. It bore some resemblance, but this guy looked younger than the image he had in his head from her verbal description. Her sketch showed a white man in his early thirties with a broad face, thin lips, cold dark eyes, and thin hair slicked straight back.

"They'll circulate the picture, although the artist said it's likely the man will have fled the area by now."

Hunter shook his head. "Maybe not. If my dad is his target for some reason, he may stick around to see what happens." Then he told them about his frozen research grant and the call from the Charlottesville police.

"So you see, the man who killed Harrison is not only a threat to you and your brother's family because he thinks you may have this notebook he wants, but for some reason he's also a threat to my dad and possibly me as well. For some reason it appears he has a personal issue with both of us."

"Or," Lannigan interjected, "he may simply be hired help and working for someone else who's pulling the strings behind all this. Someone with a motive we know nothing about."

Hunter thought about that. "It would seem that my dad's safe for the moment, in jail, but Billie, you and your brother's family aren't. What are you going to do?" he asked her. "What are your plans?"

Billie Chen was silent, her effervescence at completing the sketch suddenly replaced with fear of the killer.

"I don't know," she said in a weak voice, choking back tears.

Lannigan stepped in here. "Ed McCoy has no obvious motive to kill Harrison. Most of the information about your grandfather in Harrison's book was freely available on the internet. We can assume it was the killer—or someone working for or with him—who got into Ed's cabin, took the sword and the computer, and exchanged emails with Harrison. Whoever did that also planted the laptop back in Ed's dresser drawer here in Florida. We know this happened sometime in the last two days, because Ed said he'd go into that drawer every day and would have seen it. The bloody clothes from the murder scene hidden in the house added to the attempt to frame him.

"The timeline for the break-in at the cabin up north also suggests that the man who threatened you, Ms. Chen, is the same one trying to frame the McCoys. The big mystery is, how are the two connected?"

The lawyer stood up and addressed Hunter. "I'm going in to see your dad now and tell him what we have so far. The bail hearing is tomorrow morning at ten in the courthouse. The problem is—like I said before—he's being held on a first-degree murder charge, and the judge will undoubtedly agree to hold him without bail. I'll see what I can do but be prepared. He may have to stay there a while."

After Lannigan left, Hunter asked Billie, "Where are you staying?"

"I don't have a place yet. I came directly from the airport in my rental car to Scott Harrison's house."

"You're going to have to spend the night at least. Follow me to the Inn At The Beach, in Venice. I've stayed there before. You'll like it. They should have a vacant room."

TWENTY MINUTES AFTER LEAVING BILLIE at the hotel, Hunter pulled into the driveway of the Kingston house. On entering, he found Henry sprawled on the kitchen floor with blood pooling around his head.

What the . . .?

Henry groaned and tried to get up just as Hunter reached him. He slung his arm around Henry's waist and eased him into a chair. Henry sank back while Hunter checked his pupils. Normal and even. Next he checked the gash on his head, which was still bleeding. Taking the man's head in both hands, he said, "Henry can you lift your arms in front of you?" Still wobbly, he did. They came up even.

"Show me your teeth," Hunter said.

"Wha—? My teeth?"

"Just do it."

Henry grinned and showed his teeth. Hunter saw that his smile was even, no drooping face. In the bathroom Hunter found first aid supplies, returned, and patched up his old friend as well as he could with what he had on hand. Finally he asked him, "What happened, Henry?"

"Not sure. I had just come into the kitchen and was going out to the lanai when something hit me. I don't know what."

"Did you see anyone?"

"No," Henry pressed his bandaged head and moaned.

"Let's go, I'm taking you to Urgent Care. Someone's got to check you out."

Hunter bundled Henry into the Jeep and drove to Sarasota Hospital's Urgent Care facility in Venice.

While the staff took Henry in for repairs, Hunter closed his eyes and tried to make sense of recent events. With all the strange things going on in his life right now, whoever was behind all this might have decided to take it to the next level, and thinking it was Hunter, attacked Henry instead.

But something was still wrong here. If whoever did this really meant him harm, they'd have killed him, not just hit him in the head. This seemed more like serious harassment.

A nurse came out to get Hunter about a half hour later and invited him back to Henry's examining room, where he met the attending doctor.

"Mr. Lahti says you're with him. So I'll tell you both what we know. The wound on the head is deep but not serious, and I've patched it up with sutures. Imaging shows no brain damage or internal bleeding from the blow. I've given him some pain meds that should take care of the headache."

Addressing Henry directly, he said, "You should be fine. The sutures will dissolve on their own. Come back if you experience any complications. Otherwise, we're done here."

12

THE NEXT MORNING'S BAIL HEARING WENT pretty much as Lannigan predicted. The county DA argued that the evidence against Ed was so compelling and the crime so heinous, that no bail should be granted. Lannigan argued that the evidence was circumstantial at best—that every point made by the DA could be explained by logical alternative evidence, and that Ed, a man with no prior police record, wasn't a flight risk. Nevertheless, the judge, a strict law-and-order type, refused bail. For the time being, Ed McCoy would remain in jail. Hunter was allowed to see him for twenty minutes at two o'clock that afternoon.

"How you doing, Dad?"

"I can handle it. Lannigan stopped by after the bail hearing and filled me in. He says the grand jury indictment means nothing. They're only allowed to see the prosecution's evidence. Unfortunately, their decision means that the State can formally charge me with murder, if they choose to, and I have to stay here until trial if it comes to that. Lannigan says none of it will hold up in court."

"I agree with him. The biggest problem is that Skaggs thinks he has his man—you—and he's not looking for other suspects. That's going to be my job. Another problem is that no one can verify your whereabouts at the time the coroner says Harrison was killed. Henry was out on the boat with your two neighbors, Jim Furlow and Joe Palma, while you were home alone."

"So," Ed said, "you either find the man who threatened Billie Chen, or you find this notebook he was after. If you find the man first and turn him over to the cops, I get out of here and get this thing off my back. Or you find the notebook first and when the guy comes for it, you grab him. Have I got that right?"

"That sums it up, Dad."

Hunter knew what he said was true. There was nothing he could do for his father in jail. Lannigan would have to deal with that. His job was to do what he did best, find the real killer.

"Dad, there's something else you need to know."

He told him about the problem with his NIH grant and the confusing allegations against him at his loft apartment in Charlottesville.

Ed McCoy put his head in his hands. "Oh man, this thing just keeps getting worse. We can't afford to have you behind bars too, son. You've got to find out who's doing this."

After leaving his dad, Hunter drove to Billie's motel. She'd called earlier and left a message telling him she needed to see him, and he'd texted back saying he'd check in after the jail visit.

When he knocked at the motel, she opened the door and threw her arms around him.

"Oh, Hunter, thank God you came," she cried, burying her face in his shoulder and holding him tight.

Whoa, what's going on?

"What's happened?" he asked.

"I went to the hotel's breakfast room for coffee this morning. When I got back I found this taped to the outside of the door."

She handed him an envelope with something heavier than a note inside. He opened it and extracted a small framed photo of a young girl.

"That's my niece Kim, my brother's youngest daughter."

The photo had obviously been removed from the frame and cut with a scissors, separating the girl's head from her body. Then it had been replaced in the frame. It was gruesome, and the implied threat was obvious.

"We've got to find that notebook," Billie pleaded. "It's the only way to save her. We've got to find it."

Hunter knew she was right. He had no leads to follow that pointed to the killer directly. The only link to the man was that he wanted the damned thing.

Even that was weird. Why would he want it? It was hard to imagine the guy was interested in the treatment of juvenile diabetes. That level of altruism in a man capable of torture and beheading seemed unlikely if not ridiculous. Still, the blood-stained note and now this 'beheaded' photo of the little girl just added more support to the idea that the same man was involved.

"Call your brother. Ask him where this photo came from. If the guy was in his house, they're not safe. Can he afford to hire some security?"

"Yes, he can. I'll call him."

"You've also got to call the police in Chicago and report what's happened. You can't let this go unreported any longer."

Hunter listened to the one-sided conversation while she made the call. He was surprised when she asked her brother to call the Chicago police rather than do it herself. Still, he and his family were the ones threatened, so it made sense.

"Now you have one more call," Hunter continued. "You've got to call detective Skaggs and give him this photo and the envelope so he can check for prints. Maybe somebody got careless."

When she called the Sheriff's office, Skaggs told her to call the Venice police. It wasn't his jurisdiction, but he'd send a deputy to liaise with them.

WITH HER HOTEL ROOM NOW TEMPORARILY A CRIME SCENE and with no real leads to go on to the find the man himself, Hunter and Billie drove to the Kingston house to decide on what they could do next. While she had coffee with Henry, Hunter called Wally Osborn.

Hunter knew that while Wally was on "the other side," so-to-speak, of this business—the prosecution side—and even though it wasn't his jurisdiction, he might be able to give him some insight on Detective Skaggs. He caught Osborn at his desk.

"Hi, Wally. Hunter."

"Hi, Hunter, what's up?"

"Detective Otto Skaggs of the Sarasota County Sheriff's Department. What can you tell me about him?"

"Skaggs?" Osborn mused, as if trying to conjure up the man.

"Yeah. Otto Skaggs."

"What do you want to know exactly?" Osborn said. "You do know I might have some professional ethics issues here."

"Right. I understand. I'm only concerned that he seems to be sure my dad is guilty and therefore has no need to look for anyone else. Lannigan's talked with the prosecutor who knows that the evidence against him might not stand up in court, and he's been trying to get Skaggs to either find more evidence, drop the charges, or find another suspect. But Skaggs is apparently reluctant. I just wondered if you know enough about the man to maybe explain his unwillingness to look deeper."

Osborn coughed. Finally, he said, "I don't know for sure, but I might have an idea. You have to understand that he and I are in different departments—sheriff and municipal police—and I don't know the facts of his cases, so this is just a guess."

"Understood. Go ahead."

"About a year ago, I recall that he worked a case where he arrested a man for killing his ten-year-old daughter. The grand jury indicted the man on a murder charge, and trial was set. Before the trial began Skaggs found additional, and pretty convincing, evidence that the girl's uncle, the man's brother-in-law, was the real killer. The father was freed. The brother-in-law was arrested and protested his innocence all the time, claiming he was being framed by the girl's father. Distraught, the man then somehow managed to hang himself in jail.

"Skaggs investigated some more and found that the man he'd originally arrested had planted the evidence that framed his brother-in-law. He rearrested the father, and the man is now awaiting trial."

"I see," Hunter said.

"So maybe he doesn't want to second-guess himself again," Osborn said. "A mistake like that can get to you."

"I imagine it can. Thanks, Wally."

"Keep me informed."

"Will do."

HUNTER AND BILLIE SAT AROUND THE DESK in her hotel room. "Let's focus on the notebook for the moment," Hunter began. "You've never seen it, and except for the reference in the diary, you've never heard of it?"

"That's right." She took the diary out of her purse and started leafing through it. "I already told you and Mr. Lannigan about the first reference." She repeated it again.

"The process for refining the medicine that I've used to treat juvenile diabetes is detailed in my research notebook. The Glorious Store is linked to it in a most ironic way."

"Here's the second reference." She translated for him.

"Confirmation today. All three children following three months of treatment have maintained normal blood sugars for two months with no insulin, no special diet, and no further treatment. Blood and urine sugar values in all three appear to be normal. Details in research notebook. Thank God. It's a miracle. It really works."

"That's unheard of," Hunter said. "If he's referring to three kids with juvenile diabetes, there's no way they could go that long without insulin and have normal blood sugars. They would have been in diabetic ketoacidosis at the very least, and most likely coma."

He tried to recall what would likely have been available in Japanese-occupied China during the war to treat kids with diabetes. Insulin was in use then, but probably not available to Chen in a war zone. Maybe that was why Chen felt compelled to search for some other way to deal with these kids and then somehow made his discovery. He also had access to a means of testing body fluids for glucose, since he'd said they were normal.

"It could be that the killer wants the notebook because a discovery like this could be worth a fortune today," Billie said. "Do you think that's it?"

"Greed. Sure. That could be it, if your great-grandfather's notebook explains what the stuff is and how to produce it. People have committed murder for far less. But even if that's true, why make it look like my dad did it? And make no mistake about it, whoever did this is after him *specifically*. Even if the killer wants the notebook because it might be worth a fortune, he still has some reason to target my dad."

Billie watched Hunter quietly for long moment. Her expressions both worried and hopeful. "I've picked up pieces of conversation between you and your attorney, Mr. Lannigan," she said, "and it sounds like you do some kind of work that involves finding things. Is that right?"

"Yeah, I do, when I'm not busy at the medical school—like now. People ask me to find something that's gone missing and help them correct the consequences of that loss. I see where you're going with this."

"Yes. Good. I want to hire you to find the notebook. I can afford to pay you. In the process, you might get your chance at finding the real killer and getting your dad out of jail. What do you say?"

Hunter met Billie's eyes. "Let me tell you how this works. I don't have a fixed fee for my services. When I've found what's missing and corrected the consequences of that loss, my clients pay me what they think it's worth. It's completely up to them. I haven't been disappointed yet."

"And you won't be this time either," she replied, brightening. "Thank you."

13

HUNTER RETURNED TO THE RENTAL HOUSE and slept soundly. In the morning he returned to the Inn At The Beach, picked up Billie, and drove her to the Kingston house on Casey Key. After spending a half hour or so updating Henry on Ed's situation, they turned their attention to finding the notebook.

"So where do we start?" Billie asked.

Hunter had been wondering the same thing. Scott Harrison had undoubtedly done a lot of research to have written his book. He may actually have interviewed Hunter's grandfather and many others as well. So who else did he interview? For the first time, Hunter realized that he was at a disadvantage not having read Harrison's account of his grandfather's experience in China.

"You said you read the book, right?" he asked Billie.

"I did, yes."

"Did he mention any other names related to our grandfathers' stories?"

"Let me think." She rested her chin on her palms and stared off into space for a moment before responding. "He mentioned the guy who apparently abandoned your grandfather in the first place. I think that was the only name."

"That would be Captain Grayson Malport," Hunter acknowledged. "I know that story. Henry, can I see your copy of the book?"

"Sure, let me get it. It's in the bedroom."

When he returned and handed it to him, Hunter used the index to find his grandfather's story. It was only six pages long, so he read them while the others waited. He looked up when he was finished.

"I notice two things. First, Harrison read an article in the *Upper Peninsula Post* on my grandfather. He cites it under the references for the chapter on my grandfather. My dad actually wrote the story." He read it aloud.

McCoy, Karl, Remembering VJ Day, First of a three-part series, the *Upper Peninsula Post, August 20, 1995.*

"Secondly, and this is interesting, Harrison says that Malport's son thought the whole story about the notebook and a great medical breathrough was nonsense. So here's what we need to do. Let's check to see if Grayson Malport is still alive. If he isn't, we'll look up his son."

Hunter booted up his laptop. After a few minutes of searching, he found an obituary for Grayson Malport. The man had two sons. After searching White Pages online he was able to find one of them.

"Colin Malport is sixty-five years old and lives in Cape Coral, Florida."

"That's only an hour's drive from here," Henry said. "It's just south of Fort Myers."

Within the hour Hunter was driving the Jeep south on Interstate 75. During the drive, Billie called her brother and told him what they were doing. Hunter pulled into the driveway of Colin Malport's house a little before noon.

The old bungalow had a carport with a late model white Buick SUV parked under it. The other homes in the area were similar, no doubt built at the same time by a developer using just a few different floor plans. They were neat and well kept up, but not ostentatious.

Hunter knocked, and a woman in her sixties opened the inner door and looked out through the screen. "Hello," she said, smiling. "Can I help you?"

Must be his wife, Hunter thought.

"Hi, my name is Hunter McCoy, and this is Billie Chen. We'd like to speak with Colin Malport if he's home?"

The woman's smile faded slightly, unsure what this was about. "Okay. Let me get him."

Without inviting them in, she turned and went into the house. A moment later a stout man in his sixties, wearing white shorts and a green golf shirt, came to the door. "I'm Colin Malport."

"Mr. Malport, could we come in and talk. It has to do with your father."

"My father?" the man said, surprise obvious on his face.

Hunter continued. "I'll explain when we're inside, if that's all right with you."

Having no idea what Hunter was taking about, but seeing no reason to be rude, he invited them in. "This is my wife, Eleanor," he said as he led them into a small but comfortable living room.

Once they were seated, Malport, still looking confused, asked "So what about my father?"

"Maybe you heard that the author Scott Harrison was murdered recently—up on Casey Key, near Venice."

"Scott Harrison? Wait a minute, that's the guy who called me about a year back. He was writing a book or something—about the war."

"That's the one. Your dad was mentioned in his book, as was my grandfather, and—nodding at Billie—her great-grandfather too. Have you read it?"

"Read it?" He asked, frowning. "No. I don't generally read books. Didn't even know it was published. You say he was murdered?"

"Yes, a few days ago."

"What's this got to do with my dad?"

Billie took up the story. "Mr. Malport, my great-grandfather and Hunter's grandfather lived for a while in an abandoned convent in Wuchang, China, during the war."

Malport put his hands up to stop her. "Oh, I remember now. It's about that damned notebook, isn't it? That's why you're here?"

"Yes," Billie said, then continued. "Harrison probably interviewed Hunter's grandfather, Sgt. Karl McCoy, who was in his nineties at the time. The sergeant told him about a medicine my great-grandfather, Li Qiang Chen, had supposedly developed that might prevent the development of juvenile diabetes. He kept the information in a notebook. Hunter's grandfather died shortly after that, and then Harrison interviewed you. Apparently your father, Grayson Malport, had already passed on at the time."

"Yeah, that's right," Malport said.

"I believe you told Harrison, when he interviewed you, that—let me quote you now—'I know nothing about that damned notebook, and I don't know where it is.'"

"That's true."

Hunter jumped in. "You see, Mr. Malport, we're looking for that notebook, and even though you don't know where it is, we had nowhere else to turn, so we came here to pick your brain, so to speak."

Malport put both hands behind his head and sat back in his recliner, closed his eyes, and exhaled a big long sigh, then pointed a finger at Hunter.

"Firstly, McCoy, I know what my father did to your grandfather. Harrison told me how he abandoned him at the Japanese air base when it looked too dangerous to stay there himself. That doesn't surprise me at all. My father was that kind of man, thoughtless and cruel. He only cared about himself.

"After the war he married my mother and lived off her meager income. He was always going to start some great scheme that was going to put us on Easy Street. Nothing ever panned out, and when my mother became unable to work because of meningitis, he started drinking even more than he had before. When she died, he abandoned us—just like he did your grandfather. My brother and I were raised by my grandparents. I never saw him again. I heard he died years later.

"I learned from my grandparents, after I'd grown up, that when he returned from the war he had this notebook— the one you're talking about. Said he'd found it in China. Told my mom he was going to make a fortune because it contained information on some miracle medical cure; must be the diabetes you mentioned. Anyway, he took it around to pharmaceutical companies figuring they'd pay big bucks for it.

Billie glanced at Hunter, her eyes wide.

"Of course, it was written in Chinese," Malport went on, "and when they finally found someone who could translate it, they discovered that several pages were missing. And wouldn't you know, the missing pages, were the very ones that supposedly contained all the critical information.

"Anyway, when Harrison asked me about it, I told him what I'm telling you. I've never seen the damned thing and have no idea where it might be or if it even still exists. Or, for that matter, whether it *ever* existed."

With another big sigh, Malport dropped his hands to his sides and shook his head. "The man was a complete loser."

His wife stood up, walked over, and put her hand on his shoulder. "Just relax, Colin, remember your heart."

He patted her hand, "Yeah, I will, honey. I will."

Hunter was beginning to think this was going to be a dead end.

"Do you know the names of any of the firms he took it too?" he asked. "Did he leave any records or anything?"

"No. I was too young, of course, no more than one or two at the time he was doing this."

"What about your mother?"

"Nah, she never mentioned any, or I was too young to remember. She died when I was ten. Like I said, that's when my brother and I went to live with my grandparents."

"Colin, remember that box of your mother's stuff you got from your grandmother?" Elinore said. "It's still in the attic. Maybe there is something in there that could help," Eleanor said.

"I doubt it," he said with a shrug. "It's just old letters and things. Haven't looked in there in years."

"Mr. Malport, could you look in there now," Hunter asked, "and see if there's any mention of the notebook?"

Malport just stared at Hunter and Billie for a long moment before speaking. "Maybe it's time you tell me why you want this thing so badly. You planning to make a fortune like my old man?"

Hunter knew he had to level with him. He couldn't see any downside to telling him the truth, so he did. He told him about the man who threatened Billie's family if she didn't get it to him. How they believed this was the man who killed Harrison, and how the man, for some unknown reason, had also framed Hunter's dad for the murder. He explained their reasoning that finding the notebook could lead to capturing the man responsible for all this, protecting Billie's family and freeing Hunter's dad.

"So it's not about making money, Mr. Malport, it's about saving lives."

14

A FEW MINUTES LATER, ELEANOR MALPORT returned from the attic with a dusty box, set it on the kitchen table, and they each took a chair around it. The box was ornately decorated with a flap cover and a gold-colored string that kept it closed by wrapping around a bright red button. Colin Malport opened it and removed a stack of loose papers and folders about twelve inches high.

"Tell you what," he said. "Let's each take some of these and see what we can find."

Hunter took a stack of papers, mostly yellow carbon copies, and quickly determined they were mostly old rental forms and papers related to the house Malport's father and mother rented in Cleveland. A few were late payment notices. Each one always had a note written on it in a feminine hand, stating that she told the lender the payment would be made the next month and asked that they please extend them a little time. There were some old insurance papers, and some receipts from a church called Saint Michael's for their annual giving. In short, he found nothing.

He looked up at the others and waited.

"Here's something," Eleanor said, holding up a few yellowed receipts. "These are expenses for a car trip to Detroit, in July 1946. Then another one to Chicago, in August of the same year. Finally, a third to Indianapolis a few weeks later, in September."

"What are those cities again?" Hunter asked, suddenly perking up. "Did you say Detroit, Chicago, and Indianapolis?"

"Yes."

"Now that could be something. Eli Lilly is a major pharmaceutical firm in Indianapolis. Abbott Laboratories is a large firm in Chicago, and I think Parke-Davis is in Detroit. All three of them would have been in business in the 1940s. Do you see any others?"

They each continued looking but found nothing else of particular interest.

"I can't believe that anyone from that era would still be working at any of those firms," Billie said dejectedly.

"You're probably right," Hunter replied, wondering how he'd even go about asking if they had any record of a meeting between Grayson Malport and anyone at their firms. Still, it was a lead and he'd follow it as far as he could. Then another idea hit him.

"Mr. Malport, where did your father live after he abandoned you and your brother?"

"I have no idea. Somewhere in Ohio, I imagine. We never heard from him after he left us. My grandparents never spoke about him either. They were my mother's parents and thought he was lower than snake spit, if you'll pardon the expression."

"I can imagine," Hunter said, shaking his head. "Before we go, can you think of anything else, anything at all, that might help us track down where he lived?"

Colin Malport thought about that for a moment. "I remember something—just a vague memory—about the post office. There was some link to the post office, maybe something my grandparents said about him. I don't know. Sorry."

Hunter and Billie thanked them for their help, then drove back to Casey Key pretty much in silence. Back at the house, they told Henry what little they'd learned.

"Time for some computer work and telephone calls," Hunter said. "Billie, you see if Grayson Malport ever worked for the post office, and I'll check in with the three drug firms."

Henry brought out his laptop for Billie to use. Hunter fired up his own. Billie set up on the kitchen table and Hunter went out to the lanai.

Where to start? he wondered, finally concluding that the best place would be the drug firm's research divisions. He'd explain that he was a medical school professor doing blood vessel research, which was actually true.

He began with Parke-Davis in Detroit. After establishing his credentials, he'd tell each person that he was looking for evidence of a meeting between anyone at the company and a man called Grayson Malport. It would have been in July 1946. After being rerouted to a number of different people, he finally concluded Parke-Davis had nothing—no record that survived from that era of a meeting by anyone with a Grayson Malport.

Next, he tried Abbott Laboratories in Chicago. Again, a dead end after multiple re-routings. Eli Lilly was his last hope. One of Hunter's colleagues at the medical school had done an internship with them while getting his Ph.D. in pharmacology so he knew a little about their history.

An hour later he was talking with a woman in the records department, who told him she'd found that a Grayson Malport had an appointment to meet with a Dr. Phillip Johnson on July 17, 1946. Dr. Johnson was a research scientist with Lilly at the time. Best of all, she'd found a record of the content of the meeting in which Dr. Johnson said that Malport showed him a notebook purported to contain information on a Chinese herbal medicine that could prevent juvenile diabetes.

Johnson, who surprisingly could read Chinese, said the notebook, written by a Dr. Li Qiang Chen, described several amazing cures among his patients who used an extract from a special Chinese orchid. Unfortunately, the pages that described the extract, the orchid species it came from, and the process of refining it, were missing, torn out of the notebook. Dr. Johnson told Malport the notebook was worthless without the pages, but said that if he found them, Lilly would be happy to look into it. The record indicated that Malport left with the notebook and never came back.

Billie called from inside the house. "Hunter, I think I found something." Hunter came in and looked over her shoulder at the screen.

"Look here," she said. "Grayson Steven Malport was a letter carrier for the United States Postal Service in Hamilton, Ohio in 1955. Maybe we could call the Hamilton post office and ask them to check their records for that time and see if they have his home address listed."

"Where's Hamilton?" asked Hunter.

She checked her computer again. "Looks like it's in southwest Ohio, just north of Cincinnati."

The post office wasn't just going to give this information up to anyone asking for it. Hunter knew it was time to put on one of his other hats. It didn't take long to get the phone number of the post office in Hamilton. He put the call through and a receptionist answered.

"This is Detective Lieutenant Hunter McCoy with the Virginia State Police. Can you connect me to the postmaster, please?"

Hunter watched, amused, as Billie's and Henry's jaws dropped in astonishment at this. Hunter put his finger to his lips, indicating they should remain quiet and just wait.

After a short pause, the phone connection was made.

"This is Postmaster Eberle. Sorry, who am I talking to?"

"Detective Lieutenant Hunter McCoy with the Virginia State Police. Sir, I'm working a cold case that goes back to 1955. The person I'm interested in is one Grayson

Steven Malport, who apparently worked for the post office in Hamilton in or around 1955. Would you have access to records on this person's employment?"

"1955? If we do they would be in old paper files stored in our basement alcove. We're not a big office here, so I'd have to check that out myself."

"Mr. Eberle, I can't overemphasize how important this information is to the case."

"Well, sure then. I can do that. It might take a while, maybe an hour or so."

"That's great. We're also interested in the local address he used in Hamilton. I'll give you my personal cellphone number. Call me as soon as you can."

Since Hunter's cell had a Virginia area code, he knew the man, if he checked, wouldn't be suspicious. Hunter gave it to him.

"Right. I'll call you back as soon as possible."

While they waited, Henry asked Hunter a question that hadn't come up before. "So those nuns, you know, the ones who were sent to Burma during the war, did they ever come back to that convent where your grandfathers stayed?"

"Yeah, they did, toward the end of his stay there," Hunter answered. "He told us one of them, a Sister Mary Margaret, I think was her name, sometimes helped the doc with his patients because she had nurse's training. What about you, Billie?"

"I have no idea."

"Just wondering," Henry said.

"I've got an idea." Hunter opened up his laptop and started typing. "I'm going to see if that article, the one in the *Upper Peninsula Post* that Harrison cited about my grandfather, is available online. Maybe the article tells that."

In a few minutes he found it. The three of them read the entire article as he slowly scrolled down the screen.

"There it is," Billie said. "Sisters of Notre Dame de Namur. That's the convent where they stayed."

"Your grandfather never mentioned that in his diary?" Hunter asked. "Never said the name of the convent?"

"No, he never did. Just called it the convent."

"Well, let's check them out."

He googled "Sisters of Notre Dame de Namur." Soon he found a website that described the establishment of the convent and a school in Wuchang, China in 1926. It went on to describe how, during the war years, the nuns were moved to Burma while the Japanese occupied the country. It also said they returned after the war but were eventually forced to abandon the convent again in 1948 because of the imminent communist takeover and the stepped-up persecution of Christian missionaries. All the nuns were repatriated back to the motherhouse in Cincinnati at that time.

They were startled from their reading by Hunter's cell ringing. It was Postmaster Eberle calling back.

"Detective, I think I have what you're looking for. I was able to pull the records for Grayson Malport who did work for us for a little over a year in 1955. It's just three pages. He was apparently let go for drinking on the job. I could send a copy to you if you'd like."

"Great. Take photos with your phone and email them to me at hmccoy@vsp.gov."

"That's a Virginia State Police address?" the man asked.

"That's right. Do your records show what happened to Malport?"

"Says he died in 1956 here in Hamilton, a year after losing his job.

Can you tell me, do the papers give an address for him?"

"Yes. It's right here. But you're not going to like it."

15

WHILE HUNTER WAITED FOR THE EMAIL TO come through, Billie couldn't hold back any longer. "What are you doing? You can't impersonate a police detective. You'll go to jail."

"It's time I explain a few things to you." He told her about his background with military intelligence, the police, and Interpol.

Billie ogled him, as if he were some alien from another planet. He wasn't sure, but he thought he even detected a little fear in her expression, though he couldn't imagine why.

"So how. . ." She paused as if not knowing what she wanted to ask him.

"Don't worry about it," he told her. "My contacts will be useful in trying to find the person or persons behind all this."

The next morning, they caught a flight to Cincinnati. Billie bought the tickets and paid for the rental car at the airport. As they drove the forty miles to Hamilton. Billie was quieter than Hunter had ever seen her. He suspected the full disclosure of his credentials had made her realize how big this thing had gotten.

He identified Malport's house by a rusted mailbox on a wooden post surrounded by weeds. He wasn't heartened by what he saw. The roof of the old wood-framed house had collapsed, and with that gone the walls had obviously followed suit. And judging by the luxuriant growth of mature vegetation, this had all occurred many years ago.

Hunter now understood what the postmaster meant when he said, "you won't like it."

Still standing, although just barely, was a separate single car garage from the same era. If the wood siding had been painted at one time there was no way to tell the color, it was so weathered. As they approached it, a big crow cawed and landed on the roof. Hunter figured it wasn't a good omen.

The garage had two big doors that opened outward. He tried, but failed to open them, the roof having settled, sealing them in place. He walked around the side and found a door at the back that did yield to his efforts.

"Back here, Billie, this one's open," he called.

They carefully walked in, hoping the roof would hold. The floor was dirt. Just enough light filtered in through two small windows—the glass long since gone—that they could see their way around. The space was empty save for some old furniture in a corner, covered with years of dust. Obviously, no one had been in here in decades. The furniture turned out to be a small desk and a swivel chair lying on its side.

Hunter opened the drawers, hoping, but not really expecting, to find the notebook. In that respect he wasn't disappointed. Save for a few old pencils, they were empty. He tried under the desk and then under and behind the drawers. Again, nothing.

As they were walking out of the garage, Hunter spotted one other piece. It wasn't furniture, but a small box. He hadn't noticed it when they came in because it was on a shelf several feet above the door they'd passed through when entering. It was just out of Hunter's reach, so he went outside and found a piece of wood about three feet long that had fallen off the garage. Using the prop, he reached up and pushed the box toward the edge of the shelf and caught it as it fell.

It was a wooden box with a small padlock. He brought it outside, found a rock from the driveway and smashed off the lock. A piece of the rock broke off and hit Billie's left hand, drawing blood. He saw a large flap of skin had been torn and gave her his clean handkerchief to temporarily stop the blood.

"Sorry about that. Are you okay?"

"Sure. Fine. I'll be fine. Let's see what's in there."

They looked at each other, as if to say, "nothing ventured, nothing gained." Hunter opened the box.

There it was. A leatherbound notebook about eight by ten inches and maybe an inch thick, covered in dust. Chinese symbols adorned the cover.

"My God, Hunter, that's it," Billie shouted.

Hunter picked it up.

"Careful," Billie cautioned. "Remember it's old. Let's look at it in the car."

Back in the rental Billie repaired the back of her hand using bandages she had in her purse. Then she gently brushed the layer of dust and translated the Chinese writing on the cover. "Research notebook—Li Qiang Chen—Wuchang, China, 1939."

Relieved, Hunter now knew that what they had was the actual notebook. Billie slowly turned the pages, briefly translating out loud to Hunter the gist of the contents.

"He's thankful to the nuns for letting him treat patients out of the convent's basement. He goes on to explain how the sisters approached him to help the people in the area after his small practice in Wuchang was damaged by the Japanese.

She turned the page and read silently for a moment. "This is more of the same."

She turned more pages and continued to read, twirling her fingers, indicating still more of the same.

At last she reached a page and appeared to brighten up. "Okay, now he's talking about helping diabetics, and it's beginning to get technical."

"Read it out loud to me."

"Okay. Here goes." As she turned page after page and read aloud, Hunter saw that Chen was obsessed with autoimmune diseases in his patients. While Hunter knew that rheumatoid arthritis had long been identified as an autoimmune disease, it appeared that Chen had used herbal medicine to treat several patients with the condition. Type 1 diabetes, so called juvenile diabetes, was not known to be an autoimmune disease during the nineteen forties, but here was Chen, making the connection. Amazing.

As Billie read the next several pages, it was apparent that Chen was having success. He reported that he'd been monitoring two children several times a day for two months while treating them. Most remarkably, their blood and urine sugars were normal. But even more unbelievable, he'd withdrawn treatment and they'd been normal since then.

"This is incredible," Hunter said, awed.

She continued to read. "It's time I formally describe the source of my medicine and the procedure."

She turned the page and they both saw it at once. The next several pages were gone. The rough edges where they'd been torn were clearly visible. On examination it appeared there were a total of six pages missing. Billie went on reading the remaining eight pages after the missing section in silence, explaining to Hunter they were filled with similar descriptions of other children with diabetes. His unidentified treatment was successful with them too.

Hunter watched Billie after she'd finished the last pages. She appeared lost in thought and gazed out the front widow of the car, saying nothing.

16

CARRIE JOHANNSON THOUGHT OF HER grandmother as she and Bruce Fembro stared at the seedlings growing a pale green in the spread flasks. She was relieved to see them looking so healthy. If nothing else she and Bruce could author a paper describing the successful flasking and germination of seventy-year-old orchid seedpods.

She thought of the old Chinese doctor who'd found them and told her grandma they represented the culmination of his professional life—a treatment for juvenile diabetes. Over the past year, she'd done a lot of reading on Chinese herbal medicines. She'd also learned all she could about juvenile diabetes, now commonly called Type 1 diabetes. She knew that Chinese herbal medicine used many orchid extracts to treat all kinds of things. Maybe Dr. Chen's orchids did actually produce something that could prevent Type 1 diabetes from developing. That'd be something all right.

"Unfortunately, we don't have the equipment necessary here at Selby to chemically analyze the plants," Carrie said to Bruce. "I think you need special chromatography equipment to do that. But I might have a way around that. I've got a friend who's a pharmacognosist at the medical school in Tampa. I could check with her and see if she could examine them, once we get them flowering. Maybe she could find out if they contain any molecules of real value—run some tests on rats or something."

Bruce wrinkled his brow. "What's a pharmacognosist?"

"Pharmacognosy is the branch of knowledge concerned with medicinal drugs obtained from plants or other natural sources."

"Like our orchids here."

"Exactly. But we have another potential problem," Carrie said. "Let's say the plant does produce a valuable drug. Maybe the chemical is only found in the seedlings, like we have here. Maybe by the time the plant is mature the chemistry changes, it's not useful."

"Could be," Bruce agreed. "Or it could be just the opposite. Maybe only the mature plant contains the good stuff, not the seedlings."

"Exactly." Carrie said, nodding. "I'll call her, tell her our predicament, and see if she's willing to test both seedlings and the mature plants—when and if we get any out of these guys." She waved her hand at the spread flasks. "I think we'll have plenty of seedlings to do both."

Carrie called her friend, Dr. Stephanie Bennet, at the University of South Florida medical school. They'd been undergraduate roommates together at Ohio State University. Both were intensely interested in science and had gone on to Ph.D. degrees, Steph in pharmacognosy and Carrie in botany, specializing in orchids and bromeliads. The two had remained good friends and had gotten together regularly since they'd both accepted positions in Florida cities located only an hour apart.

Steph answered her phone right away. "Hey, hotshot, what's up?"

Carrie never was sure where the "hotshot" nickname came from, but all of her close friends used it.

"Hey, Steph. Do you have a few minutes to talk? I have a science question or two."

"Sure. I'm between classes, and the next one is an exam. It's ready to go, so no prep time needed. What have you got?"

"Do you remember the orchid seedpods I told you about before? The ones my grandma had?"

"Sure. You wanted to see if they were still alive after all those years. World War Two, wasn't it?"

"Right. I also told you that Bruce and I don't really know anything about them because the old doctor's research notebook that presumably explains it all, is missing. Grandma was supposed to have it but somehow never got it.

"Yup. I remember," Steph said.

"Well, Bruce and I have succeeded in getting seedlings from the old seedpods, and we were wondering if you could run some of them thorough your equipment to see if they contain any molecules that look like they'd be useful for treating juvenile diabetes."

"I'm sure I could fit them in, but you have no idea what you're looking for, right?"

"None. It's not my area, but I know that lots of molecules from orchids have been shown to have important clinical value. It could be anything. Grandma said it wasn't just a successful treatment and management of the disease but was able to prevent its development to full Type 1 diabetes. Not a cure as such, but a preventative. I know what you're thinking; treatment is one thing, and a cure is another altogether. Still, a preventative has to be pretty important too, right?"

"Are you kidding? That would represent a major medical breakthrough all by itself."

Carrie grinned, relieved that her old friend was getting excited about the possibility of making a notable discovery.

Steph continued. "If we find something interesting you know what has to happen next, don't you?"

"Animal studies," Carrie said.

"That's why they call you hotshot, hotshot. And correct me if I'm wrong, but you don't do that kind of thing at the Selby Botanical Gardens, right?"

"Right."

"Any idea how you're going to accomplish that?" Steph asked, in a bemused tone, indicating that she knew exactly what her friend was going to propose next.

"Well . . . I thought maybe . . ."

"Yes?"

"Maybe you could . . ."

"Yes?"

"Do it there at the med school?"

"Tell you what," Steph said. "Get me the seedlings, and I'll run them through the system at no charge to you. I'll do the same when you get the mature plants. However, you need to know that you're not going to get a research grant to pay for prediabetic rats without some pretty convincing data that you have a molecule worth testing."

Carrie paused, thinking about the difficulty of doing that. Finally, Steph jumped in.

"Carrie. I'll look into the funding. You find that missing notebook."

17

HAVING FOUND THE MISSING NOTEBOOK and with nothing else to keep them in Ohio, Hunter and Billie caught a flight back to Sarasota and retrieved Hunter's rental Jeep from the parking garage. He'd called Lannigan before leaving Ohio and said he wanted to meet with him before driving on to Venice. The attorney said he'd wait for them.

On the flight back, Hunter tried to talk with Billie about how to flush out the man who threatened her. She seemed interested but distant. Finally, he asked, "What's going on? It's obvious something's bothering you."

She looked up as if surprised by the question. "What?"

"You've been quiet ever since we found the notebook. No, even before that. I think it started after you learned about my background. Is something wrong?"

"Oh. No. I mean, I know. I'm sorry. I guess it's all of that. It's just all so ominous. I must be getting nervous now that we're possibly getting close to finding him. Do you think that's it?"

"Maybe," Hunter offered. "You have told me everything, haven't you? I mean, you haven't left anything out of the events you described?"

"What? No. Oh my gosh, no. I'm so thankful for your help, Hunter. Without you we wouldn't be this close."

"Not saying you are. Just asking."

Hunter had noticed something else. On the flight back, Billie had been reading the notebook over and over, but seemed to spend a lot of time on the page just before the six pages were ripped out.

They pulled into the small gravel parking lot beside Lannigan's office and went inside, where they found the lawyer on the phone. He indicated the lone chair, and Billie sat while Hunter stood, thinking, not for the first time, that the man needed more furniture. While the phone conversation went on, Hunter used Lannigan's printer to carefully copy the cover and all the inside pages of the notebook.

"Just making a copy," he said in reply to Billie's inquiring expression. "Just a precaution. We can't be too careful."

Lannigan finally ended his phone call. "Things are looking better for your dad, Hunter," he said. "That was the DA. My PI, Stretch Jones—you'll meet him soon—found a witness across the street from your dad's place, Joe Palma, who'll testify that he saw a black Honda hatchback, pull into your dad's driveway at about ten in the morning the day after he was arrested. Palma said that two men carried a large black garbage bag into the house after fumbling with the front door. They left a few minutes later, and the black bag was obviously empty. The men wore baseball caps pulled low that partly covered their faces. What hair he could see was black. He's not sure, but the witness thought the men could be Asian."

"Joe Palma? He's in my dad's book club. That's great. Those guys had to be planting the computer and the bloody clothes."

"It's very likely. That's what I told the DA, who now agrees with me that with Palma's testimony, the case against your dad would not hold up in court. So unless Skaggs comes up with something else really incriminating, he won't proceed with prosecution. At this point, though, Skaggs still won't drop the arrest order, so your father has to stay in jail for the time being. I'm working on that.

"Two other things. The Sarasota police say the only fingerprints on the photo of the little girl tacked to Billie's hotel room door, are Billie's. that's not surprising, since she didn't take precautions when handling it. Secondly, Harrison's calendar listing of an appointment with your dad was posted the day of the murder. I'm afraid that neither helps nor hurts his case. So, what have you got?"

Hunter told him about tracking down Grayson Malport to Hamilton, Ohio and finding the notebook in his garage. And, just as they'd been told by Malport's son Colin, six critical pages were missing relating to the Chinese doctor's medical work on diabetes. Apparently, the man who threatened Billie and probably killed Harrison and framed his dad didn't know about the missing pages, or else he was interested in something else in the notebook. In any case, it was now Hunter's job to trap him, offering the notebook as bait.

The trouble was he didn't have any idea how to do that. If he could bag the man and tie him to the break-ins at Billie's and the cabin in Marquette, the remaining case against his dad would go up in smoke.

Hunter picked up the notebook and said to Lannigan. "Do you have a safe here where we can keep this and the copies for the time being?"

"Sure, bring them over here." The lawyer led the way to a small back room and opened a large closet door that revealed an enormous metal safe about the size of a refrigerator.

"It's triple bolted to the concrete slab that holds up the house. They'll be safe in here."

As Hunter went to lay the notebook on a shelf in the safe, his thumb caught on a sharp edge of the thick leather back cover. He turned it over and examined it more carefully, pushing his fingers slowly over the surface.

"Something's weird here. Feel that, Billie."

She ran her fingers over the surface as he had. "You're right, if feels like something's inside."

"Have you got a knife, something sharp?" Hunter asked Lannigan. "I want to cut into this."

"Yeah. Bring it into the kitchen."

Hunter slit the back cover along the edge near the spine. He gingerly slid his fingers in, felt a single loose paper, and pulled it out. Examining the spine, Hunter could now see that the cover had been slit open to allow the folded sheet to be inserted and then carefully stitched back shut. One could barely see the stitches, as if they'd been done by a skilled surgeon. They were so fine Hunter hadn't even seen them the first time.

"I think Dr. Chen inserted this into the cover himself for some reason."

"Why would he do that?" Lannigan asked.

"I don't know, maybe he didn't want it falling into the wrong hands," replied Hunter. "There's not much on it. Just some Chinese characters."

"Let me see that," Billie said, reaching out for the single sheet. "I'll translate it."

Hunter and the attorney watched as Billie quickly scanned the sheet without speaking. When she was finished she sat back and thought for a moment. Then she silently went back over it a second time.

Hunter was getting anxious, also a little annoyed. "Are you going to translate it for us, or not?"

"What? Oh, yeah, sure. Sorry," she said. "It's like a poem."

Six sisters
and the Glorious Store,
the secret to China Gold
Orchid tea
A life that's free
From sugar's deadly hold

"That's all it says, " she added, looking up.

"There's 'Glorious Store' again," Hunter said. "The diary mentioned that."

"Yes," Billie said, dreamily.

"What does the 'secret to China Gold' mean?" Hunter mused out loud. "That last part clearly refers to his successful treatment for diabetes. 'A life that's free from sugar's deadly hold' is pretty obvious. Does 'orchid tea' mean anything to you?" he asked Billie

"Huh?"

Hunter scrutinized the young woman. "Are you okay?" he asked. "You seem distracted."

"No. No, I'm all right. Sorry. Just trying to make sense of all this. If Dr. Chen wrote this, why would he hide it in the cover of his notebook?"

"Does he mention any of this anywhere else in the diary? China gold, or orchid tea, or any of this? You've read it all."

"No," she answered. "No references to any of it."

Hunter wondered if it was even remotely possible that the orchid tea referred to could be the treatment for Type 1 diabetes. Was this a special orchid that produced a miracle chemical of some kind?

He turned to the lawyer. "I want to make copies of this too, and then store everything in your safe."

"Right," Lannigan said, and then added, "I heard from the police. There were no prints on the envelope or on the photo of the little girl pinned to your door at the hotel, Billie. Whoever did it was careful."

Turning to Hunter he added, "Now all you have to do is somehow find the man who threatened Billie, lure him into a trap where you catch him, and he confesses to extortion and murder."

Hunter nodded.

"Yeah, that's all. How hard can it be?"

18

BEFORE LEAVING LANNIGAN'S OFFICE, Billie told Hunter and the lawyer that she needed to check in on her travel business in Chicago. "We communicate through my laptop and it's back in my room at the hotel. I need to spend some time catching up with my office manager."

"Of course," Hunter said. "I'll drive you there now."

Then, turning to Lannigan, he said, "Let me know if Skaggs changes his mind."

On the drive back to Venice, Hunter realized that he and Billie had barely been apart, except for sleeping, since they'd met at Jenny Lahti's. When they reached the Inn At The Beach, Billie waved goodbye and said she'd call him tomorrow.

Back at the Kingston house, Henry jubilantly told Hunter about Joe Palma seeing the Asian men who planted the laptop and bloody clothes in the house.

"I know. I've just come from Lannigan's place. But even with that, Skaggs won't drop the arrest charge, so dad has to stay inside for the time being."

"What's Skaggs's problem?"

Hunter told him what Lannigan had learned from Wally Osborn, that Skaggs probably was afraid of second-guessing himself again, like he had in the child murder case a year ago.

"Well tough. That's his job. Every case is different, and he's got to get past that or he won't be worth a damn."

"I agree with you. Still, my job now is to make it easier for him to do that by giving him the real killer." Hunter went on to describe how he and Billie found the research notebook with the missing pages.

"So how are you going to track this guy down, Hunter? Do you just wait around for him to contact Billie? Isn't there anything you can do to let him know you have the notebook? I mean, that's what he wants right?"

"Yeah. I wish there was a direct way."

Hunter fixed himself a perfect Manhattan on the rocks and was just preparing the lemon twist when his phone rang. He broke into a wide smile at the image on the screen, his gloom instantly evaporating. It was Genevieve Swift.

"Hey, babe, you're just the breath of fresh air I need at the moment."

"Glad to hear it. You'll never guess where I am."

"If you're right outside my door, you're in the right place. Tell me that's it."

"Not quite, I'm afraid. I'm in Sarasota."

"What? You're here?"

"What do you mean here? Where are you?"

"I'm in Florida on Casey Key, visiting my dad and Henry. What's going on? Why are you here? Shouldn't you be at the Louvre?"

"Shouldn't you be in Virginia?"

"It's a long story."

"I'm staying at the house on Sarasota Bay, where I was last year. Come get me, take me to dinner, and I'll tell you all about it."

"It's a deal. Give me an hour and a half."

He poured his Manhattan down the drain, took a shower, and dressed in clean clothes.

On the drive, Hunter felt the anxiety of the past several days begin to slip away at the thought of once again being with Genevieve. They'd been through so much together in recent years.

During their first adventure, a lost manuscript from the Spanish Inquisition, she'd been employed as an assistant curator in the documents section of the Bibliotheque Nationale in Paris, and he was in his second year as an Assistant Professor of Physiology at the University of Virginia School of Medicine. He'd been hired for one of his "Find-and-Correct" jobs during the summer to find the book. They met when he'd employed her to help with its authentication.

While they succeeded in finding the book, the search had been deadly, and they'd both nearly been killed several times. Through it all they'd become lovers, but still ultimately had to separate to return to their jobs on opposite sides of the Atlantic.

During the following summer they were together again when Jenny Lahti hired him to find the missing body of her late husband, Charley Lahti. But the best of all, had been just last year, when Genevieve surprised him by accepting a one-year appointment as curator of pre-twentieth-century Western art at the John and Mable Ringling Museum of Art in Sarasota. By now she had changed jobs and held a similar position at the Louvre in Paris. Their plan was to spend the summer together in Sarasota, since Hunter had taken the typically non-busy summer semester off from his duties at the university.

He chuckled as he recalled how that idyllic plan went awry when an old man left a masterpiece painting, stolen during the Napoleonic invasion of Italy, on a display case at the museum and then immediately died on the grounds. What followed was the dangerous mission to save the Ringling Museum that Hunter referred to as Wicar's Legacy.

By that time, he and Genevieve both knew they belonged together. Still, they'd had to separate at the end of the summer to return to jobs thousands of miles apart. If he thought deeply enough about it, Hunter knew that part of his current decision to take a leave of absence from the medical school was to consider ways they could be together permanently.

He pulled into the driveway of the little house on Sarasota Bay, not far from the Ringling Museum. Genevieve rushed out and they fell into each other's arms and held the embrace for a long time, neither of them speaking. Finally they separated, and Hunter said, "Wow, I missed that."

Genevieve's "Me too, *mon cher*" was followed by an equally long kiss.

They went through the house, out to the lanai, where Genevieve brought out a glass of white wine for herself and an expertly made perfect Canadian Club Manhattan on the rocks with a twist of lemon that she'd prepared for Hunter.

As the setting sun cast a beautiful patina of multicolored light over Sarasota Bay, they gazed out at the glistening city skyline and the beautifully arched Ringling Bridge to Lido Key. Silently toasting each other, Hunter waited for Genevieve to begin her explanation.

"Okay, here goes," she finally began. "Neither Phyllis Durham nor I knew it at the time, but apparently our respective superiors at the Louvre and the Ringling, were thrilled with the way we acquitted ourselves last year during the curator exchange program. Apparently both institutions had been communicating with each other for some time and decided to set up similar exchanges in other areas of their museums. So, bottom line, the Ringling wants me for another year, and likewise the Louvre wants Phyllis to return for another year."

"That's great."

"I know. I'm so happy."

They clinked glasses, and Hunter said, "Now I know I made the right decision arranging to take a leave of absence this fall. Apparently I'm going to be spending most of my time here in Florida too."

"Because I'm here?"

"Yes, of course, but. . . I wish it were the only reason."

Genevieve frowned, "What does that mean? What's the other reason?"

Hunter talked for the next hour, leaving nothing out.

"Why would anyone want to frame your dad?" Genevieve asked when he finished.

"That's the big mystery. I have no idea. But now that Billie and I found the notebook in Hamilton, Ohio, it could be the key to solving all our problems. I hope to use it as bait to get to the guy who threatened her."

"That's all? Genevieve said with a smile. "That shouldn't be hard for us."

"Us?"

"Of course, us."

Hunter sighed. *Here we go again.*

Genevieve got up and taking Hunter's hand, led him back into the house where they each set their glasses on the table.

"Hunter, are you hungry?"

Never one to miss an obvious clue, he saw something in her eyes that suggested a different kind of hunger, one he, himself, had been feeling for the past few hours. He kissed her, swept her up in his arms, and carried her into the bedroom.

Over the next hour they realized just how hungry they both were.

19

THE NEXT MORNING HUNTER GOT UP BEFORE Genevieve and made breakfast out of what he found in the kitchen. He knew she'd only arrived two days ago but had somehow already managed to lay in supplies.

How does she look that beautiful first thing in the morning? he thought. He couldn't keep his eyes off her as he made them omelets and coffee. While she waited at the table, sipping her coffee, she noticed him staring.

"What?" she asked.

"Just thinking how nice it is to have you here again."

She came around the table and kissed him deeply. After another hour in the bedroom, they finally got around to the omelets. By now both were famished and ready for real food.

As they were eating, Genevieve asked him how he intended to proceed. Hunter had been so happy to have her back he'd actually put all his current problems aside for the moment. Her question brought him back to reality.

"The guy gave Billie a month to find the notebook. The month was up last week. It could be he's lying low after killing Harrison and might wait a bit before contacting her again."

He drank some coffee and killed the omelet, then refilled his cup and sat quietly for a moment.

"What?" Genevieve asked. "I've seen that look before. What's wrong?"

"I don't know," he admitted. "Something just isn't right about all this. I can't put my finger on it, but it just doesn't flow."

"What do you mean?"

"Well, for one thing, why would the guy give Billie Chen a month to find the notebook, but kill Harrison right away? Surely he could have threatened Harrison's family and given him some time as well. I mean, Billie told him she didn't have it, and I assume Harrison did too. Yet he gives her a month, not a day or a week, but a month. That suggests he knows she doesn't have it but might have the means to find it. Why not do the same for Harrison? Like I said, it just doesn't flow."

"I see what you mean. Tell me more about Billie. What do you really know about her?"

"Just what I told you. She's Chen's great-granddaughter; she's a widow who runs a travel agency in Chicago; and she's trying to save her brother's family by finding the notebook."

"Did you check her story?"

Hunter thought about that. He hadn't. He'd just accepted what she'd told him, just like Jenny had. But why would she not be on the level? She had Chen's diary. It seemed authentic. Still, admitting Genevieve was right, he answered, "Hmm. Good point. No, I haven't checked."

"Do you know the name of the travel agency?" Genevieve asked. "You could start by seeing if she really is the boss."

"I think she said it was the Gifford Agency. Let me check." He opened his laptop and googled Gifford Travel Agency, Chicago. "There it is," he said, turning the screen to her. He clicked on the Staff link and there was her name, Billie Chen, Owner. Also listed were six agents and their phone numbers.

"At least that part's true," Genevieve said. "Still, what a coincidence that you two met at the scene of the crime, so to speak."

"I know. That's what she said. But when we talked it through, it made sense. We each had a perfectly plausible reason to be there—at Jenny's—at that time."

"Tell me some more about the notebook you found."

Hunter repeated the story of how they tracked it to Grayson Malport's old, run-down garage and then how they found the strange poem in the notebook's back cover at Lannigan's office. He told her that Billie translated it, but they didn't know what it meant.

"What about the rest of the notebook? Genevieve asked. "Was there anything of importance in there?"

"Didn't seem like it. At least not as she translated it to me."

"I'd like to see it," said Genevieve.

"It's in Chinese."

"Let's get it translated."

"Good idea." After all, he'd only heard Billie's translation once. If they wanted to pore over it in detail, they'd need a good quality written translation. He and Billie might have missed something in the first reading, something that might explain why the man who threatened her wanted it so badly.

"Tell you what," he said. "I made copies of everything at Lannigan's office. I'll get the copies and have a translation made today, and we can go over it tonight. You've got to work today, right?"

"Yes, I do, and I'd better get going if the Ringling is going to continue having a good impression of me. Look at the time." She grabbed her purse, kissed Hunter goodbye, and drove off in her leased white BMW convertible.

He poured another cup of coffee and tried to recall Billie's translation of the rest of the notebook. He couldn't remember anything particularly useful. He only recalled that she seemed to spend a lot of time on the page just before the six missing pages.

He googled translation services in Sarasota and found a company that did certified translations of business and legal contracts. At Lannigan's office he made copies of the copies to take to the translator. That way the original notebook and a complete set of copies would stay in the safe.

He drove to the translator's office. The man who did Chinese translations studied the copies Hunter handed him and quickly leafed through them. "This is written in Mandarin Chinese. The grammar is excellent. The writer was clearly educated."

"How long will it take you to get me a written translation?" Hunter asked.

"I can have it back by mid-afternoon tomorrow. How's that?"

"Great."

Hunter called Billie Chen and, though he knew it was a long shot, asked if she'd heard anything from the bad guy.

"No, nothing," she answered. "Do you think he's given up?"

"Not a chance. He's already killed at least once, and his threat to you and my dad is as strong as ever. No, he's not going to give up. Have you called your brother and had him step up his security?"

"I called him yesterday. I also called my office in Chicago and reminded them again how important it is to always alarm the building when they leave."

"Did they wonder about that?"

"What? Oh—yeah. I told them that the police called me and said there'd been an increase in break-ins in the area lately and all local businesses should take extra precautions."

"Good thinking. No need to scare them," he said.

"Hunter?"

"Yeah?"

"I've been thinking about all of this and I don't see there's anything else I can do here. Maybe I should take the notebook back to Chicago and work in my office while you try to find the guy. If he does contact me, I'll call you and you can set a trap, or whatever it is you plan to do, when he comes to collect it."

Hunter thought about that. She was right. Of course, the guy would contact her, not him. Still, the notebook was evidence and its existence might be necessary to exonerate his dad. And, if things got rough here—and he was almost sure the guy was staying in the area setting up his dad—and maybe him—she'd just be in harm's way.

"I agree. With a modification. You take the copies and I keep the original. I'll call Lannigan and have him get the copies out of the safe. I'll meet you there in an hour. Oh, and bring phone numbers where I'll be able to reach you."

An hour later, the three of them were in Lannigan's office. Billie told the attorney what she'd told Hunter about there not being anything useful she could do here. And, just as Hunter had, Lannigan agreed she'd be better off in Chicago. Hunter and Lannigan went into the back room to get the copies from the safe while Billie waited in the front office.

Lannigan retrieved the copies from the safe, "I'll get a mailer envelope for her to carry them in."

While the attorney fished for a suitable envelope, Hunter returned to the front office and was surprised to find Billie talking—to herself. He couldn't hear what she was saying as it was too low. She seemed surprised by his return. Perhaps embarrassed by being caught talking to herself.

Lannigan returned with the envelope and Billie placed the copies inside. Hunter told her to be careful when she got home, and to call him immediately if she heard from the guy.

"I will, don't worry. I want him put away as badly as you do."

Later, after Billie left, Hunter and the lawyer sat quietly for a moment. Finally, noticing Hunter's vacant stare, Lannigan asked. "What are you thinking?"

"I don't know. Just an uneasy feeling that I'm missing something important."

20

LATE THE NEXT AFTERNOON WITH THE SUMMER CLOUDS gathering, it looked like rain. Hunter returned to Sarasota Translations and retrieved the copies he'd made of the original copies of the notebook and the poem, along with a neatly arranged English translation.

As he leafed through it he could readily see the guy had done a quality job. He'd even footnoted words and passages that could have multiple translations, depending on local dialects and meanings. Hunter concluded it was a professional and thorough piece of work. He paid him, thanked him, and left.

Later, when Genevieve arrived home from work, Hunter realized there was something else he had to share with her. With everything else going on, he hadn't mentioned it earlier. He told her about the phone call from Jason Turtle at his laboratory and the trouble with his NIH grant.

"Someone's been withdrawing money from the grant and putting it in your bank account?" she asked incredulously.

"It seems so. Yeah, hold on a minute." Hunter realized, he'd been so busy trying to free his dad he hadn't even looked at his bank accounts. He logged in to his bank on the phone app and pulled up his 'Find-and Correct' account. Sure enough, five thousand dollars had been deposited weekly for the past month.

"How did you not notice this?" Genevieve asked.

"I only use the account to make deposits. They don't happen that often, so there's not much reason to check it regularly."

"It would seem that someone is trying to discredit you, and it's working."

"It sure is."

He'd almost forgotten about the call from the Charlottesville police about the allegations of suspicious behavior at his loft apartment near the medical school. He told her about that too.

"Do you think all of this is linked somehow?" she asked.

"I wonder. You know, it was three months ago that the Harrison book came out."

"So, what are you saying?"

"I don't know. I'll call my bank and ask them how the payments were made to my account. If they were wired in, whoever did it would have needed the account number and the bank routing number. Since it's not a checking account, they couldn't have gotten their hands on one of my checks and taken the account and routing number from there. I'm not sure how you'd get the numbers for a savings account. I suppose a good hacker could find a way."

"Maybe you'll get lucky, and whoever did it just walked into the bank and made the deposit at the counter. Someone there might remember him, or maybe they have a video of it," Genevieve said.

"It's worth a try. The last deposit was just last Friday."

Hunter made the call and was referred to one of the officers on duty.

"Mr. McCoy, how can I help you?" the banker asked.

"Can you look at my account and tell me how a deposit was made, if I give you the account number?"

"You don't know how you made a deposit?"

"I didn't make it. Someone else did."

"I see."

The man asked for corroboration that Hunter was who he said he was, and when he had, then pulled up his accounts and asked him which one he wanted info on.

"A savings account I call 'Find-and-Correct. I'm interested in the weekly deposits for five thousand dollars."

"Alright, hold on."

In a minute he had the answer. "They were all transfers from an account in the name of Gilbert Aker to your account using a cellphone app activated by your fingerprint."

My fingerprint? How is that possible?

After hanging up, he told Genevieve what he'd learned, then added, "I'll have to find out how a fingerprint could be faked."

Just then his phone rang. The screen showed the call was from Bethesda, Maryland. Hunter knew the National Institute of Health was in Bethesda.

"Hello?"

"Dr. McCoy?"

"Yes."

"Dr. McCoy, this is Jack Busbee from NIH."

"I hope you've learned something good about my funding?" Hunter asked, amazed at the timing of this call to the one he'd just made to his bank, hoping for some good news.

"A little. We've discovered that our system here at NIH has been hacked. The name Gilbert Aker was added to the payout list of your grant. We know you didn't do this, and our IT experts are still trying to track it down."

Hunter told him what he'd just learned from his bank about the method of deposit of the money into his account and that it somehow involved the use of his fingerprint on the bank's cellphone app.

"Good. I'll give this information to our people and they'll get right on it."

"So does this mean our funding will be freed up?"

"Not yet, but it's looking better for you. I'll keep you informed."

After ending the call, Hunter sat and thought. Genevieve, who'd heard the conversation on speakerphone, said. "That's a positive development."

"Yes, it is. I'll call Jason later and let him know." Then he added, "You know, maybe I should call Billie and warn her to be on guard. Chicago's an hour behind us. She might still be at work."

Earlier, he'd written down the number of the Gilbert Travel Agency in Chicago and punched it into his cell. A friendly female voice answered.

"Hi, this is Hunter McCoy, is Billie Chen in?"

"Excuse me?"

"Billie Chen. Did she come in to work today?"

"What did you say your name was?"

"McCoy, Hunter McCoy. Is Miss Chen there?"

"I'm sorry to tell you, sir, but Miss Chen died—three months ago."

"What? Died? That can't be, I just talked with her yesterday."

"I'm sorry sir, that simply can't be true."

"I'm talking about Ms. Chen, the owner of the agency."

"Yes, sir. She is definitely dead. I identified the body myself."

"*You* identified the body?"

"Yes. I'm her partner in the agency. I'm afraid she was murdered."

"Murdered?"

What is going on here? Surely there's some mistake.

"Why. . . why didn't her brother identify her?" he finally managed to blurt out.

"Her brother? She had no brother. She was an only child."

21

DEAD? MURDERED? THREE MONTHS AGO? How can that be?

If Billie Chen is dead, who the hell is the woman pretending to be Billie Chen? Have I been fooled by an imposter all this time?

Hunter had two phone numbers for "Billie" that she'd given him when she left in the event he needed to reach her. He tried the first one and got:

Welcome to Verizon Wireless. Your call cannot be completed as dialed.

He tried the second number. Same result. Double-checking, he called the Gilbert Travel Agency and spoke to the same woman.

"This is Hunter McCoy again. I just spoke with you. I believe a woman has been impersonating Billie Chen. I believe you when you say she's dead. But I wonder if you'd have a digital photo of her that you could text me, so I can compare it to this woman?"

Hunter waited while she apparently thought about his request. "Um, I don't know if I should. I mean, I don't know you. I think you should call the police. She was murdered, after all."

"I *am* the police," Hunter said. "I'm a detective with the Virginia State Police Department, Lieutenant Detective Hunter McCoy. If you'd feel more comfortable, you could email a photo to me at <u>mccoy@vsp.gov</u>. VSP is Virginia State Police."

"I guess that would be okay. Let me see. I'm sure I have one in my photo file. Hold on."

While he waited, Hunter turned to Genevieve, who'd been listening to all of this. "I can't believe I've been fooled. I'd have sworn she was legitimate. Damn. Well, we'll have the answer in a minute or two."

"Okay, I have a good one. I'll send it to your email address."

"Thank you, Miss . . .?"

"Mrs. Nason."

A few seconds later he checked his email and there it was. He scrolled through the full facial photo. He stared at Genevieve and shook his head.

"This is definitely not the woman I know as Billie Chen."

"I'm not surprised," Genevieve said. "The question is, who is she and why is she pretending to be Billie Chen?"

"The lady at the travel agency said the real Billie Chen had been murdered," Hunter said, pausing to think through the ramifications. "And this woman now has the original notebook. She also had Dr. Chen's diary. How'd she get it?"

Genevieve's eyes widened. "Do you think she killed her and took it?"

Hunter couldn't imagine the timid, fearful woman he'd known as Billie killing anyone. He googled "Billie Chen Murder" on his laptop. He found several references to the crime on the internet and read them all. Apparently she'd been surprised in her apartment and stabbed several times. The police had no suspects and no known motive.

"I'll bet Fake Billie killed her, Hunter."

"Could be. And now everything appears to be a lie. The whole story about a man breaking into her apartment in Chicago and threatening her alleged brother's family if she didn't find the notebook—it was all a lie."

Genevieve nodded. "She wasn't after the notebook to bargain for their lives. She wanted it for herself for some reason. Any ideas what that might be?"

Still unable to completely fathom all this, Hunter said, "The most obvious one is the potential financial gain from supplying the formula to treat Type 1 diabetes. It would be worth a fortune for any drug firm to get its hands on that information."

"Didn't you say you made copies of the notebook and that she took them with her? And you stored the notebook itself in your attorney's safe?"

"I did, and she knows it. So the only way for her to be in sole possession of everything is for her to get the notebook. Good thinking. I'll call Lannigan and warn him she might be after it."

Before he could make the call, his phone rang. It was Lannigan. "Hunter, I've got some bad news. The safe's been broken into. I'm afraid the Notebook is gone."

Damn.

"Someone clobbered me from behind and got into the safe."

"Are you all right?" Hunter asked.

"I think so. I called my doc and she told me meet her at the emergency room of the hospital. I'm going now."

"Are you okay to drive?"

"Stretch is driving. I'll be fine."

"Listen, Lannigan. Billie's an imposter. I just learned the woman we know is not Billie Chen. The Real Billie Chen was murdered in Chicago. Be careful."

"Jesus."

"Right. I'll check with you later."

Hunter walked silently to the sliding doors going out onto the lanai. He stood there for a moment thinking. At last he turned and said to himself, as much as to Genevieve, "She's really played us all for fools."

"Well, there's one thing she doesn't know. She doesn't know that you have a copy of everything and an English translation."

"Yeah, She's got to think she has it all, the notebook, the copies she took, and the diary."

He pulled out his copy of the entire research notebook and the poem along with the complete English translation. The answer might be in there somewhere. He used Genevieve's printer/copier to make a second set of translated pages.

"Okay," he said, "it's probable that the financial possibilities of a medical breakthrough are her motivation. But—and I don't know what—I have a feeling there's something else as well, some other reason she wants the notebook. Maybe there's something in there important enough to kill for. Let's read through these copies and see if anything jumps out at us."

An hour later, after each of them had read it through several times, Genevieve asked, "What's the Glorious Store?"

"Exactly," agreed Hunter. "That's the odd thing. Earlier, at Lannigan's office, she told us the only thing she knew about the notebook was that it was somehow related to the Glorious Store. He asked her what that meant, and she said she had no idea. I think she was telling the truth."

"Too bad we don't have the diary or a copy to go along with the rest of this."

"Yeah. She's still ahead of us. What do you make of the poem?" Hunter asked.

> Six sisters
> and the Glorious Store,
> the secret to China Gold
> Orchid tea
> A life that's free
> From sugar's deadly hold

"There's the Glorious Store again," said Genevieve. "Maybe China Gold refers to the orchid tea. And the tea is somehow the treatment for diabetes. The phrase 'A life that's free from sugar's deadly hold' is a pretty obvious reference to the disease."

"Agreed," Hunter said, "and I'm beginning to get an idea about what the 'Six sisters' are."

"Me too. Didn't you say that there were six pages—the *critical* six pages—missing from the notebook?"

"It has to be a reference to the missing pages, and they're somehow in the 'Glorious Store,' whatever that is."

"So we've got to find this 'Glorious Store.'"

"Right. Did you see anything else of interest in the translation?"

"No," she said. "How about you?"

"No, but as I think on it, there was something about the way she translated it. Let me see. I recall she acted odd a few times. She took her time over the last page of the notebook just before the missing six. Let's have a look"

He shuffled the translation to the page before the missing pages and read it aloud. It was unremarkable until about two thirds of the way down, when he came across a passage he read aloud:

The process for extracting and refining the medicine that I've used to treat juvenile diabetes is detailed in the following pages. How ironic that the gift of health it gives was developed directly over the route to the Glorious Store. And doubly so, that this treatment owes its success not to the China Gold of the Glorious Store acquired by the son of a doctor no less, but to one of nature's beautiful gifts. Ironic and sad.

"I wonder what it means?" Genevieve said.

Hunter shook his head, not having an answer. "Do you suppose it refers to the convent somehow? That's where the doctor did his work and had his laboratory, such as it was. If that's where he made his discovery, then maybe this 'Glorious Store,' whatever it is, was there too."

22

BEFORE GENEVIEVE LEFT FOR THE RINGLING MUSEUM in the morning, Hunter told her he'd decided he needed to learn something about orchids, since orchid tea was mentioned in the poem sewn into the diary's cover.

"Go over to Selby," she said.

"Selby?"

"Right. The Marie Selby Botanical Gardens, right here in Sarasota. I read somewhere they're among the leaders in air plant research in the world."

"And orchids are air plants?" Hunter asked.

"Technically, they're called epiphytes."

"How do you know this?"

"My dad grows them."

"I need to learn something about their potential medicinal value. See what the experts know, so to speak."

"They definitely have experts. I read that the study of epiphytic plant groups is one of their specialties. I think there are something like 25,000 species of orchids worldwide."

Hunter smiled at her, saying nothing.

"What?" she asked

"You never cease to amaze me. You'll be shifting from museum curator to orchid specialist at this botanical garden next."

"I don't think so. Those people are real specialists."

Hunter thought about this as he drove to the Selby Gardens on Sarasota Bay. At the front entrance he asked to meet with one of the orchid specialists.

The receptionist asked, "Do you have an appointment with someone?"

"No."

"They're pretty busy people. Can I ask what you want?"

He showed her his detective shield and ID from the Virginia State Police. "It has nothing to do with Selby or anyone here. I just need some general information on orchids. It would be helpful to solving a case I'm working on. I promise not to take much time."

"Let's see what I can do."

After several calls to what Hunter assumed were their orchid people, she finally seemed to have found someone who was free to speak with him. A few minutes later, a pretty young woman came up to the desk from somewhere in the gardens and introduced herself. "Hi, I'm Dr. Carrie Johannson. What can I do for you?"

"Detective Hunter McCoy. Is there someplace we can talk?"

He followed her back to a lab, amazed by the incredible color and scents of the place. He understood why people might choose this area of science over others.

At her desk, she sat and offered the one other chair to him.

"So, Detective, what do you need to know about orchids?"

Hunter had thought about this. What exactly *did* he need to know? And then, how much to tell this young woman? He decided to start simply but stick to the truth as much as possible.

"I'm working a case that involves the potential medicinal value of orchids, and I admit I know nothing about them. Do they even have medicinal value?"

"Oh yes. Orchids have been used for centuries in Chinese medicine. I'm not an expert on that, but herbalists in China use them all the time. One of the most common orchid species—*dendrobium*—has been used in the treatment of fever, gastritis, diabetes, infections, dizziness, convulsions, hypertension, and stroke, just to name a few."

"Diabetes?"

"Yes. Apparently extracts from the orchids can lower blood sugar. Don't ask me how; herbal medicine is not my specialty."

He decided this wasn't the time to tell her that medical physiology was his specialty. He wanted to keep her talking.

"My case involves a descendent of a Chinese doctor who may have found an orchid—maybe a new species, I don't know—that has the potential to arrest the development of juvenile diabetes."

Carrie Johannson froze in her chair. She just stared at Hunter and licked her lips. "What did you say?"

Hunter noticed the immediate change in her attitude. "Like I said, this Chinese doctor may have found a successful treatment of some kind for diabetes."

Carrie stood up and said, "Why are you really here?"

"As I said, I need to learn about—"

"Why are you talking to me specifically?" she said in an accusatory tone. Hunter didn't knit his brow. Clearly, he'd touched a nerve somehow.

"Apparently you were the orchid specialist available. Why? What's wrong?"

Obviously shaken, Carrie sat back down, composed herself, and asked, "What, specifically, is this case you're working on?"

Hunter decided he had to open up to her if he was going to get any more information. "A woman's been murdered in Chicago. I'm working with the Chicago Police Department to apprehend her killer.

A little white lie. But that's okay.

"The dead woman is the great-granddaughter of the Chinese doctor I just mentioned. It may be that this orchid has a bearing on the case. That's why I'm here, to learn a little bit about the medicinal value of orchids."

Carrie Johannson stood up again and began to pace the lab as if she were trying to make up her mind about something. Halting, she turned toward him and asked, "What's the name of the dead woman?"

"Her name was Billie Chen. Her great-grandfather was Dr. Li Qiang Chen."

Carrie closed her eyes, put her hands to her face, and exhaled.

Confused, Hunter asked, "Dr. Johannson, do you know anything about this?"

Still seemingly in shock, Carrie returned to her desk and sat down heavily. "This is incredible," she said. "Detective, can you tell me where your Dr. Chen lived?"

Completely confused, Hunter said, "During World War Two, he operated a clinic out of the basement of a convent in Wuchang, China. Why do you ask? What do you know about this?"

Carrie opened her desk drawer and removed an envelope. Hesitating for a moment, she handed it to Hunter. "Perhaps you'd better read this, Detective."

He took the envelope. On the cover, in a woman's handwriting, was written, *"The Life Work of Dr. Li Qiang Chen."*

He opened it and began to read.

I'm recording the events that led up to my being given the sack of seedpods by my dear friend, Dr. Li Qiang Chen, while they're still fresh in my memory . . .

He read on in stunned silence right through to the end of the letter. Then looked up. "Dr. Johannson, you're not going to believe this. I can barely believe it myself."

"What?"

"US Army Technical Sergeant Karl McCoy, described in this letter?"

"Yes?"

"He was my grandfather."

"What?"

"He told me stories about living in the convent and about this kindly nun, Sister Mary Margaret."

Then, the thought just occurring to him, Hunter asked," May I have a copy of this letter? And how did you get it anyway?"

"This is too much," Carrie said, heading for her copy machine. "Now it's my turn to tell you something you won't believe. Sister Mary Margaret—Laura McCasey—was my grandmother."

They both sat stunned for a moment. Hunter had copies of Dr. Chen's notebook but knew that without the critical missing pages and any actual plant material, it wasn't much help. Now, it appeared that Dr. Chen had given seedpods from his miracle orchids to Sister Mary Margaret. What had she done with them? He was just about to ask when the botanist spoke first.

"Let me show you something I think you're not going to believe."

They walked to a greenhouse next door and she led him to a corner, where he saw several flats of seedlings. She swept her hand at them. "These are from the seedpods my grandmother got from the doctor. Can you believe it? After all those years?"

She explained about finding the seedpods and the letter in a cooler in her grandmother's basement.

"This is amazing," Hunter said. "You've managed to resurrect them?"

"Yes, and I'm working with a pharmacognosist at the medical school in Tampa to try to isolate any clinically important components related to treating diabetes."

"Who else knows about these seedpods?"

"My mother, Bruce Fembro here at the gardens, and Steph Bennet the pharmacognosist," she answered.

Her expression grew grave. "Detective, there's something I still don't understand. You said Dr. Chen's great-granddaughter was murdered. Who would do that, and why?"

"That's what I'm trying to find out."

After leaving Selby Gardens, he left a message for Henry that he was going to spend the night with Genevieve in Sarasota, but he'd call him again later. He also told him to be sure to keep the doors locked. He drove to Genevieve's house on the bay and arrived just as she pulled into the driveway ahead of him.

"How was your day?" he asked.

"Good. How about you?"

"I took your advice and went to Selby to learn about orchids."

"And?"

"I learned about orchids *and* I met Sister Mary Margaret's granddaughter."

"The nun from the war? You met her granddaughter?"

"Yup, and she's here, working at the Selby Gardens. She's a botanist and orchid specialist." Then he went on to tell her all about Carrie Johannson.

"What an incredible coincidence. And she's growing the actual orchids?"

"Yes, and here, read this." He gave her the copy of the letter Carrie's grandmother wrote.

Genevieve read it and turned to Hunter.

"Amazing."

23

IN THE MORNING BEFORE GENEVIEVE went off to work, Hunter said, "I've got an idea. I'll call Carrie Johannson at Selby and ask if her grandmother ever mentioned the term 'Glorious Store.'"

"Good idea," Genevieve replied, on her way out the door. "See you later."

Carrie answered on the first ring.

"Dr. Johannson, it's Hunter McCoy. I have a question."

"Before you ask your question, Detective, how about if you call me Carrie and I'll call you Hunter. Given the circumstances, maybe a little less formality? What do you think?"

"I agree, Carrie it is. So, Carrie, do you recall your late grandmother ever mentioning the term 'Glorious Store?'"

"It doesn't ring a bell. Why do you ask?"

"Dr. Chen mentions the term in his research notebook."

"His notebook?" she practically shouted. "You have his notebook? The missing notebook that my grandmother talked about in her letter?"

"Yes. Sorry I didn't mention it yesterday. After a long search, I recently found it in an abandoned house in Ohio. You know, now that I think about it, you need to read it. You may recognize something that Genevieve and I missed."

"Who's Genevieve?"

He knew Genevieve was at work, but tomorrow was Saturday. "Tell you what. Could we meet somewhere tomorrow morning, so we can show you our translated copies of the notebook? See if anything jumps out at you. You can meet Genevieve then."

"I'm afraid not. I'm not actually in Florida. Right after we met at Selby, I flew to Indianapolis for a two-day conference. I'll call you when I get back and I'll look at it then, How's that?"

Disappointed, but understanding, Hunter said, "Sure. Okay, see you then."

Early the next morning, he woke up next to Genevieve and for a fraction of a second was lost. Was he at the Casey Key house, his loft in Virginia, a hotel in Cleveland? Then he remembered. He was at Genevieve's place on Sarasota Bay. It was Saturday and she didn't have to work, so they were going to try to track down any other nun who might have been at the convent in Wuchang while Dr. Chen was there.

Leaving Genevieve to sleep, he made a cup of coffee, took his laptop out to the lanai, and began searching for the motherhouse in Cincinnati. He figured he'd try to get a number and as much information as he could before making the call, knowing it was probably too early to call now anyway.

He located a website for the Heritage Center of the Sisters of Notre Dame de Namur. It was the one he'd found earlier that described the history of the school in Wuchang. He got the information he needed and now just had to wait for an appropriate hour to make the call.

As he waited he thought about his dad. If Billie Chen wasn't Billie Chen, then her story about the man breaking in and demanding the notebook was a lie. That would only make his dad look more likely for the murder, and Skaggs would feel more than ever that he had his man.

Of course, Hunter knew his dad hadn't done it so who had? Whoever killed Harrison had left the sword and note, and later left a phone message threatening Billie. If the threat was real didn't the killer know that Billie was an imposter? What did those threats say? He tried to recall. The bloodstained note left with the sword was something like: *He said he didn't have the notebook either.*

Then, when the sheriff's people were working the crime scene at Harrison's house, the phone rang, and a disguised voice said to Skaggs's sergeant, *Tell the bitch she'd better find that notebook. There are other swords,* or something like that.

Hunter concluded it could go either way. But he was leaning to the opinion that these messages were phony too.

Tell the bitch she'd better find the notebook was consistent with a guy actually threatening Billie earlier, as she said. What *'bitch'* was he referring to if not the Billie imposter? Were the note writer and the Billie imposter working together? Was Billie herself the note writer? Was she also the killer? He still couldn't imagine the slight fragile woman he'd known as Billie beheading a man, and he doubted she could have assaulted Lannigan. She definitely couldn't have knocked out Henry, as he'd just left her at her hotel when it happened. And who were the two Asian guys who'd planted the evidence in the Kingston house?

He just couldn't wrap his mind around it. Why the concerted effort to frame his dad? What could anyone possibly have against him?

He heard Genevieve rustling about in the bedroom. He made her a cup of coffee and set it on the table just as she came out.

"Hi, babe."

"Hi, yourself," she answered, bending down to kiss him. "What are you up to?" she asked, sitting down and taking a sip from the cup he'd put out for her.

"Just thinking about the woman who pretended to be Billie Chen. If she's the one who broke into the cabin and stole the sword and computer, that means she somehow got to the DIA computer guy who accessed my file and got the cabin's address and security code. Oh, I didn't tell you. Yesterday I got a call from the director, They found the guy dead in a wooded area behind the DIA building. He was murdered.

How did she know to get to that guy? If all that's true, she probably wrote the threatening notes too. That would mean there was no intruder who threatened her to find the notebook. It has to be like we thought before. For some reason she wanted it for herself. But what I don't get is why would she specifically be trying to frame my dad?"

"And," Genevieve jumped in, continuing his thought, "maybe it's not just your dad. She could be behind the problem with your research grant.

"If so she's got a lot of hi-tech skills," Hunter observed.

Genevieve nodded. "So like I said before, the real question is, who is this woman and what is she after?"

They both looked up at the same time, suddenly hearing birds squawking outside. The noise seemed to be coming from her carport. They went out the kitchen door, where they saw that the hood of Genevieve's white BMW was completely covered in red. Crows were pecking at it, flying off with red feet as Hunter approached.

It appeared to be blood, and someone had just recently poured it on. He ran to the street, looked both ways, and did a quick tour around the house. No one.

Back at the car Genevieve cried, "Hunter, look."

Taped to the window was a note obviously addressed to her.

It's not healthy to be close to the McCoys Sword

"Mon Dieu, Hunter. Look at that."

"Don't touch anything," he said. "I'll call the police."

Who to call? He instinctively knew this was related to everything else going on with his dad, the murders, and his problems. Skaggs was handling this with the Sarasota County Sheriff's Department. But Genevieve's house was in the city of Sarasota, not the county, so the local police would handle the call. Wally Osborn was with the Sarasota Police Department, but Hunter knew he couldn't start with the homicide detective. So he called the police line and talked to the person who answered.

"This is Hunter McCoy. A car in our driveway has just been vandalized. I believe blood was poured all over it."

"We'll send an officer out as soon as we can, sir."

While they waited he called Lannigan. "How's the head?"

"It's okay. A few stitches, that's all. Listen, Hunter, we've just gotten some bad news, I'm afraid. It seems that Detective Skaggs has just come into some additional incriminating evidence that your dad is guilty. I just got off the phone with the DA."

"What evidence?"

"He's got records showing that Ed McCoy bought a ticket on American Airlines out of Fort Myers to Chicago and then transferred to Regional Southwest Airlines to Marquette, Michigan on September twentieth—one day before the sword and computer was stolen from the cabin. Then he returned on the twenty-second."

"But that's impossible," Hunter practically shouted. "There must be a mistake."

"It gets worse," Lannigan went on. "No one can vouch for your dad's presence here during that time. His friend Henry was on a three-day trip to Key West with Jim Furlow and Joe Palma. Your dad didn't go because he said he was waiting for you to come down from Virginia and he wanted to see you when you got here."

Hunter thought about that. It was true. He had planned to fly to Florida about that time. But then, when he decided to build the sauna at the cabin, he'd called his dad and told him he was going to delay the trip for a few weeks, saying he had some things to do at the med school. The sauna was going to be a surprise.

"This frame-up is getting tighter, Hunter."

"Yeah. And don't forget the freezing of my research grant and the complaints about illegal activity at my apartment. Then, just a few minutes ago, Genevieve Swift—you'll meet her soon—was also sent a threatening message for being associated with the McCoys. It seems someone, for some reason, has a personal stake in ruining us. I'm seriously beginning to think that the fake Billie Chen is behind all this."

"Unfortunately," the lawyer added, "that leaves your dad as Skaggs's only viable suspect for the murder of Scott Harrison."

The Sarasota police arrived and took photos of the bloody car and the note. Before leaving, they took statements from both Hunter and Genevieve. The officer said they'd be in touch if they learned anything.

Hunter didn't expect they'd learn anything useful. He was more convinced than ever that he'd have to solve this thing on his own.

24

HUNTER AND GENEVIEVE ARRIVED AT THE JAIL at ten in the morning on the sixth day of Ed McCoy's arrest. Lannigan was already there. After Hunter introduced the lawyer to Genevieve, the three of them went in to see Ed.

Ed and Genevieve hugged, and the guard told them to separate, sit down, and have no further physical contact.

Lannigan immediately took over.

"All right, this is what we need to do. I've got Stretch tracking down the airline ticket fraud." Addressing Ed, he said, "We can only prove it wasn't you by finding whoever did get on that plane to Marquette and back. The man's a bloodhound. If it exists, he'll find any evidence that you were actually here during that time.

"Now Ed, I need you to sit back and tell me everything you can remember about the sword. I want it all, even if it seems superfluous to you. I want to know how your dad came into possession of it during the war, and I want to know how you learned about the killing of Scott Harrison. Start from the beginning, and don't leave out anything."

"Okay, if you think it'll help. But be prepared, it might take a while."

"Go ahead."

"Let me see. I think I'll start with the men's book club. We were meeting at Jim Furlow's place, just down the road a bit from where Henry and I live. Jim Furlow had been a fishing boat skipper all his life. He and his business partner, Joe Palma, who lives across from us, had commercially fished the Gulf of Mexico waters for nearly forty years before they decided it was time to retire."

The attorney had activated his recorder so as not to miss any of this.

"Jim and Joe had always been voracious readers," continued Ed, "often good-naturedly arguing over books on the open water when they were fishing. They both agreed their literary wrangling helped pass the time and relieved the hard and often dangerous work of fishing for a living.

"When Henry and I rented the place next door, Jim and Joe introduced themselves and we quickly became friends. When they learned that Henry and I were also readers, they asked us if we'd like to form a men's book club. We said sure.

"In order to keep the discourse civil, we decided on a few simple rules. We'd select only nonfiction works, and as much as possible, avoid books that focused on religion or current politics. When Joe read us a review of Harrison's book, we were fascinated by its premise and decided to make it the club's first 'selection.'

"Most people only know about the well-publicized formal Japanese surrender in August of 1945 on the battleship *Missouri* in Tokyo Bay. You know, the one with General Douglas MacArthur; the one you always see in print and in the movies, with the Japanese guys in top hats and tails."

Lannigan and the others nodded.

"You mean there was more than one surrender?" Genevieve asked, incredulously.

"Oh yes, my dear. Harrison's book points out that there were almost fifty ceremonies, some very formal, some not so much. Communications weren't always so great in those days, you know, so each surrender served to make sure everyone in that region involved in the fighting knew the war was really over. Some of those little islands out in the Pacific were pretty remote and isolated."

"And your father's story was one of those other surrenders?" the lawyer asked.

"Yes, it was."

Then, his voice, dreamy in remembrance, Ed McCoy related the story of his father's experience during that time; the story he'd written for the *Upper Peninsula Post* several years earlier.

"My dad, Technical Sergeant Karl McCoy, had been in the Army Air Corps with the 1980th Truck Company in China in 1945. They were tasked with transporting equipment in truck convoys along the Burma Road to the Allies' forward airbases in Southern China.

"Following the formal Japanese surrender in August 1945, several officers in his company were ordered to fly to an airbase in Wuchang, China, then occupied by the Japanese. My dad was ordered to accompany the commissioned officers on the mission, which was designed to prepare the airfield for the Allied forces that were expected to move in soon.

"When their C-47 cargo plane landed on the still camouflaged Japanese air field at Wuchang, my dad—and I'm sure the officers on board the plane—were surprised to be met by a fully armed Japanese ground crew.

"Captain Grayson Malport, the senior American officer on board the plane, quickly determined that the Japanese were not yet ready to accept the American team. Captain Malport decided they were going to unload their cargo and fly on to Shanghai. He ordered my dad to stay behind, telling him there was nothing to worry about—the war was over.

"'We'll be back,' he called down to my dad. Then they flew off, leaving him unarmed and alone to make first contact with an enemy force that he sincerely hoped knew the war was actually over."

"That had to be scary," said Genevieve. "One guy, unarmed, with no backup surrounded by all those armed

Japanese. Do you think those enemy soldiers even knew the war was over when your dad was dropped off there?"

"I think so," Ed said. "I remember my dad telling me that at first, when Malport left him there alone, he wasn't sure. But he said they treated him okay and didn't threaten him in any way, so he figured, yeah, they probably did.

"That first night the Japanese brought him to an abandoned Catholic Convent in Wuchang. He stayed there for many weeks and became a friend and helper to an old Chinese doctor who lived there and treated patients out of the basement. With no word from his unit or the officers who'd left him there, he was convinced he'd been abandoned.

"There was really nothing for him to do, so one day, not sure what to expect, and with nothing to lose, he ventured onto the Japanese airbase and walked into the headquarters building. He was stunned when all the military men in the room suddenly snapped to attention. Then the officer, a Japanese colonel of unusually short stature, ceremoniously reached behind him and unsheathed his samurai sword.

"Now you've got to understand, my dad was a twenty-one-year-old sergeant who stood six-foot-three, but he was still more than a little worried. He had no idea what the man was going to do with that sword. His fear subsided when the colonel stepped forward, resheathed his sword, bowed, then formally presented it to him and saluted. Later, when my dad told me this story, he laughed and said, 'The guy must have thought I was General MacArthur himself.'"

Lannigan nodded. "Did your dad meet with Harrison to give him all this information for his book?"

"I don't know; he never mentioned it to me. He could have gotten it all from the article I wrote for the *Upper Peninsula Post* that would have been available in a web search. I wrote it based on conversations with my dad. The paper published it in three installments.

"But wait a minute," Ed scratched his head as if something had just occurred to him. "I never wrote in that article, nor did I even know about, the other stuff Harrison wrote. I knew about the Chinese doctor and the nun who helped him when she came back from Burma, Sister Mary Margaret, but I didn't know about my dad's role in the arrest of the Japanese general, Tomoyuki Yamashita that Harrison described in his book. He never told me that."

"I don't remember hearing that story either," Hunter said. "Harrison must have learned that by actually interviewing him. They must have gotten together at some point, unless he heard that part from someone else."

"When did you learn about the murder of Harrison?" the attorney asked Ed.

"It was during the book club meeting, when we were discussing the surrenders. Jim Furlow's front door suddenly opened with a bang, and Joe Palma's son Jeff rushed in, carrying a copy of the *Venice Herald Tribune*. He asked if any of us had read the paper that morning. We all said no.

"Jeff went on to tell us that, according to the paper, Scott Harrison, the author of *Surrenders In The Pacific,* had been murdered the day before at his home. A neighbor found him when he went over for their regular Wednesday afternoon cocktail hour. According to the paper, he'd been beheaded by a Japanese samurai sword. It was found lying next to the body.

"Shortly after that, the cops arrived and arrested me."

25

AFTER LEAVING THE JAIL, HUNTER DROVE GENEVIEVE to her office at the Ringling Museum since her car was temporarily out of commission while they cleaned it up. Then he rejoined Lannigan at his office.

"Was my dad's long story helpful to you?" he asked the graying attorney.

"Well, it supplies several witnesses to your father's surprise at learning about Harrison's murder. That could be useful in a jury trial if it ever comes to that. Beyond that, I'm not sure. But it always helps to have the whole picture.

"Hunter, you've got to focus on something else. You need to find this fake Billie Chen. If she really is behind the murders, the notes, and framing your dad, and now possibly putting you and Genevieve in her sights, finding her is key to proving his innocence.

"It's obvious this woman, this Billie imposter, had some reason to find the notebook, but she also has some reason to target you personally. I think it's almost as important to find out her motive for all this as it is to find her."

"Agreed."

Hunter left and headed for his Jeep. He knew he couldn't go on referring to the imposter as Billie Chen, so Genevieve had come up with an appropriate alternative name—Fake Billie, the same term Lannigan had used. The problem was, where to begin? Maybe Mrs. Nason at the Gilbert Travel Agency could be useful again. If he could somehow get a picture of Fake Billie, he could show it to her and ask if she'd ever seen her. If she was the person who killed the real Billie Chen, who knows, she may have stopped in the travel agency on a scouting trip ahead of time. The only problem with that was, he didn't have a picture of her.

Just as he got behind the wheel, his phone rang, and his problem was solved.

"Hey, Henry, what's up?"

"Hunter, I'm over at Joe Palma's place. It's the green house, directly across the street. You might want to get over here. He's got something you'll find interesting."

"Give me forty-five minutes."

He pulled into Palma's driveway thirty-five minutes later.

"Tell him what you've got, Joe," Henry said to Palma, after he'd brought Hunter a cup of coffee at the kitchen table. "Tell him what you did. He'll be happy."

Curious, Hunter watched as Joe Palma brought out a black compact digital camera.

"Now you have to understand, Hunter, I wasn't snooping, I was trying to catch a photo of a black and white warbler I'd been following. I'm kind of an amateur birder and the little stinkers never sit still long enough for me to get a good shot, always jumping behind branches and leaves. Anyway, the one I'd been following flew from my tree to the tree in front of Henry's place.

"Now this little camera has a pretty good zoom lens on it—you know, so I can get those closeups of the birds? Anyway, just as I shot it, you and that woman Henry was telling me about came out the front door. I got all three of you in it, you, her and my warbler. As it turned out, the photo of the warbler wasn't too good, but I got a pretty good shot of you and the woman."

Hunter was stunned. *This is just what I need.* "Talk about a lucky shot, Henry." Reaching for the camera, Hunter asked, "Can I see it?"

"I can do better than that." Henry handed Hunter a high-resolution photo. "I like to print out my good bird photos, so I always use this high-quality paper."

The photo clearly showed Billie, or rather Fake Billie, in a full-frontal shot. It was just what he needed.

"Joe this is great. You can't believe how important this is."

"I think I can. Henry told me she was an imposter. I sure hope this helps get your dad off the hook. The three of us—Jim, Henry and I—want to help in any way we can. We're here if you need us."

"Well, this sure helps, Joe. Can you text me the digital version of this photo?"

"Easy, I'll do it right now."

Within a minute Hunter had it on his phone. He'd be able to send this image to Mrs. Nason, to see if she recognized her.

Henry said, "Hunter, just so you know, Joe, Jim, and I are going to do some thinking about this frame-job on Ed. Reading a new book right now, with him in jail, just seems less important than trying to get to the bottom of what's going on here."

"Good. Never hurts to have more minds on the problem."

"Guys," Joe said in a loud whisper from one of the windows. "Over here. Come here. Look."

Startled, the two men rushed to the front window to join Joe and looked out.

"Over there. See that black hatchback?"

Hunter saw a black SUV with what looked like two men in it, parked about a hundred yards away on the street.

"That's the one I saw right after they arrested Ed. I told the lawyer, Lannigan, about it."

Hunter nodded.

"It was the day after the arrest when I saw two guys get out of that same black SUV carrying a large black plastic bag. They walked to your front door, Henry, and went into the house."

"Joe, get your camera," Hunter directed. "Try to get a picture through the window. Don't let them see you."

"Okay."

He took several shots. Not happy with the way they looked, he said, "I can't see their faces clearly, angled like this through the window. If I go upstairs, I can get a better shot."

"All right, do it, but be careful; don't let them see you."

While Joe went upstairs to take the shot, Hunter and Henry continued to watch. Joe came back from upstairs. "Got'em. I got the car, and closeups of the two guys. They're both Asian. I told the lawyer, the guys I saw go in the house looked Asian. I'm sure of it now."

"How about a license plate?" Hunter asked, "did you get that too?"

"No. Florida plates are only in the back, and they're facing us."

"Okay, go back upstairs and keep watching. When they leave you might get a clear shot of the back."

"I'm on it," Joe said, and ran back upstairs.

Just as Hunter was figuring out how to approach the two men, they left, did a U-turn, and drove away. He shouted upstairs. "Joe, did you get the shot?"

"Damn," he said. "No, I couldn't do it."

Hunter called Lannigan and told him that Joe Palma had just taken photos of the two guys in the SUV that matched the ones Joe had seen carrying the bag into his dad's house.

"That's great. Do you think Palma will be a good witness?"

"No question about it. He'll be credible. Also, and this is big too, he got a great photo of Fake Billie one day when she left the Kingston house with me." He explained how that happened while Joe was trying to get a clear shot of the elusive bird.

"This is good," the lawyer said. "Now we each have something to work with. Palma's eyewitness account will cast considerable doubt on the prosecution's evidence, and you have photos to use to go after the girl and the two guys. Send me copies of those photos."

"Right," said Hunter. "I'll do it now."

"You know, Hunter, there's a coincidence here that might just be helpful."

"I know," said Hunter. "Fake Billie and the two guys in the SUV?"

"Yeah. All three are Asians."

26

THAT NIGHT OVER DINNER, HUNTER AND GENEVIEVE speculated on all the questions they didn't have answers to.

"I've been thinking about the note threatening you for being associated with us, my dad and me," Hunter said. "It strongly suggests that while the initial threat may have been against us, it's now been widened to include you because of your association with us—most likely me, specifically."

"And don't forget Henry," she said.

"Right. He's also close to us."

"This is looking like a vendetta," she said. "Like it's personal."

———————————

IN THE MORNING, STILL TIRED from a poor night's sleep interrupted by weird dreams, but coming alive after two robust cups of coffee, Hunter called the Gilbert Travel Agency in Chicago.

"Mrs. Nason, this is Detective McCoy. I'm afraid I need your help and your cooperation again."

"Okay…?" she said slowly, ending the word with a question mark.

"I have a digital photo of the woman pretending to be Billie Chen. I'd like to text it to you and ask if you've seen her before. Maybe she stopped in the office before Billie was killed, or—I just don't know. But if you or your staff recognize her, it could be important."

"Well, sure. I could do that."

She gave him her cell number, and he texted it to her and waited for a response.

He didn't have to wait long.

"Yes. Yes. She was here. I remember. Several months ago, she came in looking for a job. We didn't have an opening at the time, but we always keep records of applicants in case one opens up. I specifically remember *her* because she said no, she didn't want me to do that. If we didn't have an opening, we didn't have an opening, she said. She didn't want to be on an indefinite waiting list."

"Okay," Hunter said. "Can you tell me anything else, anything at all?"

"Well, I remember after I told her that, she said she'd like to talk to the owner, Billie Chen."

"I told her I was the co-owner and that wasn't possible. Then she shoved me and left."

"She shoved you? You mean like physically shoved you?"

"Yes. She pushed me back and I almost fell over. Is she the killer? Detective? Did she kill Billie?"

"I don't know, but it's beginning to look like a real possibility."

After ending the call, Hunter was trying to figure out what to do next when Genevieve appeared at the bedroom door, stretched, and came into the kitchen. It was Saturday and she wasn't working. Over coffee he told her what he'd learned from Mrs. Nason.

"You know what you need to do next, Hunter." She said this as a statement not a question.

"Yup. I've got to call the cops in Chicago. Tell them I have information on a possible suspect in one of their murder cases."

"You know what I like best about you?" she said, standing behind him and leaning his head back and pulling him close for a kiss?"

"Is it my rugged good looks?"

"No."

"Is it my incredible skill in bed?"

"Not entirely."

"How about my earning power?"

"No."

"My…"

"Hunter?"

"Yes?"

"Shut up."

"Hmmm"

"What I like best about you is—"

"You know, before you tell me," Hunter interrupted, standing and slipping off her robe, "I have an idea of my own. Let's revisit the question of my incredible skill in bed."

THREE HOURS LATER HUNTER MANAGED to get a late morning flight out of Sarasota to Chicago, arriving at two that afternoon. By four o'clock he was sitting at the desk of Homicide Detective Wilbur Jenkins of the Chicago Police Department. He was handling the Billie Chen murder case. Jenkins was a fit-looking fortyish, no-nonsense cop. Hunter had worked with a lot of guys like him.

"So, Mr. McCoy, the desk sergeant says you have some information on one of my cases. What is it?"

"I have a photo of a person who may be Billie Chen's killer, or at least is associated with the killer in some way."

"Really? And how is it you have such a photo?"

Hunter told him about Scott Harrison's murder, the appearance of the fake Billie Chen, his discovery that she was a phony, and that Mrs. Nason at the Gilbert Travel Agency recognized her. Then, to add as much credibility to his story as he could, he also told Jenkins about his own background and showed him his credentials.

"That's quite a story, McCoy. Let's see the photo."

Hunter handed him the print that Joe Palma had taken of Fake Billie and him leaving the rental house on Casey Key.

Jenkins took it, still eyeing Hunter with a slight air of disbelief. Then he looked down at the photo and his expression immediately changed to one of shock and obvious recognition. He returned his gaze to Hunter. "When was this taken?"

Hunter gave him the date.

"Stay here. Don't move. This could take a while. Have some coffee. Over there." He pointed to a side table with a coffee machine and paper cups. On his way out the door with the photo, Jenkins talked to another detective, and Hunter assumed he told the man to make sure he didn't leave.

Almost an hour later, Jenkins came back. Sitting down, he clasped both hands on his desk and leaned across toward Hunter. "Firstly, McCoy I had you checked out. Much to my surprise you're legit—DIA, Virginia State Police Detective, and this I still can't believe, a medical school professor?"

"I know, strange but true," Hunter said.

Jenkins took a deep breath and exhaled slowly, as if what he was going to say next would take a huge effort.

He placed the photo on the desk and tapped it with his index finger several times. "You really don't know who this is, do you?"

"That's why I'm here, Detective, I don't know."

He sat back and began. "Her name is Leiko Yamashita. She's thirty-three years old, a stonecold killer, and the head of a ruthless Japanese crime family in Chicago."

"Yamashita?" Hunter asked, recognition slowly dawning. "Is she related to General Tomoyuki Yamashita?"

"So you know about that, do you?" Jenkins said. "She's his great-granddaughter. We've been after her and her family for years. She took over running the organization from her father about three years ago, when he died."

Hunter mulled this over. He simply could not reconcile the wisp of a girl he'd thought was Billie Chen, crying and afraid, with the image Jenkins had just put in his mind. How could he have been so completely fooled? With his training and experience he should have been able to see through her act, but he hadn't. She was that good.

Seeing Hunter's confusion, Jenkins said, "What are you thinking, McCoy?"

"I'm wondering how she fooled me so completely."

Jenkins nodded in sympathy. "Understood. And I can't begin to imagine her as the weak, vulnerable woman you described."

The two men regarded each other quietly for a moment. Finally, Jenkins said, "All right, then my task is clear," Jenkins said. "I plan to question her regarding the murder of Billie Chen. Another detective is handling Chen's murder case, but since it involves Leiko, I'll question her. What you haven't told me, McCoy, is why you want her. It can't just be your bruised ego for being so badly fooled."

Hunter told him everything he hadn't told him before. When he was finished, Jenkins said, "You've got a lot on your plate, man. Let me give you some advice. If you run into her again before I do, just remember she's not even remotely the mild-mannered, frightened girl you knew. Don't ever lose sight of that. The woman is a deadly viper."

Hunter asked. "Did you ever get anyone for Billie Chen's murder. For that matter, how was she murdered?"

"As I said, I'm not handling that case, but as I recall she was stabbed multiple times."

The two men shook hands and as Hunter left, Jenkins added, "Oh, and McCoy, I might have a small but hopefully welcome surprise for you later tonight."

Hunter had taken a cab from the airport, so he called for another one and had the cabbie drive him to the Palmer House, where he'd booked a room, since his return fight wasn't until eleven the next morning. On the way he wondered what Jenkins had up his sleeve.

After dinner in the hotel's dining room he moved to the bar, where he ordered a perfect Manhattan on the rocks. A pianist was quietly playing a slow, jazzy version of "Stormy Weather." Hunter began to relax and thought about Genevieve and how good it felt to have her back in his life again.

"Excuse me."

Startled, Hunter looked up and saw the one person in the entire universe he never expected.

Fake Billie Chen.

27

"BILLIE?"

"No. My name's Lana. The woman you know as Billie is my twin sister, Leiko."

Twin Sister?

Regaining his composure he examined the young woman closely. The voice seemed subtly different. Billie was always tentative and unimposing, but this woman stood tall and straight. Still. . . He looked around to be sure she was alone. The bar was empty except for a young couple at a table and two women at the other end of the counter.

Before he could ask her to sit, she said, "I need to talk to you. Please, can we sit at a table in the corner? I'll explain."

Hunter picked up his drink and chose a booth against the wall where he could see everyone coming and going in the room. The woman slid next to him so she could survey the room as well.

"McCoy, you have to know that you're in grave danger from my sister. She's not who she says she is."

Hunter shifted slightly away from her. "I know she's not Billie Chen."

"That's not what I mean."

"I've learned she's Leiko Yamashita, great granddaughter of the Japanese General Yamashita, and not the granddaughter of Dr. Li Qiang Chen."

"That's right, but there's more. And you can relax, I'm really not her. I'm a homicide detective with the Chicago PD, and I work with Jenkins. The name's, Lana Sato." She showed Hunter her credentials. "I'm the 'surprise' Jenkins told you about earlier."

"You're her sister and you're a cop? How does Leiko feel about that?"

Lana gave a tight smile. "About like you'd imagine. She's tried to have me killed more than once. Now, with you interfering in her plans, you're a target as well."

"I have to admit, she had me completely fooled. I know what she led me to believe, but I don't know what she's really after. Do you?"

"I think so, or at least I have a good idea. But first let me give you some background. Jenkins asked me to fill you in. It didn't take long to find out where you were staying."

Not with the entire Chicago Police Department behind you, no, it wouldn't.

"Okay, go ahead."

"Leiko and I are identical twins. Until the age of fourteen we lived with our mother, Mika, and our father, Masaaki Yamashita. Leiko's personality was shaped by and most closely aligned to our father's. They were extremely close. I, on the other hand, instinctively didn't like or trust the man and spent as little time with him as I could."

"What happened at fourteen?' Hunter asked.

"Our mother died. Her death was suspicious, and I think Leiko was responsible. In any case, when I accused her of it, my father threw me out."

"You were only fourteen. What'd you do? Where'd you go?"

"I knew we had an aunt somewhere, my mother's sister. We'd never met, but I was able to locate her, knocked on her door, and told her my story. She took me in and raised me. Got me through high school, college, and helped me join the Chicago PD."

"Lucky for you."

"Yes, it was."

"How'd you get the name Sato?"

"I took my aunt's last name. I officially changed it from Yamashita to Sato."

"Why do you believe Leiko killed your mother?"

"You're perceptive, McCoy, that's good. When it became apparent that Leiko was leaning toward the criminal side of the family and our father was actually grooming her to take over some day, I believe our mother was going to tell her something, something that our father didn't want her to know, something powerful. I don't know what it was, and I don't believe she did tell her, but she intended to.

"I believe he found out somehow and told Leiko a made-up story that our mother was planning some kind of treachery against the family. She was much closer to him than to our mother, so she bought into his lie completely."

"This happened when you were both fourteen."

"Right. I accused her of murdering our mother. I didn't have any proof, just a feeling. Things she said afterward. Things like 'Our mother had it coming to her,' and 'She deserved it because she was a traitor to the family.'"

"So your father, Masaaki, heard about this and threw you out?"

"Exactly. That very day I was out on the street with nothing but the clothes on my back. My sister actually smiled when she saw this. We've never met nor spoken since."

Hunter said, "That's quite a story."

"Yeah, and it's not over yet." She signaled for the waiter to come over. "Bring me a Dewar's on the rocks." She looked inquiringly at Hunter's half full Manhattan.

"I'm good," he answered.

When the waiter returned with her drink, she continued. "Of course I've been following my sister's career, if you can call it that, ever since I joined the department. Since making detective, I've made it a priority to stay up to date on her activities. I know she left Chicago and went to Florida, where she met up with you. What I don't know is why. What can you tell me about that?"

Hunter told her everything, including his suspicion that she might be behind the murders of Billie Chen and Scott Harrison. He also suspected, but couldn't imagine why, she was specifically going out of her way to frame his dad for the murder of Harrison. He also told her that somebody was discrediting him as well, getting his grant frozen, planting rumors about illegal activity at his apartment, threatening his girlfriend, beating-up Henry. He wondered if Leiko was behind all this as well.

"Did you say Harrison's book specifically named your grandfather, Karl McCoy, as the man who ultimately turned in General Yamashita?"

"Yes, that's quite clear in the book."

"And it also specifically named This Dr. Li Qiang Chen as the man who spotted the General and told your grandfather about it?"

"That's right."

"There's your answer, McCoy. Leiko's definitely behind the frame of your father, and the personal troubles you're having as well."

"I don't understand."

"Before he died three years ago, Masaaki Yamashita, my father, had been trying to find the names of the two men who were responsible for the general's betrayal—as he saw it—leading to his ultimate trial and execution. He'd been looking for this information his entire life. Family honor required him to avenge the general's arrest, trial, and execution.

"And since Scott Harrison's book was published *after* his death, he never got those names. But Leiko read it and found them. And now that she's the head of the family, the responsibility to restore its honor, in her warped mind, falls to her.

"McCoy, you said your grandfather is dead and so is Dr. Chen. That means the vengeance gets redirected to the descendants. I'm afraid that includes you and your dad on the McCoy side, and apparently Billie Chen on the Chen side."

There it is. That explains it.

He took a long drink of his Manhattan and sat back, pondering what he'd just heard.

"If this is all true, Detective Sato, you've explained almost all the strange events that have happened since this thing began. Almost, but still not everything."

"What don't you know?" Sato asked.

Hunter explained. "If Billie Chen was a target, your sister succeeded by killing her. And that makes sense according to your vengeance theory. What I don't know is why she took Billie's grandfather's diary and why she wanted Dr. Chen's research notebook so badly—which she now has, by the way."

"What else can you tell me about this notebook?"

"You know, I think it would be better if you read it. You might spot something that we didn't because you know her. I had a translation made—unless you read Chinese?"

"No, but Leiko does."

"Okay, I'll have a translated copy sent to me here in the morning. You can see it then. I'm scheduled to fly back to Florida tomorrow but I'm going to cancel the flight and stay for a while. Where can I meet you in the morning?"

"Come on down to headquarters. There's something else you need to see. You might as well know what you're really up against with my sister."

28

LEIKO SAT QUIETLY, DEEP IN THOUGHT, on her ornate sofa covered in red silk embellished with intricately embroidered gold designs of Japanese nature scenes. It was 1:30 a.m. and she was gazing out at the city skyline still ablaze with lights even at this early morning hour. She was contemplating her success so far.

The father had been arrested for murder, she'd completely fooled the son, and his reputation was being smeared. His girlfriend, the Swift woman, had been threatened. She smiled in satisfaction, knowing how humiliated Hunter McCoy would be at having been made a fool of so completely. She savored the feeling of vengeance and absolute superiority.

This is better than simply killing them, she thought.

While all the men in her family had been tall, going all the way back to the general, Leiko was small and slim. Nevertheless, more than once she'd used her agility and physical strength to kill a man with her bare hands. And, in the tradition of her ancestors, she'd been equally lethal with a variety of weapons.

On his deathbed her father had told her that it was now her responsibility to avenge the family honor. She'd shown from an early age the dexterity and cunning required to be the rightful successor to the crime family she'd been running in Illinois since inheriting it three years ago.

Early on she'd shown that she had what it takes to lead. She'd killed her first man when she was sixteen. The man was no pushover, either. Her father had selected him deliberately because he was a worthy opponent. Of course, the killing had also been righteous, since the man had committed the one crime against the organization for which there was no forgiveness—he'd dishonored the family name of Yamashita. She had personally killed her own mother for the same reason—without a moment's hesitation.

Revered by her family, the general had been betrayed by two men, a Chinese doctor and an American soldier. He'd been tried for war crimes, sentenced to death, and executed by hanging in 1946. Both she and her father had thoroughly read the exhaustive records of the war crimes trial of her grandfather, searching in vain for the names of the two men. The trial records clearly spelled out the Chinese doctor's and the American soldier's roles in considerable detail, but never mentioned their names. During the war they'd been living in an abandoned convent, out of which the doctor had been treating patients.

Over the years Leiko's father, the general's only grandson, had tried in vain to learn the identity of the doctor and the soldier. Family honor required him to seek revenge, but he'd died without learning their names. She'd been headed for the same ignominy until she'd read Scott Harrison's book. The American historian had given her what she needed, their names: Li Qiang Chen and Karl McCoy.

She soon learned that Chen was long dead, and Karl McCoy had died last year. Nevertheless, she hatched an elaborate plan to restore the family honor and avenge her great-grandfather. She'd go after the descendants of the doctor and the American soldier.

She learned that Karl McCoy had two living descendants: a son, Edward, and a grandson, Hunter. With vengeance uppermost in her mind, Leiko decided to add to this list anyone the two men seriously cared about.

Genevieve Swift, and the man, Henry Lahti, fit that role perfectly.

As for Dr. Chen, the man who recognized the general and then told Sergeant McCoy about it, Leiko learned that he'd died in Wuchang, shortly after the surrender. But Chen had one direct descendant still alive, a great-granddaughter living in Chicago, Billie Chen.

Even though she ran a vast criminal empire, Leiko knew she had to execute the plan herself, as it would be a betrayal of the family honor to entrust it to anyone else. Her slight physique betrayed a lightning fast lethality coupled with an intrinsically psychopathic nature. So far she had completed the first steps of the plan for revenge. By digging into Ed McCoy's personal life, she'd been able to learn about the cabin on Lake Superior in Michigan's Upper Peninsula.

In the process of acquiring knowledge about Hunter, she'd had to eliminate a government official to get the former DIA intelligence agent's link to the cabin and it's security code.

She'd read Harrison's book about the samurai sword the Japanese colonel had surrendered to Hunter's grandfather, so when she saw the sword on the wall, she reveled in her luck. She took, it along with Ed McCoy's laptop computer, to use in her plan.

The other death at her hands, Scott Harrison, was not directly related to avenging her grandfather. Instead it was related to Yamashita's treasure, the name given to the alleged war loot stolen in Southeast Asia by the Imperial Japanese forces during the Second World War and hidden in caves, tunnels, and underground complexes, most likely in the Philippines. In spite of many efforts since the war by treasure hunters from many countries, no one had found any evidence of it.

But after reading Harrison's book, Leiko realized that the historian had referred obliquely to the treasure and its link to a missing research notebook of the Chinese doctor's. Then, when she was Unable to extract the information from him about the whereabouts of the missing notebook she'd beheaded the man herself with Ed McCoy's sword.

Leiko smiled at how simple it had been to completely fool Hunter McCoy into leading her to the notebook. And now she had it, along with the only copies. Now all she had to do was figure out how to use it to get to her real goal, the location and recovery of Yamashita's golden treasure.

Meanwhile, she would continue to carry out her campaign to take her family's long-awaited revenge on the McCoys.

29

IN THE MORNING, HUNTER CALLED LANNIGAN and told him everything he'd learned in Chicago so far.

"That's good stuff, Hunter. The one thing we've been lacking in defending your dad is a motive for framing him. But this vendetta by Leiko Yamashita fills in most of the gaps. Let me talk to the DA, see what he thinks."

"That'd be great. Dad's got to be going nuts in there."

"He's a tough guy, but yeah, it's no fun. Stretch, my guy looking into the airline tickets, has a lead he's following. Hopefully we'll know more later today. If we can find out who took those flights in your dad's name, we'll have some concrete evidence of the frame to go along with the rest of it. If we get that, I know the DA will drop the case and suggest that Skaggs look elsewhere. The good news is, we even know who to point him at—Leiko Yamashita."

Next, Hunter called Genevieve to update her and asked her to email him copies of the translated pages. He wanted Detective Sato to see if anything in there might explain why Leiko wanted it so badly.

"A whole crime family? Be careful, Hunter."

"You know me, babe. I will."

He took public transportation to the station and was immediately directed to Detective Sato. As he looked at her now, he could see the difference between the two sisters, at least the differences Leiko wanted him to see. As Billie, she'd been small and defenseless. But now he supposed that was all an act and she was in reality more like what he saw now when he looked at Detective Sato, confident, ramrod straight, and determined.

As Hunter sat in front of her desk, she brought out a large file about two inches thick and patted it. "This is everything I've collected on my sister's criminal organization. I'm not allowed to work the cases directly because she's my sister. Jenkins runs the task force dealing with their homicides. But I stay current on things because he uses me as a sounding board when he needs to.

"The murder of Billie Chen has been added to this list and the detective who'd been working her case was glad to turn it over to Jenkins. but she's just the latest in many murders linked to my sister since she's taken over the organization. Leiko runs protection rackets, money laundering, drugs, and murder for hire. And, just so you know, ever since she's taken over, the violence has increased considerably. You've got to understand what you're up against with her. Get in her way and she'll kill you and anyone associated with you. You, your dad, and your girlfriend are not safe, not by a long shot. The fact that you're not dead now, means she's just playing with you for a while."

Hunter nodded in acknowledgment of the obvious. "I understand. So how about you? Can you move against her now that you have an eyewitness showing her checking out the travel agency?"

"It would never hold up in court. We've been stymied in the past by the DA's office. They insist that any case would need to be ironclad before they'd be willing to move against her. But her personal links to events in Florida—meeting with you and all—this is a departure. Normally she doesn't get involved herself. So this is definitely different.

"Also, if Jenkins can identify the men who carried the laptop and bloody clothes into your dad's place as being part of her organization, the case against her gets stronger.

The photo of the two men in the SUV will be a big help. Over the years he's collected a large file on her associates. If those men are among them, he'll know it soon."

Jenkins came into the squad room, nodded at Hunter, and began talking to two men, giving them orders. Shortly he came over and said, "I see you and Detective Sato have gotten acquainted."

"We have," Hunter acknowledged. "She's been a big help as far as my understanding of Leiko goes."

"Good," he said. "I would assume she's brought you up to speed on the nature of the problem you face going after her."

"She has. I rarely underestimate threats, Detective, but I have to admit, Leiko's in a league of her own."

"She is. Today I'm going to her compound with two officers to question her about the Billie Chen murder. You have no jurisdiction here, so you can't come along, but I'll wear a wire, so you can hear my questions and her answers. I'll also be wearing an earpiece, so if you hear something that suggests a question I should ask, you can say it and only I will hear it. What do you say?"

"Where will I be?"

"Out on the street in a squad car."

"Deal."

Jenkins returned to the two men he'd been talking with earlier, and Detective Sato tapped Hunter on the arm. "My sister is smart. She's thoroughly evil, but very smart. It won't take long for her to realize that Jenkins has been talking to you. As soon as she puts that together, and it won't take long, your survival chances will nosedive."

"Right," he said. "My guess is it's already tanked now that my usefulness is over. I'm convinced she was simply using me to find that notebook. She knew I'm good at finding lost things and I was safe as long as we were still looking. But now, even without the missing pages, I'm probably too close to her. She'll want to get on with her plans for vengeance.

FOR THE NEXT HOUR AND A HALF, so that Jenkins would be completely familiar with Leiko's phony activities as Billie Chen, Hunter told him and his sergeant everything that he and Fake Billie had done from the time of her arrival at Jenny Lahti's house on the Casey Key until she left Lannigan's office with the notebook. Then they went over all the questions the detective would ask Leiko.

Hunter's phone buzzed, and he saw that Genevieve had emailed him copies of the notebook translations. He asked Jenkins where he could print them out.

"We're done here for now. Go see Sato, she'll help you."

Back at her desk she told him to send the copy from his phone to hers, and she'd print it right there.

"What I'd like you to do," Hunter told Lana, "is to read it over carefully to see if there is anything in there that your sister would want badly enough to kill for. I think we both agree it's not the cure for a disease that would attract her attention. I have a feeling it's something else. Something that you might recognize but wouldn't necessarily mean anything to me."

"I'll do that while you and Jenkins are at the compound. Jenkins already knows her well. He's questioned her several times before. Unfortunately, he's never been able to make anything stick strongly enough to arrest her. You, on the other hand, will no doubt be hearing someone you won't even recognize."

30

LEIKO YAMASHITA LIVED IN a fifteen-thousand-square-foot stone house on two acres in one of the most expensive areas in the city. The hilltop mansion gave her a view of the Chicago skyline. Her security chief and his staff occupied two outbuildings on the site, which was completely surrounded by a ten-foot stone fence.

Two Chicago Police cars pulled up to the fortified front gate of the compound at one o'clock that afternoon. When a security guard approached the first car, Detective Jenkins showed him his credentials and said he was here to see Leiko Yamashita.

"Do you have an appointment?" the guard asked with a perfectly straight face.

"I don't need an appointment. I'm the police. Contact her now and tell her we need to speak to her."

The stone-faced guard returned to his small guardhouse, and Jenkins watched while he used the phone. Shortly the guard came back, looked at the two cars, and asked, "How many of you?"

"Just my sergeant and I will enter the house. The others will stay in the second car— unless I need them," he said, the implied threat clear.

The Guard nodded, and the gate opened. "Drive up to the house and someone will come out to meet you."

The cars parked in front of the main entrance just as the door opened and an Asian man wearing livery stepped into the doorway and signaled for the two men to approach.

Jenkins had been here twice before and knew what to expect. During neither of those visits had he been able to arrest Leiko because his evidence, for whichever current murder he was investigating, was scanty at best. He'd just wanted her to know he was watching. This time, though, he had a little more ammunition. He'd see how things went and take it from there.

The manservant brought them to a large study where Leiko, wearing a brilliant red kimono decorated with yellow embroidered flowers, stood and greeted them.

In a voice cold and flat, she said, "Detective Jenkins, what do you want this time?"

"I have some questions about your activities during the past few weeks."

"My activities are none of your business."

"I want to know why you've been in Florida impersonating a woman named Billie Chen?"

Leiko stared hard at Jenkins before answering. "I don't know what you're talking about, Detective. I've never been to Florida."

"We have a photo of you and a man named Hunter McCoy, exiting a house on Casey Key five days ago. Here, take a look." He handed the photo to her.

Without taking her eyes from the detective, she accepted the photo. Then, looking down, she examined it. After a moment's pause she said, "There's a vague resemblance, but that is not me, and I've never seen that man before. What did you say his name was?"

"McCoy, Hunter McCoy."

"Don't know him. Never been to Florida. That's not me."

Jenkins knew it was time to begin his programmed questioning even though Leiko hadn't asked them to sit.

"We have an eyewitness ready to testify that you went to the Gifford Travel Agency and asked for a job. When you were told there were none currently available, you demanded to see the owner, Billie Chen."

"Nonsense. I've never been to this Gifford Travel Agency, whatever that is. I certainly never asked for a job. Look around you, Detective. Do I look like I need a job?"

"Hunter McCoy claims that he and you, posing as Billie Chen, searched for and found a research notebook belonging to Billie Chen's great-grandfather dating from World War Two. He claims that you took the notebook, and copies that were made of it, with you when you returned to Chicago."

"Again, Detective. I have no idea what you're talking about. I haven't been out of Chicago in recent months, and therefore would have no reason to return."

Hunter's voice came into Jenkin's ear.

Look at her left hand. The back. I just remembered she cut it when we were in the garage in Ohio getting the notebook.

Jenkins looked down, but Leiko's left hand was not visible as she held it behind her back.

"Show me your left hand, please."

"My left hand? Why?"

"Just show me, please."

She extended her left hand, palm up."

"Show me the back, please."

As if she finally knew he was on to something, she put both hands behind her back.

"That's quite enough, Detective. Unless you have something else, this interview is over."

Back in the squad car on the drive back to police headquarters, Hunter said, "That's the same voice. I don't doubt it's her. But I never heard it full of the steel she used with you. Why didn't you bring her in for questioning?"

"We have nothing to charge her with yet that would stick. You could pick her out of a lineup as the woman you worked with who pretended to be Billie Chen. But then what? We have no evidence that she killed her. Even if the woman at the travel agency picked her out of a lineup, no. We need some evidence that will hold up in court. But don't worry, McCoy, I won't stop until I get her. We'll keep digging. There are surveillance cameras everywhere. I'll get her boarding a plane to Florida or something. There's always a trail. I'll find it."

Back at headquarters, Detective Sato told Hunter she wanted a few minutes with him when he was done with Jenkins. Twenty minutes later, he sat down at her desk.

"You're right," he said, without preamble. "That 'little girl voice' your sister used with me was effective but nothing like the cold flat reality of her real voice."

"How do you plan to deal with this going forward?"

"The only way to prove my dad is innocent of Scott Harrison's murder is to find the real killer. And it looks increasingly like that person is Leiko. Or at least she's behind it. With the information you've given me, it appears that her motivation is this family vendetta against the McCoys and Billie Chen, unless of course you found something else when you looked at the translation of the notebook."

"I think I did."

"Really? What?"

"What do you know about General Tomoyuki Yamashita?'

"Not much. Only what I read in Harrison's book, that the doctor and my grandfather turned him in to the Allies, after which he was convicted of war crimes and executed."

"What do you know about his alleged looted treasure?"

"Treasure? What treasure?"

Lana sat back, sipped her coffee, and began to tell him an amazing story. "Let me give you some background. The story goes that in 1927, when Japan declared war on China, Japanese forces allegedly looted gold, jewels, and other valuables from Nanking, then the capital of China. General Yamashita, a colonel at the time, led the raid.

"Some historians claim that the looting was done with the knowledge and blessing of the highest levels of the Japanese government, including the emperor himself. The thefts of gold and jewels continued throughout Japanese-controlled Southeast Asia—the theory being that the Japanese government intended to use the booty to finance the war effort.

"It is believed that many of those who knew the locations of the treasure were killed during the war, or later tried by the Allies for war crimes and executed or incarcerated, including Yamashita.

"According to various accounts, the treasure was initially concentrated in Singapore and later transported to the Philippines.

"There is even a theory that American military intelligence operatives located much of the loot and then used it to finance American covert intelligence operations around the world during the Cold War.

"Treasure hunters have been looking for Yamashita's treasure since the end of the war. To date, the bulk of the treasure has never been found."

"Okay, so what does this have to do with Leiko?"

"The general's grandson, our father, Masaaki Yamashita, referred to the loot as the 'Glorious Store,' a term he'd learned from the general himself. If there's even a slight possibility the treasure actually exists, she'd move heaven and earth to find it."

"Does this mean you found something in the notebook about the treasure?" asked Hunter.

"Yes. And I know the real reason she recruited you to find it."

"And what's that?" Hunter asked.

"The key to Yamashita's treasure, of course."

31

"THE KEY TO YAMASHITA'S TREASURE?"

"I think so. Let me show you," Lana answered. She leafed through translated sheets until she found what she was looking for.

"Here, in the section just before he describes how to make his magic tea."

Hunter saw it was the same section he and Genevieve had studied earlier, the one Leiko—then Fake Billie—had spent considerable time rereading.

The process for extracting and refining the medicine that I've used to treat juvenile diabetes is detailed in the following pages. How ironic that the gift of health was developed directly over the route to the Glorious Store. It's ironic, indeed doubly ironic, to me that this treatment owes its success, not to the China Gold of the Glorious Store acquired by the son of a doctor no less, but to one of nature's beautiful gifts. Ironic and sad.

"Let's take this apart," Lana said. "The term 'China Gold' could refer to the plant he used to extract his medicine, the one that he used to treat juvenile diabetes. He writes *this* 'China gold' gives the gift of health. But here's where it gets interesting. We can assume he developed his medicine in the same place where he worked. And where did he work?"

"Out of the convent," Hunter supplied.

"Correct," Lana said. "And notice that he says this development occurred *over* the 'route to the Glorious Store.' He also writes he's not referring to *the China Gold of the Glorious Store acquired by the son of a doctor,* but to *one of nature's beautiful gifts,* presumably the plant that supplies the treatment for diabetes. Maybe the irony is that he also calls his orchids China Gold. General Yamashita's father was a doctor. So he was the *son* of a doctor."

"Okay," Hunter said. "And you think the Glorious Store is Yamashita's treasure, *his* China Gold, and it's buried under the convent in China?"

"Yes, I do, at least some of it—probably the gems and jewels—and let me tell you why. When I read this section in the notebook, something sounded familiar to me. I wasn't sure what. So while you were meeting with Jenkins, before your trip to see Leiko, I went over everything I have concerning my time with my mother and sister before my father threw me out. It's not much. Remember, I left with just the clothes on my back. But the phrase, 'Glorious Store' rang a bell. I was sure I'd heard the term before, and it was during my time with my mother, my sister, and my father, Masaaki Yamashita.

"Then it came to me. I hadn't actually heard it, I'd *seen* it, in Masaaki's study. There was a framed photo of the general on the wall behind his desk. Below the picture, also framed in bamboo, was the phrase 'The Glorious Store.'

"I asked Leiko if she knew what it meant. She said, 'Yes, it's the general's treasure.'"

Hunter nodded. "So when Leiko saw that phrase in the notebook, she knew what it meant. That explains why she spent so much time over that last page just before the section that was ripped out. That's where he wrote this passage about the Glorious Store and told her exactly where to look for it—under the convent."

"And that, McCoy, is the exact moment when she didn't need you anymore."

"You're right. She left shortly after that and took the copies of the notebook and poem with her."

Before either could comment further, Jenkins came up to the desk. "Leiko is gone. Her private jet just left Midway ten minutes ago. I'm trying to get the flight plan. See where she's going."

"I think we might have an idea," Lana said.

Jenkins pulled up a chair from the adjacent desk. With the three of them together, Jenkins addressed Hunter. "What do you plan to do about Leiko?"

"I'm convinced she's behind the murders and the attempt to frame my dad for Harrison's killing. In addition, it's highly likely she's behind the threat to me and Genevieve Swift. The note threatening her was signed 'Sword.'"

"There you go. No question about it," Lana said. "Masaaki Yamashita gave her the nickname 'Sword' on his deathbed to mark her as the vehicle to carry on the family's vengeance."

Hunter nodded. "Also, she's been trying to discredit me with the medical school and the Charlottesville Police Department."

"So, you're going after her?"

"Unrelentingly."

32

THE LEARJET 70 HEADED EAST OUT OF LA toward Cleveland, Ohio with its only passenger, Leiko Yamashita. Although now she was unrecognizable, once again in disguise.

It hadn't taken Leiko long to figure out how McCoy had learned who she was. He'd have checked with Chen's travel agency and found out that Billie Chen was dead. She also realized she shouldn't have made up the story about a brother, knowing that Billie Chen had no brothers. If there were any, they would certainly have been on her list for retribution.

She was sure she'd made the transfer from her own private jet to the rental Lear without being seen. When her personal pilot finished fueling up her jet and headed for China, the authorities—if they were following her—would assume she was on board with him.

She wasn't sure if Jenkins knew she'd be looking for her great-grandfather's treasure. She and her father had known about it for some time of course, and there would be nothing illegal about searching for it. After all, treasure hunters had been looking for Yamashita's treasure—or Yamashita's Gold as it was sometime called—incessantly since the end of the war. But now, with the notebook's reference to the 'Glorious Store,' she had a specific place to search. Somewhere that all those the treasure hunters didn't know about—the convent in Wuchang.

Her pilot, Kim Zhang, had a visa to enter China, but she didn't. She'd told him that his mission was to locate the convent and report back. She stressed to him how important this information was to her, but not why. And Zhang, long in her employ, knew enough not to ask. When he returned with a full report including photographs, she'd decide what to do.

Meanwhile, she was headed to the motherhouse of the Sisters of Notre Dame de Namur in Cleveland.

HUNTER DECIDED IT WAS TIME TO CALL IN INTERPOL. He dialed a number only available to a few people, and after a series of identification checks, got through to Eduard Gautier.

"Am I speaking to the famous professor himself, the one and only Hunter McCoy?"

"In the flesh, Eduard. Or more correctly, in the 'ether,' I suppose."

"What can I do for the man who single-handedly solved the case of the freeport fraud and got me a big promotion in the process? And, I might add, a very substantial pay raise.

"Single-handedly might be pushing it a bit, but it's still always good to have you willing to help."

"At your service. What can I do this time?"

"I need to know if a convent run by the Sisters of Notre Dame da Namur in Wuchang, China is still there. It was established in 1926 and was occupied through 1948. I don't know if your reach extends to mainland China or not, but if it does, any information you could give me would be a big help on a case I'm working."

"I'll see what I can find. What's it all about?"

Hunter explained about Billie Chen, Leiko Yamashita, the Chicago crime gang, Harrison's book, his dad's arrest, Dr. Chen's treatment for juvenile diabetes, Yamashita's treasure, and the importance of the convent.

Eduard sighed. "You do know, don't you, Hunter, that some professors, actually just 'profess,' right?"

Hunter laughed. "I do, and believe me, that's the norm. But I need you and your incredible skills when I'm hunting bad guys. Or in this case, a bad girl."

"Got it. Your Find-and-Correct work, right?"

"Right."

"I'll call you when I have something."

Hunter thanked him. His phone rang immediately after he ended the call to Interpol headquarters.

"McCoy, it's Jenkins. I've got some information on the two guys your man photographed outside the house on Casey Key in Florida. We know them both, Ryuki Ono and Akito Hano. They're in the employ of Leiko Yamashita. Give me the name of the detective running your dad's case. I'll call him and tell him what we have. Unless he's a real hardass, this will strongly indicate a frame and should get your father out. You can call his lawyer and tell him the same thing."

"That's great. I'll call him right away."

Hunter gave him Detective Skaggs contact info, thanked him again, then called Lannigan.

"Got anything new?" the lawyer asked.

"I do. The Chicago police identified the two men who stashed the computer and bloody clothes in my dad's house. He gave Lannigan their names. They both work for Leiko Yamashita—Fake Billie. The detective working the case, Wilbur Jenkins, said he'd call Skaggs and fill him in."

"That's great. I'll call the DA. It's time for Skaggs to let Ed out."

"Hallelujah," Hunter said.

FOUR HOURS LATER, GENEVIEVE Swift was on her way home from work at the Ringling Museum of Art. Hunter's revelation that Fake Billie was really a crime boss in Chicago by the name of Leiko Yamashita left her concerned for both her and Hunter's safety. The blood splashed on her car and the threatening note from the woman was scary, to say the least. Hunter had told her that Leiko Yamashita went by the nickname 'Sword' and that he'd learned this from her twin sister, who was actually a Chicago homicide detective.

The drive from the Education Center at the museum to her home on the bay was less than five minutes, but during this brief ride she considered that life with Hunter was never dull. In fact, when they were together working on one of his cases, their lives were often in danger, like now. She sighed and dreamed of a day when they'd just relax and have fun together with no one trying to kill them.

This last pleasant thought was in her head as she pulled into her carport at the home on the bay and was violently thrown back against the seat of her BMW. Before she could react, she felt the car being pushed rapidly forward through the back of the carport, splintering the wood frame, and across the lawn toward the bay. She recovered enough to look in the rearview mirror and see an enormous vehicle; she thought it might be a truck. Before she recovered her senses enough to apply the brakes or turn the wheel, her convertible went over the retaining wall into the bay and rapidly sank below the warm waters.

HUNTER DECIDED THERE WASN'T MUCH MORE he could do in Chicago, so he caught a late flight from O'Hare to Sarasota. He figured he'd better check in with his dad and Genevieve, since they were both targets of Leiko Yamashita. While in the air, he tried to consider the mental state of his opponent.

Was Leiko rational? He had to assume she was. She'd successfully played an entirely different person when she was with him, so consistently that he'd been completely fooled. There was a rational reason she did this, and that was to get the notebook. Once she'd had it, she had no more use for him and ran. But she would still want his hide.

He tried to imagine what she would do next. What was more important, going after Yamashita's treasure or continuing her vendetta against him and his dad? He had to finally conclude that she was perfectly capable of doing both at the same time.

33

IN HER DREAM, GENEVIEVE FLOATED THROUGH SPACE, tumbling over and over, her arms and legs extended as if she were flying. Except for the pain in her head, it was a wonderful sensation. She would see a bright light, then it would turn dark, then bright again, then dark once more, until finally she gasped a big inhale as she cleared the surface.

Water? Am I in the water?

Then, remembering what had just happened, she began to paddle and desperately looked around.

There was her house, about twenty yards away. She swam toward it and reached the retaining wall, only to find there was nothing to hold onto and the wall was too high to grab and pull herself up. Fighting back panic and tiring, she swam toward the dock, where the boat was up on a lifter. She reached the structure and was able to pull herself up by stepping on the struts. After managing to get up on the dock, she lay on her back and hyperventilated.

Thankfully, she'd just undone the seat belt as she pulled into the carport, just before the truck or whatever it was, rammed her from behind. This was no accident, she knew. Suddenly fearful whoever it was might still be there, she stood up and quickly looked back at the carport. The truck was gone. But, she thought, so was the Beamer. She walked to the edge of the retaining wall and looked down. There was no sign of the car, just her shattered carport. She hadn't realized before how deep the water was just off the wall.

She went to call Hunter, but as she reached for her phone she realized that her purse with the phone inside, was in the car at the bottom of the bay.

LEIKO'S PILOT, KIM ZHANG, LANDED AT Wuchang/Nanu airport after a twelve-hour flight from LA. He spoke fluent Chinese, and with his American passport was likely to get along well with the Chinese he encountered. Given the hostility that most Chinese still felt toward the Japanese, his surname and language fluency would be an advantage, and one he knew would certainly not be extended to his employer, Leiko Yamashita.

After a few questions at the airport, he'd rented a car and been given the address of the city's historical building. But first he needed to sleep. Wuchang was a modern city that had several fine hotels. He found one, parked the car, went to his room and promptly fell asleep for ten hours. When he awoke it was noon local time.

After lunch In the hotel, he set out for the Wuchang Uprising Memorial Hall. It turned out to be a red brick building at the foot of a hill next to the Yangtze River. Known to local people as the Red Chamber, the building was the first hub of the Wuchang Uprising that led to the Xinhai Revolution, which subsequently brought down the Qing dynasty. Kim hoped it would also have some historical information on the convent.

The receptionist greeted him warmly. "Welcome to Memorial Hall. We have a new guided tour beginning in fifteen minutes. Would you like to join it, sir?"

"No, thank you," Kim responded. "I am looking for information on an old site in the city."

"Oh, I see. What are you looking for?"

"I believe there was a Catholic convent and school run by the Sisters of Notre Dame de Namur that was started in 1926. I know it's a longshot, but I wonder if the convent is still standing and where it's located."

"I'm not familiar with it but let me check the directory."

Kim waited while she spun her chair around and pulled a large ringed notebook off a shelf.

"This contains a listing of all the historic sites we've been able to identify in the city. If we know about it, it will be in here. You say the Sisters of Notre Dame—what?"

"The Sisters of Notre Dame de Namur."

"Okay. . . here it is. The convent was built in 1926, and the school was built the next year. The school was torn down in 1950 and the convent in 1951. The area is now a park. Would you like the address?"

Dejected by this news, knowing Leiko would not be happy, Kim nevertheless answered, "Yes, please, if you would."

Outside, he programmed the address into his phone's GPS system and set off to what he imagined would be nothing of importance. After an hour drive, carefully following the guidance from the GPS, he arrived at the bank of the Yangtze River. The road ended at the river and he could see the park, off to his right.

It was about the size of a football field, no more than one hundred yards long by fifty yards wide. It was very hilly, with trees that offered shade to people who were sitting on benches and picnic tables. There appeared to be a small concession stand at one corner of the park that was backed right up against a very steep grassy hill.

Kim began to take pictures, figuring he needed to show Leiko something, even though the convent was gone. He walked to the concession stand and spoke with the proprietor, a young man in his twenties.

He looked at the concessionaire's nametag. "Gui, do you know of any caves or underground caverns in this area?"

"You mean like that one?" The young man pointed to a sign behind the stand over an entrance into the hill. It said "CAVE."

"That takes you into a cave?' Kim asked, astonished.

"Sure, it takes you under the convent that used to be here. The building's been gone forever, but the cave is still here. You can go down and have a look. It's lit up even. You really didn't know that?"

"No."

"That's why this little park is called Cave Park."

Kim couldn't believe it. "So I can just walk down there and look around?"

"Yes, sir, go on, knock yourself out."

Kim entered the opening under the sign and found himself walking down a flight of wooden stairs that ended about thirty feet below the surface. From this point on he followed a well-lit dirt path that meandered for another hundred feet before ending against an earthen wall. There were no side paths of any kind, so there was no way to get lost. He turned around and walked back to the stairs. He knew he'd better record this, so he used his cell's camera and photographed everything. Once again climbing the stairs, he photographed the entrance with the CAVE sign.

Kim wondered, not for the first time what he was doing here. What did Leiko care about a Catholic convent in China and whether it had caverns or caves below it? Oh, well, she paid him generously, so he took more photos of everything in the park and the bank of the river for good measure.

Rather than just get on the plane and fly home with the possibility he might have missed something, he called her using Facetime to tell her what he'd found.

"Where are you?" she asked.

"I'm in Wuchang, at the site of the convent. The site is now a park. Here, let me show you." He reversed the screen camera so it no longer looked at him, but instead showed whatever he pointed the phone at.

"Walk around and show me everything you can see."

Kim repeated his journey from the riverfront through the park, and into the cave below the old convent. Leiko seemed particularly interested in the cave and had him repeat the underground walk several times, focusing on the floor, the ceiling, and the walls. Finally he said, "If I knew what I was looking for, it might help."

Leiko paused, then instructed, "Find out whatever you can about the underground cave. Get as much of its history as you can. The Memorial Hall might have records. Dig deep. Then call me when you have something."

She ended the call.

What the heck am I looking for, he wondered? *What's so important about this that she'd send me halfway around the world?*

34

WHEN HUNTER ARRIVED AT GENEVIEVE'S HOUSE after his evening flight from Chicago he was alarmed to see the shattered carport but no car. Inside, he found her sitting on the sofa, wrapped in a blanket.

"What happened, babe?" he asked, moving to her side.

She just hugged him tightly and said nothing.

"What's wrong?" He asked more gently this time knowing instantly that something terrible must have happened. His first thought was that it involved one or both of her parents in England—but then he thought of the shattered carport.

Inhaling deeply, she finally said, "I wanted to call you, but I lost my phone."

She lost her phone? Why would that have her so obviously upset.

"What happened?"

Meeting his worried eyes, she said, "Hunter, someone tried to kill me tonight."

"What? Are you okay?"

"Yes. I was pulling into the carport when a truck or something, it was black, came up behind and pushed me through the back, over the wall, into the bay. I thought I was going to die."

He held her tightly.

"The top was down on the car and I'd already unhooked my seatbelt. That was a good thing, because I must have hit my head and was a little out of it. I found myself floating to the surface. Once I crawled onto the boat lifter and the dock, the truck, or whatever, was gone. I went to call you and then realized my purse with the phone was at the bottom with the car. I went to the neighbors and called the police. They were here earlier.

Leiko did this.

"Leiko's behind this, I'm sure," Hunter said through clenched teeth. "First dad, then me, then Henry, now you. Her mission, it seems, is to cause as much anguish as possible."

Genevieve stood and threw off the blanket, and recovering some of her swagger, said with venom, "You know, Hunter, this woman is really beginning to piss me off."

In spite of the seriousness of the situation, Hunter couldn't hold back a grin at the sound of the crude American idiom in her elegant French accent—peeese me off. "Me too, Genevieve, me too."

Then, more seriously, "We don't know where she is right now. The Chicago police traced her and her private jet to LA and they suspect she's flown to China looking for a treasure she believes is under the old convent. Jenkins identified the two guys who framed Dad by planting the bloody clothes and his computer at the Kingston house. They work for her. We know they're here, and they could have done this to you."

That night Hunter wrapped Genevieve in his arms as they slept.

IN THE MORNING, HE WAS ABOUT TO CALL LANNIGAN, when the attorney called him first. "Hunter, they're going to release your dad at eleven this morning. The murder charge has been dropped, but the DA wants him to remain in the area until this is all settled."

"Great."

"The icing on the cake, after what you found in Chicago, was that Stretch managed to get a still shot from the surveillance camera at the airline gate of the guy who boarded the flight to Marquette under Ed's name. It's clearly not your dad. That, along with the eyewitness account of the planted evidence, convinced the DA they had no case. So, they're dropping the charges against him."

"I know that's going to make him happy. I'll pick him up."

"Okay, but you know this is also going to make him an easier target for Leiko."

"Right," Hunter said. "Can the sheriff's office keep an eye on their place? It should be the least they can do given that we've identified the real killer for them.

Lannigan said, "I'll call and see about protective surveillance."

"We know she's still operating in the area," Hunter continued, "because she targeted Genevieve just last night."

"What happened?"

He described the attack and told Lannigan that the police had shown up almost immediately after she'd called 911. They'd taken her statement and examined the shattered carport and tire tracks of both her car and the vehicle that pushed her, before they left. She told them she didn't need medical attention."

"Got it, Lannigan said. "Now I have something else, Hunter, and you're going to like this. I just got off the phone with Detective John Bolt, of the Charlottesville PD it looks like your troubles with him are over."

"Really? How'd that happen?" Hunter asked relief obvious in his voice.

"Apparently the whole thing began when the police received complaints from two of your neighbors. After the cops started investigating they learned that the two had moved into one of the lofts only one week before they filed their complaints. Bolt said they'd only learned this later, or they would have dismissed the allegations completely. The two men, who gave their names as Chris Ahorn and Stan

Aki claimed you'd been running a human trafficking ring out of your apartment and promised they had photo evidence to back it up.

"The cops ran their fingerprints and discovered they're real names are Ryuki Ono and Akito Hano and they work for a criminal organization in Chicago known as the Yamashita crime family. They've got arrest warrants out for both of them, but so far haven't been able to apprehend them."

Hunter thanked the attorney for intervening on his behalf and told him he'd keep in touch.

So Leiko was behind my trouble with the Charlottesville PD.

Earlier this morning Genevieve had called the car leasing agency, explained what happened, and they said they'd take it from there and get the car pulled out of the water.

Now over coffee on the lanai and back to herself, she said, "So Hunter, what do we do next about the dragon lady?"

"We?"

"Of course, 'we.' Your little friend has made this personal for me now too."

Hunter knew from past experience he wouldn't be able to dissuade her but gave it a shot anyway.

"You're going to have to work every day, so I can do the investigating and we can talk at night."

"Nice try. As it turns out I have the next two weeks off."

Surprised, Hunter asked, "How did you manage that?"

"Director Bertram called me personally and told me to take as long as I need. He appreciated what a harrowing experience I went through last summer, helping you to save the museum from disaster. So he said I could start with two weeks at full pay, and we'd negotiate after that if more time was necessary."

"Wow," he answered, acknowledging defeat.

At eleven o'clock they picked up Ed McCoy at the jail and drove him to the rental house, where he and Henry were reunited.

"I've never been so glad to see you," Henry said.

"Same here, buddy."

"I'm cooking tonight. Hope you like grilled grouper."

"You bet," Ed said, laughing. "Cuisine at the county lockup did leave a little to be desired."

Hunter and Genevieve laughed as well, happy to see the two old friends reunited and in such good moods.

They went out to the lanai overlooking the intracoastal waterway where Henry had prepared lunch for the four of them, large gulf shrimp salads and iced tea followed by key lime pie. Later, when everyone had been fed and the conversation began to slow down, Ed turned the talk to what Hunter planned to do about Leiko Yamashita now that she had morphed from the innocent waif who'd been threatened by a fictitious bad guy to the evil instrument of all their problems. He told them what Lanigan had learned from Detective John Bolt.

"Genevieve and I have been thinking about just that. Where do we go from here? We've concluded that Leiko has two objectives. One is to exact revenge for what she considers the betrayal of General Yamashita. She's already taken care of part of that by killing Billie Chen.

"She's working on the other part by orchestrating everything that's happened to us."

"You said she has two objectives. What's the second one?" Ed asked.

"We believe her second goal, and the real reason why she wanted Dr. Chen's research notebook so badly, was that she thinks it would point to the location of Yamashita's treasure."

Hunter explained what he'd learned about the war loot from Detective Lana Sato.

"Old Dr. Chen was pretty clever about the way he used the term, 'China gold.' On the one hand he used it to refer to the new species of orchid that might contain a treatment for Type 1 diabetes, but then he also let the term imply the treasure buried by Yamashita. We believe, and I'm sure Leiko does too, that the phrase 'Glorious Store' is the location of the treasure, or at least part of it. Everything suggests it's located under the convent in Wuchang."

Then, stating the same conclusion that Hunter had come to earlier, Henry said, "And she seems perfectly capable of working on both objectives at the same time."

"Agreed," Hunter said. "And let's not forget that she doesn't need me anymore since she has the notebook and the diary. And if she doesn't need me she doesn't need the rest of us either."

"Jeez," Ed said. "And I was just starting to enjoy being out of jail."

35

LEIKO RENTED A CAR AT THE CLEVELAND AIRPORT and drove to the motherhouse of the Sisters of Notre Dame de Namur. Other than knowing they had a convent and school in Wuchang during the war, she hadn't been able to get any information useful to her goal from their website, so she'd decided to make a personal trip. She also knew the authorities were probably looking for her after Jenkins came to her house and questioned her, so she'd have to travel incognito.

She'd actually enjoyed playing the wimpy Billie Chen and seeing the influence she'd had over Hunter McCoy. The man had been completely taken in by her act. It had given her the confidence to play another part today. Now she was Karen Applewood, Harvard historian, writing a book about Christian missionaries in China during their civil war. She'd done enough homework that she was sure she could fool anyone she needed to.

She drove to what appeared to be the administration building, parked, and wearing a professional-looking business suit and carrying a briefcase, approached the front entrance. She was let in by a young novitiate, who took her to the front desk.

"Hi," she said to the middle-aged woman at the desk, extending her hand. "I'm Karen Applewood. I'm a professor of history at Harvard University. I wonder if you could help me? I'm researching a book on Christian missionaries in China during the civil war between the communists and the nationalists. I know your order had a convent and school in Wuchang and I wonder if you have anyone here who could help me with historical information during that time."

"The person you need to talk with is Sister Claire. She keeps the archives of the order and could probably answer most of your questions."

Leiko knew all this already. She knew their archives were substantial and that this Sister Claire really was the keeper of the keys, so to speak. She was playing dumb and modest in order to get them to want to help her. Apparently it was working, at least with this woman.

A few minutes later she entered another building where she encountered an elderly nun who introduced herself as Sister Claire.

"I understand you want to do some research in our archives? Is that correct?"

"Yes, Sister. I'm particularly interested in the school and convent your order maintained in Wuchang, China from 1926 through 1948. I know the chances of any of the nuns from that time still being alive to interview personally is pretty slim, so I thought you and your archives would be the next best thing."

"Well, my dear, you're right about there not being any sisters left from that time. The last one died three years ago, right here in Cleveland. Sister Mary Margaret left the order shortly after returning from China in 1948 and eventually married."

Taking out a notebook and pen, Leiko asked, "Do you know her married name?"

"Her name was Laura McCasey. She stayed faithful to the Church and raised a family. In the early years, she would even come here for reunions with some of the other nuns from that time. I met her several times over the years. A lovely woman."

Then, apparently thinking she was rambling a bit, Sister Claire asked, "What is it you want to know?"

"In my research I've come across the interesting fact that a Chinese doctor treated patients out of the basement of the convent in Wuchang during the Japanese occupation of World War Two. I know the nuns were moved to Burma for their safety during that time, but I wonder if he was still there when they returned after the Japanese surrender in 1945."

"Too bad you didn't start your book three years ago. You could have asked Sister Mary Margaret herself. Still," the old nun said, scratching her chin, "let me check. We might have something."

She turned to her large desktop computer and began typing. While Leiko waited patiently, the nun pounded away, seemingly checking references. Eventually, she stopped, walked into an adjacent room, and returned with a file folder. "I'm afraid this is the best we can do for you. Several years ago one of our nuns wrote a history of the Catholic missions in China during the war. It was never published, but this is it. It includes the history of the mission in Wuchang. What you're looking for may be in here. You can read it and examine it here, but I'm afraid you can't take it with you. Would that be all right?"

"Of course. Can I work at one of these desks?"

"Certainly."

While the old nun retreated to the front room, Leiko opened up her briefcase, took out a laptop computer, and set it on a desk. Then, taking a seat, she opened the file folder and began reading. The section on the Wuchang school and convent took up about nine single-spaced pages. She got what she was after within minutes. There was an overlap between the date the nuns returned and the death of Chen. They returned in October 1945, and he died three weeks later. As she expected, there was no mention of General Yamashita, or any buried treasure. But there was a brief mention of an American soldier staying there without naming him.

Returning to the front room with the file, Leiko handed it to Sister Claire, thanked her, and asked, "Sister, would you have the address of any of Laura McCasey's children or grandchildren—if she had any—so I might interview them?"

Leiko could see her contemplating this for a moment, then deciding. "I guess that would be all right. She had a daughter, Emma Johannson. I know her quite well. A very nice lady. I'm sure she'd be willing to meet with you."

An hour later Leiko drove to downtown Cleveland to Emma Johannson's high-rise condo.

"Mrs. Johannson?" Leiko asked the elegant woman who answered the door.

"Yes?" she said, tentatively.

"Mrs. Johannson, my name is Karen Applewood. I'm a professor of history at Harvard University, and I'm writing a book on missionary programs in China during the war. I wondered if I could ask you a few questions about your mother's experience there. I understand I'm a few years too late to ask her directly."

"I'm afraid you are," Emma answered. "But please, come in."

Inside, over tea, Emma Johannson answered all the young woman's questions. She only hesitated when the professor asked if her mother had brought any papers back from that time in China.

"What do you mean, papers?"

"You know, letters, diaries, anything like that."

"No. Nothing like that. Nuns don't generally keep diaries."

"How about papers that might have belonged to the doctor who worked out of the convent?"

"No, just the seed pods. Oh, and there was a letter with them."

"Seed pods?"

"Yes, when my daughter Carrie and I were cleaning out her house after her death, we found an old cooler with a sack of seedpods, along with a letter my mother had written to explain them. It seems they were special orchid seedpods given to her by the doctor on his deathbed. There was supposed to be a research notebook to go along with them, but she never got it, only the sack of seedpods."

"Do you have the letter?"

"No, my daughter has it."

"Do you remember what was in the letter?"

"It was something about the seedpods being valuable for treating diabetes, I think. Oh, and the doctor asked her to hold them until his brother showed up; then she was supposed to give them to him."

"And did he get them?"

"No. He apparently never came since she still had them when she died. Anyway, my daughter's trying to do something about them now."

"Your daughter?"

"Yes, her name's Carrie Johannson. She's a botanist at the Selby Botanical Gardens in Sarasota, Florida."

36

At nine the next morning Hunter's phone rang. "Hunter, it's Carrie Johannson. I'm back from the conference and I'll be glad to look at that translation you told me about."

Hunter had almost forgotten about the young woman botanist, with all that had happened since their last meeting.

"Sure. Thanks for calling."

"How about if we meet in your lab at Selby, say, in an hour?"

"We?"

"Right. I'll have Genevieve Swift with me."

"Oh, right, I forgot. Okay. See you then."

At ten, the three of them sat down at a lab table. Hunter introduced the two women to each other. On the drive over, he'd decided the best way to explain Genevieve's involvement would be to tell Carrie his full background and that Genevieve had helped him solve several international crimes.

Carrie took a moment to absorb all this. All he'd told her earlier was that he was working with the Chicago Police to solve a murder. "But how did you get involved in this business with the missing notebook." She asked. "Is this all some kind of international crime?"

"Probably not. I'm afraid it's more personal than that."

"What do you mean? Because it involves your grandfather?"

"No. Because it involves my father."

"I don't understand," she said, looking confused.

Over the next fifteen minutes he told her about Scott Harrison's book and his father's arrest for his murder. He also told her about Fake Billie.

Looking suddenly nervous, Carrie asked, "Does this Leiko woman know about me?"

"I can't imagine how. I mean, I only learned about you quite by accident. But again, you have my number. Please call if you ever feel nervous about anything related to this. I'll be there, or I'll get someone to help you as soon as possible."

Genevieve said, "Carrie, believe me, you can trust Hunter on this. I know from experience, he won't let you down."

Carrie eyed them closely, "So are you two more than colleagues. Are you . . .?"

"Yes, we are," Hunter and Genevieve said in unison.

"Okay then. Let's look at the notebook."

When Hunter handed her the copies of the translation, he explained that Leiko didn't know he had them.

Hunter and Genevieve left her alone to read while they temporarily retreated to another table.

Genevieve smiled and whispered. "I think she might have had her eye on you, big boy."

"I've only got eyes for you, Babe."

"Seriously, do you think she's in any danger?"

"She's got the only living orchids from Dr. Chen's research that we know of. If that's what Leiko's after, yes, she could be."

"But how would Leiko know about her? Like you said, you only learned about her by accident."

"Who knows? I'll ask Carrie if she knows whether any other nuns from that time are still around. It's possible Leiko might take that approach and could find her that way."

They watched as Carrie gathered up the papers and came over to their table.

"Find anything?" Genevieve asked.

"Maybe. It's about the phrase, 'Glorious Store,' that you asked me about earlier."

Excited that she might be onto something, Hunter leaned in.

"I told you I'd never heard my grandmother use that phrase. It meant nothing to me. And it still didn't until I looked at your translation. More precisely, I looked at the notes your translator included with his translation. Notice that next to the phrase 'Glorious Store' he added the Chinese words for it. I suppose he did that because the phrase was repeated several times and he figured it was somehow important. Look here."

Glorious store (Guāngróng de shāngdiàn)

"Now I don't know how to pronounce that exactly, but it looks a little like something my gram used to say, '*gangshandian.*' I didn't know if it was Chinese or not, only that she used the word to describe something that was very expensive or very nice. Like if she got an expensive present at Christmas, she might say 'very gangshandian.'"

"So you're thinking that maybe she was repeating what she recalled as the actual Chinese for Glorious Store?" Genevieve asked.

"I don't know. Maybe."

"If that's true," Hunter went on, thinking out loud, "she must have heard the Chinese for 'Glorious Store' somewhere.' And since Dr. Chen used the same phrase, either she heard it from him or, somehow she knew about it herself. It's too bad your grandmother didn't keep a diary. She might have explained it in there."

"I can see that now," Carrie said.

"What about your mother?" Genevieve asked.

"What do you mean?"

"Just wondering if she has any papers that might have belonged to your grandmother. If she does, maybe she mentions the phrase in one or more of them."

Carrie said, "I don't think so, but let me give her a call and see."

A few minutes later her mother was on the line, and Carrie put her on speakerphone.

Carrie told her who Hunter and Genevieve were and that Hunter had found the missing research notebook that Grandma never got, but that six critical pages were missing.

"Mom, do you know if Grandma had any other papers or anything from that time? And you remember how she used to say 'gangshandian?' Did she ever tell you where that came from? It could be important."

"Gangshandian. Yeah, that was her favorite word to describe something great, or beautiful, or even glorious. I remember asking her what it meant, and she said it was Chinese."

"How about any old papers, or anything like that," Carrie prompted.

"I remember her telling me that anything like that from her time in China was turned over to the motherhouse in Cleveland. The only thing I have from that time is her bible. She gave it to me when she turned ninety. Said she hoped it would give me as much comfort as it had her. I'm afraid that's all I have."

Carrie looked questioningly at Hunter and Genevieve to see if they had any more questions. Both shook their heads, 'no.'

"Okay, thanks. I'll call you later."

The three of them looked at each other for a moment. Hunter spoke first.

"I think it's time for a trip back to Ohio. Genevieve and I could examine that bible and then call on the motherhouse and see what they might have on her. There might be nothing there, but it's the only lead we have now. And you could be an asset in talking to the nuns," he told Genevieve.

"Me? How would I be an asset talking to the nuns?"

"Well, you're a woman. They're women. Can't hurt. Carrie, can you ask your mother if we could meet her and examine the bible?"

AFTER DEPARTING THE CLEVELAND AIRPORT, they found their way to Emma Johannson's high-rise condominium building. After being cleared by the security guard at the ground floor entrance, they ascended to her fifteenth floor, three-thousand-square-foot penthouse condo. Emma greeted them at the door and invited them in. Upon entering, they were immediately stunned by its opulence and breathtaking view of the city in four directions.

Emma was a small woman, elegant and refined with an engaging smile that was both welcoming and reserved at the same time. It was late afternoon, and she offered them coffee and small pastries.

"Your home is spectacular, Mrs. Johannson," Genevieve said.

"Thank you. I know it's really more than I need, but it is lovely, and my husband liked it. He and I lived here only a few years before he died. That would have been just two years before my mother died."

"And she died, what, three years ago?" Hunter asked.

"That's right. That's when Carrie and I cleaned out her house and found the seedpods and my mother's letter explaining them. Can you tell me what you're actually looking for and hope to find here? I understand you're going to go to the motherhouse as well."

"We think it's possible that your mother's use of the term 'gangshandian,' may actually be the congruence of two Chinese words she may have heard, perhaps from Dr. Chen." Hunter answered. "The two words are Guāngróng de shāngdiàn, which translates in English to Glorious Store. We believe the term Glorious Store, as used by Dr. Chen, refers to the location where two things are located. One of these is a treasure, or perhaps part of a treasure, sequestered by a Japanese war criminal, General Tomoyuki Yamashita.

"Dr. Chen also hints that the missing six pages of his research notebook, describing how he successfully treated Type 1 diabetes, are there as well. All the evidence so far suggests this Glorious Store is under the convent where your mother was during the war. We're wondering if either her bible that she left you, or anything she may have left with the motherhouse, mentions the term or suggests where the 'Glorious Store' is."

37

"No, I'm afraid I don't know anything about a 'Glorious Store,' and if my mother knew, she never told me."

"Maybe there's something in her bible. Have you checked that?" Genevieve asked.

"I looked through it after Carrie's phone call. I didn't see anything. Here, let me get it so you can see for yourself."

She left the room, returned shortly, and handed the bible to Genevieve. While she began going through it, Hunter decided on another approach.

"Do you know if the motherhouse has any of your mother's material from her time in China?"

"I believe so. I know she turned a box of material over to them when she formally quit the order. She told me that was the standard thing to do. Since she'd been in China, I'm sure much of it related to that time."

"Can you tell me where the motherhouse is? We'd like to go there next. Maybe they can show us what she left with them."

"I'm sure they can. But it's funny, you'll be the second one to do that in the last two days."

"What?" he asked, suddenly on alert. "What do you mean?"

"Yesterday, a professor from Harvard stopped in here after visiting the motherhouse. Apparently she is writing a book on the history of Christian missionaries in China during the war."

"She stopped in here?"

"Yes, Like you, she wanted to know if my mother brought any papers back with her from her time in China. She was particularly interested in anything related to Dr. Chen."

Hunter got a sinking feeling in his gut. "What was her name?"

"Her name was Karen Applewood."

"What did she look like?"

"Her looks didn't go with her name. She was Asian."

The sinking feeling got deeper as he took out his cellphone and brought up the picture of Leiko Yamashita. "Is this her?"

"Why, yes. That's her."

Damn, she's still a step ahead of us.

"I'm sorry," Emma Johannson said. "What am I missing here? Do you know her?"

"I'm afraid so. Her name is Leiko Yamashita. She is not a college professor. She's the head of a crime family in Chicago, and she's already been responsible for several deaths associated with this business."

"Oh, my God. What have I done?"

"What do you mean?" Hunter asked

"I told her about the seedpods and my mother's letter, and I told her that Carrie had the letter and was growing the orchids at Selby Gardens, in Sarasota."

Hunter got on the phone and called detective Otto Skaggs.

"What do you want, McCoy?"

"Detective, I believe that Leiko Yamashita may be heading your way. Specifically, she may be heading to Selby Gardens and a young woman who's on the staff there, named Carrie Johannson. I'm at Carrie Johannson's mother's house in Cleveland right now. Leiko was here yesterday, posing as a Harvard professor. Carrie's mother has positively identified her as Leiko Yamashita. She was using the alias Karen Applewood."

"Why would Leiko Yamashita be interested in this Carrie Johannson?" Skaggs asked.

"She's a botanist at the gardens, and her grandmother was the nun who worked with Dr. Chen in China during the war. Her mother believes Leiko was heading there next to see what her daughter knows. Leiko may be there already. She was here yesterday."

Hunter knew that Skaggs wanted Leiko for the murder of Scott Harrison now that it was obvious she'd framed his dad for the murder. He didn't like being made a fool of. Who did?

"Thanks, McCoy. I'll contact the Sarasota Police and we'll get some people over there right away."

Hunter turned to Emma. "That was a detective with the Sarasota County Sheriff's office. He's got an arrest warrant out for this woman. He'll get over to Selby and look after your daughter right away."

Next, Hunter called Carrie, told her what they'd just learned and that he'd alerted the police.

Genevieve said, "I don't see anything of interest in your mother's bible—no loose papers, no notes in the margins, nothing highlighted."

"Okay, I guess that's it, then," Hunter added. "Thanks, Mrs. Johannson, your daughter should be safe now with the police on their way. Can you tell us how to get to the motherhouse?"

An hour later they arrived at the same building Leiko had visited the day before. When Sister Claire met them and learned what they were interested in, she said. "Why this sudden interest in Sister Mary Margaret?"

Hunter explained everything he could, including that the woman who'd been there yesterday posing as Karen Applewood, Harvard professor, was nothing of the sort.

She was a criminal and a killer. He showed her his credentials with the Virginia State Police.

"Could you show us what you showed her yesterday regarding Sister Mary Margaret?" Genevieve asked.

"I showed her the history one of our nuns wrote about that period. I'll get it for you."

As she went off to another room to retrieve it, Genevieve asked him, "Do you think Carrie is going to be safe?"

"Skaggs wants Leiko pretty badly." Hunter said. "My guess is he'll stay very close to her in hopes Leiko shows up."

Sister Claire brought back the same folder that Leiko had seen the day before and they sat down at a desk and went over it. A half hour later they concluded there was nothing it that they didn't already know. Sister Claire had retreated to the front room while they examined the document, so Hunter went out to bring her back.

"We're finished with this, Sister, you can put it away. But first I want to ask you something else."

"What?" she asked

"Emma Johannson told us that her mother stayed here after returning from China, before she left the order."

"That's correct. She was here almost a year before renouncing her vows."

"She also told us," Hunter went on, "that some of her personal things were in a box that she left here when she moved out. She explained that was not uncommon. Is that true, and does any of it still remain here at the motherhouse?"

Sister Claire, seemingly growing nervous about this whole thing, digging up the past. "Detective McCoy, maybe you should tell me why this is so important to you," she said.

"Sister Mary Margaret may have known where Dr. Chen stored six critical pages from his research notebook describing how to extract a medicine from orchids to prevent Type 1 diabetes. He left a note that suggests these six pages were hidden in something he called the 'Glorious Store.' We think the hiding place is under the convent, possibly in caves. So, if Sister Mary Margaret left anything personal here at the motherhouse, it might contain something that could point to the location of this Glorious Store."

Sister Claire studied him for a long moment as if deciding what to do. "Wait here."

38

SISTER CLAIRE RETURNED ABOUT TEN MINUTES later wheeling in—to their astonishment—a dolly with a wooden box carefully balanced on it. She stopped next to a large table.

"This is all we have from Sister Mary Margaret. She chose what to leave with us in the event she ever returned, so I suspect it's mostly her personal habits and such, but you're welcome to look through it all."

Hunter removed the box from the dolly and placed it on the table. It was about the size of a foot locker and neatly labeled on the top with "Sister Mary Margaret, SNDdeN." Heavy twine wrapped around the box kept the lid closed. Sister Claire handed him a pair of scissors, and he cut the twine. Just as she'd guessed, it was filled with religious habits of the same type Sister Claire wore. They carefully looked through pockets or any other areas that could hold something. They found nothing. No notes, books, ledgers, or papers of any kind. They repacked the box and tied it closed again.

Finally, determining that there was nothing more to be gained, they thanked Sister Claire and were preparing to leave when the old nun startled them by saying, "Wait. There is one more possible place to look. I don't know why I didn't think of it earlier."

"Where's that," Genevieve asked.

"Sister Mary Margaret would have written a letter to the Mother Superior when she decided to leave the order. It would be in her files, I imagine. Let me go check. Why don't you wait here? Coffee and cups are out front. Have some and wait for me."

After she left, Hunter said, "Well, I'll say this for her, she's certainly trying."

"She is at that," Genevieve agreed.

Almost twenty minutes later Sister Claire returned with a file. "Our Mother Superior told me I can't let you have this or even read it yourself. Instead she asked me to read it, and then let you question me about its contents. I'm to decide if your questions are appropriate to answer."

"Fair enough," Hunter said. "Have you read it?"

"Yes, just a few minutes ago."

"Does she mention Dr. Chen at all?"

"Yes."

"Does she make any reference to the Glorious Store or use any other language that might suggest Yamashita's treasure?"

"She does."

"And what is that?"

"Mr. McCoy, Mother's orders were quite direct. I'm to answer your questions but not to volunteer information."

Hunter swallowed his frustration, knowing he had to proceed carefully if he wanted her continued cooperation. "I understand. Does she mention the missing pages from his notebook?"

"Yes."

"Are they together with the treasure?"

"Yes."

"Does she explain what his plans are for the treasure?"

"Yes."

"Can you tell us?"

Here Sister Claire paused and thought it over. At last she nodded. "Sister Mary Margaret explains that the vast bulk of the treasure—gold bars and gemstones worth tens of billions of dollars allegedly looted by the Japanese Imperial Army, after the Japanese declared war on China in

1937—was buried in caves. She goes on to say that Dr. Chen found a map to this vast treasure in a cave under the convent's basement shortly after he spotted General Yamashita and turned him in to Sergeant McCoy—your grandfather. He found no treasure himself, but the map clearly shows where it's buried. He referred to the map as 'the Glorious Store.' It gave directions to the looted China Gold.

"After the war, if China was again a free country, he intended to inform the authorities of its location. He explained that, like the map to the treasure, he wanted to protect his secret for the diabetes treatment until it was safe to give to the West. To protect both the map and the six pages, he'd moved them to a safe place—far from the enemy.

"When Dr. Chen was dying, he asked Sergeant McCoy to give Sister Mary Margaret the seedpods and his research notebook. Then the old man died. The sister goes on to explain that Dr. Chen hadn't told her where he'd moved the treasure map or the six pages, and she had no idea where they were."

Genevieve interjected here. "It's strange that he would give her the seedpods and planned to give her the notebook to go along with them, but not the missing pages. He had to know that without them, the notebook would be incomplete and probably useless."

Hunter asked the nun, "Is there any explanation in the letter for that?"

"Maybe."

"Maybe?"

"You both have to understand that this is a long letter. It's personal, and its primary purpose was for Sister Mary Margaret to explain why she was leaving the order and renouncing her vows. This is a very serious thing for us and not to be taken lightly. The bulk of the letter deals with that."

"Did Dr. Chen have anything to do with her decision to leave?"

"Not that I can see from her writing."

Pausing to consider what he should ask next, Genevieve filled the gap. "So, Dr. Chen's plan was to give her the seedpods and the notebook, a notebook that was incomplete. And yet we can assume that he wanted her to have the missing pages. Does she offer any explanation for this incongruity?"

"He told her he'd see to it that she had everything his brother would need to succeed in extracting the medicine from the orchids."

"Could he have given it to her without her knowing about it?" Genevieve mused out loud.

"But why would he do that?" Sister Claire asked.

"Maybe he wanted his brother to be the only one to have all the pieces of the puzzle for some reason," Hunter suggested. "Maybe he was trying to protect her somehow."

"Protect her from what?" Genevieve asked. "Who'd not want a treatment for diabetes?"

"Don't forget, we saw the lengths that Colin Malport went to get the formula. He abandoned my grandfather a second time to get the secret. What would he have done to sister Mary Margaret if he'd thought she had it?"

He turned back to Sister Claire. "Is there anything in there that even hints at the location of the map and the missing pages, Sister?"

"No, I'm afraid not," she answered. "As I said, the letter is mostly about her personal reasons for leaving. I can tell you that none of what she wrote regarding that has any bearing on the issue you're concerned with. She explains that the reason she even included the story of Dr. Chen in her letter is because of the kindly man's importance in her life at the convent."

Knowing they were pretty much at the end of their inquiries here, Hunter said, "Sister, if you come across anything else that might have a bearing on our search, would you call us please?" Then Hunter gave her his business card.

"Of course," she said, seeing them out.

39

LEIKO YAMASHITA WATCHED AS HUNTER AND Genevieve left the motherhouse. She'd heard the entire conversation between them and the old nun over the listening device she'd planted under the nun's desk the day before. Her hunch that McCoy and the woman would be tracking the same leads had paid off. She regretted now that she hadn't also bugged Emma Johannson's place earlier.

So there's a map she thought. The Glorious Store was a map, a map to her great-grandfather's treasure. He must have been either hiding the map in the old convent or coming to retrieve it when Chen spotted him and betrayed him to the American soldier. Then the old man moved the map and the missing notebook pages to a location—how did he say it—far away from the enemy?

She sat back in her car, closed her eyes, and thought about that. How could he get far away from the enemy? Did he mean far as in distance? If so, they could be anywhere. But he was an old man. He was sick, and he died shortly after. He couldn't have traveled very far on his own. He'd have needed help. Someone had to do it for him. Who could it have been? If by "far away" he meant a slim chance of the enemy finding it, he could just have buried it in a deeper and more secure site at the convent. Leiko considered that but didn't buy it. No, he had help.

It had to have been either the soldier, Karl McCoy, or the nun, sister Mary Margaret. He had to have entrusted one or both of them to do it. The war was over, both would be returning to the States. But which one was it?

The doctor had asked Sergeant McCoy to give the sack of seedpods and the incomplete notebook to the nun to take back to America. The notebook never made it, but the seedpods eventually got to her granddaughter.

Leiko and Hunter McCoy had found the notebook with its missing pages and the cryptic poem hidden in the cover. She recalled the poem.

Six sisters
and the Glorious Store,
the secret to China Gold
Orchid tea
A life that's free
From sugar's deadly hold

The poem implied that the missing notebook pages and the map were stored together.

She didn't care about the orchid cure, of course. What she wanted, above all else, was Yamashita's long-lost treasure. Nothing and nobody would stand in her way. Recovering that treasure was another way to avenge the treacherous treatment of her grandfather.

Now that she and Hunter McCoy had the same information, they'd both be looking for the location of the map and the pages. She wanted the map; he wanted the missing pages. She smiled as she vowed to herself, only one of them would succeed, and it wasn't going to be him. But she knew about McCoy's vaunted skills at finding things. Perhaps the best course was to follow him and to allow him to do what he did best. Then take it.

LEIKO'S PILOT, KIM ZHANG RETURNED TO the Memorial Hall. The receptionist recognized him immediately as the tall, good-looking man who'd been in earlier asking about that old convent. She greeted him with a warm open smile as he approached her desk.

"Back again? Did you find what you were looking for?" she asked, brushing her long black hair behind her left ear in a flirtatious gesture.

Too tired to even acknowledge it, he said, "I found the park but not what I was looking for, I'm afraid."

"And what is that, exactly?" She smiled, showing concern.

"That's just it. I don't really know what I'm looking for."

"I don't understand," she said with a pretty frown. "You found the park, but you don't know what you're looking for?"

"Yeah, crazy, I know. I was sent here to find the old convent that's apparently long gone. There's a cave under the site that's open to the public. My boss wants me to examine it thoroughly and report back. But she won't tell me what I'm supposed to be looking for."

"Sounds intriguing," the young woman said with a smile and a flirtatious toss of the head. "Maybe I can help."

"How could you do that?"

"We do have other archives in addition to those that we allow the public to see."

"Who can use them?"

"Scholars, people with government permits to do research, people like that with proper permission. They can examine more detailed records of many of our sites."

Perking up at the possibility he might still find something, Kim asked, "Do you have more detailed records on the convent?"

"I don't know. I'd have to check. Are you a scholar?"

"I read a book, once," he said with a smile.

"Close enough. Come with me and we'll check."

Kim followed the cute receptionist into a room filled with file cabinets. She stepped up to one and asked, "Sisters of Notre Dame de Namur? Is that right?"

"Yes."

She opened a drawer and began to leaf through it, finally pulling out a folder. "Here we are, Convent and School of the Sisters of Notre Dame de Namur."

As Kim reached for it, she pulled it back and held it to her chest. "Before I can let you examine this, you'll have to convince me of your scholarly credentials, say over dinner this evening."

Finally Kim got it. He really *must* be tired. *Well, what the heck*, he thought. This had been a pretty boring trip so far. A little R and R with the lovely receptionist wouldn't be out of order. And he'd get to check out the file too. It might be another dead end, but at least he was trying.

"I'd be delighted."

"Good. I'll give you my address. You can get me at eight. I'll make the reservation, and I'll have the file."

Promptly at eight, after a shower, a shave, and a quick nap, Kim picked up the receptionist and they had a lovely dinner, followed by cocktails at her apartment, and a night of wonderful sex. He'd almost forgotten about the file, but when he got up in the morning, there it was on the kitchen table. He had just opened it when she came in from the bedroom and asked if he'd like coffee.

"Yes, please. But I may not have enough energy left to lift the cup." He grinned.

"No fear. I can attest to your energy level," she said with a coy smile. "So, Mr. Scholar, did you find what you were looking for in the folder?"

"I don't know, I just picked it up now."

He could see that the single content of the file was a booklet, apparently prepared by the order of sisters, that appeared to be a history of their mission in Wuchang. As his companion prepared coffee, he read. It was pretty boring until he got to the part on the arrest of the Japanese General, Yamashita, at the end of World War Two.

Yamashita? Was that what this was about? Was Leiko related to this guy?

He continued to read, now with more interest. Apparently this General Yamashita may have hidden a map in the convent and may have been on his way to get it or hide it there—the narrative didn't say—when, a Dr. Li Qiang Chen, who was associated with the convent, recognized him and turned him in to an American soldier, Technical Sergeant Karl McCoy. General Yamashita was later tried as a war criminal and executed by the Allies.

It all started to come together for Kim when he read that the map supposedly gave the location of a vast treasure that the general had looted and stored somewhere during the war.

So, this is what she's after, he thought. It was all becoming clear now.

Reading on, he learned a lot more. Then, deciding on a course of action that he knew could get him killed if he weren't careful, he decided to tell Leiko that the doctor had found the map and planned to move it to a secure location in the United States with the cooperation of Sister Mary Margaret, SNDdeN.

With a fist pump in the air, convinced this information was what Leiko was looking for, Kim got up to leave only to have the beautiful receptionist slip out of her robe and say, "I believe I need to check your scholarly credentials one more time before you go."

"I understand," Zhang said. "One can't be too careful."

40

ED McCOY, HENRY LAHTI, JOE PALMA, and Jim Furlow were meeting at Jim's house two doors down from the Kingston house. The members of the men's book club—like they'd told Hunter earlier—weren't going to just sit around and wait for trouble to find them.

Ever since Joe had captured the headshot of Leiko Yamashita on his camera and turned it over to Hunter, the men had decided that the real-life adventure of helping to capture the woman and the Asian guys who'd tried to frame Ed would be much more rewarding than trying to select and read another book. So they'd put the book-reading part of the book club on hold for the time being.

Joe asked Ed, "Have the police been able to identify the guys I photographed who planted the phony evidence in your house?" Joe had been very proud of being able to get those shots.

"Yeah, great job, Joe. Hunter told me the Chicago police identified both of them and they definitely work for Leiko. The Chicago Police, the Sarasota County Sheriff, and the Sarasota PD all have arrest warrants out for them now."

Earlier, Ed had told the book club about Leiko's relationship to the notorious General Yamashita and that she had sworn to take revenge on the families and close friends of Dr. Chen and his dad for their role in her grandfather's trial and execution for war crimes. Ed and Henry also brought Joe and Jim up to date on the issue of

Yamashita's treasure, the missing notebook pages, and the orchids that Carrie Johannson was growing up at Selby.

Jim Furlow shook his head. "So this Leiko is not only after Ed and Hunter, but anyone they're close to as well— just to spread the pain around?"

"That's what Hunter's learned, yeah," said Henry.

"Well I don't like it," Jim said. "What kind of sick person would do that? And these two guys, the ones Joe photographed. They work for her?"

"Yup," Ed said. "Those are the guys who tried to frame me for Scott Harrison's murder. Since then they've attacked Genevieve and tried to drown her. They also left Henry with a serious lump on his head."

Jim Furlow got up and paced his living room for a moment before stopping and facing the other three. "Here's what I think. I think they're not going to stop just because their attempt to frame Ed failed and he's been released. If this Leiko's serious, Ed, she's going to continue going after you and Hunter, and Genevieve and Henry too. And I'd say it's likely that Joe and I will also be in her crosshairs."

Jim poked his fingers in the air. "Now let's think about this. What do we know? We know she knows where Genevieve lives and where Ed and Henry live. And Hunter's either at one or the other of those two places. It also looks like she's likely to continue using these two guys to do her work."

"And?" asked Henry.

Jim began to smile, and a sinister smile it was. "I have an idea. Now hear me out. Joe and I have had a lifetime of experience catching fish that—one has to assume—didn't want to be caught. Let me tell you my plan, and be advised, there's a part in it for all of you."

GENEVIEVE AND HUNTER CAUGHT THE NEXT AVAILABLE flight from Cleveland to Charlottesville, Virginia, early the next morning, after their visit to the motherhouse. Hunter decided he needed to check in with Jason Turtle at his lab and find out how things were going with the NIH grant. Genevieve was happy to accompany him, since she'd never seen where he lived or been to the medical school.

They went to his loft after the flight from Ohio, and Hunter decided to check in with the police first. He called the number Detective John Bolt had given him, and the detective answered.

"Ah, Dr. McCoy. I'm glad you called. We believe we have the complaint against you taken care of. It's been quite fascinating. If you come down to the station house on McCardle Street, I'll be glad to explain it all to you. But just so you know, you're off the hook."

"I'll be right over," Hunter answered, relieved that at least this confusion was going to be cleared up.

He and Genevieve arrived a half hour later and were ushered to Detective Bolt's desk immediately. The two men shook hands, and Hunter introduced Genevieve. The detective invited them both to sit while he told his story.

"This whole thing began when we received complaints from two of your neighbors. We later found out that each of them had moved into separate lofts on the same day only a week before they filed their complaints. We only learned this later, or we would have dismissed their allegations completely. One of these two men, who called himself Chris Ahom, but we later learned was really Ryuki Ono, claimed he'd seen you selling drugs openly from your apartment and decided he couldn't take it anymore. The other man, who called himself Stan Aki—who was actually Akito Hano—claimed you'd been running a human trafficking ring out of the apartment. He promised he had photo evidence to back it up.

"When we became suspicious we ran their fingerprints and discovered they're from Chicago and work for a criminal organization known locally as the Yamashita crime family. We've got arrest warrants out for both of them, but so far we haven't been able to apprehend them."

Hunter and Genevieve looked at each other and shook their heads in amazement. Hunter made a mental note. *Now I can add the Charlottesville PD to those who have arrest warrants out for these two.*

"Detective, I think it's time I tell you a story," he said. Over the next hour, he told him everything. When he was finished, Detective Bolt rans his fingers through his sparse head of hair and exhaled long and hard.

"Not much surprises me anymore on this job, but I have to say, your story is a doozy. So this Leiko Yamashita is after you and your father to avenge the arrest and execution of her war criminal great-grandfather?"

"Yes. And I believe she's also behind a problem I'm having at the medical school with one of my research grants. We're going over to my lab next to try to straighten that out."

Detective Bolt stood and reached out to shake Hunter's hand. "Good luck with that. Again, doc, I'm sorry we had to put you through this."

At the medical school Hunter gave Genevieve a small tour of the campus as they made their way to his laboratory, where they found Jason Turtle entering data in a notebook. When he looked up, a big smile spread across his face.

"Hey, boss, good to see you. So you finally decided to do some work again instead of leaving it all to us peasants?"

"Some peasant," Hunter said to Genevieve. "Jason here is an M.D. and he's working on a Ph.D. in my lab as well."

"I'm still a peasant compared to him," Jason said, indicating Hunter. "And who is this beautiful lady? Wait. Don't tell me. This must be the famous Genevieve Swift I've heard so much about."

Hunter made the introductions.

"Nice to meet you, Jason. Hunter's told me all about you too."

They sat on stools around a lab bench.

"What's new on our grant problems?" Jason asked Hunter.

"I'm going to call Jack Busbee, the NIH guy who froze our grant, and get an update. I've instructed my bank to accept no more deposits into that account until I personally authorize them."

"At least we know they've figured out that part of the fault lies with them, since the NIH got hacked and Aker's name was added to the three of ours," Jason added.

Hunter nodded in agreement. "Now it's time to call him and find out what else they've learned."

41

JIM FURLOW'S PLAN INCLUDED USING THE SKILLS of Joe Palma's son Jeff, since none of the four club members, Ed, Henry, Joe, or Jim, knew much about "techie" surveillance stuff. However, Jim and Joe were experts on other aspects of the plan.

They decided to start with the Kingston house. The setup was perfect, as both the front and back doors had a small portico with a covered roof. Even though Jim and Joe weren't commercially fishing anymore, they still maintained a small building at the commercial dock where they kept their boat, and it contained everything they needed.

It took all morning to rig up the portico at the front of the house, but only an hour to do the back. By then they had mastered the setup and tested it to make sure it worked.

Henry had played the intruder and swore mightily when the net dropped, closed around him, and yanked him upside down and off his feet.

"I don't know," Jim Furlow said, looking at the inverted, struggling, and swearing, Henry Lahti, "I think I'll toss him back, Joe. He doesn't look like good eating."

"Jeez, get me out of here," Henry yelled.

Joe activated the winch motor, slowly lowered Henry to the ground, and freed him.

"Looks like it works," Jim said as Henry disentangled himself from the heavy netting and slowly stood up.

Henry glowered. "Oh, yeah. It works all right. Hey—Jim?"

"Yeah?"

"How about we test the back door with *you* being the intruder this time."

"No. I'm pretty sure we need my expertise calling the shots out here."

"Hmmm," Henry muttered.

By the end of the day, they'd similarly prepared the entries to Genevieve's and Carrie Johannson's houses in Sarasota.

AFTER BUYING GENEVIEVE LUNCH IN THE medical school's cafeteria and during the walk back to his lab, she said, "It's a beautiful campus. It looks like you have everything here you could possibly want."

Hunter squeezed her arm and looked at her. "Not quite everything." She smiled and kissed him on the cheek.

Back at the lab he called Jack Busbee, their grant administrator at the NIH.

"Mr. Busbee? This is Hunter McCoy, calling from the University of Virginia School of Medicine about our NIH research grant number 584900132. Have you learned anything new since you got hacked and the name Gilbert Aker was added to our payout list?"

"Hold on, Dr. McCoy, I believe I have some good news for you. It just came across my desk an hour ago. One moment."

Hunter put his hands together in prayer and looked heavenward. Genevieve smiled and crossed her fingers.

Hunter put the phone on speaker as Busbee returned. "Our fraud department is very good, Dr. McCoy, and they've closed the case and you'll be getting a formal written report sent to you immediately, but here's what we found.

"The fictitious Gilbert Aker sent in all requests for his salary from a single computer we've traced to a house in the Chicago suburb of La Grange. Through some pretty sophisticated computer hacking, the requests appeared to our disbursement department to be coming from an address in Charlottesville, Virginia, where this Dr. Gilbert Aker supposedly lived. The checks were sent there made out to Gilbert Aker, Ph.D., who then deposited them in his account at your bank.

"Now here's where it gets interesting. To make this look like fraud on your part, he had to transfer these funds from his account into your account. So once a week, the day after he deposited the check for five thousand dollars into his account, he'd write out a check to you for five thousand dollars, endorse it, signing your name on the back, and deposit it using the bank's cellphone app.

"He had to hope you used the fingerprint feature to log into your account, which you did. Then he installed your bank's app on his phone. After that, all he had to do to deposit the check would be to supply your fingerprint to his cell phone. Somehow, he lifted your fingerprint—maybe from a water glass, who knows—with a special tape and used it to open your account. Then, to deposit the check, he followed the bank app instructions. He'd take a photo of the front and back, type in the amount, indicate which account to put it in, and bingo. He's done, and you're screwed."

"So how did you figure out it wasn't me doing all this?"

"Easy. The time of the transfer is recorded, as is the identity of the cellphone used to do it. The phone wasn't yours, and seven of the eight times the phone used to do the transfers was located somewhere you weren't based on cell tower records of your own movements.

"Now granted, you could have had someone do this for you, to try to throw us off, but when we found out the identity of the phony Dr. Aker, from his fingerprints in the house in La Grange, we contacted the Chicago Police Department. And guess what? He turns out to be a

Japanese-American man in the employ of the Yamashita crime family. That got us talking to Detective Wilbur Jenkins., who told us the family is out to get you. Jenkins then picked up the man and arrested him. He's in custody now and has confessed to the fraud.

"So, Dr. McCoy, you're off the hook with us and your funds will be unfrozen immediately. But you'd better watch your back with a crime family after you. Jenkins wouldn't tell me much about that, only that you're innocent."

"Glad to hear it," Hunter said.

KIM ZHANG HAD THE GULFSTREAM 680 on autopilot and was having a sandwich and coffee as he flew over the Pacific. Before he left Wuchang for the States, he'd called Leiko and told her what he'd learned. He'd explained that through an incredible amount of digging he'd been able to access a file that he believed had what she was looking for. He left out how he'd come by the file and that the work wasn't exactly painful all the time. No need for her to think he was actually enjoying himself.

He told her he'd come across information on the arrest of Japanese General Tomoyuki Yamashita who'd hidden a map in the convent at the end of World War Two that supposedly gave the location of a vast treasure the general had stored somewhere during the war.

Apparently a Dr. Chen found the map in a cave below the convent and moved it to a secure location in the United States with the cooperation of one Sister Mary Margaret, SNDdeN. He told her he'd read the rest of the document to the end and found no further information concerning this map.

Leiko had seemed pleased with what he'd found and told him to get back to Chicago and await further instructions.

As the jet flew, effortlessly eastward, Kim Zhang smiled at the thought that there was one bit of crucial information concerning the treasure map he hadn't told his boss, Leiko Yamashita.

He knew *exactly* where it was.

42

HUNTER AND GENEVIEVE FLEW BACK TO SARASOTA, picked up her new leased BMW, this one a dark royal blue to replace her drowned white one, and drove to her house. The next morning they picked up Carrie Johannson in Hunter's Jeep and went to the Kingston house, where Hunter had arranged for all the principals to meet at ten o'clock to discuss the risks going forward. He had invited Jim Furlow and Joe Palma to join his dad and Henry, along with Genevieve, himself, and Carrie.

With everyone seated, Hunter began. He reviewed everything they'd experienced and learned since the murder of Scott Harrison. He explained that he wanted everyone to be familiar with all aspects of the events since then, even though each of them may have been involved in only a small part of it and unaware of how it fit into the larger picture. Potentially, all of them were at risk from Leiko Yamashita's vengeance against the McCoys and their friends—which presumably now included everyone present.

"As to the threat," Hunter continued. "it definitely continues, even though so far we've stopped her. Her attempt to frame Dad for Scott Harrison's murder didn't work in the long run, although she caused a lot of anxiety while it was going on. And here we need to remember that's part of her plan too—to make life miserable for those in her sights.

"The sheriff's office and Detective Skaggs are now convinced that Leiko and her two thugs are behind all the events here in Florida. Those include the murder of Scott Harrison, framing Dad for it, and the attacks on Genevieve and Henry. The evidence is now clear that she was also behind the interference with my research grant at the medical school and the attempt to set the Charlottesville police on me."

"She's got to be pissed at failing at all that," Joe Palma said.

Hunter nodded in agreement. "And I don't believe for a moment that she's abandoned her vendetta against the family while she goes treasure hunting. Even if she's right now in China looking for it as Detective Jenkins seems to believe, we know the two men that work for her, Ono and Hano, are likely still here in the area, with instructions to keep up the pressure."

"Can we get protection from Skaggs?" Ed McCoy asked.

"I've checked with him about that. He'll send cars by our houses periodically, but he doesn't have the manpower to assign people around the clock."

"So," Jim Furlow said, "it looks like we may have to take matters into our own hands."

"No, I'm not saying that," Hunter said. "We just need to be particularly careful and observant, try to catch whatever signals we can."

Jim Furlow cracked a sly smile and said, "Right."

"That goes for you too, Carrie," Hunter said. "We don't think Leiko's interested in the orchids or the diabetes treatment at all. We think her goal is to find Yamashita's treasure. Still, it's not out of the question that she might think you know something about that, or possibly have something of your grandmother's that might suggest where it is.

"Genevieve and I learned through a letter from Sister Mary Margaret that Dr. Chen found a map in a cave under the convent's basement that clearly showed where the treasure was buried. Dr. Chen referred to this map as 'the Glorious Store' that would lead to the looted China Gold. To protect both the map and the six notebook pages, he moved them to a safe place far from the enemy. We don't know where that is."

"You think this Leiko has two goals then," said Jim; "one, to find this treasure—although she's not aware it's just a map to its location—and two, her vengeance thing."

"That's pretty much it, Jim," Hunter agreed. "And while Detective Jenkins of the Chicago PD believes she's in China right now, trying to track the treasure down, none of us are safe. She can work on both goals at once. Don't forget her two goons are probably still here and planning something."

"I sure hope they try," Jim said, eyeing the guys in the men's book club.

Uh oh, thought Hunter. *What are these old rascals up to?*

43

LEIKO HAD BEEN ENERGIZED BY ZHANG'S phone call. She now had information that McCoy didn't. She knew the map had been returned to the States. She didn't have to search China. It was here somewhere, and the key was the nun. What had she done with it? Apparently it wasn't in the motherhouse. Emma Johannson only knew about the seedpods, the letter her mother had written, and box of clothes left at the motherhouse. She'd said there was nothing else of her mother's there. If either she or that Sister Claire were lying, they'd pay the price.

The only link she hadn't talked with was Emma Johannson's daughter, the botanist at the Selby Gardens. Leiko was in Charlottesville, having followed McCoy and the Swift woman there after Ohio. She'd been able to learn that her attempt to discredit him at the University and with the local police had failed. Heads would roll over this, she vowed.

She chartered a private flight to Sarasota and arrived in time to drive to the Selby Gardens where she asked to see Carrie Johannson. She knew she couldn't use the Karen Applewood-Harvard history professor persona again, so she'd told the people at the front desk that she was Anna Naguchi, a book rep with a botanical publisher. They directed her to the botany building, an old house on the property that housed the botany staff.

They had no receptionist, but one of the other staffers told her that Carrie had the day off and she thought she had a meeting of some kind on Casey Key. If she'd like to leave a business card, she'd see to it that Carrie got it.

"Tell you what," Leiko said. "How about if I write a note and leave it on her desk?"

"Sure, I'll show you her office."

The woman left Leiko at Carrie Johannson's desk, and as Leiko wrote a note she looked around for anything that might be of interest. The small bookshelf was stuffed with texts on botany, orchids, and greenhouse management, but nothing about China that she could see. She quickly rifled through the desk drawer files and found nothing. Just as she was getting ready to leave she saw a small statue of a Chinese warrior on a shelf. She picked it up and examined it. Turning it over, she snorted in disgust when she saw that it was from a gift shop in Disney World, Orlando. She put it back.

Seeing nothing else, she left the office.

Leiko had already learned Carrie Johannson's home address and drove there immediately, figuring she wouldn't be home if she was at a meeting on Casey Key. She wondered what that. Casey Key was where Ed McCoy lived, and where Scott Harrison had been questioned and then killed at her command. Was that just a coincidence or were they connected somehow?

Certainly, McCoy was aware of Carrie Johannson, since he'd interviewed her mother and the nun at the motherhouse. It was possible Carrie was meeting with him at his father's house on the Key.

Leiko smiled as she thought of the next phase in the plan for vengeance. Ono and Hano would put it in place in the next day or two. She quietly enjoyed the fact that unknown to them, McCoy and Swift, were actually helping her get to the map while she, at the same time, was toying with them. Well, that 'toying' was about to get a little more painful.

Carrie Johannson lived alone in an apartment in downtown Sarasota, within walking distance to the Selby Gardens. Her unit was on the first floor of a two-story apartment building, and it took Leiko no more than a minute to get inside. She quickly determined that the one-bedroom flat was unoccupied at the moment. Being careful to leave no trace she'd ever been there she thoroughly searched the place.

IT HAD BEEN A LONG DAY, AND CARRIE JOHANNSON was tired. Hunter and Genevieve drove her back to her apartment after the meeting on Casey Key. On the way she considered how much more there was to all of this than simply growing orchids from Dr. Chen's seedpods and hopefully finding his treatment for diabetes.

She'd been shocked to learn about the murder of the author, Scott Harrison and that this horrible woman, Leiko Yamashita, was behind it. And amazingly her own grandmother, was in the middle of it all. Had she helped him move the missing pages from the notebook and the treasure map to a safe location far from the enemy? She wondered where that might be.

Genevieve noted how quiet she was on the return trip.

"It's a lot to take in, isn't it?"

Carrie sighed. "It is. I thought my grandmother's role was just to get the seedpods out. Now with everything Hunter went over today, I'm frightened. I hope my mother is safe."

"I don't think anyone will be completely safe until we catch and convict this woman," Hunter said in an uncharacteristically somber moment. "But the police in two states have an arrest-on-sight warrant out for her, and that's a lot of manpower on our side."

When they arrived at her place, Carrie said goodnight to Hunter and Genevieve at the curb. They drove away as she walked to her front door. Inside, she flipped on the hall light and laid her purse on the side table. After checking her image in the mirror above it, she remembered something she was going to ask Genevieve. She took out her cell and called her number. While it rang she walked into her living room and immediately sensed she wasn't alone.

44

"SIT DOWN," SAID THE WOMAN SITTING IN HER CHAIR with the small but deadly looking pistol pointed steadily at her chest.

"Who are you?" Carrie demanded in a voice implying more courage than she had, but instinctively fearing she knew who the woman was. "What are you doing here?"

"Sit down and you *might* not get killed."

Carrie looked around automatically searching for a way out of this. She realized there was nothing she could do, but her phone was still in her hand with her jacket over it, so she flipped her phone to silent mode and slipped it in her pocket, hoping the woman wouldn't notice—but that Genevieve would. She sat down opposite the woman who had to be Leiko Yamashita.

Leiko stared at Carrie and Carrie stared at the pistol.

"You are Carrie Johannson, daughter of Emma Johannson and granddaughter of Laura McCasey who was once known as Sister Mary Margaret.

"So what? And stop pointing that damned gun at me."

"My name is Leiko Yamashita, but I suspect you already know that. Your grandmother took a bag of orchid seedpods out of China at the end of the war at the request of Dr. Li Qiang Chen. She was also to have removed his research notebook but couldn't find it. The notebook has since been found, but six critical pages are missing. I've recently learned that those six pages, along with a map, were moved by Dr. Chen to a secure location far from the enemy.

"I've been to the motherhouse and met with Sister Claire and later met with your mother at her condo. At the time I didn't know what had happened to the pages and map. Now I do. I know that your grandmother moved them from China to the United States at Chen's request.

"Now let's be clear. I'm going to get the map. I'm starting with you, now, here. Where is it?"

"How would I know? How do you know he gave it to my grandmother?"

"Miss Johannson, I have a very large organization looking into this, that's how I know. If you have any information about this, I'd advise you to tell me now."

"I don't. I only know about the seedpods and the letter my grandmother left explaining them. Her letter said nothing about a map. I can show it to you if you'd like."

"Don't bother, I've already read it. There's nothing in there. But there must be something else, something your grandmother brought back, that has this information."

"There's nothing. She either left things at the motherhouse or—"

Suddenly Leiko got up, walked quickly to the kitchen, and disappeared.

Carrie was stunned. Then she heard the back door close silently, just as Hunter appeared through the front door with a gun in one hand and finger to his lips.

Carried nodded toward the kitchen. Carefully Hunter entered. Carrie stayed put. Soon she heard the back door open and close. She continued to wait. Several minutes later Hunter came back in.

"She's gone."

Carrie sat back and exhaled a deep sigh. "Thank God."

Genevieve came through the front door and moved to hug Carrie. "You can turn your phone off now. Thanks to your quick thinking, we heard everything."

"Carrie, was she wearing gloves?" Hunter asked.

"Huh?"

"Was she wearing gloves? If not, we can get fingerprints and prove she was here."

"Let me think—yeah, yes, she was. Wow. All I could see was that gun pointed at me, but yes, she was wearing gloves."

"So, why'd she leave?" he asked.

"I don't know," Carrie answered, shaking her head. "She just stopped in mid-sentence and went to the kitchen. It was like she sensed something. Maybe she heard you coming."

"Did you hear me coming?" Hunter asked.

"No, but with her gun in my face, I was pretty focused on that."

"Understood."

"Well, we know one thing for sure," Genevieve said. "We know she's here and not in China."

Hunter nodded. "She told you that she knows that the missing pages and the map were brought back to the States by your grandmother. How does she know that? She didn't learn that from Sister Claire at the motherhouse, and she didn't learn that from your mother, either."

"Right," Genevieve added. "She said they'd been moved to a safe place far away from the enemy. And we knew that too."

"Wait a minute," Hunter said, with a shocked look on his face, "that's it. Her words, the words she used. She told you—and I quote—*'I've recently learned that those six pages, along with a map, were moved by Dr. Chen to a secure location far from the enemy.'*"

Genevieve got it right away. "A secure location far from the enemy. We just heard that exact same phrase, but it came from Sister Claire after reading Sister Mary Margaret's resignation letter."

"Right, and Leiko never had access to that letter."

"So how did she get it?" Carrie asked, near tears.

"She either had a bug on us or had one in the motherhouse. And she just heard that yesterday, because that's when we heard it. But then she went on to say that even more recently she'd learned that Dr. Chen arranged for your grandmother to take both the missing pages and the map to the United States."

"Yes, that's right," Carrie said, now getting into the debriefing. "And she said she'd learned this from the fact that she has a large organization, or something like that."

Hunter paced the room, scratching his head. "She must have meant by that phrase that someone in her organization had just learned it. Who would that be?"

"We know the pilot flew her jet to Wuchang," Carrie pointed out. "He must have learned something there and called her."

"What did you learn from Eduard, your man at Interpol, Eduard?" Genevieve asked. "Didn't he say the convent was long gone and there was a city park there now? Something like that?"

"He did. He said they tore down the school and convent in the fifties and turned it into a park. He said there was a concession stand there and an attraction featuring a small cave under what used to be the convent. Maybe her pilot checked it out and found something."

"Could be," Carrie said. "And if so, we just heard her say what it was. That my grandmother brought the pages and the map back to the States. She didn't know where they were though, since she'd just started to ask if I did, when she beat it."

"Beeet it?" Genevieve said, her French accent, unsure what the phrase meant.

"It means she took off," Carrie answered.

"Took off?"

Hunter jumped in. "They're both slang phrases meaning suddenly left. She beat it, she took off, she suddenly left."

"Cool," Genevieve said, understanding now.

"Cool?" Hunter said.

"All right, enough fun at my expense, let's get back to sleuthing."

Hunter was smart enough to leave "sleuthing" alone.

"If Leiko has information that your grandmother brought the pages and map out of China to the US, she'd have to assume, just like we would, that they're currently in the possession of the motherhouse, your mother, or you, Carrie. Now, it's likely that none of you know about this. They might be concealed in something that your grandmother brought back—something you've had around all these years but didn't know about. Can you think of anything like that?"

"Boy, I don't know. I hope it wasn't something we threw out after cleaning Grandma's house after she died. Mom and I went through everything, and as I recall, separated stuff into three piles—stuff to keep, give away, or throw out.

"I was almost ready to throw out the old cooler that contained the seedpods and the letter when I decided to open it and look inside. Good thing I did, or they would have been gone."

"Did you save anything else?" Hunter asked.

Carrie closed her eyes and sat back.

"Let me think."

45

JEFF PALMA HAD JUST COMPLETED THE MONITORING SETUPS at the three houses. Both the front and back doors at the Kingston house on the Casey Key, as well as Genevieve's and Carrie's houses in Sarasota. Twenty-four/seven video monitors outside the house would clearly show anyone standing at the entrances of the six locations. The members of the men's book club had decided it would be best to have a single control station from which the sites could be monitored and the nets activated.

They'd picked Jim Furlow's place. The men would take turns at the monitoring station, working in four-hour shifts. If any of their targets—Leiko, or her two goons—showed up, the man on duty would spring the trap. Then they'd call either the sheriff or the Sarasota police, depending on the house and tell them to get to the location.

In addition, each man had an app on his phone with a split screen showing all six doors. They could monitor activity, but only the man on duty at Jim's house could spring the trap.

Jeff had just finished testing the system when Jim Furlow and Joe Palma came into the den, where the monitoring station had been set up.

"How ya doing, Jeff?" his dad asked.

"It's ready, Dad. Hi Jim. I have to tell you guys, I'm not sure this is really such a good idea. I mean, these people will have guns, even though they're caught in a net. They could still shoot somebody."

"Don't worry, Jeff," Jim said, placating the young man. "Believe me, being suddenly caught in a net, flipped upside down, and feeling the net tightening around them, any weapon they have will be useless. Just ask Henry."

"I hope you're right. But, don't you think you should bring Hunter in on this? From what I've heard, he's at least some kind of law enforcement guy. I think I'd feel better if he were in the loop."

"You could be right," Jim said, "but consider this. If we tell him, and he says it's too dangerous, what are the alternatives? We wait for the next break-in and someone *definitely* gets hurt? Remember, these people are out to get us, to make us suffer. That's their goal, and probably to kill us in the end, when they're done messing with us. The police can't protect us twenty-four hours a day. And, besides your dad and I are experts with this stuff. We'll get them and turn them over to the authorities."

"Hunter's good at what he does, but he can't be everywhere," Joe told his son. "We're just extending his reach, so to speak."

"Okay then. You're all set to go. Who gets the first watch?"

KIM ZHANG HAD RETURNED TO CHICAGO, hangered the jet, and headed back at his place to sleep off the jet lag. It wasn't until the taxi ride back from the airport that he'd made his final decision to find the map to Yamashita's treasure on his own. What he'd told Leiko was accurate; the nun had taken the pages and the map out of China and back to the US. But he hadn't told her the rest of what he'd learned.

Thanks to the incredibly detailed report he'd been allowed to read after sleeping with the receptionist, he knew exactly what to look for. He even had some pretty good ideas where to look.

HUNTER CALLED WALLY OSBORN, while Genevieve and Carrie looked on.

"I just missed Leiko Yamashita."

Hunter had previously told Wally all about Leiko and the warrants out for her arrest with the Sarasota Sheriff's Department, the Chicago Police Department, and the Sarasota Police Department.

"She just held Carrie Johannson, a botanist at the Selby Gardens, at gunpoint in her own apartment," he went on. "I heard it because Carrie had called Genevieve and had the presence of mind to leave her phone on. It was definitely her, but somehow she got spooked and left just before I got there."

Hunter explained Carrie's role in the business.

"Can you get some forensic people out to her place? If we can tie her to Carrie's apartment, the case against her personally gets a lot stronger. Carrie said she was wearing gloves, but my guess is she searched the place thoroughly before Carrie got home and found her sitting in a chair waiting for her with a gun. They should sweep for bugs at the same time and get Carrie's prints for comparison."

"Okay. Tell everyone there not to touch anything."

Ending the call, Hunter said to Carrie, "I have a suggestion. The police will send a team out here to find any evidence that can put Leiko here—possible prints, hair, anything. You might not be safe here."

Genevieve jumped in before Hunter could bring it up. "Carrie why don't you pack what you need and come stay with us for a while at my place on the bay? You can go to work from there, but otherwise be with us. It'll be safer."

Carrie looked at Hunter questioningly.

"Just what I was going to suggest. I have a feeling this is all going to be over soon, and you can go home then. What do you say?"

"Sold."

After the forensics team arrived and took Carrie's prints, and before they left, Hunter took a flashlight out of the glove box and got on his back and checked under the Jeep. He found it within minutes. The bug was a GPS receiver. It wouldn't pick up conversation but would give an accurate reading of his location. He knew Leiko must have had the receiver on her and that's what alerted her to leave so abruptly.

He carefully removed it, bagged it, and gave it to the forensics people inside to check for fingerprints. He was sure the Chicago police had her prints on file.

LEIKO YAMASHITA KNEW SHE'D BEEN LUCKY. The bug she'd planted under McCoy's Jeep had pinged the vibrating receiver in her pocket just in time to alert her that he was approaching the apartment. She knew it wouldn't take him long to figure out how she knew it was time to leave. He'd look for, and find, the tracking device.

Zhang had done well in China, getting confirmation that the nun had transported both the notebook's missing pages and her grandfather's map back to the US. It made sense that they would be with the nun's family somewhere—or at the motherhouse. After all, she'd spent almost a year there before quitting the convent. In fact, the more she thought about it, the more likely it seemed that they might be there.

She decided to leave Carrie Johannson alone for the moment and go back to Ohio. However, this time she wouldn't be Karen Applewood, Harvard professor. She had another plan.

ED MCCOY AND HENRY LAHTI DOCKED THE BOAT at the Spanish Point Tiki Bar on the mainland side of the intracoastal waterway, about five miles north of the Kingston house. They found a table in the shade with a great view of Casey Key across the water.

"Stephen King, the writer, has a place over there somewhere," Henry said.

"Yeah, I know. Hunter told me that Jenny Lahti's house and Scott Harrison's aren't far from his."

Henry watched as Ed twirled his spoon around his fingers while gazing silently out at the water. The silence dragged on until Henry said, "Okay, what's up? I know you too well to not know that something's going on."

Ed made a fist, put it up for a "fist bump" and Henry responded in kind.

"You *do* know me pretty well."

"Yes, I do. So, what's going on?"

"Okay, you know I've been bothered about not telling Hunter about our rigging the houses with the nets."

"Right."

"Well. . . I told him."

Henry waited.

"I told him what we'd done, that we tested it, and that it worked. I told him that Jim and Joe were experts with this stuff and that I thought it was a good idea. He thought about it for a moment and asked how it was triggered. I explained about the control station at Jim's house and the whole setup. How we were all going to take turns monitoring the six doors."

"What did he say?"

"He asked more about the triggering mechanism. Then he got up and paced for a bit. Then he told me that since none of us were going to be anywhere near those doors when, and if, the system was activated, it was probably safe. His only insistence was that if we trigger it, we call the police, *and him*, right away."

"So he's on board?" Henry piped up gleefully, then looked around to see who might have heard that.

"Yeah, and I'm glad he is. Makes me feel better."

"Me too. Good work, Ed. Now we have to let Jim and Joe know."

46

LEIKO APPROACHED THE MOTHERHOUSE OF THE Sisters of Notre Dame de Namur for the second time in four days. This time, rather than the confident Karen Applewood, professor of history at Harvard University, she was a timid cleaning woman with the Ascot Cleaning Service. She was filling in for the woman who usually came on Tuesdays, a woman who had suddenly taken ill thanks to Leiko, and couldn't make it. She'd told the nun her name was Lisa.

Sister Claire told her that they need the cleaning help because most of the nuns were too old and frail to do the work themselves. Then, she showed her around and pointed out what needed to be done in the records house. Leiko had managed to give herself a small but noticeable scar on her left cheek and wore a wig that completely altered her appearance from the professor the elderly nun had encountered three days earlier. She also assumed the nun didn't see well, since her glasses were extremely thick.

The records house was old and dusty but consisted of only four rooms. Other than Sister Claire and herself, Leiko quickly found that there was no one else around. It seemed the archives weren't a popular spot. So while the nun busied herself in the front room at the desk, Leiko began "cleaning" and had the place to herself. She quickly found the file she'd read earlier and looked through the cabinet to see if there was anything else. Since the nun had no reason to doubt her validity as the professor earlier, she didn't expect to find anything of value in there. Sister Claire would have shown her everything she had. Of course, she hadn't shown her Sister Mary Margaret's resignation letter, but then Leiko had heard what was in it when she'd read it to McCoy.

Still, she thought, McCoy hadn't had actually seen it. The nun had said she'd been instructed to only answer questions about it, but he couldn't see or read it himself. She needed to get that letter and read the whole thing. Then she remembered, it wasn't here; the nun had to get it from the Mother Superior's office. On the other hand she'd check the nun's desk out front later, when the old lady wasn't there.

Meanwhile she kept cleaning and looking for anything else. She found Sister Mary Margaret's wooden box that contained the clothes McCoy and the Swift woman had examined. She undid the string and did a thorough examination of the clothes and any pockets. She found nothing. Unlike the research notebook, nothing was sewn into the hems.

She got back to mopping just as Sister Claire appeared.

"Lisa, I'm going over to the main office for a bit. I'll be back shortly."

"That's fine, Sister, I have plenty to do here," Leiko answered in her disguised voice.

She waited a few minutes after the nun left. Then began going through her desk. She found the letter immediately in the center pull-out drawer. She began reading. Most of it was her explanation for leaving the order. It was personal, sincere, and offered nothing new. As she'd heard earlier, the information on Chen, and the missing pages, and the map, was included because it meant so much to her, just as the old nun had said. There was nothing she hadn't heard before.

She slipped the letter back in the drawer and returned to the back room, where she continued searching for anything related to the nun from China. Finding nothing, she returned to the box of clothes and examined the box itself. Again, nothing there, no hidden compartments. Frustrated, she left before Sister Claire returned.

THE NEXT MORNING, HUNTER DROPPED THE GPS receiver off with the police to check for prints. If Leiko hadn't used gloves to search Carrie's place they might get lucky. He and Genevieve spent the rest of the morning learning as much as they could about Leiko and her criminal organization through news stories on the internet. Eduard Gautier called about noon.

"Eduard. What do you have?"

"What makes you think I have something? Can't this just be a social call, you know, like from two old friends who've never actually met each other in person?"

"True enough. One of these days we're going to rectify that."

"Until then," Eduard said, "I believe I have a useful little nugget for you. I dug around for what I could find on that convent of yours in China. It turns out there's a very useful facility called the Memorial Hall in the city of Wuchang that keeps old records on the city's historical past. Using my incredibly persuasive Interpol clout, I got into their files and have here, in my very hands, a digital copy of an illuminating history of the convent and school written by one of the nuns. Not your Sister Mary Margaret, but a friend of hers at the time, Sister Bernadette."

"I'm impressed," said Hunter.

"You shouldn't be, knowing my amazing powers as you do."

"I stand corrected."

"I'll email you a copy right now."

"Thanks, Eduard. What would I do without you?"

"It'd be ugly. Don't even think about it."

When the email arrived a few minutes later, he printed it out on Genevieve's printer. They made two copies, and both began reading. Hunter found the first ten pages of the narrative were indeed a fairly tedious history of the establishment of the school and convent starting in 1926. More interesting, was the description of the efforts to close the facilities in 1948 and for the nuns to return to the United States, specifically the motherhouse in Cleveland, Ohio. At this point the narrative got personal, as Sister Bernadette described the activities of each of the nuns as they prepared to leave this part of their lives.

It was obvious that Sister Bernadette and Sister Mary Margaret were close friends as well as colleagues. She described how, in 1942, Sister Mary Margaret, at the request of the Mother Superior, asked Dr. Chen to operate his medical practice out of the convent's basement. This was before they'd left the war zone for Burma. In return he was to care for the nun's health. When they returned in late 1945, after the surrender, Dr. Chen was dying and asked Sister Mary Margaret to do something for him.

He gave her a sack of orchid seedpods from a new species he'd discovered, a species he named China Gold. He said that treatment with China Gold could prevent juvenile diabetes. He also gave her his research notebook explaining how the orchids were to be used. He told her his brother, Huan Chen, would later come to the motherhouse in America to collect the research notebook and the sac of seedpods from her. He would then see to growing the China Gold orchids from the seeds and arrange for the treatment to be made available to everyone.

He'd also given her a small statue of a fat Buddha that he wanted her to take back to America. He said it was an old family heirloom that he wanted her to keep safe for his brother. He told her it contained the six sisters and a map to the Glorious Store.

There it is, Hunter thought, recalling Dr. Chen's poem sewn into the cover of the research notebook.

So this Buddha contained the six sisters—the six missing pages from the research notebook—and a *map* to the Glorious Store.

A map.

Six sisters
and the Glorious Store,
the secret to China Gold
Orchid tea
A life that's free
From sugar's deadly hold

"The treasure hasn't been moved, it's the *map* to the treasure that's been moved far away from the enemy," he said aloud.

"So we need to find this Buddha," Genevieve said, having reached the same conclusion as Hunter at the same time he did.

"Right. The question is, does Leiko have this information?"

"Her pilot flew to Wuchang, according to Jenkins," Genevieve replied. "He may have found it and told her."

"You're right. At least we have to assume that she knows."

"You know what that means, Hunter?"

"Yes. Carrie, her mother, and the nuns at the motherhouse are now squarely in Leiko's crosshairs."

47

ED MCCOY WAS TAKING HIS FOUR-HOUR SHIFT monitoring the doorways from Jim Furlow's command center. He was in his last hour and couldn't stomach another cup of coffee. The surveillance had been completely uneventful. The only thing he'd added to the group's logbook was that two little Girl Scouts selling cookies knocked on the door at Carrie Johannson's place. They were dressed in their uniforms, and of course no one answered the door since Carrie was at work.

With fifteen minutes left in Ed's shift, Joe Palma, who was scheduled to take over for him, came in. Joe sat down next to him and was just about to ask if he'd seen anything, when both men suddenly saw it at the same time.

"There. Look. It's them," shouted Joe, "The two Asian guys."

"Damn, you're right, they're at her back door," Ed said, the excitement obvious in his voice.

"Look, one of them is trying to pick the lock. Let's do it."

Ed hit the button, and both men hooted at the scene that unfolded in front of them on the screen. The net shot down on both of them, tightened around their feet, and yanked the intruders into the air, where they hung upside down, struggling and helpless.

Ed called the prearranged number for the Sarasota Police and told them that two men who were on their "arrest on sight" list were neatly packaged and available at the address he gave them. He told the officer they needed to get someone over there immediately. Then he called Hunter.

———————————

HUNTER AND THE POLICE ARRIVED AT THE SAME TIME, and Hunter had to stifle a laugh at the confusion on the Sarasota cops faces as they looked at the two struggling men in the net at Carrie Johannson's back door. He showed them his detective shield.

"Hunter McCoy, Lieutenant Detective, Virginia State Police. I'm working with Detective Wally Osborn, of your homicide division. Call him, and he'll tell you that there's an arrest warrant out for these two."

"We know that, McCoy, we called in on our way over here." Then one of them, scratching his head, pointed at the two men swearing and dangling in the fishing net, "And what the hell is that?"

"That's an ingenious method of fishing that apparently worked like a charm."

"Well, let's get them down," the officer said.

While Hunter lowered the net, the two officers handcuffed the captured men, who appeared equally terrified and pissed. After removing their weapons and wallets, the officer in charge determined that the two were Ryuki Ono and Akito Hano. He read them their rights, then arrested them on charges as described in the arrest warrants. These included planting evidence in a homicide investigation, attempted murder with a motor vehicle, and as of a few minutes ago, breaking and entering.

Hunter regarded both men. "You two have as much to fear from the authorities as you do from Leiko Yamashita. I'd cooperate if I were you. And as often as you've screwed up, the last thing you want is to be set free so Leiko can get at you."

Akito and Ryuki looked at each other and swallowed hard, apparently agreeing,

Hunter called Jenkins in Chicago.

"Detective, the Sarasota Police have just arrested Akito Hano and Ryuki Ono."

"How'd they find them?" he asked.

Hunter explained, in exquisite detail how the men's book club had pulled it off. When he was finished, Jenkins was still laughing out loud. "Wow. Good for the old guys. Did you know they were doing that?"

"Not at first."

"Well, they did a great job. Thank them for me. Are we any closer to Leiko?"

"We haven't spotted her yet, but I think I know where she'll be looking."

"Be careful, McCoy. She won't be as easy to catch as those two."

"I know."

HUNTER AND GENEVIEVE DROVE TO THE SELBY GARDENS to tell Carrie what had happened. Genevieve took the lead.

"They've captured the two men who worked for Leiko. They won't bother any of us again."

"How'd they do it?"

"The fish nets."

"That really worked? I can't believe it. Whose door?"

"It was your backdoor. Hunter's dad spotted them on their monitor and sprung the trap."

"So they were coming after me, then."

"We don't know what their plans were yet," Hunter answered, "but we will. I have a feeling they'll both be talking. But yes, it was your house."

He and Genevieve had been standing in the doorway to Carrie's office. "How about if we sit down, Carrie," he added. "There's more."

As they sat, Carrie, looking worried again, asked, "What do you mean? What more?"

"I have a colleague who works with Interpol. He just sent me a copy of a history of the convent and school."

"Interpol—the international police?"

"Yes."

"You *do* get around," she said, admiration in her voice.

"It seems the history was written by another nun in the convent at the time your grandmother was there—a Sister Bernadette."

"I never heard my grandmother mention her. What did you learn?"

"Sister Bernadette wrote that Dr. Chen also gave your grandmother a small statue of a fat Buddha that he wanted to keep safe for his brother. He told her it contained the six sisters and a map to the Glorious Store."

"The six sisters? That's the six missing pages from the research notebook, right?"

"That's right."

"But wait. What else did you say was in the Buddha?"

"A map to the Glorious Store."

"Leiko told me she wanted a map."

"Which raises the next concern," Hunter said, knowing he had to make Carrie fully aware of the risks her family was now facing.

"We don't know whether Leiko knows about the existence of this Buddha statue, but we have to assume she does, since she's looking for a map. We also have to assume that the places she's likely to be looking for it are all associated with your grandmother and her family. That includes you, your mother, and the motherhouse as well."

"So you're saying that bagging those two guys is not the end of it. We've got to be on the lookout for the dragon lady too."

Genevieve chuckled. "Dragon lady" was the exact term *she'd* used to describe Leiko.

"The question is, Carrie, where is this Buddha statue? Have you ever seen it?"

"Not that I remember."

"You never saw it at your grandmother's house or your mother's?"

She shrugged. "I don't recall ever seeing it. Of course, that doesn't mean much. It could have been around when I was a kid and I never noticed it."

"Give your mom a call and ask her."

"Okay."

A minute later her mom was on the phone.

"Mom, I'm here with Hunter and Genevieve, and they've discovered something that's linked to a small statue of Buddha that Grandma may have had. Do you recall ever seeing it?"

"Let me think. It's not likely a nun would have a statue of Buddha."

"Apparently Dr. Chen gave it to her to bring back to the States. She was supposed to give it to his brother—the one who never showed up. Any idea what might have happened to it?"

Emma Johannson paused, thinking. "You know, Carrie, I wonder if it was there in Grandma's house when you and I cleaned it out," she said. "I think maybe there was an ugly statue that I put in the give-away pile. Remember we had those piles?"

"Yeah, Mom. So did you give it away?"

"I think so. It's been three years, so I could be mistaken. But yes, I think I did."

"Who did you give it to?"

"The Salvation Army."

THE MEMBERS OF THE MEN'S BOOK CLUB were at Jim Furlow's when Hunter came in. They greeted him with cheers and high fives. They'd been celebrating the success of "Furlow's Nets," as the trap system had become known. Ed McCoy was also being celebrated as the "lucky guy" who got to pull the trigger, so to speak. Hunter knew he had to get them to settle down.

"Guys, guys," he said holding his hands up to bring their joviality to a halt. "You've done a great job. Thanks to Joe and Jim's expertise with the nets, you've removed two bad guys from our watch list. But let me remind you that the real threat is still out there."

The men reluctantly stopped shouting and began to listen.

"Leiko Yamashita is most definitely our biggest problem, and I want to tell you now—seriously—you will do *nothing* to try and set a trap for *her*. Her level of potential threat is way beyond Hano and Ono. What you did there was great, but I don't want you to try trapping her. She's in a league all her own. Let the police do it."

"But you'll still be going after her?" Joe asked.

"Yes, but remember I *am* the police, in a way. Now, just to keep you in the loop and up to date on everything we know, let me tell you what we've learned since yesterday."

He went on to tell them about his contact at Interpol and what Eduard had told him. He explained about the Buddha and that he thought Leiko would be going after Carrie's family, figuring they'd have it, or know where it is.

What he didn't tell them was his own plan on how to catch her.

48

LEIKO WAS REGISTERED UNDER AN ASSUMED NAME at the new Westin hotel in downtown Sarasota. Not wanting to leave a digital trail for the police, she'd paid cash for a three day stay. This left her short of money, so she found a bank machine and inserted her debit card. There was a two-hundred-dollar withdrawal limit for a single transaction, so she'd need to do this several times to build up some walking around cash.

Shocked, she stared at the screen—Account Frozen.

What the. . .?

She withdrew the card and inserted it again. Same result.

Withdrawing her card a second time, she stepped away from the screen, glowering. *McCoy*. She knew that with his federal credentials he'd probably be able to pull this off. Damn him.

She immediately went up to her room, grabbed her things and left the hotel in case the authorities were monitoring her use of the card. She drove south and stopped at a modest motel where she called Solomon Ito, her lieutenant, who—in her absence—ran her operation in Chicago.

"Solomon, report."

"It's not good. The police are all over the place. They've got a car permanently stationed outside. I've also gotten word that the Chicago police have a warrant out for your arrest. We haven't heard from Hano and Ono, either.

They may have been arrested, I'm not sure. What's going on?"

Hano and Ono arrested? she thought. If that was true it meant the police in Florida were probably looking for her as well.

"I need cash. I think the feds have blocked my bank debit card. Get ten thousand dollars in cash and mail it to me overnight, to Taylor Min, at the"—she looked at her receipt—"the Manatee Motel in Osprey."

"Taylor Min?"

"Just do it."

Ending the call, she considered her options. It could be McCoy who'd blocked her card, or it could be the Chicago police, or even the local police, if they'd caught Hano and Ono here in Florida. Any of them would probably have the authority to get her bank accounts frozen.

She had to assume they had warrants out for her arrest as well, so she couldn't use a credit card, as that would give away her location if they were tracking her. She'd have to rely on Solomon to keep her funded. The man had been with her for the three years she'd been running the organization and had always proved himself to be dependable and loyal.

What were her options? The map was most likely in Cleveland at the motherhouse or with the nun's daughter, Emma Johannson. Her bet was on the daughter. She'd go there and apply pressure until she got an answer.

THE NEXT MORNING, AFTER GETTING the cash from Solomon and using her Taylor Min credentials, she flew to Cleveland, rented a car, and drove to Emma Johannson's apartment.

"You! What do you want? I'm calling the police," the elegant woman started to close the door.

Leiko shoved her backwards, and Emma fell to the floor. Mouth agape, Emma watched as Leiko shut the door and stepped forward holding a small pistol, which she pointed directly at the terrified woman.

"Get up and sit in that chair. You'll call no one. Instead you're going to answer my questions."

Terrified, Emma did as she was told.

"I assume you know who I am. Is that right?"

Recovering and showing a surprising level of spunk, Emma answered. "I know you're no professor at Harvard. You're a criminal of some kind from Chicago, and your related to that Japanese war criminal."

Leiko moved so fast, Emma never even had a chance to raise her hands in defense against the slap in the face that nearly carried her out of the chair.

"He was no war criminal. The real criminal was the man who betrayed him, Dr. Chen—your mother's friend."

Her short-lived bravado now completely gone, Emma said nothing.

"Your mother had something that belongs to me—a map. It was accompanied by some missing pages from Dr. Chen's research notebook. I believe you know where they are and you're going to tell me now."

"No, I— "

This blow was harder than the first, and Emma did actually fall out of the chair. Leiko waited, staring hard at the woman on the floor. As Emma hesitantly got up and arranged herself, Leiko continued to stare. When Emma sat down again, Leiko continued.

"As I said, I believe you know where they are and you're going to tell me."

Hesitant to speak lest she get hit again, Emma finally said slowly, "Why do you think I would know this?"

"I know that your mother brought them back to the States when she returned from China. They're not at the motherhouse, and I don't think your daughter has them. That leaves only you. If you don't tell me, I'll have no choice but to confront your daughter and, as you can see, I'm not easily dissuaded."

Leiko waited as she watched Emma desperately trying to figure out what to do. It was obvious the woman knew something, and she wouldn't want her daughter harmed.

"It's possible the things you're looking for are hidden in a small statue of Buddha that my mother brought back from China," Emma said. "I had no idea it contained anything of value, and when my mother died I gave it away to the Salvation Army, along with lots of other stuff. That was three years ago. I have no idea what happened to it after that."

"What made you think there was something inside?"

"When I picked it up, I could tell there was something loose inside. I just figured it was stuffing or something like that. It was old and ugly."

"And you gave it to the Salvation Army?"

"Yes."

"Which branch?"

"What?"

"Where exactly did you take it?"

"I don't know. I called their number and they sent a truck to pick up all of that stuff."

"Give me the number you called."

Emma looked it up in her computer and gave it to her.

Leiko left a frightened, but relieved Emma Johannson and called Solomon.

"Contact Kim Zhang and have him fly to Cleveland immediately and contact me as soon as he lands."

"Okay, but what's going on?"

"Just do it."

———————————

SOLOMON HAD A PRETTY GOOD IDEA what was going on. He thought about the conversation he'd had with his cousin, Kim Zhang, when he'd returned from China.

Kim had told him that he'd discovered a document in Wuchang that said a doctor Chen had found a map to Yamashita's treasure, and placed it into a statue of the Buddha, and given it to a nun to take it to America. After the war she'd returned to Cleveland.

That explained why Leiko was in Cleveland, Solomon thought. She'd just called him and asked him to send her more cash.

Solomon called his cousin. "Leiko wants you to fly to Cleveland immediately and contact her as soon as you land."

"Why?" Kim asked.

"I don't know," Solomon answered.

This wasn't true, as Solomon had learned that one of Leiko's men, a man referred to only as the "Filipino," had been secretly researching the treasure. He believed the bulk of it was buried in caves in the Philippines. She'd sworn the man to keep their search a secret, especially from Solomon. She'd told him that if they found it, she'd get ninety-five percent, and he'd get five percent. If its value was anywhere near what was speculated, the man's five percent would be enormous.

"Have you told her about the Buddha?" Solomon asked.

Here, Zhang paused. "Not really. I told her that the nun was instructed to bring the map and the research notes back to the US with her after the war and wait for the brother to pick them up."

"But you didn't tell her they were inside a statue of Buddha?"

"No."

"Be very careful in Cleveland, cousin. I don't want to know why you didn't tell her."

49

SOLOMON KNEW MORE THEN HE'D LET ON TO HIS COUSIN.
He knew what Leiko was planning. He'd secretly installed
a listening device in her office over a year ago. The risk
he'd taken doing this was enormous. She'd kill him with
her own hands, if she ever found out. But the risk had been
worth it.

Leiko had a habit of talking out loud to herself when
alone. He'd discovered this once when he'd dared to enter
her office without knocking and found her in mid
"conversation" with no one else present. He'd been
severely reprimanded and never did it again.

Still, the opportunity to know what she was thinking
was too good to pass up. Once a week she had fresh
flowers delivered by a local florist. The delivery person
would bring them to Solomon, and he'd knock on her
office door, enter when she responded, and place them on a
credenza in her office. It had been their habit for a long
time.

What she didn't know was that he'd become highly
skilled at reaching behind the credenza as he placed the
vase to retrieve the previous week's voice-activated
memory stick recorder and replace it with a new one.
Fortunately for him, her requirement that he personally
bring in the flowers was just one of her ways of letting him
know who was in charge.

He hadn't learned anything of real importance until
she'd started the revenge project against Billie Chen and
the McCoys. He had several useful recordings. Knowing

she was in Ohio, safely away, he'd listened to the most
damning recording again:

I get rid of the McCoys and take what's mine.
—pause—
I'm going to do it. Why not?
—pause—
I get everything this way.
—pause—
I'm a blood relative. It's all mine.
Screw the organization.
—pause—
The Filipino can help, until I don't need him anymore.
Get rid of him; Solomon too.
—pause—
I take it all. Then turn them over to the cops.
(She laughs
I'm long gone with my fortune and my new identity.
Screw em all.

Solomon was not going to take this lying down. He'd
made a bargain with the devil and fully intended to carry
out his part of it.

EMMA CALLED HUNTER IMMEDIATELY AFTER LEIKO LEFT
and told him what had happened.

"She left after slapping me around. I knew if I didn't
tell her about the Buddha, she'd go after Carrie."

"That's okay. You did the right thing. Are you all
right? Are you hurt?"

"Only my pride. I'm okay. She's an awful woman."

"Yes, she is. So you told her about giving the Buddha
away to the Salvation Army?"

"Yes."

"Good. That means the motherhouse is safe and Carrie
too. There's no reason for her to go there or to contact

Carrie. She'll be after that Buddha. I suppose you didn't see the car she arrived in being way up in your high-rise."

"No, I'm afraid I have no information to give the police."

"Actually, you probably do. You can describe what she's wearing, how she's doing her hair, things like that. She'll absolutely stay in the area, looking for information on the fate of the Buddha. I'll call the local police, and they'll send someone out to take that information from you. Is that okay?"

"I can do that. I'll start writing down what I remember right now, before I forget."

"Good, and don't worry, Carrie will be alright."

———————

LEIKO GOT LUCKY ON HER FIRST TRY AT THE Turneytown Shopping Center. The middle-aged man at the counter actually remembered the Buddha.

"Yeah, I remember that. It was an ugly thing. Still, my aunt Hilda liked it. She actually bought it, said it fit her personality. She was right about that."

Leiko was excited. This could be it. She had to play this carefully.

"Oh my. I can't believe it. Do you think she'd sell it back to me? My mother gave it away three years ago and I'd always wanted it. It belonged to my grandmother."

"I don't know, you'd have to ask her, but good luck with that."

"What do you mean?" Leiko asked.

"She's retired and lives in Florida."

"Where in Florida? Do you have her number?"

"Somewhere on the Gulf of Mexico, I don't really know."

"Do you have her name? I'd really like to contact her and ask if she be so kind as to sell it back to me. It would mean so much."

"Hilda Byers, her name's Hilda Byers, B Y E R S. I don't have her phone number. I remember she said something about the circus. I don't know—she lived somewhere near that, I guess."

"Thanks, you've been a big help. I'll try to get a phone number and give her a call."

"Okay, but I wouldn't expect too much."

"What? Why?"

"Aunt Hilda's not very friendly. She never liked her relatives, and she likes strangers even less."

50

Using White Pages, Leiko found one person named Hilda Byers in Sarasota who was in the right age range. She called her and said she was a friend of her nephew in Cleveland.

"So, what do you want?" the woman asked in the gruff, unfriendly manner her nephew had warned her to expect.

"I understand you might have purchased a Buddha statue from the Salvation Army store in Cleveland that my mother donated three years ago. Is that correct?"

The woman paused before answering. "What did you say your name is?"

"Carrie Johannson," Leiko lied.

The woman paused again, this time even longer. "So what?"

"I'd like to buy it from you."

"Whatcha willing to pay for it?"

Good, Leiko thought. "What are you asking? It has lots of sentimental value to me, so I'd be willing to pay a hundred dollars for it. Do you have it?"

"Yeah, I think it's here somewhere. A hundred dollars, you say."

"Yes," Leiko answered, suspecting the woman was thinking over her counteroffer.

"Tell you what," Hilda Byers said, "Come on over here and we'll talk about it."

"I can be there tomorrow. What's your address?"

Leiko returned to her hotel room to pack just as Kim Zhang called to say he'd landed at the Cleveland airport.

Perfect, Leiko thought. *Back to Florida.*

After checking out of her room, Leiko drove to the airport and thought about what the Filipino would be able to do if the Buddha statue actually contained all it promised. She didn't care about the missing pages; it was the map she wanted, and she knew the man was an expert at maps. Over the years, he'd been her "go-to" guy when finding something hidden was the goal.

If something was missing and the Filipino couldn't find it, it didn't exist anymore. He was her Hunter McCoy.

More importantly he was one hundred percent loyal to her. If the map pointed to Yamashita's treasure and there was any ambiguity, he would work his way through it to the specific location or locations. Of course, after that his usefulness would be over, and as loyal as he was, he'd become expendable.

By the time she reached the airport and returned the car, Zhang had refueled the plane and filed a flight plan for Sarasota. After she boarded they were airborne within minutes.

Leiko stepped into the onboard bathroom, closed the door, took out her phone, and called the Tanaka brothers— the Hano and Ono replacements—who were already waiting for instructions in Sarasota.

"I want you to pick her up now. Take her to the location we talked about earlier and hold her there until you hear from me. Do you understand?"

"Yeah, boss. We've got it covered."

Back in her seat she began to talk out loud to herself.

"So, a Buddha."

—pause—

"The map's in the Buddha."

—pause—

"Hilda Byers has it."

—pause—

"Tomorrow I get it for a lousy hundred bucks."

—pause—

—laughter—

"She obviously doesn't know what she has."

Leiko sat back, closed her eyes, and went to sleep.

———————

DETECTIVE WILBUR JENKINS HEARD the entire conversation Leiko had with herself, thanks to the voice activated recorder his tech people had installed in the main cabin after Zhang had returned from Chicago and before he took off for Cleveland. There was no mike in the bathroom, only the cabin.

He immediately called Hunter to tell him about Hilda Byers and the Buddha, and that Leiko was on her way to get it.

"I'll go there now and beat her to it. How much time do I have?"

"She's airborne but just left the Cleveland airport. It's about a four-hour flight."

"Can you get me an address?" Hunter asked.

"Hold on."

Within two minutes Jenkins had it and gave it to him.

"Thanks, I'm on it," Hunter said, grabbing his key fob and heading out.

———————

HILDA BYERS LIVED IN A DOUBLE WIDE mobile home in a small community of similar homes off US Highway 41 just south of downtown Sarasota. It didn't take long to find her place. He knocked, and an overweight woman in her seventies with visible tattoos on her arms and neck answered the door.

"Yeah?"

"Mrs. Byers? Hilda Byers?" Hunter asked.

"Who wants to know?"

Hunter showed her his credentials. "Detective Lieutenant Hunter McCoy, Virginia State Police."

"Police? Virginia? Whatcha want? I didn't do nothin, never been to Virginia."

"Are you Hilda Byers?" Hunter asked again.

"Yeah, so what?"

"Look, Mrs. Byers, you've done nothing wrong. We're not interested in you. You're not in any trouble. But you can help us. A woman is coming to see you about a small Buddha statue. She is an extremely dangerous criminal. The FBI and the police in three states have warrants out for her arrest.

"It's a big break for us that we know she will be coming here to get the statue. We intend to arrest her when she does. But you need to be somewhere else when that happens for your own safety. Do you have someone you could stay with for a day or two?"

"Jeez. I didn't know. Yeah, I guess. My brother. I could stay with him."

"Would you get the Buddha, please? Let me see it?"

"Yeah, hold on."

Hilda Byers disappeared, returned a moment later with the statue, and handed it to Hunter. It was lacquered black, about a foot high, and heavy. He didn't want to examine it now and alert the woman to anything, even though he wanted to turn it over, shake it, and check it out thoroughly.

"Mrs. Byers, I'm going to have the authorities stake out your house so we can arrest this woman when she shows up. We know she could be here as early as four hours from now, but, most likely not until tomorrow. Are you willing to go to your brother's while we do this—and leave the Buddha here with us as bait?"

She scratched the tattoo of a huge flower on her left arm and chewed her lip. "Okay, sure. I can do that. Do I still get the money she was going to pay me?"

"We can take care of that, don't worry."

Before he called Wally Osborn to get the ball rolling on setting up the ambush to grab Leiko, he got Hilda's brother's name, address, and cellphone number. She also gave him her cellphone and the number. His plan was that a policewoman would imitate Hilda's voice if Leiko called before showing up.

By the time Hunter finished his calls he was sure that if Leiko came anywhere near this house, he'd get her. It took Hilda Byers an hour to pack and drive to her brother's house during which time a female Sarasota PD detective arrived and spent time with Hilda, doing the best she could to learn to imitate her voice.

Once she was gone Hunter began to examine the Buddha. Shaking it, he thought he could detect that there was something inside. He'd hoped for a plug or something in the bottom that could be removed giving way to a hollow interior but there wasn't any obvious opening. Had the doctor sealed it up somehow? He wondered.

Finally he found it. It was the head. It screwed off. Apparently the doctor had applied a thin coat of black lacquer to the entire statue, successfully hiding the narrow line between the head and the rest of the body. He carefully unscrewed it and removed the head.

It was too small an opening to reach in, so he turned it upside down and shook out the contents onto her kitchen table. What emerged could best be describe as ash and bits of what might have been paper at one time in the distant past.

Damn. It's all disintegrated.

He examined the pile on the table. The quantity of material that came out might have been enough to account for several pages of paper at one time. If the map and missing pages had been intact when the doctor put them in there in the 1940s, age and God-knows-what had turned them into useless rubble.

He didn't care so much about the loss of the map, but the missing pages might have held the secret to a medical miracle.

Well, Carrie and Stephanie Bennet, you're on your own now. At least you have the orchids. You'll have to take it from there.

He refilled the Buddha with the useless remnants and screwed the head back on.

51

HUNTER KNEW THAT THINGS WERE COMING TOGETHER. He had the Buddha and knew that Leiko was on her way to Florida to meet with Hilda Byers. He planned to set a trap she couldn't wiggle out of.

Because of his connection to Hunter, Wally Osborn had been put in charge of organizing the Sarasota PD's efforts to capture her. This kept Hunter fully in the loop as plans developed. The female detective with Hilda's phone would appear to be the only one in or near the double-wide when Leiko arrived. If she called ahead of time, she'd think she was talking to Hilda. Once Leiko was within the capture perimeter, men would appear and spring into action, and they'd have her. Now, they just had to wait.

KIM ZHANG BROUGHT LEIKO'S PRIVATE JET into final approach at the Sarasota/Bradenton International Airport. After a smooth landing and a short taxi to the private plane area of the tarmac, Leiko exited. She told Zhang to fuel up and stand by for her instructions.

She checked into a hotel. The next morning she got a rental and set out to Hilda Byers's house in South Sarasota. On the way she called the woman on her cell phone.

"Yeah?" the lady detective answered in her best gruff voice.

"This is Carrie Johannson. I'm on my way to your place now to see the statue."

"Good, I'm here. You got some money?"

"Yes, I do."

"Where's you now?"

Leiko hesitated. "Why?"

"When you gonna be here?"

Leiko paused again before answering. "Maybe half an hour."

"Okay, see you then."

Leiko had been driving and following the GPS to the address. She had an uneasy feeling but couldn't put her finger on it. Something was off.

She pulled over into a Culver's parking lot and sat back, thinking for another minute or two before picking up her phone and calling Kim Zhang.

"When was the last time you swept the plane for surveillance equipment?"

"Umm, let me see. It would have been right after getting back from China. Yeah, I did it at the airport before leaving the plane. Why?"

"Do it again, right now and call me back."

Leiko went into the Culver's and got a small coffee to go. No sooner was she back in the car when her phone rang.

"We were bugged. I found a high-powered transmitter in the perforated wall panel in the cabin near the sitting area."

"Destroy it, file a flight plan for New Orleans, take off, but then divert to Tallahassee without telling air traffic control and wait for my call."

HUNTER AND OSBORN'S SWAT TEAM had been in position all night. Hunter had called Genevieve late yesterday afternoon to tell her he wouldn't be home because of the stake-out. She hadn't answered, but he'd left a message.

The Hilda Byers imposter was alone in the house with the Buddha. Osborn had the team positioned outside the mobile home, well-hidden but in earbud contact. Hunter was stationed so that he had a clear view of the front door and would be able to identify her. When Leiko drove up she wouldn't see anything unusual.

Funny that she'd introduced herself to Hilda Byers as Carrie Johannson, Hunter thought, while he waited. She must have somehow found the Salvation Army location where the Buddha and the rest of Emma Johannson's donated stuff was delivered. He assumed she'd told the clerk on duty a story about needing to get the Buddha back for some reason. He or she must have somehow come up with Hilda Byers as the person who bought it from them. They must have asked Leiko her name and she just said Carrie Johannson, Emma's daughter.

Suddenly Wally Osborn's voice came through everyone's earbuds.

"Everyone ready. A car's just entered the mobile home community. This could be it."

Hunter watched as a tan Chevy sedan drove slowly toward the home. It slowed as it approached and then just as slowly drove past and pulled into a driveway five doors down. An elderly man, carrying two sacks of groceries, emerged and entered the house. False alarm.

Unable to relax, Hunter thought about how good it would be to arrest Leiko Yamashita, after all the harm she'd caused. More than anything, after they had her in a jail cell, he wanted to ask her why. Was it really all to avenge the death of her great-grandfather, a convicted war criminal?

If everything he'd learned about her was true, she'd be more interested in herself than retribution for someone else, even a distant relative. But then, who knew what went on in the mind of someone as depraved as she was?

"Another car coming. Get ready."

Instantly, Hunter put aside his reverie and looked up as a dark blue SUV—it looked like a Cadillac—approached. He could see the driver, who looked like a woman, and no passengers.

The car slowed and pulled into Hilda Byers's driveway. Hunter could feel the team's tension, awaiting orders. He could see the driver in silhouette without detail. It could be her, but he wasn't sure. The driver didn't exit the car, but just sat there.

Hunter lowered his voice and spoke to Osborn and the rest of the team. "It's a woman, alone. I can't be sure it's her yet. Let's wait."

Hunter watched as the woman brought up a cellphone and called someone. Was she calling their Hilda imposter inside? He could see her talking to someone. She put the phone away, opened the car door, and stepped out where Hunter could see her clearly.

"Chris, did she just call you?" Hunter asked the detective posing as Hilda.

"Yeah, she's outside and coming in."

"It's not her."

"Say again?"

"The woman's not Leiko Yamashita. She must be a decoy. Play it by ear."

"Right."

"Team. Hold in place."

The woman knocked on the door and "Hilda" answered it.

"You Johannson?"

"Yes," said the decoy, who was clearly not Asian. "Do you have the statue?"

"Yeah, come on in."

Hunter and the team could hear the conversation clearly even though they couldn't see inside the house.

"I have two hundred dollars for the statue."

"Two hundred, eh? Let's make it one thousand," said "Hilda."

"No, I'm authorized to go to—

"Authorized? What do you mean authorized? Who's authorizing you?"

"I—I can't say. Look, I'll give you five hundred. That's it."

"You're not Carrie Johannson. Who are you?"

"Oh, God, look, I'm just trying to make some money here. Give me the statue, and I'll give you five hundred."

"Who paid you to do this? 'Hilda' demanded. "Who told you to pretend you were Carrie Johannson?"

The woman began to cry and broke down. "I don't know her name. She offered me a thousand dollars to pretend I was her and do this."

"What did she look like?"

"She was pretty—and Asian."

Hunter made a decision. "I'm going in. Team, stay in place."

Leaving his vantage point, he entered the front door and surprised the decoy.

"Who—who are you?" the woman asked when Hunter burst in.

"My name's Hunter McCoy, and this is detective Carla Brecht, of the Sarasota Police Department. Now you can cooperate with us and you'll be fine, or she'll arrest you for participating in a criminal activity."

"Oh, my God. No. I was just trying to make some money."

"So, you'll cooperate?"

"Yeah. Sure."

After verifying that she was unarmed, Hunter said, "Detective Brecht, check her for a wire."

It didn't take long to find the small transmitter under the lapel of her jacket.

"We're coming for you, Leiko," Hunter said, speaking directly into the mike.

TWO MILES AWAY, SITTING IN THE BACK SEAT of the parked car, Leiko thought about what she'd just heard.

It was a trap. They bugged the plane and heard me talking on the flight from Cleveland. They knew I was coming for the Buddha and set a trap. They must have the real Hilda Byers, and that means McCoy has the Buddha. He knows I want it, and I'll be coming for it. He thinks all he has to do is wait.

Well, he's in for a surprise. I have something he wants even more than the Buddha.

52

GENEVIEVE'S HEAD WAS POUNDING. On top of that, her back hurt. Her arms and legs hurt, and her neck was stiff. Then, realizing that her eyes were closed she opened them. The last she remembered she was about to get in her car after work at the museum. *Was that yesterday?*

She heard road noises and realized she was in the back of some kind of vehicle, maybe a van. She tried to get up, but found she was restrained. She could reach her left wrist with her right hand. Chains. Also, a chain around her waist.

She could see out the side windows. It was light outside and she saw lots of pine trees, but no palms. Somehow this didn't look like Florida. Had she been unconscious all night? Suddenly the vehicle must have left the pavement, because the ride got softer. They must have turned onto a dirt road. The vehicle drove forward for another few minutes and stopped.

She could hear voices, male, at least two. The back door swung open, and the bright light made her squint. They had her sit up, thrust a newspaper into her hands, and told her to hold it in front of her. After photographing her, they unchained her and led her out of the vehicle. They were Asian. Firmly, they led her to what looked to be a log cabin in the pine woods. And it was cold. This was definitely not Florida.

"Who are you?" she demanded. "What are you doing?"

"Shut up and you won't get hurt."

"I demand—"

The one who had told her to shut up slapped her across the face, hard enough to make her eyes water.

"You'll demand nothing. With any luck you may survive this. If not, you won't."

Instead of leading her to the cabin, they followed a path around to a small wooden building about the size of a large tool shed. There was a single door in the front.

After they pushed her inside, she could hear them locking it from the outside. She stumbled further in, realizing how much she ached. Her head was still pounding but she thought it was a little better. Where was she?

She saw no windows, but still the interior was lit. Looking up, she saw why. There as a small skylight in the ceiling and two small windows high on the wall, enough to illuminate the room. They offered no way out even if she could reach them. They were too small, apparently for illumination only.

She was in the smaller of two rooms. There were benches against two of the walls and a divider separating a toilet and sink. Everything was knotty pine—the walls, the benches, the floor, and the ceiling.

The larger of the two rooms held much the same, except the benches were on two levels and in one corner an iron stove stood adjacent to a container of large black stones.

For the first time she noticed heavy-duty light fixtures in the ceiling of both rooms. Then she saw the light switches. They worked. What was this place? Then it came to her. This was a sauna. She'd never been in one before, but she'd read about them.

Genevieve tried the door. It was definitely locked. She could see no other way out. Resigned for the moment, she sat on a bench and checked her arms and legs. Everything moved, and except for bruise marks where she was chained, apparently unhurt. She guessed the aches in her back and limbs were from the bumpy ride in the back of the van. The headache was probably from whatever they'd drugged her with.

They. Who were they? It had to be Leiko. What did they expect to get by kidnapping her? Hunter had told her about the Buddha and that Emma Johannson had donated it to the Salvation Army and that Leiko had found that out too.

What had the guy said? "If you're lucky, you might survive this?" So if Leiko thought Hunter might get the Buddha first, she could be holding her to trade for the statue if it came to that. Convinced that was the answer, she turned her attention to how to get away. She examined the structure again, this time focusing on any weak spot that might conceivably be an escape route.

She started in the small room with the door to the outside. She saw no hinges. They had to be on the outside. Maybe she could pick the lock with something in her purse. Where was her purse? It was gone. No tools and no cellphone. The walls looked strong and solid, and the floor appeared to be pine planks over a concrete slab. Both rooms had a drain set in the floor.

Just as she was about to sit on a bench in despair, she heard someone at the door.

"Step back into the back room and put your hands above your head."

She did as she was told just as the door opened and one of the men stood there pointing a gun directly at her. The other man came in and set a grocery bag on the bench. He went back out and appeared again, this time with a woolen blanket that he tossed on the other bench. They left and locked the door again.

She opened the grocery bag and found two cans of beer and something hot wrapped in paper. She unwrapped the paper and revealed what looked like a pastry crust around lumpy hot material inside. She tore off one end and discovered it was cooked meat and potatoes, maybe some onion, she couldn't tell. It smelled good, and she suddenly realized she was hungry. How long ago had they taken her? When was the last time she ate?

She took a bite. It was good, and knew she had to keep her strength up, so she began to eat the rest. She didn't drink beer, so she opened one can, poured it out onto the drain in the floor in the larger room with the stove, and filled it with water from the tap.

As if she didn't know, the blanket told her she was going to be there overnight. Fortunately, she'd worn slacks to work and a long-sleeved blouse, but that's all she had. If the temperature dropped, she hoped the blanket would be enough.

The light through the skylight and small windows was starting to get dim. She turned on the light switches, and both rooms lit up. At least she had that, she thought. She turned her attention to the iron stove. Next to it were several appropriately cut logs that would fit the opening and a small amount of kindling. Genevieve knew how to start a fire, as in England, her parents had a similar stove. But what about matches?

She looked and looked but saw none anywhere. Finally, she spotted what she'd missed before because it fit so perfectly into the knotty pine walls. Near one of the benches was a small drawer, seemingly of a piece with the wooden wall panel. She pulled it open and found a full box of kitchen stove matches.

Then she noticed something else. Everything in here was new. So new, it was unused. She opened the stove and looked in. Spotless. There'd never been a fire in it.

Then, both to test it, and because she had to use it, she tried the toilet. It flushed. So, everything worked—the plumbing, the electricity, and presumably she could even make a fire to keep warm, at least until the stack of wood gave out.

Gratified by that, it suddenly came to her—this was Hunter's. Hunter had told her he'd been in Michigan building a sauna as a surprise for his dad. That was it, this was his sauna. She was in Upper Michigan. No wonder it was cool outside.

53

HUNTER AND WALLY OSBORN interviewed the woman pretending to be Carrie Johannson and gleaned all they could from her by noon.

Wally Osborn said, "I've put an APB out for the car they were in, based on the description the woman gave. But without a state or plate number, chances of picking her up are slim to none."

"One thing we can be sure of," Hunter said, "she'll be coming for me, figuring I've got the Buddha. Call me if you hear from Jenkins and he has any information."

"You got it."

Hunter drove to Genevieve's house and decided to lie down and nap. When he awoke and looked at his watch he found it was after seven. Where was Genevieve? She should have been home by now. He called her number again. Still no answer.

Something's wrong.

He called Genevieve's co-worker at the Ringling, the resident curator of pre-twentieth-century Western art.

"Genevieve hasn't come home," he told her, "and she doesn't answer her cell. Was she at work today?"

"No, she wasn't in all day. In fact, I wondered about that, because we had plans to work on a project together. Do you think something's wrong?"

"I don't know. Maybe. If you hear from her, call me, okay?"

"Of course. Now you have me worried. Where else could she be?"

"I don't know, but I'm going to keep looking. I'll call you if I learn anything."

He hung up and called Carrie Johannson, on the odd chance that she might have heard from her.

"No," Carrie answered. "I haven't heard from her. Maybe you should check with your dad."

"Good idea. I'll call him next."

"Do you think it's Leiko?" his dad asked when Hunter told him Genevieve was missing.

Hunter closed his eyes, sighing deeply. "I hope not. But if it is, that woman will wish she'd never been born."

"You be careful, Hunter."

It was now eight-thirty. She'd certainly have called him by now if she been able to. Leiko must have grabbed her somehow. But where would she keep her? If she had her she was undoubtedly planning to use her as a pawn in exchange for the Buddha. Leiko knew he had it and would want to trade. By now she'd know that the mobile home park was a trap, since her surrogate hadn't returned. He tried Genevieve's cell again but didn't even get the messaging service this time. It had either been turned off or was out of power.

What could he do? The police were looking for Leiko's car, but that was a longshot. It made no sense for her to leave town, since what she really wanted was the Buddha and he had it. So she'd likely stay here and make contact with him. He hated to just wait but couldn't come up with an alternate plan.

Frustrated at waiting, he felt he had to do something, so he called Detective Wilbur Jenkins in Chicago.

"I know Leiko is here in Sarasota," he told him. "I think she's taken Genevieve Swift. I believe she wants to trade her for a statue of a Buddha that I have. She thinks it contains a map to a treasure she's been looking for. I managed to get the statue before she did. I'm fairly certain she's taken Genevieve and plans to trade her for it."

"Hold on a minute, McCoy."

Hunter waited. In a few minutes, Jenkins was back on the line. "What I'm going to tell you now is strictly between you and me and Lana. It's too sensitive to go any further than that. Okay?"

"Sure. What do you know?"

"One of Leiko's lieutenants, Solomon Ito, contacted me last night on my personal cellphone. I have no idea how he got the number. Anyway, he told me he believes that Leiko is on the verge of uncovering a huge treasure of some kind—must be the one you're talking about. He apparently bugged her office and overheard her saying that she was going to find it and keep it for herself. After that she'd disappear and sell the organization down the river, including Ito and her pilot, Kim Zhang.

"I asked Ito what he wanted," Jenkins continued. "He said he'd cooperate with me if I could guarantee him and the pilot some kind of immunity from prosecution."

"What did you tell him?"

"I said I'd have to talk with the DA. Which I'll be doing in—twenty-five minutes. It looks like the wheels are finally starting to fall off the wagon for Leiko Yamashita."

"Yeah," Hunter said, "and that makes her all the more dangerous. Where's her pilot now?"

"We know he flew to Sarasota yesterday. We had her plane bugged and knew about the planned meeting with Hilda Byers because she talked openly about it on the flight. Seems the lady has a habit of talking to herself—out loud. That's something new. We didn't know that before. After they deplaned in Sarasota she must have gotten suspicious, because the next morning she had the pilot search the aircraft and he found the bug. Then he filed a flight plan for New Orleans but never showed up. We're still trying to find out where he is."

Hunter paused. "He'll be somewhere in Florida. She'll want to keep him and the plane close for a fast flight to parts unknown."

"I expect you're right."

"Like I said, she knows I have the Buddha, so she'll be contacting me for an exchange with Genevieve. I just wish to hell I had a way to get to her first."

"Now don't take this the wrong way, McCoy, but will you trade with her?"

"Of course. She can have the damn thing."

54

LEIKO SMILED TO HERSELF AS SHE SIPPED coffee in her room at the old one-story strip motel along Route 41 just south of downtown Sarasota. She'd ditched the car.

She checked the bedside clock—8:43 a.m.

Finishing the coffee she'd made using the equipment in the room, she called the two Tanaka brothers on the burner phone she'd purchased the night before at a Dollar Store while wearing a disguise.

"Tell me everything is under control."

"It is. We're holding the woman in the sauna. There's no way she can get out. We just now brought her some food. She's pissed."

"Good. If she gives you any trouble, rough her up a little, but not too much. I need her to bargain with. I'll call you later with further instructions."

She turned her thoughts to the Filipino. For his sake, he'd better be up to this. He'd told her he knew the Philippines like the back of his hand. Every corner of it. "If the map points to the treasure, I'll be able to get us there," he'd said.

Even though the man was a Japanese citizen, he'd grown up in the Philippines. His father had been abandoned there at the end of the war by the defeated Japanese army. Not wanting to attempt returning to Japan, he'd created a new identity and married a Filipino woman—the Filipino's mother. Unable to get work in the war-ravaged country, they'd started their own business, guiding anyone who could pay to sites of interest. Often this was the home village of some relative the client hadn't seen in a long time. Also, the Americans needed direction, and he became an expert at touring them around.

After his father died, the Filipino continued doing this work for an increasingly varied clientele. He'd even done some work for Ferdinand Marcos himself, who'd heard of his amazing knowledge of the country.

Leiko needed him to make sense of the map she expected to have soon. This map, possible written by her great-grandfather himself, would lead her to the Glorious Store. The references to it in the diary, the notebook, and the bamboo-framed saying on her father's wall, all convinced her the treasure was hidden in the Philippines. Once she had the map, and with the Filipino's help, she'd locate the fortune and disappear.

She'd been working on the plans for remaking herself, with a new identity, a new face, and a new country, for some time now. Everything was in place and only awaited her locating the Glorious Store to activate it. She'd no longer be Leiko Yamashita from Chicago, wanted by the police, but instead an unrecognizable new person with a new identity and a vast fortune in a faraway place.

One thing she hadn't yet decided on was how to complete the righteous vengeance for her great-grandfather's betrayal. She'd already done this for the Chen family, when she'd killed Billie Chen, but the McCoys were another matter. Hunter had managed to interfere with her plans for convicting his father for the murder of Scott Harrison. The police were now focused on her. She had to give him credit for accomplishing that. She hadn't thought it possible. Well, she wouldn't underestimate him again.

She considered the possibility that her vengeance would have to be delayed until after her transformation. The problem with that was that she planned for "Leiko Yamashita" to be killed in a highly visible way with no body found. She hoped that this would stop the police from continuing to look for her and she could get on with her new life and identity unencumbered by looking over her shoulder all the time.

But if things started happening to the McCoys and their friends after that, they might re-evaluate whether she was really dead. She'd have to give this some thought.

By now McCoy would have noticed that his girlfriend was missing and assumed that she had her. He would know that an exchange was the only possibility. He had no way to contact her; he had no choice but to wait for her to call him.

He would have only one motivation—to get Swift back safely, she thought. He knew that she has two motivations. One was to get the map the other was the family vengeance. Before he turned that map over, she'd have to convince him that the Swift woman would be safely returned unharmed.

He had to be convinced that Leiko was done seeking vengeance and her only interest was in the map. He would demand that she stop all hostility toward his family and friends. She'd agree to that, but he would demand proof.

She began to smile as she thought, *I know a way.*

GENEVIEVE WAS COLD, ANGRY, AND ACHING. She'd spent the night wrapped in the blanket on the top bench in the sauna. The hard boards only further amplified the pain in her muscles and joints she'd developed during the long ride from Florida to Michigan chained in the back of the van. The two guys had brought her food an hour ago, so at least they weren't planning to starve her to death.

She'd thought about her predicament continually during the night and was now fully convinced that she was here as a bargaining chip. Hunter would give Leiko the Buddha she wanted so badly, and Leiko would give her to Hunter in exchange. She had to admit the dragon lady had planned it pretty well. The trouble was, Genevieve didn't believe her for a minute. While the woman might want this treasure or whatever it was, badly, she wasn't going to give up on her quest for vengeance against the McCoys.

Genevieve knew that Leiko held all the cards and wasn't going to give them away in a straight barter. Whatever she arranged with Hunter was going to be a trap. No doubt about it. Someone as demented as her wouldn't give up so easily. Genevieve had to get out of here on her own and shift things in their favor.

Once again, she started a complete examination of the sauna's two rooms. There had to be a way out. If she could find it, she could safely escape through the woods and get help. This time she noticed that the bottom bench in the sauna room, unlike the one above it, had boards across the front as well as the seat. She got down on hands and knees and tried to see what was behind them. It was dark in there, even with the overhead lights on, but she thought the wall behind looked different than the rest.

She scanned the room for something to use as a pry bar. She spotted a sturdy-looking metal bar holding the wood-burning stove to the wall. It looked like it might do the job, but how to get it unbolted from the wall and the stove? She tried turning the bolts with her fingers. No luck there. She needed a tool. She found a fork that had come with her breakfast, held the tines up to the bolt, bent back two of them in the middle, and shoved the space against the head of the bolt. It might work as a wrench. She tried the makeshift wrench and with a little effort the bolt began to turn. She discovered that she could turn it the rest of the ways with her fingers.

Leaving it in place she did the same with the second bolt. Not wanting the men to notice anything, she left the bolts in place, but loose. Then she straightened out the fork and replaced it on the tray. Returning to the metal bar, she removed the bolts with her fingers, freed the bar, and tried it on the wood boards on the bench. She pried one end loose and pulled it forward, so she could look behind it.

The wall was definitely different here. Instead of knotty pine boards, she saw two-by-four studs separated by sixteen inches. Apparently, the only wall here was whatever the outer wall of the building was made of.

This could be a way out.

55

SOLOMON ITO RECEIVED A PHONE CALL FROM PILOT KIM Zhang shortly after he landed at the airport in Tallahassee. He'd had to do some fast talking with the tower as to why there was no flight plan. He told Solomon he had made up a story that the owner of the plane—his boss—was always fearful for his life and liked to remain hard to get. The local authorities hadn't bought it but eventually relented.

"Listen, Solomon, when we landed in Sarasota, Leiko had me search the plane for recording devices. I found one near the passenger seats. She's convinced it had to be that Chicago PD detective, Jenkins. Was it him?"

"It must be. He's been after her for a long time. I don't know who else would do it." Solomon had never told Kim about bugging Leiko's office, so his cousin would have no reason to suspect that he'd done it. But in fact, he hadn't, so it probably was Jenkins.

Zhang paused, before getting to what was really on his mind. "Is she really going to do it? Is she going to dump us?"

"Yeah, I'm convinced she is," Leiko's lieutenant replied. "I've heard her say it out loud to herself. She didn't know I heard, but I did."

"She said it to herself? Maybe she was just kidding," Kim said, grasping at anything that might suggest she wasn't planning to throw them all under the bus.

"Kim, listen to me. You and I have kept our hands cleaner than anyone else in the organization over the years. So we're probably the least vulnerable to serious legal charges. But we're not blameless and in the clear either. Still, I think I see a way out for us."

"What are you talking about?" the pilot asked.

Solomon paused. "Where are you right now?"

"I'm in my room at the Holiday Inn. Why?"

"Okay, Kim. We've got to talk about this."

"I'm not going to like this, am I?"

"She's going to sell us all down the river as soon as she has this treasure she's looking for. That even includes the Filipino as soon as his contribution is over. The only way out for you and me is to cooperate with the cops."

"What? Are you nuts?"

"Calm down and just think about this for a minute. She's about to get the Buddha and the map, which means she's about to get the treasure. At that point she doesn't need us at all. In fact, we're a liability. If she gives us up, we could all go to prison for life. I say we beat her to it. We give her up first. I'll talk to Jenkins and tell him we can supply information in return for immunity or leniency. They're liable to deal with us because, like I said, we're less culpable than almost anyone else."

"Jeez, Solomon, I don't know. That's a hell of a risk. They could just grab us right there and arrest us. No deal, no nothing."

"I've thought of that. Our only hope is to promise something so big against her it'll stand up in court."

"You've got something like that?"

"I do."

"What?"

"I don't want to talk about it on the phone. You stay put and wait for her to contact you. Then do whatever she asks. If she asks you to pick her up and fly her somewhere, call me and tell me where. I need to know where she is at all times. Do you understand?"

"Sure. I can do that. That's easy."

Solomon sat back in his chair. Part of him couldn't believe what he was about to do. Another part told him he had no choice. He picked up his phone and called Detective Wilbur Jenkins for the second time.

Two hours later, after a cab ride, a trip on the subway, and another cab ride to avoid being followed, Solomon ended up at the police station and was immediately taken to Detective Jenkins. Solomon found himself sweating. He'd never been in a police station before.

"Mr. Ito. What do you want?" Jenkins asked.

Solomon was surprised at himself. He never quivered when dealing with Leiko, in spite of what he knew about her capacity for cruelty. But here, out of his element, he fidgeted nervously.

"If Kim Zhang and I give you information that can put Leiko Yamashita behind bars, can you guarantee immunity for us?"

Jenkins met his eyes and Solomon squirmed. "The District Attorney says she'll listen to your offer. Are you ready to talk to her now?"

"Now?"

"Yes, now. Her office is upstairs."

"I—yeah, sure. Now is good."

Wilbur Jenkins made a call, then said to Solomon, "Okay, let's go."

In the elevator Solomon rehearsed what he was going to say. Once he talked, he knew there'd be no turning back. He and Kim would be out there on their own, at the mercy of both Leiko and the Chicago PD.

Once they entered her office, Solomon instantly recognized the District Attorney from TV and the newspapers. She was a tough woman in her early fifties who won most of her cases and didn't like to lose. She didn't rise from her chair behind a huge desk, but simply eyed Solomon and let him stand.

"Mr. Ito, I'm not a woman who likes to waste time. Tell me what you have to offer on Leiko Yamashita and I'll tell you what we're prepared to do for you and your cousin. Please, have a chair."

Solomon sat. He knew he couldn't give it all away but had to tell her what he could deliver in exchange for a break for him and Kim. He'd thought this over carefully.

"I've been working for Leiko Yamashita for the past three years. I brought in my cousin, Kim Zhang, as her pilot at that time, as she'd decided she needed her own plane. My job was to organize her office. My background before taking the job had been as an office manager for one of her father's front companies, Yamashita Properties, Inc. I'd been with them five years before moving to Leiko's office three years ago.

"While I was working for Yamashita Properties, I had no idea of the family's criminal activities. It wasn't until after I moved to the main office and brought my cousin onboard that we both came to realize what kind of outfit we worked for. During the past three years, I've learned enough about the criminal activities of the operation and Leiko's involvement in running it that if I turn it over to you, you would have no trouble bringing her down."

"What concrete evidence do you have?" the DA asked.

"I've made copies of letters, notes, bills of sale, payoffs to assassins within her group. Believe me, it's a treasure trove. I've got all of it in a secure place, and I'll deliver it to you in exchange for immunity for Kim Zhang and myself."

The DA sat back and stared at Solomon for a long moment before speaking. "Why this sudden change of heart? Why are you coming to us with this now?"

"Six months ago, I began bugging her office. It was risky, I know. But I did it for my own protection. I didn't learn anything of interest until she read Scott Harrison's book, *Surrenders In The Pacific*. She has a habit of talking to herself out loud. She started railing against someone name Karl McCoy, saying he'd betrayed the general. I knew she meant her great-grandfather, General Tomoyuki Yamashita, who was tried and executed for war crimes at the end of World War Two. She also screamed out against someone called Dr. Chen. I didn't know what she meant or who these people were until I read the book myself.

"About a week later I heard her talking to herself again. She said 'Well, Billie Chen, you've just paid for your grandfather's betrayal. The McCoys are next.

"One day she brought in Akito Hano and Ryuki Ono, her two most trusted gunmen. I heard her tell them to get to Sarasota, Florida, check into a room, and wait for her instructions. She told them she was going to have a personal talk with Scott Harrison about a missing notebook. Two days later, Scott Harrison was murdered in Florida.

"She was gone for two weeks. I don't know what was going on during that time. I was out of touch with her. But when she returned to the office, she called in a man known as the Filipino. That's when I heard all I needed to know. The transcript of their conversation alone will put her in prison for life. But what shocked me and the reason I'm here now is what I overheard her say about her plans for the organization once she got her hands on a certain map.

"She told the Filipino that if he helped her use the map to find her\ great-grandfather's treasure, his reward would be very generous. They wouldn't have to share the fortune with anyone else because she planned to betray them all to the authorities. This included—and she named us specifically—me, Kim Zhang, and the rest of the organization. All of this is recorded, and I have it, along with the incriminating papers. I'm prepared to give it all to you in exchange for immunity for Kim and myself."

The DA looked at Jenkins, then back at Solomon.

"Mr. Ito, you have a deal."

56

HUNTER, FRUSTRATED AT SEEING NO WAY TO PROCEED on his own initiative against Leiko, paced the living room of Genevieve's house when his cell rang.

"McCoy, it's Jenkins."

"What do you have?"

The detective went on to explain about the deal with Solomon Ito and Kim Zhang. "They can supply us with enough evidence to bring her down for good. Once we have her in custody, The DA will see to it that she and her organization are finished. I know this is good for us but not necessarily for you. Still, it gives us leverage we didn't have before."

"Great," Hunter agreed. "So if she contacts the pilot to take her somewhere, we get her."

"That's right. He's in Tallahassee, waiting instructions from her. We believe she has no idea that he and Ito have turned on her. She won't be careless, she never is, but she won't suspect anything either. That should work in our favor. We told Solomon Ito that we believe she's taken Genevieve to hold as ransom for the statue. We asked if he had any idea where she might be keeping her."

"Did he know that she's been taken?" Hunter asked.

"No, he knew nothing about it. I believe him. The same with the pilot."

"What about where she might keep her?" Hunter asked.

"No idea. But he told us about two warehouses she owns that we didn't know about before. I've got men checking them out now. We'll know within the hour."

"So that means she's still here, unless she's gotten a car or flown out under an assumed name."

"Another thing, McCoy," Jenkins continued. "She's paying cash and not using credit cards. Ito told us he'd shipped her a large sum of cash so she should be able to stay below the radar until that runs out. If she needs more cash, she'll have to contact him. If she does, we'll get her when she picks it up. Also, the Florida Highway Patrol, the Sarasota County Sheriff, and the Sarasota Police have been updated on the new information and all have arrest warrants out for her."

"Thanks, Jenkins. I appreciate it."

"We'll get her, McCoy."

Hunter walked out on the lanai overlooking Sarasota Bay and considered his options. Just sitting around and waiting for a call from Leiko didn't sit right with him. He had to do something, so he called Hilda Byers.

"Ms. Byers? This is Hunter McCoy. If no one's told you, you're free to return to your house. You've been a big help. We didn't catch her yet, but we will."

"Thanks. I am home. Detective Osborn called and said I could return."

"That's great. Would you mind if I came over for a few minutes? I have a couple of questions you might be able to help me with."

"Yeah. Come on over. This has been quite an adventure. I'll be here."

Hunter could have asked his questions over the phone, but he needed to do something and was too wound up to just sit and wait. Twenty minutes later he pulled into her driveway at the mobile home park. He got right to it.

"I want you to think back to when you first got the call from the woman who said she was Carrie Johannson. Did she say or give you any idea where she was?"

"Let me think. No. But now that I think about it, she must have been out of town, because when I said to come over, she just said 'I'll see you tomorrow.' I mean, I got the call just after lunch, so there would have been plenty of time to come over that day, especially as she seemed pretty hot to get the Buddha."

"That's good, Hilda. That helps," Hunter said, knowing that her assessment fit the facts as they knew them. Her pilot had flown her from Cleveland to Sarasota that evening. Then he took off again for New Orleans but detoured to Tallahassee. Leiko had apparently rented a car under an assumed name and stayed somewhere that night. The next day they trained the substitute Hilda and set up the meet, only Leiko took a page from their playbook and sent a substitute Leiko instead. She was clearly playing this very carefully.

Before Hunter could ask another question, his cell rang. It was Wally Osborn.

"I've got some news. A woman fitting Leiko's description rented a black Nissan Sentra from Hertz under the name Connie Tomoyuki. The clerk identified her from your photo. She registered under that name at the Starlight Motel south of downtown the same night she flew from Cleveland. She paid cash both times. She checked out of the place, ditched the car and we don't know how she's moving about."

"If she checked out this morning," Hunter said, "she must still be in the area."

"That's my guess. We have people watching at the airport, the bus station, and the car rental agencies. She's got to be feeling the pinch."

"Good. That means she'll have to contact me sooner rather than later. She must still have cash, or she would have asked Solomon for additional money by now. Jenkins will let me know if and when she does."

Hunter thanked Hilda for her cooperation and left. With nowhere else to go, he returned to Genevieve's house. After parking in the demolished carport, he walked to the side door and stopped dead in his tracks. Taped to the door was a note.

I've got her.

He crouched, pulled out his gun, and scanned the yard. Nothing. He carefully covered the entire yard around the house from the street to the retaining wall on the bay. Nothing. Back to the door he carefully tried it. Locked. Apparently, she hadn't gotten in. He used his key to open the door, then slowly, carefully entered and began a search. He found nothing. No more notes. Nothing disturbed.

Taking a tissue from a box on the kitchen counter, he returned to the door and carefully removed the note. He'd get this to Wally to check for prints, although he doubted they'd find any. It wasn't signed, but he had no doubt it was from Leiko. Why didn't she call? he wondered. Was she just going to play with him for a while? Maybe this was part of her vengeance thing.

She'll call soon, he thought. She'll want to trade for the Buddha. Obviously, she was afraid to use the phone for fear of being tracked—that's why the note.

He called Osborn. "Wally, she just left a note saying 'I've got her' taped to Genevieve's door. You can check it for prints. If she's going to use notes to communicate, she must be nearby and maybe she has Genevieve actually with her. There are two big mansions on this street whose owners must be gone, since their hurricane shutters are up. It would be a perfect place for her to hide. Can you get into them?"

"Don't know the law on that. Let me check. I'll call you back."

While he waited, Hunter walked down the street and checked the addresses of the two homes. Both were on the bay and had to be worth several million each. He had a feeling about this. It would be a perfect way for Leiko to be close and not be seen. The huge stone Mediterranean-style mansions both had boat docks on the bay and yachts up on lifters. The owners probably had other homes they were currently visiting. Since the hurricane season in Florida extends from June through November, they were prepared while they were away.

Wally called. "The judge says that if we have probable cause, we can enter. Wait for me. I'll be right over."

A half hour later, Hunter, Osborn, and two uniformed officers entered and carefully examined both shuttered homes. Thorough searches clearly showed that no one had been there recently.

Hunter was no closer to getting Leiko or finding Genevieve.

57

GENEVIEVE PULLED BACK THE TWO BOARDS that formed the front of the bottom bench in the sauna room. She crawled in to examine the back wall. Unlike the rest of the room it wasn't covered in knotty pine. Once she got in there she discovered that nevertheless, it was a solid surface, very solid. Seeing no way out through it, she retreated and replaced the boards so as not to alert the guards to her attempt.

Frustrated but unwilling to give up, she searched again for another way. She tried behind the toilet. Nothing there. The two high windows in the entry changing room were too small for her to fit through even if she could get them open. She couldn't even see out through them as they were too high. *Still, it would be nice to see where I am*, she thought. She noticed that the little box next to the toilet containing toilet paper and cleaning materials could be moved. She pushed it over below the windows and stood on it. Perfect. She could see out.

There was the cabin, about twenty meters away, nestled in a heavily wooded setting. If she leaned far enough she could even see the big lake. Hunter had told her it was Lake Superior. It looked as if a storm was on its way. The sky was gray. She stiffened when she saw the door of the cabin open and the two men who'd brought her food earlier step out onto the porch. They started on the path to the sauna.

Quickly she stepped off the box, pushed it back in place, then returned to the sauna room and sat on the lowest bench. Speaking perfect English but with a Japanese accent, one of them shouted, "Step back from the door into the back room."

"I'm already there," Genevieve answered.

It was only mid-morning, too early for lunch. What did they want? She heard them fumbling with the door, and finally it opened.

"What's the combination to the safe?" One of them barked.

"What safe? What are you talking about?" she asked, confused.

"The large safe in the house. What's the combination?"

"How would I know? I've never been here until now."

'You lie. This is your boyfriend's house. Tell us."

"I've never been here and don't know anything about a safe, and I certainly don't know its combination. But, I do want to know why the hell I'm here," she demanded.

They retreated back a few steps from the door and conversed quietly with each other. Finally the leader, or at least she assumed he was the leader, stepped forward, entered the sauna room, and slapped her hard in the face. Not expecting this, Genevieve fell backward and hit her head on the iron stove, then lay on the floor, quiet and unmoving.

"Is she dead?" the smaller one asked, fearfully .

"No, she's just stunned. Get some water and splash it in her face."

The smaller one took the shower hose, coiled and hanging on a hook, and sprayed in it in her face. Genevieve coughed and turned away from the spray. She put her hand to the back of her head, and it came away bloody. And it ached. He sprayed her hand and watched as the blood flowed off.

The taller man, the leader, reached out, pulled a towel from the rack and tossed it to her. She pressed it to the back of her head.

"Why am I here?" Genevieve asked again. "What do you want from me? Who are you?"

"You'll know why you're here when we do. Now shut up and listen. Our orders are to feed you, that's all. If you step out of line, you'll get a hell of a lot worse than a slap in the face. Understand?"

With that, they left and locked the door behind them. She quickly pushed the box over to the window and, fighting dizziness, watched as they walked back to the cabin and disappeared inside. She examined the window again. It was definitely too small to get through.

Sighing, she stepped down to the floor and sat on the box, considering what the tall man had said. "You'll know why you're here when we do." So, they didn't know what this was about either. They were just following orders. She had no doubt whose orders those were—Leiko's. She now officially loathed the woman as much as Hunter did.

By now she was sure Leiko had told Hunter she had her and was demanding the Buddha and map in return. If she could just get out of here and contact him, he wouldn't have to cooperate with her, especially since the map and pages had apparently disintegrated over the years anyway. But how could she get out? He'd built the place like a fort. She'd found no weak spot. The only way in or out was the door.

The door. She turned her attention to it again. The only hardware on the inside was the door lever. How were they keeping her in? If they'd locked it with a key from the outside, all she'd have to do is turn the release to unlock, move the lever up or down, and open the door. She could easily move the lever, but still the door wouldn't open. They must have installed a crossbar or something. Hunter certainly didn't build it so someone could be locked inside.

Maybe she could see through the window. She got up on the box again and tried. No way. She couldn't get enough angle to see the door below her. She did notice, however, that the sky had turned dark and it was beginning to rain.

Maybe whatever they'd built or put up wasn't that strong. She could try kicking it. But how would she do it? She had to turn the lever and hold it open while she tried. But that would have her right up against the door, and she needed to start some distance away to get enough force in her kick. Damn, she thought. If she had tape or something, she could maybe keep the lever open while she stepped back for a go at it.

She looked in vain for anything she could use. What about her prybar? Could she use that somehow? Bringing it out of the back room where she'd propped it up to look like it was still in place, she tried every way she could think of. Nothing worked. The lever always fell back to the closed position. Certain she could do this if she could only find a way to solve this problem, she kept looking for something that might work.

Suddenly she heard a crack of thunder and the pounding of rain on the roof. *This could be good* she thought. *If I ever get this damn thing locked in the open position, they shouldn't hear me slamming at the door.* Energized again to get this to work, she got an idea. The lever was maybe three feet off the floor, and the prybar hadn't work because it was too short. but the boards she'd taken off earlier from the front of the bench were longer. One of them should do the job.

Excited she pulled one of them off easily, since she'd had no way to nail them back in place. She tried it. It worked. It easily propped the lever in the up open position.

The thunder was coming in regular rolls now. This was it. She tried kicking with the bottom of her foot. This wasn't going to work. She couldn't generate enough force. What could she use? Looking back in to the sauna room, she spotted the oak logs that were stacked next to the stove. One of those would be perfect. She selected a sturdy one about a foot and a half long. At the door, she brought it back as far as she could with both hands and then slammed it forward, like a battering ram, with all the force she could generate. At that same instant, a huge crash of thunder erupted overhead.

The door flew open.

58

LEIKO WAS ON THE MOVE. IT HAD BEEN SIX HOURS since she'd left the note on McCoy's door. He should be getting very anxious by now. The thought gave her pleasure. As much as she wanted the treasure, she also wanted the personal satisfaction of avenging her great-grandfather. She, of course, had never met the general; nor had her father, oddly enough. He'd only been a very young boy during the war and had no personal recollection of him. His mother had given him all the information he needed to know about the man.

She'd told him that the general was a kind man, always respectful of her, and an inspiration to the men under his command. He'd been a leader of men from his earliest days in the Imperial Army. Rising rapidly through the ranks, he became General of all Japanese forces in the Philippines shortly after the invasion of the islands. His mother told him that the treasure he'd amassed and hidden was for the use of the government to pursue the war to ultimate victory. It was never intended to be used by him personally. The whole idea that it was, was ludicrous.

The trumped-up charges against him at his trial after the war were just an excuse for the Allies to find and take the gold, and anything else that made up the so-called Glorious Store, for themselves. That such an honorable man would be betrayed by Chen and McCoy and turned over to the enemy was a crime beyond imagining. Leiko's father had reminded her of all this on his deathbed and sworn her to avenge the family's honor. She fully intended to do that.

GENEVIEVE RAN OUT INTO THE RAIN AND DOWN the gravel driveway to what she assumed led to the main road. She knew she didn't have much time. She didn't know if they were planning to give her lunch or just something at night, but she had to assume lunch, so she figured that gave her— at the most—only an hour. The rain was torrential, and she was instantly soaked through. Still, she ran until she found a paved road that looked as if it would take her—if she could get a ride—to a town where the authorities could help.

She decided on a direction and tried to flag down a passing car. After being passed up by three of them, a pickup truck slowed, then stopped and backed up. The driver held open the passenger door while she jumped in. The driver, a kindly looking elderly man, said. "Good lord. What are you doing out in this?" as he started heading down the road.

"Oh, thank you. Can you take me to the police? I've just escaped from kidnappers."

"What? Oh my God. Kidnappers? Yeah, sure. The sheriff's in Marquette. That's where I'm going. Are you all right?"

"Yes. I'm okay," she answered, while reflexively checking the back of her head

He reached behind the seat and gave her a towel. She dried herself up as much as she could. She had no purse or comb, so she used her fingers to do the job on her hair.

"You have an accent," the man said. "Where are you from? By the way, my name's, Will."

"Genevieve. The accent is French. I'm from Paris."

Two minutes later a van passed them on the left. Genevieve glanced over. It was them.

The man not driving pointed to her. There was no doubt they recognized her. Damn, she thought, how had they discovered her missing so quickly?

"That's them," she shouted to Will, "The kidnappers."

Will sped up his old pickup, but it was no match for their van. The driver kept nudging them over to the right. The rain had started again, heavily. Genevieve looked out the window to the side of the paved road. There was no shoulder, only a dip into a storm gutter and then the white birch forest. The van sideswiped the pickup with a scraping noise.

"Shit, they're going to force us off the road!" will shouted.

The van moved left about two feet, and both Genevieve and Will saw what he was going to do next. He'd slam into them and force them off. Will hit the brakes just as the van swerved right so the kidnapper only caught the left front bumper of the truck. Still, it was enough to send them into the ditch and the trees.

Sometime later Genevieve woke and found herself lying on the road with an emergency medical team lifting her onto a stretcher. She saw the circling red lights of their vehicles and slowly she remember what happened. "Will? Is Will all right?"

"If you mean the man in the truck with you, yes, he'll be all right."

"What about the van that hit us? There were two men."

"Now you just relax. There'll be time for questions later."

"Dammit, they kidnapped me. I was escaping. Where are they?"

"Kidnapped? Just a minute." They set her down and the EMT rushed over to a policeman standing nearby. "The lady says she was kidnapped by the two men in the van."

The officer came over, and as the two men picked up the stretcher again, asked her, "What's your name, ma'am?"

"Genevieve Swift."

Noting her accent, he asked, "Where are you from?"

"I work at an art museum in Sarasota, Florida. The two men in the van kidnapped me and drove me to what I think is Hunter McCoy's cabin. I escaped and Will—the man driving the truck—was taking me to the sheriff's office in Marquette when they ran us off the road."

Then, as the thought just occurred to her, she asked. "Did you get them? The kidnappers?"

"In a way."

"What?"

"They're both dead. You almost were too. We're only fifty yards from a concrete bridge abutment. You missed it, they didn't."

"Two Asian men, maybe in their late thirties or early forties?"

"Yes."

The officer went back to his patrol car, presumably to phone this in while the medical team lifted her into an ambulance.

It wasn't until the two attendants started working on her that she noticed the intense pain of her dislocated right shoulder.

59

GENEVIEVE SLOWLY CAME TO IN A CLEAN BED with fresh sheets. Foggy for a moment about where she was, she quickly remembered what led up to this. She'd escaped and been in a truck crash. She tried to reach up to push the hair away from her forehead, but her right arm was wrapped and restrained.

"Welcome back," a friendly nurse said. Then, in answer to Genevieve's unasked question, added, "Your shoulder was dislocated, and it's been put right. It'll be sore for a while, but it'll be fine. You're pretty lucky nothing else happened. The truck you were in was badly damaged."

"And the man who was driving?" Genevieve asked.

"His face is bruised and we're keeping him for observation. He's in the room next door. His biggest problem has been explaining to his wife what he was doing with a beautiful young woman in his truck."

She said this with a smile and a wink.

"The sheriff's been waiting to talk with you. I'll tell him you're up. He's next door talking with your driver."

While she went to get him, Genevieve closed her eyes briefly and thought, "I hope this whole nightmare ends soon."

A large uniformed man in his sixties came into the room.

"Ms. Swift, I'm Sheriff John Destramp. I'm a friend of both Ed and Hunter McCoy. Tell me what happened to you."

"I've heard Hunter mention you."

Genevieve went on to explain all she could remember, starting from when she left work at the Ringling and was apparently grabbed by the two men in the parking lot until she woke up on the side of the road with the medical team hovering over her.

Then she gasped. "I've got to call Hunter, right away. He doesn't know what happened to me. He'll be frantic."

Destramp put up his palms. "Don't worry. I've already called him and told him you're all right and safe with us. I also told him your kidnappers were dead. We've identified them, with the help of the Chicago Police. Hunter also told me the whole story about Leiko Yamashita."

Genevieve lay back. "Thank you for calling him," she said.

"Now I have a proposal for you." The Sheriff said. "I've talked this over with Hunter and he agrees it's the best way forward." The sheriff explained the plan. Genevieve closed her eyes and nodded yes.

HUNTER WAS OVERJOYED TO KNOW THAT GENEVIEVE was safe. The call from Destramp was like being thrown a lifeline after falling off a ship. She was out of Leiko's grasp and safe in Marquette. Her two kidnappers were dead, but there was no way Leiko could know this. That was going to work in his favor.

His phone rang; it was Genevieve.

"Hi, Babe. How's the shoulder?"

"Oh, Hunter. It'll be fine. It's so good to hear your voice."

"Yours too, believe me. You were amazing, getting out of the sauna, hitching a ride, and taking care of your kidnappers too."

"Yeah, about that sauna. You're going to need a new door when this is all over. I smashed it down."

"Do I even want to know how you did that?"

"Let's just say I put some muscle into it."

"So that's why your shoulder is dislocated."

"Nope. Dislocated it in the crash on the highway."

"Then how'd you break down my door?"

"I'll tell you when we get together. I hope that won't be too long."

"Me too. Meanwhile, Sheriff and Mrs. Destramp get to enjoy you as an exquisite and entertaining houseguest."

"Take care, my love, and put the dragon lady away."

60

LEIKO HAD DRIVEN ANOTHER RENTAL TAKEN OUT UNDER one of the alternate names and driver's licenses she traveled with to Arcadia, a small town about fifty miles inland from Sarasota known as the rodeo capital of Florida. She planned to hole up there and use the town as a base of operations for the next phase of her plan. After the drive through the flat Florida countryside, she'd arrived and checked into a room at the Bucking Bronco Motel. *Good cover,* she thought.

Once in her room she considered her next move. Pasting another note on Hunter's door would be too dangerous. She knew that, while a burner phone couldn't be traced to an exact location, the police could tell which tower carried the signal, giving them a known radius from that tower. Too close. She planned to drive about a hundred miles away from Arcadia, calculating that would put her in another tower's reach. Then, she'd use a burner to send a text to McCoy.

Before leaving, she called to tell her two men at the Michigan cabin to take a new photo of Genevieve Swift holding the current edition of *USA Today* and text it to her immediately. She got no answer. Next she tried the 360 app to verify where they were. They were still at the cabin, and both phones were charged.

Why the hell don't they answer? She thought.

She would have to send the picture of the woman holding the paper from two days ago that she had on her phone. McCoy would want something more recent, of

course. Well too bad. That was all she had, and it would
have to be enough. Far from Arcadia she sent the proof-of-
life photo to McCoy and then tried her two men again. *Why
weren't they answering their phones?* She was going to
enjoy getting rid of those two losers. She had no intention
of turning over the woman to McCoy either. Killing her
would be part of her vengeance. If her plan worked as set
up, she'd get the Buddha and map, and the McCoys and the
Swift woman would die.

HUNTER'S PHONE SOUNDED A TEXT ALERT. The message
said, "instructions to follow." It contained a photo of
Genevieve, restrained in the back of a vehicle of some kind
holding a newspaper from the day she was apparently
kidnapped. Seeing her chained, even though he knew she
was now safe and unharmed, fired up his anger again.

You're going down, Leiko.

He thought about this. Leiko didn't have Genevieve,
but she obviously wasn't aware of it. The kidnappers must
have found Genevieve gone and just took off after her.
They wouldn't have taken the time to call and tell Leiko.
Nor would they have had the balls. She would think her
two goons still have her locked up in the sauna at the cabin.

He was glad he'd thought earlier to ask Sheriff
Destramp to have one of his men bring the dead men's
cellphones up to his cabin and plug them in. He wanted
Leiko Yamashita to think they were still there for as long as
possible.

Of course, she wouldn't know why they weren't
answering, but at least she'd have to assume they still had
her. One of the sheriff's guys would periodically check to
see if she called and left any messages. Those messages
could be valuable incrimination if she mentioned the
kidnapping. Even without it, Leiko was going down.

Next, he called Detective Wilbur Jenkins in Chicago and brought him up to date on everything that had happened.

Hunter thought about the "proof-of-life" photo of Genevieve in the back of the van holding a two-day old copy of the Sarasota *Herald Tribune*. Destramp had checked on it, and it was definitely the vehicle the two men had died in.

He had to assume that Leiko had been trying to contact them for a more current photo in order to make a deal with him to swap Genevieve for the map.

Both of them had been operating under the assumption that the Buddha statue that the nun brought back contained the missing pages to Chen's research notebook as well as a map to the "Golden Treasure," whatever that was.

He considered the irony of the situation.

She thinks I have the map and will try to swap Genevieve for it.

I know the map and the missing pages are useless dust.
She doesn't know this.

I know she no longer has Genevieve.
She doesn't know this either.

So when she contacts me for the swap, I'll agree, knowing that she has nothing to deal with.

Then I take her down.

THE NEXT MORNING, HUNTER AWOKE TO HIS PHONE'S RING. It was Jenkins again.

"McCoy. Get ready to move. Solomon Ito just got a message from Leiko that she needs some cash."

"Great. Where does he send it and how?"

"She's given him the name of a hotel in Arcadia, Florida. Do you know where that is?"

"Yeah, it's about forty-five miles inland from here."

"Good. The name of the hotel is the Bucking Bronco Inn. The name she gave him is Taylor Min. This morning he'll express mail her a money order for nine thousand dollars made out to that name. She should get it tomorrow."

"That's great. That means she should be there until the mail arrives. We'll get on it right now."

Neither the Sarasota Sheriff's Department nor the Sarasota Police Department had jurisdiction in Arcadia. He'd need the cooperation of the Arcadia police. He called Detective Otto Skaggs. The man was desperate to get Leiko for the murder of Scott Harrison in his jurisdiction on Casey Key. The newspapers had been giving him a hard time for not having made an arrest yet. He'd do everything he could to help.

"I believe I know where Leiko Yamashita is," he told Skaggs." She's out of your jurisdiction in DeSoto County, but you can help."

"Tell me how."

Skaggs was aware that she was also wanted in Chicago for murder and running a criminal gang because he'd cooperated with the man in charge of that investigation, Detective Wilbur Jenkins. He'd coordinated with Detective Wally Osborn of the Sarasota Police Department's homicide division as well.

"Two principals in her organization are cooperating with the Chicago PD," Hunter told Skaggs. She's at the Bucking Bronco Inn in Arcadia, waiting for a money order from one of the men cooperating with the police. I don't know anyone in the Arcadia PD. Can you grease the skids and set something up that involves me being part of the team?"

"Yeah, for sure. I know the DeSoto County Sheriff well. He's a good man. I don't know the police chief, but he will. This will take an hour or two to set up. Where are you now?"

"I'm in Sarasota."

"Well, get down here to my office and we'll drive over there together. Being your creds. You're right, I don't have jurisdiction, but you'll be more believable showing up in a cop car with me than waltzing into the chief's office on your own. While you're driving here, I'll start setting things up."

"Thanks, Detective. See you in forty-five minutes."

ON THE HOUR-LONG DRIVE FROM VENICE TO ARCADIA, Skaggs and Hunter talked about Leiko Yamashita.

"That woman's a real piece of work," Skaggs said. "Jenkins told me about this crime gang she runs. They're into murder-for-hire, drugs, loan sharking, running a protection racket, and God knows what else."

"Yeah," Hunter agreed. "And while she was pretending to be Billie Chen—who we believe she murdered—she was as sweet and defenseless as a lamb. She had me and everyone else totally fooled.

"Equally amazing," Hunter continued, "her sister, Lana Sato, is a homicide detective in Jenkins's department. The two sisters haven't seen each other since they were fourteen, and Lana says Leiko has tried to kill her several times."

Skaggs shook his head. "Sounds like a wonderful family. You know, McCoy, I always thought college professors were supposed to be quiet intellectuals leading boring lives. Where did you go wrong?"

Hunter thought about that. Certainly, the Find-and-Correct work he occasionally did was never boring. Tracking down Leiko Yamashita was certainly not boring.

What about his job at the medical school? Was that boring? No. He loved doing research on vascular smooth muscles and working with the highly inspired post-docs in his lab—young men and women with MD degrees working on their PhDs, or vice versa. The intellectual stimulation involved in designing experiments to unlock the secrets of how blood vessels behave in response to disease was riveting and highly rewarding work. Nothing boring there.

What about teaching medical students? Not boring either. His classes on physiology were attended by some of the brightest students in the country. They always kept him on his toes with insightful questions and novel ideas. Preparing classes for these people required hard work and innovation. Again, nothing boring there.

Hunter turned to Skaggs and addressed his question. "I don't know, Detective, just lucky, I guess."

61

WHEN THEY ARRIVED AT THE DESOTO COUNTY SHERIFF'S office, Hunter was impressed. Skaggs had done his job. The Desoto County sheriff, a man named Norton, was in the process of organizing a task force to surround the hotel, cutting off all escape routes. They'd be in place and ready in another hour. The plan was that Hunter and Skaggs, along with Sheriff Norton, would move in and take her. With six armed men strategically placed around the unit, she'd have no way out.

The sheriff had identified all the cars in the lot. Leiko's rental car, parked in front of the unit, had been registered in the name of Taylor Min. The hotel manager said she'd called the desk and said she was checking out that morning but hadn't done it yet. He was surprised because she had said she expected to be there several days when she'd checked in just the day before. He assumed she was still in her room since her car was there.

Skaggs, Hunter, and the sheriff, all armed and wearing tactical vests, approached the door of the unit. With weapons drawn, the sheriff shouted, "Open up, this is the sheriff."

Nothing.

"Open up, this is Sheriff Norton."

Still nothing.

The sheriff put a key in the lock and standing aside, opened the door.

Skaggs and Hunter burst through, weapons panning the room.

Nothing. No one in the bathroom. The room was empty. Leiko wasn't there.

They scoured the room. No luggage, no clothes in the closet, nothing. Then he saw them. On the nightstand were some plastic cards. One was a driver's license in the name of Taylor Min. Beside it was a VISA card also in the name of Taylor Min. The tape on the back showed that it had probably never been activated.

"Damn," Hunter said, frustrated and angry. "She knew we were coming. Somehow she knew it and leaving these behind was her way of saying she's still way ahead of us."

Norton radioed his men. They'd seen nothing. She hadn't slipped out and past them.

"The car's still here, but I'm sure she isn't," said Hunter. Still, you'd better have your men scour the area and nearby stores to make sure she hasn't walked somewhere."

Norton gave the order, and then the three men returned to the sheriff's office.

"The check from Solomon Ito isn't supposed to turn up until tomorrow," Hunter said, "so she may have a plan to get it then. The owner told me earlier he has a room with two double beds next to the room Leiko rented." Then addressing Skaggs, he said, "You and I could take that room, plant a listening device in hers, and wait it out. What do you say?"

Norton nodded. "I'll call the judge and get permission. When we have it, I'll have my men set up the equipment for you."

Skaggs agreed. "Sounds good to me."

"I'll also have a man in the office when the mail comes in tomorrow," the sheriff said.

Hunter and Skaggs stayed hidden outside and watched the door to Leiko's room until two a.m. She never returned. After that they took turns sleeping while the other stayed outside and watched.

She hadn't shown up by the next morning either. The hotel owner said that the mail usually arrived about eleven am. When it came at eleven-fifteen, they examined it. No overnight express mail addressed to Taylor Min. No overnight express mail at all.

The car was still there, untouched.

She'd fooled them and abandoned the car.

After thanking the sheriff and his men, Hunter and a dejected Detective Skaggs headed back to Venice.

"Do you think she could intercept that overnight letter somewhere along its way?" Hunter asked Skaggs. "Would it have to clear through Sarasota or Venice before it reaches Arcadia? If she somehow knew the route, could she show identification and pick it up at a way station?"

"I don't know," Skaggs said. "I suppose it's possible. I can check when we get back to the office."

"Because I'm thinking," Hunter continued, "she still needs that money. We don't know if she found out we were coming or decided she'd been in one place too long for comfort. Either way, Solomon is her only avenue for cash. I don't think she can afford to let it go. The fact that it wasn't in the mail this morning would mean the USPS isn't doing its job."

"Right, and any time I've used their overnight express service, it gets there," said Skaggs.

"I'll find out all I can about the overnight delivery process and whether she could have intercepted it somewhere along the way. I'll call you when I get something."

"Thanks detective."

HOW DID SHE KNOW WE WERE COMING?

He couldn't get that question out of his head as he drove to the Kingston house. It seemed like ages since he'd checked in with his dad and Henry. For that matter he wondered how Carrie was doing. He'd have to call her later.

As he pulled into the carport at the rental, all the members of the men's book club were already there, sitting in lawn chairs under the shade of a huge live oak tree. He saw Jim Furlow leading a discussion with his dad, Henry, and Joe Palma.

"Hunter," Jim called out as he exited the car and approached the group, "we've just been talking about you, wondering what was going on with the case."

Henry brought out another chair, unfolded it, and indicated it was Hunters.

Hunter sat, took a deep breath, and related events since the guys had sprung the netting trap on Ono and Hano and he'd just learned about the Buddha.

"What about Leiko?" Hunter's dad asked when he finished. "Are you any closer to finding her?"

The other men leaned in to hear his answer.

"We traced her to a hotel in Arcadia, but when we busted the place she was gone. We're still following leads. We'll get her."

The men asked questions for another half hour or so and then disbursed. In the house, Hunter, Henry, and Ed McCoy continued the conversation.

"Hunter, were they keeping her at the cabin? You didn't give any details out there."

"Yeah, they were. I was going to let you discover this on your own, Dad, when you got back up north, but I've got to tell you now. I built you a sauna while I was up there for a few weeks before you called and told me you'd been arrested for murder."

"A sauna?"

"Yeah. They kept her locked in there. She told me she used one of the oak logs I had cut and piled in there for you. She rammed it into the door and knocked it open. She said to tell you she was sorry for wrecking it for you."

"Jeez. That is some woman you've got there, Hunter. Don't ever think of letting her go."

"Don't worry, Dad, I have no intention of letting her go."

62

HUNTER HADN'T SLEPT WELL. HE KEPT ASKING HIMSELF questions. How did she know we were coming? Something spooked her, but what? She certainly hadn't seen the police because she called to say she was checking out before he and Skaggs even got to Arcadia. Somehow she'd been alerted early this morning.

Okay, he continued musing to himself, I've got to think this through. Who knew we were coming early yesterday morning? Checking his phone, he saw he'd gotten the call from Jenkins at 9:30 telling him Leiko was at the Bucking Bronco Inn in Arcadia.

He called the Bucking Bronco Inn and got the manager.

"This is Detective McCoy again. Can you tell me the exact time you got the call from the woman we were after yesterday, saying she was checking out?"

"Sure. Let me check. Okay, here it is. That was at 9:42 a.m."

Hunter thanked him and ended the call.

9:42. Twelve minutes after I got the call from Jenkins.

A very unpleasant thought began to creep into his mind. He sipped his coffee, considering that it could just be a coincidence and he was making something out of it that just didn't exist. Still, he couldn't get it out of his mind. Finally, knowing he needed an answer, he called Detective Jenkins in Chicago.

"I have a question for you," he told Jenkins. "When you called me yesterday morning to tell me Leiko was going to be in the Bucking Bronco Inn in Arcadia?"

"Yeah?"

"Who else heard you make that call?"

"Let's see. Sato was here; we'd been going over plans on how to deal with Solomon Ito. That's it. Nobody else, just the two of us. Why?"

That's got to be it.

"Is she with you now?"

"What? No. Why?"

"Did she stay with you after that or did she leave right away?"

"She left right away. Said she forgot she had a meeting uptown. What are you getting at, McCoy?"

"Think about this. Exactly twelve minutes after your call to me, Leiko told the hotel manager she was checking out. twelve minutes. Something spooked her—*or*—she was alerted we were coming."

"Now wait a minute, McCoy, are you seriously suggesting that Lana called her?"

"Check her phone records. See if she made a call to Florida during that time. Here's another question. When did she learn that Leiko was going to be at the hotel? Did she know this before she heard you say it to me, on the phone?"

"Damn," Jenkins said. "No. She didn't know it. She was with me when I got the call from Solomon telling me about it. I called you immediately, before I even told her what he'd said."

Neither man spoke for a moment, considering the implications of this.

"She knew we were coming, detective. We had the place surrounded. We moved in, and she was gone. And, she had at least a two-hour head start. The authorities are scouring the area but haven't found her yet."

"Lana's been with me three years, McCoy. Her sister's tried to kill her several times. This can't be true."

"Think about this, Jenkins. If she's been working with Leiko all this time, it could explain why you've never been able to get enough dirt on her for an arrest. Lana tips her off ahead of time. And here's something else. If she is a mole, that means that everything Solomon Ito has been giving you, she'd relayed to Leiko."

"Goddammit it, McCoy. If that's true, she also knows that your girl has escaped and is staying with your sheriff up in the UP."

The same thought had just occurred to Hunter.

"Check out Lana Sato, Detective. See if she made that phone call. I'm calling Destramp."

———

LEIKO WAS TRAVELING WEST, IN THE FIFTEEN-YEAR-OLD pickup she'd bought for $1,000 from the farmer the day before she got the call from Lana. She's parked the vehicle near the hotel in Arcadia just in case she needed to make a quick getaway, and it had come in handy. Now, using another of the several aliases she carried, she should be safe until she could contact McCoy, get the map, kill him, and get away.

While she drove, she seethed again at the treachery of Solomon Ito and Kim Zhang. Through Lana, she'd only just learned that the two men were cooperating with the district attorney and the police to set her up. Fortunately, a year earlier, she'd set up an offshore account in Jamaica and had placed enough funds in there for her and Lana to live on comfortably. They could both disappear there now and never return to Chicago. But that wasn't enough. Not by a long shot.

Great-grandfather's treasure would set them up for a life of opulence for as long as they lived. Plus, it was their birthright. All of her plans for their future—the plastic surgeries, the new identities, the new location—all were based on getting the treasure. The only thing that stood between it and them was Hunter McCoy. He had the map because he had the Buddha. Thanks to Lana she knew that the Swift woman had escaped and was in hiding with the sheriff in Marquette. So a trade for the map was out. She'd have to take a more direct route.

She tried to imagine what Hunter would do with the map. Would he keep it with him, or would he store it in his attorney's office, as he had with the notebook? Probably not, since she'd successfully gotten into the safe and stolen it. No, he wouldn't make that mistake again.

He'd make copies of the map and the pages for sure. She'd seen him do it with the notebook. He might keep the copies with him, but he'd surely store the originals somewhere safe. She and the Filipino would need the original map.

Genevieve Swift didn't have it. At least it wasn't on her when she'd had her kidnapped. Hunter wouldn't think her house was safe either. Nor, for that matter, any of the houses he was associated with. Not the one where his dad and friend were staying; not the houses of the other two men they were friends with. He wouldn't store it in the botanist's house; he knew Leiko'd broken in there easily enough as well. No, she was sure all of the houses were out. What did that leave? Bank vaults? The police? No, she thought, he needed quicker access in the event she contacted him with instructions.

There was only one possibility, he'd have the map with him, and she'd have to get him to bring it to her.

———————————

JENKINS CALLED HUNTER.

"Lana's down in the evidence room now, working on a case. And McCoy? If she called Florida at the time you said, she didn't use her own cellphone. There's no record of a call at that time. Of course she could have used a burner. But it had to have been her."

"I'm sorry, detective, I know how you feel. It looks like we've both been completely fooled by these women."

"Yeah. I swear to you, McCoy, if Lana's a dirty cop, she won't get away with it."

63

THREE HOURS AFTER HIS EARLIER CALL, JENKINS called Hunter again.

"McCoy, listen. I'm at Lana's duplex. Something's happened. She may be dead—a bomb in her car in the driveway. The blast completely demolished the vehicle, and the body inside was burned beyond recognition. The forensics people are going over it now. They're trying to make a positive identification, but they tell me it's going to be next to impossible with what's left."

"Jesus. Do you think it's a setup? Could she have staged this?"

"Or—and this is a real possibility—she's been threatened before because of a case she'd been working. The guy she was after is a bomber. This could be his work, and that's her in that car."

LANA HAD PUT HER LONG-PLANNED ESCAPE SEQUENCE into operation after leaving work. First, she'd propped the drugged woman in the driver's seat of her car and set the timer on the explosive device. Next, she'd walked the five miles to the car parked in the first-floor storage unit paid for by a fictitious woman named Carol Brown. She had the full-sized late model Lexus hatchback fully gassed up and prepacked with food and other supplies. The car carried a Colorado license plate, and in the glove box were a full set of credentials for Carol Brown and a credit card in that name, along with fifty thousand dollars. She didn't plan to use the credit card and would pay for anything she needed with cash. She estimated it would take twenty-four hours to drive to Florida. She'd spend one night on the road and drive the rest of the time.

Using the first of several burner phones, she called Leiko.

"Does Jenkins suspect you?"

"I don't think so," Lana answered. "When I turn up 'dead' in my car, he'll be convinced it was a hit on me in retaliation for a case I've been working. I told him I've been threatened several times earlier. He'll be convinced that's what it was."

"All right. Get down here as fast as you can."

After ending the call with her sister, Lana continued driving. She knew that her departure was permanent. It would completely sever her ties with the Chicago PD. She was now fully in league with Leiko and her goals. She'd known this day was coming, had in fact planned extensively for it. But now that it was here, she couldn't help experiencing a small sense of panic.

Jenkins was a good cop who never left a stone unturned. If she and Leiko were going to pull this off the way they'd planned it, everything had to go perfectly. What bothered her most was that Hunter McCoy was an equally dogged and intelligent force working against them. But she and Leiko would set up a trap to get the map from McCoy and any copies he might have made, then get rid of him and disappear. Then phase two of the plan would slowly begin.

She recalled McCoy telling her he couldn't believe how Leiko had fooled him so completely with her innocent act as Billie Chen. Well, that was nothing compared to the "honest cop" act she'd been playing for Wilbur Jenkins. And she'd been doing it for three years.

Jenkins had never suspected a thing, even though every time they were ready to move in on Leiko, Lana had alerted her and often planted evidence ahead of time, that when uncovered would show that she wasn't involved.

Lana had kept Leiko in the loop and fed her the information she needed to remain in the clear. It had been a perfect setup. It had worked flawlessly until McCoy got involved.

Both she and Leiko had underestimated the man. Well, they wouldn't do it again.

TWENTY MINUTES LATER HUNTER MET CARRIE AT HER OFFICE. She led him back to the greenhouse where the China Gold orchids were growing. By now they had healthy-looking seedlings taking up at least a ten-square-foot area of benches. Carrie explained that there had been more here, but her friend Steph was examining several of them up at the med school in Tampa. In fact, she was getting close to having some exciting data to present.

"What's she finding, do you know?" he asked.

"A little. She says that both the leaves and the stems contain some interesting molecules that they're testing now."

"I've got some bad news to tell you, Carrie. The map and the missing pages stored in the Buddha, if they were in there, had disintegrated to powder and unrecognizable bits of paper. I'm afraid they're gone for good. You and Steph Bennet are on your own."

"I didn't have much hope for those pages anyway," she said. "But Steph is working on the assumption that the active molecules are water soluble, since Dr. Chen administered his treatment in the form of tea."

"That makes sense. How is she going about it?' he asked, intrigued by what her research technique might be.

"It has to do with the fundamental way the beta-cells of the pancreas are destroyed, leading to diabetes. The beta-cells are the ones in the pancreas that normally produce insulin, right?"

"That's right," Hunter said. "The disease arises when some of the proteins in the normal pancreatic beta-cells change slightly. When that happens, the immune system begins to think they're foreign proteins and sets out to destroy them. Of course, in the process they destroy the beta-cells themselves."

"So then the beta-cells stop producing insulin and the person gets Type 1 diabetes."

"Correct," Hunter said. "Has she isolated some of these compounds from the orchids?"

"Yes, and she's even doing some inhouse experiments now on prediabetic rats to see if they can fool the immune system and protect the beta cells. She's paying for this out of department funds at this point. If these studies bear fruit, she'll be going after an NIH or American Diabetes Association grant."

"That's great, Carrie. Your grandmother and Dr. Chen would be proud of you."

"Thanks. Hunter?"

"Yeah."

"What about the other issue?"

"Leiko?"

"Yes."

He spent the next half hour bringing her up to date on Genevieve's kidnapping and escape. He told her that two of Leiko's people in the organization were cooperating with the police, and that Leiko learned about it from her sister, who they believe was a mole in the Chicago PD.

"My God, that's horrible. Poor Genevieve. Is she really all right?"

"She's fine, but we have to assume that Leiko now knows that she's escaped and where she is. So we're moving her."

AFTER HUNTER HAD CALLED GENEVIEVE TO SAY THAT HER location had been compromised, John Destramp had taken over. He immediately called his older brother, Butch Destramp, a widower who lived alone in a nice house off Main Street in Iron Mountain, an hour's drive from

Marquette. Butch was a retired Michigan State Trooper and knew how to take care of himself.

John Destramp asked Genevieve and his wife, Bonnie, if they would be willing to stay with Butch until this was settled. His brother was more than happy to have the two women as houseguests. John would remain at home and take care of any threat that came that way.

Once in Iron Mountain, Genevieve had called Hunter. There's not much I can do to help up here in the UP," she said, "so I'm going to do some research on the Yamashita girls. Bonnie Destramp is letting me use her computer. I'm going to learn everything I can about those two, every nut and bolt of their lives that I'm able to find on the internet."

"Okay. Love you, Babe."

"Love you too, Hunter. Be careful."

When they ended the call, Genevieve got right to work. She started by looking up General Tomoyuki Yamashita. She found a tremendous amount of information on the general.

"Genevieve," Bonnie Destramp called from the kitchen. "Check this out."

Intrigued, Genevieve closed her laptop and stepped into the kitchen to a beautiful place setting for three and a variety of wonderful aromas.

"Butch, is preparing a venison dinner for us," said Bonnie. "I didn't tell you that he is a master chef on top of everything else. I think we're going to be in good hands."

Genevieve nodded and inhaled the rich scent of fresh bread baking.

"Why don't you two ladies go relax outside on the porch. I'll pour you each a glass of Lucas & Lewellen Syrah Noir Vertical Blend. The connoisseurs say, 'Its rich and lingering flavors of smoky mesquite and peppered bacon are balanced by nuances of mulberry and blackberry fruit with structured tannins.'" He winked as he read from a magazine for wine lovers. "Sounds like a perfect companion to the savory venison I'm preparing for you. What do you say to that?"

The two women looked at each other and smiled. Outside, soaking in the beautiful fall colors and tantalizing smells coming from the kitchen, Genevieve and Bonnie toasted their men, sat back, and dreamed of life returning to normal.

64

AFTER DINNER GENEVIEVE RETURNED TO HER LAPTOP AND PICKED up where she'd left off, with General Tomoyuki Yamashita. She found plenty of information on a variety of websites: Wikipedia, History Net, World War II Database, History Learning Site, and many others. She started to read.

She learned that General Yamashita was born in 1885 and early on chose the military path. He eventually became an Imperial General in the Japanese army during World War II. He led the invasion of Malaya and Singapore, and by conquering both within seventy days, earned the grudging praise of British Prime Minister Winston Churchill, who called him the Tiger of Malaya. Later, while unable to stop the Allied advance on the Philippines, he was able to hold on to part of Luzon until after the formal Japanese surrender in August 1945.

After the war Yamashita was tried for war crimes committed by troops under his command during the Japanese defense of the occupied Philippines in 1944. He was found guilty in a controversial trial, even though there was no evidence that he approved or even knew of them, and indeed many of the atrocities were committed by troops not actually under his command. This ruling—holding the commander responsible for his or her subordinates' war crimes as long as the commander did nothing to try to discover and stop them from occurring—came to be known as the Yamashita Standard. The general was sentenced to death and executed by hanging in 1946.

Genevieve could find nothing about his family life. Was the man even married? Did he have children? She continued searching sites until she came across this stunner.

Yamashita was the son of a village doctor and his wife. He had two sisters, and an elder brother who followed in his father's footsteps and became a doctor. Yamashita, on the other hand, took on the rigid life of a military man, dedicated to service in war. In 1916 he married Hisako, the daughter of General Nagayama. They had no children.

They had no children? Genevieve thought. If he had no children, he couldn't have any great-grandchildren. Were Leiko and Lana imposters?

She continued searching, finding no references at all to children. Finally, while reading an account of the actual execution, she came across this.

Lieutenant Charles Raroad, a military police officer charged with executing the condemned man, waited at the top of the stairs to the gallows. Raroad prepared Yamashita's passage, working with quick, confident movements. First, he placed leather straps around Yamashita's arms and legs, followed by a black hood over his head. Finally, he dropped the noose around Yamashita's thick neck, 'the bulging knot pulled taut under the left ear.'

Raroad asked, 'Have you any last words to say?'

There is a brief, muffled reply from Yamashita: 'I will pray for the Japanese emperor and the emperor's family, and national prosperity. Dear father and mother I am going to your side. Please educate well my children.'

Please educate well my children?

What children? Genevieve wondered. She sat back and thought about it. Did the man have children or not? Maybe the children were his wife's by a previous marriage. If that were the case the Yamashita girls weren't even blood relatives. Boy, would they hate to hear that. Especially if they didn't know it already. Genevieve kept digging.

She googled a wide assortment of questions. Did Yamashita have a mistress? Nothing came up. Did his wife have any children by a previous marriage? Again, she found nothing, no evidence of a previous marriage. How about Yamashita's brother, the doctor? Maybe Leiko was his offspring and not the general's. She was unable to find anything on him.

An hour later, unable to find any more information on possible offspring of the General, Genevieve was almost ready to close the laptop and call it a day when one of her searches brought up a page from a very small print publication dated January 1925 with the name Tomoyuki Yamashita highlighted in yellow. Intrigued, she proceeded to read

Tomoyuki and Jasmine had been friends since school days. Their families lived on neighboring farms in Osugi in Kochi, Japan. Though he later attended a military school for boys they remained good friends and once, he defended her from a gang of three boys who were harassing her. Even after marrying Hisako Nagayama, the daughter of retired General Nagayama, Tomoyuki stayed in contact. Following the early death of Hisako, Tomoyuki supported Jasmine and her young son, Akihiro, financially even though they never lived together, their relationship remaining one of good friends. With no legal status, Jasmine gave her young son the surname Yamashita to honor her good friend, Tomoyuki.

Was Akihiro Yamashita's natural son? Genevieve wondered. Later on, in the narrative, she got the answer.

. . . . . *Akihiro grew into a strong young man, going to work for his natural father, Ito, a village cobbler, who never married his mother, Jasmine.*

There it is. Tomoyuki Yamashita is not Akihiro's natural father, she thought. So if the line that Leiko and Lana trace to the General is through Jasmine's son, Akihiro Yamashita, they're not blood relatives at all.

Later, lying in bed, she thought about Hunter and the danger he was in. Leiko was seeking vengeance on him and his dad—including anyone close to them—because of Karl McCoy's role in Yamashita's arrest and execution by the Allies. Leiko called it a betrayal. But even that was weird. A betrayal would suggest that Karl McCoy was on the same side as General Yamashita in the conflict. They weren't. But now, with this possibly credible evidence that she wasn't even a blood relative at all, her vendetta looked all the more misguided.

Be safe, Hunter, she thought.

65

AT THREE THE NEXT MORNING HUNTER AWOKE IN bed at
Genevieve's house to his ringing cellphone.

"If you want her back alive, be at the beach off the
Ringling Bridge across from the entrance to Bird Key in
twenty minutes. Have the Buddha and its contents—you
know what I mean. Be alone."

Click.

Hunter jumped out of bed, threw on some clothes and
put the Buddha in the Jeep. As he started driving toward the
Ringling Bridge, he left a message for Wally Osborn and
opened an app on his cellphone and reflexively rubbed a
spot on his left upper arm.

Sixteen minutes later he parked in the lot across from
the Bird Key entrance and looked around. There were no
cars or people at this time in the morning; nothing. He
waited. Technically, he was one minute early. Leiko would
have learned from Lana that Genevieve was free so Leiko's
offer to trade her for the Buddha was only to keep Lana's
cover as long as she could.

Five minutes went by, then ten. Nothing.

Then he heard it. A power boat. He couldn't see it yet,
but could tell it was moving slowly, the engine throttled
back. Finally it came into view, a thirty-foot outboard. It
stopped and idled about ten yards off shore. Leiko was at
the helm, holding a gun pointed at Hunter.

"Step out here, walk in the water, and place the
Buddha gently in the boat. Do it now."

Hunter stepped into the water and walked the ten yards to the bow of the boat. The water was up to his knees.

He placed the Buddha in the boat and stepped back.

"Walk to the shore and wait there."

He did, and then he turned to see her move forward and take the Buddha back to the helm.

"You unscrew the head," Hunter called out. "Everything it contained is in there."

He could see her do it. When she examined it and all that came out was powder, she pointed the gun at him again.

"Don't mess with me, McCoy, where is it?"

"That's all there was. Disintegrated material, nothing more."

"Well. I can see you don't value your ladyfriend's life very much, do you?"

"Cut the bullshit, Leiko. We both know you don't have her. You've got nothing to trade. And, as it turns out, neither do I. What you see there is all that the Buddha contained. There was no map and no missing pages."

Leiko stared at him for a long moment with the gun pointed directly at him from ten yards away. They continued to stare at each other. Hunter dove, the instant she pulled the trigger. He heard the round whip by his left ear.

He rolled, pulled out his Beretta, and fired six rapid shots at the receding boat, which roared away, heading north across Sarasota Bay.

Hunter got out his cellphone and checked the positioning app. He could see the red dot that represented the location of the boat as it headed up the bay. When he put the Buddha in the boat, he'd also attached a receiver to the outside of the bow. Next, he called Wally Osborn. Even before he could say anything, Osborn said, "We've got her, heading north across the open water of the bay."

"Right, I've got her on my app too."

Back in the Jeep, he roared out of the lot onto the Ringling Bridge and headed east to highway 41, where he turned north.

So far the plan he'd worked out with Wally Osborn and the Sarasota Police seemed to be working. They knew where she was and could track her as long as she stayed in the boat. He'd had to make a decision as to which route to use following her. If she pulled up somewhere on Siesta Key, he'd be on the wrong side of the intracoastal. He figured she'd pull up somewhere on the mainland instead. It offered more routes for escape.

Wally was back on the phone. "You still tracking her, McCoy?"

"I'm heading north on 41. I'm following her on the app."

"Right. Let's hope she stays with the boat. If she leaves it and doesn't take the Buddha, we'll lose her."

"I don't think she'll take the Buddha. The tracker we placed in there would be too obvious. She's not dumb. Without the map, it's of no value to her."

"Uh oh," Wally said. "Looks like she's pulling in near the east end of the Manatee Avenue Bridge on Perico Island, west of Bradenton."

Stay in the boat, Leiko, Hunter thought. *Stay in the boat.*

As he raced toward the bridge, he kept glancing at the app. The Buddha hadn't moved. It was still with the boat. Was Leiko there too?

LANA HAD BEEN WAITING BY THE BRIDGE FOR A LITTLE OVER an hour and having a hard time staying awake. She'd been driving continually since leaving Chicago and could barely keep her eyes open, even though this step was critically important. She'd been looking south across the bay, hoping to see Leiko's boat any minute.

Finally, there it was, pulling in at the base of the east side of the bridge. Leiko got out and looked around.

"Over here, Leiko," Lana said from twenty feet away in a loud whisper. "Up the bank. The car is up here."

Both women hugged and then got in the car, and by prior arrangement, Leiko drove out of the lot and headed east.

"Did you get it?" Lana asked.

"No. I got the Buddha, but nothing was in it but dust. McCoy said the paper disintegrated. I left it in the boat. I'm sure they hid a tracker in there somehow."

"What about McCoy?"

"I shot him, and he went down. I don't know."

"You shot him? What if he lied about the map? How are we going to get it now?"

"He fired six shots at me when I pulled away, so he must be all right. We need to take him alive and get him to tell us where the map is. I don't believe for a moment it wasn't in there."

"Good," Lana said.

"I'll park the car a block away, out of sight. Then, we're going back to wait for him. I'm sure he also put a tracker on the boat. If he did, he'll show up. Then we grab him."

Hunter raced toward the east end of the Manatee Bridge in Perico. It was still dark, with only a quarter-moon to halfheartedly light the landscape. He'd be on his own when he approached the boat, as Osborn and his partner had taken the Siesta Key side of the intracoastal.

He slowed when he was two blocks away from the location indicated by the red dot. In spite of driving furiously since the beach, he thought about what Leiko would do. She wouldn't believe for a minute that he didn't have the map, even though it was true. Her plan would be to get him to tell her where it is.

She'd be waiting for him to show up, sure that he be tracking her. *She's waiting now*, he thought. *Better be careful.*

He parked, inserted a new clip, and crept to the target, staying in the shadows. His night vision was improving, and more detail was coming into focus. Continuing to stay in the shadows, he moved closer and closer to the end of the bridge. He could see a small gravel parking lot surrounded by trees and shrubs. Lots of cover to hide in. She could be anywhere.

Then he saw a slight movement in the bush just ahead of him. He froze. And waited. He saw her head move up slightly and point her gun in the direction away from him.

She was close enough that he could place his gun barrel against the back of her head.

"Move and you're dead. Drop it, now."

She froze, making no move at all.

"Drop it now, Leiko."

She did, and put her hands in the air, then stood up and turned to face Hunter.

"That's enough," a woman's voice said from behind him. "*You*, drop it, McCoy."

Lana. Dammit.

66

MCCOY SET HIS GUN ON THE GROUND AND TURNED TO face Lana. Leiko collected it, then retrieved her own gun and joined her sister in pointing it at Hunter. They marched him to Lana's Lexus, where she cuffed his hands behind his back. They took his phone and searched him for a wire or tracking device. Apparently satisfied, they shoved him into the back seat and drove off. Ten minutes later they pulled into a parking lot on the north side of the road. Hunter saw a sign that said Perico Preserve. The sign said it was a birding area and showed a map of numerous dirt trails back into the woods.

They got out of the car and marched him into the preserve. After five minutes or so the women must have felt they were far enough from the road that any passing traffic wouldn't notice them.

"Stop here," Leiko said, standing some ten feet away with Lana. "Where is it, McCoy?" she demanded.

"I do have a story to tell you, but first let me to tell you something you already know. You had me completely fooled as Billie Chen, and I'm not easily fooled. But you did it. I expect the same is true of Wilbur Jenkins. He's no fool either, but you, Lana, managed to do it for three years."

"Cut the crap, McCoy," Leiko barked. "We know how good we are. Bravo, we get Academy Awards. Now where's the map? And don't tell me it wasn't in the Buddha."

"I thought it would be in there too. But when I opened it all I found is what you saw, disintegrated dust. But then something happened. Something I didn't expect. I got a phone call from Sister Claire at the motherhouse. You remember her, of course, 'Professor Applewood?'"

"Yes," Leiko said coldly.

"She told me she thought of something after my last visit to see her that might be helpful."

"Get to the point."

"She checked to see if any of the other nuns who returned from China with Sister Mary Margaret in 1948 might still be alive. And she actually found one. Her name is Sister Bernadette. She's ninety-six years old and lives in a nursing home in Cleveland.

"Sister Claire called her and asked if she remembered much from those days. She said she did, and she agreed to talk with me. We did—over Skype. I also recorded it, so there's a record.

"I told Sister Bernadette I was anxious to talk with her about Sister Mary Margaret and their days together in China after they returned from Burma in 1948. I asked her if she'd prefer for me to ask questions, or would she rather just tell me her story?

"She said she'd prefer to tell me her story, and I could interrupt and ask questions whenever I wanted to."

"Is there a point to this, McCoy?" Leiko asked with more than a hint of exasperation.

"Yes, a very good one, as you'll see. She told me that she and Sister Mary Margaret met in China at the convent. She had been there for about a year already when Sister Mary Margaret arrived. They instantly became good friends. Like Sister Mary Margaret, she'd also had nursing training. But Sister Mary Margaret was much closer to Dr. Chen than Sister Bernadette was because the Mother Superior had specifically asked her to be the liaison between his clinic and the nuns in the convent.

"After the nuns packed everything they could in preparation for their return to the States, they were driven to Shanghai, where they boarded the ship that was going to take them back. It took ten days to reach Los Angeles. She and Sister Mary Margaret shared a cabin during the voyage. She knew that Dr. Chen and my grandfather were responsible for capturing *your* great-grandfather, General Yamashita.

"During their conversations onboard the ship, Sister Mary Margaret mentioned that Dr. Chen had told her he believed he knew where General Yamashita had buried the treasure his armies had stolen from the Chinese and the Filipinos. He told her he had a map describing how to find it, but she didn't know where it was. He'd never told her. Sister Bernadette couldn't believe he'd die without telling someone.

"I asked Sister Bernadette who she thought Dr. Chen might have told. That's when she told me that first, she'd better tell me who *she* was."

"What does that mean?" Lana asked.

"She explained to me that when nuns take their final vows, they also take a new name. The name she chose was Bernadette. When she was a layperson, living in the Philippines, her name was Myrna Marcos. Her older brother, by four years, was Ferdinand Marcos."

"*The* Ferdinand Marcos, the dictator?" Leiko asked, astonished.

"The very same. And what I'm going to tell you now will explain the action Sister Bernadette took then. She told me that her brother wasn't always the criminal dictator he became later. During the war he was a revered resistance fighter for the Filipino people against the Japanese who'd invaded the islands. His resistance groups cooperated extensively with the American troops. In those days she— and most other Filipinos—considered him to be one of the great resistance leaders of the war, as well as the most decorated Filipino fighter working with the U.S. armed forces.

"Of course, she had little communication with him during that time, as you can imagine. But what she did learn was that he needed funds to fight the Japanese. That's when she thought about the map to the treasure that General Yamashita had purportedly buried in caves in the Philippines. She considered it war loot stolen from the Chinese and the Filipino people to support the Japanese war effort. She thought it would be appropriate to have her brother find the treasure and use it to finance the resistance against the Japanese. If ever there was poetic justice, that would be it.

"As I said earlier, she couldn't believe Dr. Chen would die—and he did know he was dying—without telling someone. So, she thought, since he hadn't told Sister Mary Margaret, whom he was closest to, who else would it be? The only one she could come up with was his younger brother, Huan, who was supposed to collect the seedpods, the notebook, and the Buddha that Sister Mary Margaret was bringing back to the States."

"She opened the Buddha," Leiko said, stating the obvious.

"Yes, she did. And she found the map. Eventually she was able to contact her brother, Ferdinand. She sent the map to him, hoping he'd find the treasure and use the funds to help rebuild the country destroyed by the Japanese. Instead he became a selfish criminal dictator, and the world learned all about him."

"So you're telling us that *he* found the treasure?" Lana asked.

"Yes, all of it. The map said there were several underground areas where parts of the treasure were stored throughout the Philippines, but the map only pointed to one. And it said this one was by far the largest. The map indicated it contained one hundred tons of gold bars.

"In 1992, Marcos' widow, Imelda, first publicly commented on the source of her husband's vast wealth. It was built, she admitted, on Yamashita's gold. According to Imelda, her husband had become so rich from the looted gold that it would have been 'embarrassing' to admit it. She estimated their true fortune to be close to one trillion dollars, not the usually cited sum of one hundred billion."

"So," Leiko said, "the cave indicated on the map is empty? Marcos had already gotten it, years ago? Is that what you're telling us?"

"I'm afraid so. So you see, Leiko, it seems the Glorious Store—is empty."

The two women backed off several more feet and whispered to each other, out of Hunter's earshot.

Everything happened so fast after this that Hunter took several seconds to respond. In those seconds, four men charged out of the bushes on either side of the women and tackled them, pinning them to the ground. Their weapons were confiscated, and they were cuffed, arms behind their backs.

Wally Osborn stepped out onto the path and approached Hunter.

"Good work, man," Hunter managed to get out, unable to disguise his relief. Does this mean the tracking chip we planted under the skin in my arm actually worked?"

"Sure did. That tracker helped us follow you all the way. Thankfully, your story took so long that we had time to get up close and in position. Nice going, Hunter."

"Well, you know professors. We're longwinded if nothing else."

67

HUNTER MET GENEVIEVE AT THE PASSENGER ARRIVAL GATE at the Sarasota airport at 10:30 the next morning. He hadn't seen her since before the kidnapping. Overwhelmed with joy at seeing her safe and having her with him again, he enfolded her in a prolonged hug.

"Whoa, big boy, I have to breathe."

The kiss was equally breathtaking.

When they separated, Genevieve asked, "Is it really over, Hunter?"

"It is. Wally Osborn is holding them both in jail while the various jurisdictions work out who gets first crack at them. I just got off the phone with Jenkins; he'll be catching a flight down here from Chicago later today. Skaggs also wants Leiko for murder."

"Let's go to my house," she said. "I need some of my own clothes. Bonnie Destramp was kind enough to loan me some and I bought a few things up there, but now I want my own."

"I can imagine."

Back in the Jeep they drove from the airport to her house in fifteen minutes, and Hunter pulled into the still-damaged carport. With all that had been going on, there hadn't been time to deal with it. Inside, Genevieve walked from room to room breathing deeply and sighing.

After changing, Genevieve said, "Let's have lunch at Marina Jack. I want to see that beautiful view of the bay from downtown."

"You got it."

A half hour later they were sitting at a table in the open-air section in the shade with a gentle breeze blowing through. Over lunch they talked about what would happen next.

"According to Wally Osborn, the three law-enforcement jurisdictions are cooperating with each other. They all just want Leiko behind bars for the rest of her life. Still, she may face trials in all three. Lana, of course, is especially wanted by the Chicago PD. She is an accessary to all of the charges against Leiko. Like I said earlier, Jenkins is flying down today to see about that. And of course the DA in Chicago has the most damning evidence against Leiko, thanks to the cooperation of Solomon and Kim."

"So, they're both going to prison for a long time?"

"Oh, yeah, a long, long, long time."

"Hunter?"

"What?"

"I haven't had a chance to tell you what I found when I looked into the Yamashita family history."

"Oh?"

"You do remember that Leiko tried to have me killed."

"How could I forget?"

"She also tried to kill you, as I understand it, and almost succeeded on the beach."

"Yes."

"She killed Billie Chen and has gone after your family, all to avenge her family's honor."

"Where are you going with this?" he asked.

"I'd like to talk to them in jail."

"I would think Wally Osborn could arrange that, but why?"

"How about we make it my little surprise?"

". . . .Okay."

"Trust me, you'll enjoy it," she said with a smile.

After lunch they drove to the jail, where Wally Osborn met them and took them back to the holding cell where the sisters were being kept. Lana was pacing and Leiko sat staring at the floor. When the three of them approached, Lana halted and tapped her sister on the shoulder. Leiko looked up and glared directly at Hunter with unmistakable hatred and rage. Yet she kept quiet.

Lana said. "What do you want?"

Ignoring Lana, Genevieve addressed Leiko. "My name's Genevieve Swift, Leiko. You tried to have me killed by having your men drown me in my backyard."

"Too bad they failed," she said.

Hunter smiled at this admission. More ammunition to put her away.

Genevieve continued. "For a smart woman, you've been conned all your life and didn't even know it."

This seemed to get her attention and she narrowed her eyes.

"Your vengeance aimed at Billie Chen, a descendent of Dr. Chen, and your attack on Hunter's family as descendants of Karl McCoy, was based on the premise that you are actually a descendent of General Tomoyuki Yamashita."

Both women were now staring directly at her.

"As I'm sure you both know, General Yamashita and his wife, Hisako, had no children. This information is easily available on the internet in most references to the general. So, if he had no children, how does he have two great-granddaughters?

"My guess is, you both know that your great-grandmother was not Hisako, the general's wife, but instead Jasmine, his lifelong friend."

"We know that," Lana hissed, "We're the descendants of their son, our grandfather, Akihiro Yamashita."

"Well, you're half right," Genevieve said. "You are the descendants of Jasmine's son Akihiro, but not *their* son

Akihiro. You see, the general didn't father Akihiro at all. The village cobbler did that little task. You two aren't relatives of Tomoyuki Yamashita at all. You have absolutely no blood relationship to him. None."

Leiko rushed to the bars and thrust her arms out to grab Genevieve by the throat. Fortunately, she was standing back just far enough.

"You bitch. It's a lie. You're lying."

"I'm afraid not, dragon lady. After an intensive internet search of everything Yamashita, I found a photocopy of a letter written by Jasmine to the general. It lays it all out. I had it translated. Let me read it to you.

My dear friend Tomoyuki, blessings and gifts to you. All my life you have been my friend and my protector. You have honored me with your presence in my heart even when you've been away. Since childhood, we've known each other. From our early days on the farms even to the present, you've been there to help me when I was at my most vulnerable. The mistake I made with the cobbler was mine alone and due to the innocence of a young girl. Akihiro, the son he fathered through me, is now two years old and a lovely boy. As you know, his father and I never married. It was for the best. We both agreed not to compound the problem by marriage, as we were so young and unsuited for each other.

When I asked you for your permission to give Akihiro your last name in honor of your faithful good works toward me, I was humbled beyond imagining when you said yes. Even though you are not his father, I will always think of you that way in my heart.

Jasmine

"So there it is," Genevieve concluded. "You're not a true Yamashita at all."

"Lies," Leiko screamed. "That's a lie. We know about Jasmine, she's our great-grandmother."

"Yes, she is," answered Genevieve, "but Tomoyuki is not your great-grandfather. So much for avenging the family honor. How does it feel to know that all that effort and killing you did to find a treasure that's been long gone, and to avenge the family honor that you're not even a part of, is going to send you both to prison for the rest of your lives?"

The two prisoners sat back down and glowered, silently.

"Oh, I almost forgot," Genevieve continued. "Lana, remember when you told Hunter that you believed your mother was going to tell Leiko something—something that your father, Masaaki, didn't want her to know, something powerful? You said you didn't know what it was. You believed that Masaaki found out her plans somehow and told Leiko a made-up story that your mother was planning some kind of treachery against the family. I think it very likely that she was going to tell what I've just told you now—that you weren't blood relatives of the general at all.

"So, Leiko, you killed your own mother because she was going to tell you the truth about your heritage. And now you get to rot in jail knowing that if you'd listened to her—instead of killing her—you might have avoided all of this."

"Bitch," Leiko screamed, slamming her palm into the wall and glowering.

"Have a nice day, ladies."

Hunter, Genevieve, and Wally Osborn left the holding area and walked out the front door into the sunshine. After saying goodbye to Wally, they strolled quietly, hand in hand, to the Jeep.

"Now it's over, Hunter. Now I know it's really over."

68

THE NEXT AFTERNOON AT FIVE O'CLOCK, HUNTER AND Genevieve arrived at the Selby Gardens in a buoyant mood. Carrie Johannson had arranged for a celebratory get-together and dinner on the grounds of the famous gardens under a huge Banyan tree in front of the Selby House. Already present were, Wilbur Jenkins, Otto Skaggs, and Wally Osborn. The three lawmen were drinking beer, snacking, and chatting with Joe Palma and Jim Furlow. There was enough shade under the tree for everyone to sit comfortably.

Jim Furlow and Joe Palma had supplied the fresh grouper they'd caught earlier that morning to the Michael's Restaurant team who had been preparing the place for an outdoor fish dinner to be served around six o'clock.

No sooner had Hunter and Genevieve pulled into the parking lot, when Carrie Johannson and another woman drove up.

"Hey, Hunter, Genevieve, meet my friend Steph."

"Hi, Steph," Hunter said. "I want to talk with you later about your work with the orchids."

"I'll be happy to. We're learning some amazing things. I understand you're a physiologist."

"That's right."

Genevieve took the women in to visit Ed and Henry who were relaxing under the banyan. Hunter went over and joined the group of lawmen.

"Well, Detective Jenkins, I see you've met our two local heroes." He indicated Wally Osborn and Otto Skaggs.

"I have and we're catching up on everything that's gone on down here in Florida."

"How about us?" said Joe Palma, nodding to include Jim Furlow. "We're local heroes too."

Everyone laughed.

"So you are," said Hunter. "Best man trap ever built." He turned back to Wilbur Jenkins.

"Did Wally tell you how Genevieve confronted Leiko yesterday in the jail?"

"Yeah, he did. That had to really piss her off, learning she's not even a blood relative."

"I don't think she believes it yet."

"Yeah," Wally said. "But maybe even bigger, was her learning that she was never going to get that buried treasure. Ferdinand Marcos beat her to it by sixty years. All that effort, all those murders, all that treachery, all for nothing."

"And," Otto Skaggs added, "she'd have been better off to have never heard about Scott Harrison and his book. That's when it all started going wrong."

"Right," Jenkins agreed. "With her rotten sister working right under my nose—in my department—to feed her information, we were never able to pin anything on her, even though we knew, beyond any doubt, she ran a criminal operation in the city. But when Harrison's book identified Dr. Chen and Karl McCoy as the two men responsible for her great-grandfather's arrest and conviction, she set out for revenge and in the process learned about the supposed treasure."

"Hey, gentlemen, can a humble lawyer join this august group of lawmen?"

They all turned and watched as J. Michael Lannigan walked toward them, leaning on his cane, accompanied by a middle-aged man no more than five feet tall.

"Hey, Lannigan good to see you," Wally Osborn said, then turned to the diminutive man with him. "Nice work on this case, Stretch. Lannigan's lucky to have you."

"Glad you two could make it," Hunter said to the attorney and Stretch. "My dad and I are forever grateful."

The Michaels catering staff invited everyone to sit. It was time for dinner.

As people made their way to the tables an elegant woman walked onto the grassy area where the tables were set. When Genevieve saw who it was, she ran to her and embraced Jenny Lahti, Henry's sister-in-law.

"Genevieve, what a delight to see you, my dear," Jenny said.

"It's so good to see you too. Come and sit with us."

The dinner was wonderful, and the wine was good. Everyone was having a great time celebrating the end of an ordeal. While they were waiting for dessert, Hunter raised his glass and offered a toast.

"To justice, which has a way of prevailing. But only due to the efforts of all of you. My dad and I thank you and salute you all."

"Hear, hear," was the common response.

Then Carrie Johannson's friend stood up. "Hi, everyone, I'm Stephanie Bennet. I'm a professor at the University of Florida College of Medicine in Tampa. By now, I'm sure everyone here is familiar with the story of Sister Mary Margaret and the seedpods from Dr. Chen's amazing orchids. We all owe an extreme debt of gratitude to Carrie here for rescuing them and, amazingly, bringing them to life after so many years.

"What's even more miraculous is that chemical extracts from the leaves of the China Gold orchids actually do produce useful molecules that seem to inhibit the development of Type 1 diabetes. We're in the early stages of testing at this point, and our rat models are not what they should be, but they're getting better. Still, it looks like the reports Dr. Chen wrote in his notebook about incredible success with some of his young patients might just be true.

"I just want to say to you, Hunter and Ed, and to you, Carrie, that your forebearers, were two heroic people. Because of their concern for Dr. Chen and his work, we may be on the verge of a great breakthrough.

"So I'd like to offer a toast to Karl McCoy and Sister Mary Margaret."

"Hear, hear."

Genevieve leaned over and whispered into Hunter's ear, "Still thinking about retiring from medical research?"

Hunter scratched his head.

"Let's sleep on it."

Epilog

Two weeks later
On board the *Marina*, a ship of the Oceana line
Cruising the Caribbean Sea.

HUNTER, WEARING A SPORT JACKET AND OPEN SHIRT, smiled as he gazed at Genevieve, who sat across from him at the table next to the window, watching the turquoise water rolling by. She was wearing a red and black sundress and sporting that same enigmatic smile he'd found so irresistible when he first saw it three years before in Paris. They were in the sky lounge, having cocktails before dinner on the first evening of their seven-day cruise.

Genevieve set down her glass of wine and took his hand. "I knew, if I waited long enough, we'd eventually have some time together with no one trying to kill us."

He stretched over and kissed her. "It *is* nice, isn't it?"

"And," she said, squeezing his hand, "I could get used to it with no trouble at all."

"Me too, Babe. Me too."

They sat back and sipped their drinks, with neither speaking again for several minutes. The dinner reservation wasn't for another hour, so they had plenty of time to relax. Their cabin was midship on the tenth deck and they'd been pleasantly surprised when they found a welcome bottle of champagne, along with fruit and appetizers and a card from the four guys in the men's book club, wishing them the best.

Hunter immediately thought of his dad's words; "That's some woman you've got there, Hunter. Don't ever think of letting her go."

His dad was certainly right there. He had no intention of letting her get away.

Hunter set down his glass and began to speak at exactly the same moment as Genevieve. They each heard the other's words.

"Hunter, how are we going to—"

"Genevieve, I think we need to—"

They laughed, each knowing the issue the other was going to bring up. They'd been avoiding it until now because there'd always been something else they needed to take care of first. But now they'd finished all that, and it was just the two of them.

Genevieve went first.

"Hunter, I have some news about my job at the Ringling. Director Bertram has offered me a permanent position if I'm interested. He said there's enough work for two of us in the department, so when Phyllis Durham returns from her year at the Louvre, we'd be working together. I'd need to get a green card, but he said that'd be no problem given my credentials and the offer of a permanent position."

He beamed. "That's great news. He obviously knows talent when he sees it. So, what are you . . .?"

She put up her hand to stop him. "What were *you* going to say?"

Hunter had been thinking about this ever since he'd taken the leave of absence from the medical school. But now this offer to Genevieve from the museum in Sarasota added a level of incentive that hadn't existed before.

"Carrie's friend, Steph Bennet, told me about an opening for a physiologist at the College of Medicine at the University of South Florida in Tampa."

Genevieve gasped. "Oh, Hunter, we'd only be an hour apart. Are you going to apply?

He smiled. "I already have."

Author's notes to readers

This story is a work of fiction. Nevertheless, certain aspects of it are based on actual historical events and figures. My wife's uncle, Army Technical Sergeant Karl Hyypio, was the inspiration for Karl McCoy. Sergeant Karl Hyypio was indeed left behind in Wuchang, China following the Japanese surrender, much as described in this story. The Japanese told him he could stay in the abandoned convent there. The description of the Japanese colonel surrendering his sword to Karl Hyypio was chronicled in a short history in the *Upper Peninsula Post* in August 1995, written by his son, David Hyypio. David, his sister Karol, and my wife, Pauline, are first cousins. I thank David for allowing me to borrow heavily from his account in the *Post*.

The samurai sword described in this story is currently in the possession of David Hyypio, who graciously gave me permission to photograph it and use on the cover. I also am thankful to David and Karol Hyypio for allowing me to create a fictional story based on some aspects of their father's history. For purposes of this story, I gave Karl Hyypio the name Karl McCoy and made him Hunter McCoy's grandfather.

General Tomoyuki Yamashita, known as the Tiger of Malay, was indeed arrested, tried, and executed as a war criminal for crimes committed by troops under his command. He was thought to have amassed a huge treasure of war loot and buried it in caves in China and the Philippines. The bounty came to be referred to as Yamashita's Treasure or Yamashita's Gold.

With the one exception of Ferdinand Marcos, it's never been found. Marcos is thought to have located and usurped part or all of the treasure. In 1992 Imelda Marcos, the widow of the Philippine dictator, offered a fascinating account when she publicly commented on the source of her husband's vast wealth. It was, she admitted, because of Yamashita's gold. According to Imelda, her husband had become so rich from the looted gold that it would have been "embarrassing" to admit it. She estimated their true fortune to be close to one trillion dollars, not the usually cited sum of one hundred billion.

I'd also like to thank Jerome T. Hagen, Brigadier General, United States Marine Corps (Retired), who graciously sent me a copy of the three-volume set he wrote entitled *War In The Pacific.* In volume one, entitled *America At War*, he describes the other surrender ceremonies that occurred in the Pacific following the ceremony aboard the USS *Missouri* in Tokyo Bay on September 2, 1945. He states that few Americans are aware that the ceremony aboard the *Missouri* was neither the first nor last surrender ceremony of Japanese forces in the Pacific.

General Hagen's report was the inspiration for my fictitious World War Two historian and author, Scott Harrison, and his fictitious book *Surrenders In The Pacific.* All the remaining characters and events depicted in this novel are equally the products of my imagination.

And, even though orchid extracts have been used for centuries in Chinese medicine, an orchid-based treatment for preventing the development of Type 1 diabetes—formerly called juvenile diabetes—unfortunately does not exist.

Acknowledgements

The more I write the more I realize how much I depend upon others for their feedback and inspiration. I'd especially like to thank my longtime friend Rick Morrow for starting us both on the writing road. His encouragement over the years has been greatly appreciated. My friends and neighbors have also been helpful in so many ways. I'd also like to thank Dr. Antonio Toscano de Brito, curator of the Orchid Research Center at The Marie Selby Botanical Gardens for reading and critiquing the section on flasking orchids.

I'm deeply indebted to my editor, Carol Gaskin, of *Editorial Alchemy*. I can't even imagine a finished product without her invaluable critiques and insights. I'd also like to thank the many writers in Florida's Chapter of the Mystery Writers of America. Their encouragement is always greatly appreciated. A special thank you also to my tenacious proofreaders, Monica Hoover, Pat Polazzo, and Billie King.

Finally, and most importantly, I wish to thank my wife, Pauline for putting up with my constant interruptions of her own work to listen to my ideas. Her early editing of the manuscript was extremely valuable, but her constant encouragement is her greatest gift.

Also By Don Stratton

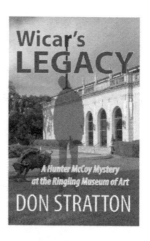

A Destitute Old Man Leaves a Valuable Painting in a Gallery at the Ringling Museum of Art and Triggers a Countdown to Disaster

A cryptic note left with the painting links it to Genevieve Swift, a visiting curator from the Louvre, and her father, a professor of history at Cambridge . . .

In Gallery 3 something unknown is eating the paint on the face of a small lion in one of the museum's sixteenth-century paintings . . .

A young girl who touches the painting becomes deathly sick . . .

Professor Hunter McCoy investigates the strange events and uncovers a link to a secretive and deadly group called the Legacy. As he peels away layer after layer of the Legacy's secrets, McCoy realizes that a countdown has already begun—a countdown that if unchecked, could cost countless lives and ruin the Ringling Museum of Art itself.

Available in paperback and Kindle from Amazon.com

Also By Don Stratton

A Widow In Florida Discovers The Body In The Coffin At Her Husband's Funeral Isn't His

Following emergency surgery for a head injury, a woman develops virtuoso-like piano skills . . .

While on holiday in Italy a man suffers a stroke and inexplicably becomes an accomplished juggler . . .

An embalmer with a secret past and his daughter face an unimaginable choice in Brussels . . .

In a secret laboratory in Sorrento, marketable skills become a valuable commodity . . .

Hunter McCoy is asked to locate the missing body and anticipates a simple find-and-correct job. However his search quickly turns deadly when he uncovers a sinister plot linking an international funeral business and a world-renowned neurological institute—a plot set in motion by a powerful and mysterious man, fueled by decades of hate and revenge.

Available in paperback and Kindle from Amazon.com

Also By Don Stratton

Young scientists scheduled to begin work at the Large Hadron Collider near Geneva are being systematically murdered . . .

Hunter McCoy discovers that their deaths are somehow linked to his search for a lost book—a book written by a Spanish physician who was burned at the stake by the Inquisition in the sixteenth century . . .

A shadowy group with ties to high-energy particle physics has its own compelling and deadly reasons to find the book first . . .

McCoy, trying to stay one step ahead of ruthless unknown adversaries is running out of time as his partner, a beautiful French archivist, is set to become the next victim—unwittingly unleashing a cataclysmic international disaster.

Available in paperback and Kindle from Amazon.com

About The Author

Don Stratton is a biomedical scientist born and raised in Michigan's Upper Peninsula. He was a professor of physiology for many years at Drake University. His research on blood vessel physiology was reported in over thirty-five scientific publications and his textbook Neurophysiology was published by McGraw Hill. Don was granted an endowed chair and named Ellis and Nelle Levitt Distinguished Professor of Physiology and Biology. He now lives as professor emeritus in Venice, Florida with his wife Pauline and dog Gracie where he's writing his next mystery novel

Made in the USA
Columbia, SC
28 March 2019